André VandenBroeck's

BREAKING THROUGH

"**Breaking Through** is exactly the right title for this book: it tells us not only what the book is about, but what it does. Every word, sentence, page, breaks down, dissolves, and momentarily reforms consciousness—only to begin the process again at another level. Its direction is inward, into the depths of our being —indeed, quite literally, into bone consciousness. Remarkably, in this journey into the very matter of flesh and bone, the concrete matter of the skeletal structure of the Earth, the silence of rock, begins to speak, and we discover human existence as a metamorphosis of the Earth's being. Time as succession collapses; space becomes at once interior and exterior. Both are incorporated into the word, the original word; the beginning we discover, is still beginning—now and every moment. While this work narrates the alchemical process, it does not take a position outside the process. In an astonishing feat of language, VandenBroeck has managed to do alchemy."

—Robert Sardello

"With this novel of Hermetic philosophy, VandenBroeck has revived the great tradition of *Séraphita* and *Zanoni*. But his language and his setting are thoroughly modern, even postmodern, and this has enabled him to escape from the dual bondage of belief and revolt. He writes as if he is a witness to the beginning of our world, describing hypernormal states with a conviction that must stem from experience. The story climaxes with Tallini's vision of the prehistoric encounter with "philosopher's stones," and the arising of human language and eroticism out of this meeting. Admirers of VandenBroeck's memoir of Schwaller de Lubicz, *Al-Kemi,* will be gratified by further insights into the mysteries of the "fixed salt" and the destiny of the human entity."

—Joscelyn Godwin

"In this virtuoso performance, André VandenBroeck improvises the space where experience begets language and language generates experience. And, since both experience and language are narrative, he tells a story that is nothing less than the birth—or rebirth—of our humanity. The stakes, then, are high, and we turn his pages with something of the breathless attention that takes hold of us during a high wire act or one of Beethoven's late quartets. Miraculously, or so it seems, he succeeds. *Breaking Through* is masterful. The theme of Hermetic transformation is studded with vignettes—a dream sequence with surreal overtones set in an early de Chirico painting, a stageplay with harlequinade, an amusing dialogue on the gardens of Goethe and Schiller as contrasting expressions of intuitive conduct and Kantian theory. These apparent digressions entertain, yet upon reflection deepen our appreciation of the theme. Thus the book performs the timeless function of art, being at once deeply metaphysical—language after all is nothing if not the expression of ideas—prophetic, and grounded in the universals of the human condition. At the same time, however, it is truly contemporary: epistemological, ecological, and psychological. The hero, Tallini, has a place in twentieth century writing somewhere between Thomas Mann's Hans Castorp and Castaneda's Don Juan—a juxtaposition that situates this text in the no-man's land between literature, philosophy, and the New Age. In this sense, *Breaking Through* may be considered the thinking person's 'Celestine Prophecy.' "

—Christopher Bamford

BREAKING THROUGH

PHILOSOPHICAL GEOMETRY

■

AL-KEMI

A Memoir: Hermetic, Occult,
Political, and Private Aspects
of R. A. Schwaller de Lubicz

André VandenBroeck

BREAKING THROUGH

A NARRATIVE OF THE GREAT WORK

CITY LIGHTS
SAN FRANCISCO

© 1996 by André VandenBroeck
© 1996 Introduction by Colin Wilson
All Rights Reserved
10 9 8 7 6 5 4 3 2 1

Library of Congress Cataloging-in-Publication Data

VandenBroeck, André
Breaking through: A narrative of the great work/
with an introduction by Colin Wilson
p.   cm.
ISBN 0-87286-319-0
PS3672.A42815b74   1996
813',54–dc20   96-16387   CIP

City Lights Books are available to bookstores through our primary
distributor: Subterranean Company, P.O., Box 160, 265 S. 5th St.,
Monroe, OR 97456. 541-847-5274. Toll-free orders 800-274-7826.
FAX 541-847-6018. Our books are also available through library
jobbers and regional distributors. For personal orders and catalogs,
please write to City Lights Books, 261 Columbus Avenue, San
Francisco, CA 94133.

CITY LIGHTS BOOKS are edited by Lawrence Ferlinghetti and Nancy
J. Peters and published at the City Lights Bookstore, 261 Columbus
Avenue, San Francisco, CA 94133.

FOR
GOLDIAN
WHO WAS THERE

CONTENTS

Introduction

by Colin Wilson

This is the most remarkable first novel I have ever read, either published or unpublished. It belongs to the type of novel I have always found most interesting: the novel of ideas. And I must confess that it has set me on a line of thinking I have found immensely fruitful.

The basic plot is simple. A filmmaker of some renown, Piero Tallini, leaves for Spain to make a documentary about Paleolithic caves and their inhabitants. Somewhat less commonplace is the twist that has this project actually putting him in touch with the earliest humans. But this is a novel, at least on the surface of it, and though something of a *roman à clef*, only a spoiler would paraphrase the yarn of what can happen in the depths of such caverns.

Why is Tallini so obsessed by the "first humans"? He feels that they embarked on the greatest adventure humanity has ever known. And no one can dispute that we have advanced a long way in half a million years or so. Yet have we not, in the process, lost most of that original impetus and vision, and the freedom that went with it? The question is encapsulated in VandenBroeck's amusing description of a fashionable party in the opening chapter. A father scolds his child, who is reading a book: "What are you doing there? Why aren't you watching the telly?"

The author's concern with language becomes evident almost immediately, not only as a theme of the novel (he wants to narrate a return to the "origin of language in the divine and primal Summons for Light") but in the text's own use of language. VandenBroeck's expression seems only partly aimed at communicating the story. The other part draws our attention to the language itself, which forces us to a slow reading and re-reading until it shows its worth. It is as if the author was unwilling to leave his hero's difficult undertaking to a reader's all too easy, careless grasp. This convergence of purpose of story and language lends an uncommon cohesion to a work that at times reminded me of the late writings of Henry James, and at times of Robert Musil. VandenBroeck is attempting to "work" language as our most ancient ancestors worked stone.

The inspiration for this may have come from the eighteen months he spent in daily contact with the maverick Egyptologist René Schwaller de Lubicz, a sojourn whose details VandenBroeck developed in his *Al-Kemi*. An important hint as to what lies in the back of his mind can be found in a passage concerning the Ancient Egyptians. They developed a demotic script for discussing everyday concerns, whereas their hieroglyphic symbols conveyed a different kind of reality, a "sacred reality." This was de Lubicz's starting point: that there are certain things that can be "said" only in symbols. Ordinary writing creates abstractions in our heads, while symbols somehow conjure up objective realities. As Tallini's erudite friend Benji asserts, cave drawings were the direct precursors of Pharaonic hieroglyphics. Our own phonetic writing has moved steadily away from that mentality. "By the time [the glyph] reaches our words, we're four times removed from what we were talking about."

VandenBroeck's language is undoubtedly influenced by such considerations, and may therefore be considered a critique of social discourse as well. The book begins with a parody of "salon culture," and Tallini's horror of "salon talk" is manifest. It pains him to see the means of self-expression and self-realization debased into a mere communication tool for abstract concepts, rendering them useless for the ends of cognition and creativity.

Yet Tallini senses that he is "on the verge of being set free," and it is clear that his creator feels the same way. "Now things were different: far more was at stake—his immediate future, the nature of his next film, and perhaps the very course of his life, all because he had asked himself new questions and something ancient was answering." What Tallini is seeking is a real breakthrough, a rebirth.

As the story progresses, it might be said that what he wants to know, to experience, is the very *nature of stone.* "Wherever stone has been worked, no matter how little, the presence of a hand is manifest, and a gesture can be gauged, a gesture that negates the acceptance of pure necessity through a modification of the given."

More than an intuition, it is a stunning ancestral summons that draws Tallini to an Andalusian fishing village where his quest begins to unfold. In the chapter describing his first day's excursion into the hills above the village, it becomes clear that, no matter how unusual its approach, this novel belongs to the great "existential" tradition originating with Goethe's *Wilhelm Meister,* and continuing through Musil and Proust and Sartre and Camus. Tallini remembers how often, as a child, he asked his mother, "What should I do?", and realizes that this question has remained fresh and new throughout his life. "It was easy to find something to do, but how was one to know that it was the thing that *needed* to be done?"

This is, of course, the question that preoccupied me in my first book, *The Outsider* (1956), and has continued to preoccupy me ever since. Like VandenBroeck's Tallini, all of the major figures in that book were obsessed by the question of what they ought to be doing with their lives, and by the feeling that mere living was not the answer. The teenage T. E. Lawrence went off to Syria in search of Crusaders' castles, but what he was really looking for was an answer to Tallini's question. In Laura del Rivo's *The Furnished Room*, one of my favorite novels of the Sixties, the same basic question is posed. The hero sits in his room, staring up at a cobweb, feeling totally unmotivated. He feels that the world around him is a kind of illusion, a falsehood, yet he has no idea of how to penetrate to reality.

The Furnished Room was influenced by Sartre's *Nausea*, whose basic theme is that the "reality" lying behind our human curtain of language is meaningless. We distinguish its meaninglessness by using it as a mirror to reflect our own emotions and purposes. VandenBroeck is at the opposite pole from Sartre. He believes that the underlying reality is more meaningful than our minds can ever grasp. Yet he seems to feel there *is* a way of experiencing it directly—almost bypassing the mind.

Few of the "outsiders" I have written about actually achieved "breakthrough." Van Gogh is one of the rare exceptions. As you look at a canvas like "Starry Night," you realize that, for a few hours, the artist had broken through the banal surface of reality, and was seeing something closer to "what reality is." The same is true, in an even more basic sense, of Cézanne. As you look at *his* rocks and stones, his fruit and bottles, you are aware that they are not the objects you would have seen if you had been standing beside him as he painted; he is attempting to surmount ordinary reality to show an underlying reality, somehow more "real" than what we behold.

I have always been aware that a sudden emergency can snap us out of the state of everyday reality so similar to sleep. But at their present stage of evolution, human beings lack the power and imagination to induce this sense of urgency, this concentration that seems to force a breach to a more profound perception of reality. To show us a model of humanity's ultimate adventure of beginning, VandenBroeck chose what is arguably its most significant transcendence to date: the breaking through to language, humanity's supreme gift. Retraced by Tallini, every step of human experience since then—from these remotest ancestors to Pharaonic Egypt, Pythagorean number, and contemporary Hermetism and alchemical science—appears to have been molded in the matrix that informed the originary ideal of transcendence or liberation.

All this explains why I consider VandenBroeck's novel so important. There remains to read the book. It demands as much effort from the reader as from the writer. But when both share the same purpose, then breakthrough ceases to be an intellectual concept and becomes a promise of reality.

BREAKING
THROUGH

Only the ardent aiming of words
at the heart of innermost silence
attains to the true effect.

Walter Benjamin

ONE

CONTACT

Tallini came to know southern Spain almost despite himself. He had been in the north of the country when young, not yet twenty, as assistant to a well-known press photographer covering the civil war for a socialist Paris paper; with the Loyalist defeat, he had sworn not to return before Franco's demise. But he had not counted on a newfound interest that declared itself after his recent return from India, where he had been the cameraman for a full-length feature about India's holy men.

The project brought him into close contact with the practices of Eastern wisdom schools, and he had pursued a meditational discipline ever since, which may have accounted for the radically expanded sense of time that seemed to have captured his consciousness. As the time-space world of four dimensions came to broader public attention after the Second World War, he had made the effort to acquire a basic knowledge of the new physics, but he had recently revisited his notions of the subatomic world in quite a different spirit. For as he traced the particles of this microcosmos back to the elementary photon, he now took the imperceptible step that turned this energetic quantum into a world of *light,* stopping time's clock.

He came away from this thought experiment with a twin realization: the origin of language in the divine and primal Summons for Light sounded more persuasive than the biggest of bangs; and this call could be fully experienced only by a being on the verge of humanity who was undergoing a comparable illumination. With this understanding Tallini was pulled far beyond mere abstract cogitation; he became preoccupied with the earliest states of humankind, with its first glimmers of consciousness. How did these beings communicate? How did they live? Shadowy as such entities appeared to his mind, he yet felt their need for place, for space: a sky, a landscape, shelter.

In a remarkably short time, a casual interest grew into a veritable passion. Soon the entire day revolved around his paleoanthropological endeavor, and he could be found until closing time at the Bibliothèque Nationale. His research began with accounts of explorations in the famous caves of the Dordogne, but soon narrowed to lesser known recent discoveries. These, though not as spectacular, often benefited from the systematic approach of modern excavation, with carefully compiled and illustrated catalogs of rudimentary artifacts that frequently proved early Paleolithic occupancy. For it was not the relatively recent Cro-Magnon civilization that intrigued Tallini; nor was it the tribes that roamed the limestone hills of southern France and northern Spain ten thousand years ago. Tallini was now counting years in the *hundreds* of thousands, intent on tracking origin, inception, the earliest human presence. He absorbed detailed descriptions of caves in which layer upon generational layer allowed a documented voyage back through time to the edge of human evidence. And this research would eventually cause him to break his promise to himself. For he was drawn more and more to an important recent find on the southern coast of Spain.

He soon realized the special feeling that had emerged for him with the cave idea had little to do with contemporary humanity. His curiosity was ignited by the first people to have lived in caves, by the coalescence of the primitive with the human that formed the first generations of the truly human, the original "speaking animal." And this primacy seemed to touch some intimate emotional spring to which he had been unable so far to lend any kind of satisfactory form. At times it was as if he were discovering traces of distant relatives with whom he had lost touch ages ago, about whose condition he knew nothing, and who might, for all he knew, need assistance of some sort. He was riled by certain illustrations he ran across in his studies that represented hairy simian brutes, armed with clubs and setting upon some prehistoric beast. Even if reason might condone such images, he was convinced they bore no relation to what he might discover: something deeper than contemporary fancy could ever contrive. Nor was he much cheered by a visit to the Musée de l'Homme, where he was offended by the romantic way humanity's infancy was presented. Missing was any sense of the kind of inventiveness required to surmount the terrible obstacles to survival. He mused about this faculty when walking the city streets. It was certainly long since dormant in the fashionable figures sharing the sidewalk.

As happened frequently in his scholarly efforts, a dilemma intruded that tended to undermine their effectiveness. The lives and tribulations of the earliest humans had become his prime concern, but he was keenly aware that however much he might fantasize about their existence, precious little factual information was available concerning those roving bands. And while he was collecting a great deal of evidence about their eventual habitat, without this newly human presence it reduced to no more than lifeless data.

He came to conceive this impasse as a challenge to the creative function of the camera, his chosen tool for the task of "peopling the caves." The camera would have to bring both cave and landscape alive, and this could be achieved only by an evocation of the early human beings who inhabited them. He had yet to formulate the nature of this evocation, for his interest lay not only in the imageable—any photographer's preoccupation—but also in the *imaginable*, by which he raised a purely practical concern into the realm of theory, of contemplation. For he was convinced a certain truth was carried by whatever could be imagined, and by that very fact, the imaginable situated itself within the domain of the possible.

3

Abstract as such considerations may seem, they were solidly wedded to his professional know-how. Tallini was a devoted craftsman who had evolved his own ethics and aesthetics of beginner's mind, the mind devoid of memorized cerebrations, of opinions, rationalizations, and preconceptions, in which the imaginable knew no academic limits. Without consciously elaborating the thought, he was already working on his next photoreportage.

This was not at all what he had planned. After the turmoil occasioned by the unexpected success of the India film, he had looked forward to some leisurely travel in his new Ferrari, a surprise bonus from the Franco-Italian consortium that had produced the film. The difficult climate of the Indian subcontinent had been physically exhausting, and the editing sessions back in Milan had led to sharp disagreements and emotional strains. Strangely enough, however, it was the triumph of the work, both critical and financial, and the social whirl it inevitably occasioned that had been the most trying for him. The two weeks in Cannes—where he was honored with the Festival's award of excellence for documentary cinematography—at least offered the practical advantage of contact with producers interested in his future plans. But his nerves were sorely tried by the fanfare and unavoidable publicity that accompanied the Paris opening and by the unending series of parties at influential salons which the politics of business obliged him to endure.

It was the only chore connected with his craft that Tallini truly minded, the gatherings in plush Paris apartments whose architectural proportions seemed to demand rigor of speech whereas in fact only clever banalities were bounced off walls and ceilings. The final irony was that the film's subjects— dedicated searchers who disdained what in the West passed for rationality in order to cultivate their intuitions and sacred traditions, and whom Tallini had mostly found to be of superior intelligence as well as of considerable learning—these "living saints" (as they had been christened by the consortium's publicity people) had now become a hub of attraction

4

not so much for serious inquiry as for a segment of bored and idle camp followers who sensed that saintliness was herewith à la mode.

So, with the Ferrari parked in a suburban garage, it was with some trepidation that Tallini found himself footing it to an afternoon reception given by Axel Ladsnik, director of CINEDOC, a producer of documentary features. Tallini had heard of the man for years through the professional grapevine, but had met him only recently in Cannes, where Ladsnik attempted to impress upon him the advantages of a collaboration. The producer's career had been distinguished by crassly commercial ventures, most recently a short film on the history of beachwear, financed by a group of manufacturers and undertaken, as Ladsnik volunteered apologetically, "to pay for better things." Presumably it was for such things that he was soliciting Tallini's collaboration.

At this first meeting Tallini had been suitably reticent, professing to have no plans as yet for any future work. He had no intention of soon sharing his private concerns with *anyone* in the business, least of all with this fellow. Furthering contact with Ladsnik despite the man's shortcomings would have to be a carefully weighed tactical move. For although Tallini was aware of his recently acquired potential for dealing with larger and more prestigious firms, he also realized that CINEDOC could offer one invaluable advantage: an opportunity at last for absolute control, down to the final edit, over the visual material. For this coveted liberty, he might be willing to endure all the rest.

His destination was a massive edifice on one of those tree-lined avenues radiating from the Trocadéro. Both sides of the street were lined with stone houses transformed into luxury apartments. At the one he sought, he rang the lower bell marked Ladsnik/CINEDOC. A female voice, metallic through the apparatus: *"C'est qui?"*

"Tallini," he answered. "Piero Tallini."

Her buzzer sprang open the glass and cast-iron portal. Ignoring the elevator's fancy cage, he strode up the red runner centered on a curving marble staircase. The door to the mezzanine apartment opened as he approached, and a woman intercepted the butler to greet Tallini personally. She introduced herself as Axel's wife. Although garbed in a sari (devoid of the traditional demure blouse), she was, he had heard, Brazilian, the main model for the beachwear commercial filmed around São Paulo. Ladsnik had brought her back and married her; she was acquiring culture and ran a salon for artistic hopefuls. "So much I have heard about you," she said, "so happy you arrive. I, also, am interested extremely in East. Please to call me Samba, everybody does," she went on huskily, taking his arm and heading with her trophy toward the drawing room. "My friends are dying to meet you, *de verdad.* Everybody is here. Germaine Crotti also, from cosmetics Crotti, *sabe como é, vary* rich people, but she does yoga, is *vary* spiritual advanced, and she *loved* your film. Everybody *loves* your film." If anything, she was voluble. "And Bruto is here, the artist, *você sabe,* the one made such a beeg *escandalo. Um grande sucesso,* he made on the *tela,* how you say, the canvas, *sim,* he made what nobody ever had made before, holes. Such genius . . ."

Axel Ladsnik interrupted their advance. "Let's go to my study for a moment, before you're buttonholed by all those people who want to meet you. I've had some thoughts." From the nearby room, Tallini clearly heard the polyglot din of the crowd, above which incongruously floated the Bhairavi, a *morning* raga. Tallini used to listen to it in Benares where it was sung by the Bauls, wandering minstrels mad in their thirst for God. Now here it was, emanating from the salon's stereo speakers, inexplicably overlaid with a bluesy clarinet and drowned out by the guests' rising laughter. Tallini was disconcerted; he could hardly stomach this desecration, but failed to act quickly enough on his impulse to flee.

They entered Ladsnik's study, where a young boy was curled up on a couch reading a book. "Sacha," he heard Axel scold, "what are you doing here? Why are you not watching the telly? Go to your room now, but first say hello to Signore Tallini. He is a great photographer and maybe he will work with us." Then he turned his attention to the captive Tallini and began to expound on the success of CINEDOC, describing several projects that would present fine opportunities for Tallini's talents. And he went on and on until Samba stuck her head in the doorway, lamenting that the guests were waiting. And during this interlude, Tallini pondered ways to escape, but he was cornered.

At that moment, the pictures he had seen at the library and the dioramas of cave life at the museum flashed through his mind along with the certitude that they bore no relation whatsoever to his affinity with the reality of the cave people, and this reality thus became a little bit clearer. These early beings had been inherently free, with a freedom perhaps no longer to be experienced anywhere on earth. Furthermore, the terrors they undoubtedly faced were redeemed through this near absolute freedom, which must have ennobled them to an extraordinary degree.

These reflections filled Tallini with a vague longing and a sense that he may have found an escape after all. For if there was no horizontal escape, and he couldn't very well sink into the ground, there nevertheless remained above him a vast open space, an upward opportunity the possibilities of which he had never before considered. So struck was he by this thought that he was hardly conscious of Samba as she led him to the salon, like a lamb to slaughter. In a moment he was surrounded and yanked about by a flurry of introductions, none of which he registered. Then came the usual inane questions: had he observed miraculous events performed by the living saints, had he evidence that any of them could read his mind, how long could they fast, were they truly chaste, did he think any of them had really reached nirvana? But as there was nothing spectacular he cared to relate, and his annoyance at being entrapped in this absurd situation rendered him monosyllabic, the lionizers seemed to lose interest.

So it was, that when Bruto, whose perforated canvases were acclaimed as a metaphysical statement, derided Madame Crotti for a casual reference to the notion of truth, and she triumphantly countered, "Mais, monsieur, la vérité, c'est *toujours vrai, n'est-ce pas?"* Tallini recoiled, and no one noticed. But as he began to retreat from this dismal scene, it seemed to him that someone was addressing him familiarly. He turned, but there was no one close by. As he looked about, he once again heard a faint call, yet immediately realized it was neither a hearing nor a calling. It had been the faintest of touches, no more than a vibratory disturbance around his head. Even the notion of touch seemed an exaggeration. A sensation between sound and feeling. Like the feelings that would surge quite suddenly and unpredictably from his reveries and meditations about the earliest people, such sensations were imbued with tactile qualities. There was recognition in the feeling, a hint of an unknown or of the unremembered.

All at once, the space above him, which had seemed open and empty and on which he had based a hope for evasion, was occupied as well. Or at least it appeared to be, judging by a current that reached down to him, somewhat like a draft, save that it didn't pass by him, over him, or through him. Nor did it engulf him. No, it was rather like an electric field that stopped precisely where he started, so it didn't touch him, and yet he sensed it. And while thus totally absorbed by this event, he walked straight through the Ladsniks' drawing room, and nobody addressed him, nobody seemed to notice him. It was as if his concentration toward the space above had rendered him imperceptible. He made his way to the foyer, picked up his hat and coat, descended the marble stairs, and with each downward tread, the boisterous noise he had been exposed to became fainter, and the contact with the space above more certain.

Tallini opened the heavy entrance door and stepped out into a moment of unnatural silence. It lasted but a fraction of a second, the time for the door to clank shut behind him. But in that total silence, he found himself in a place he didn't recognize, but about which he was certain of one thing: it was Spain, and he was there just long enough to realize it. Then the door closed and he walked into the Paris street. But he understood the message and where it came from, and with it came a sense of personal assignment, a distinct beckoning, the burden of an undefined responsibility. It swept over him that the early ones had reached out to him, and they were in Spain. And they wanted *him* in Spain. With that decision having been reached for him, he headed for the Left Bank and his hotel, where he would set the decision into motion.

◗ ◐ ○ ◯ ◑ ◕

As suddenly as it appeared, so the contact was withdrawn. It lingered but a moment in its message, and like an afterglow in his feelings, but by the time Tallini had taken a few paces, the presence above had vanished completely. Yet it left him with an impression of great certainty concerning the event: it had been a communion with an other beyond him. Because of its striking nature and its contrast with the uncommunicativeness experienced with the Ladsnik people, it somehow left him with an uncommon sense of reality. Aware of the elusiveness of inspiration, he made no effort to recapture the evanescent touch, but he did hold fast to the hint of personal transcendence that clung to the event, unlike anything he had ever experienced in the contact with a human being. For the photographer in him, immanence was practically a professional deformation, and a creative transcendence through contact with an other was not only new, but altogether revelatory.

With Spain on his mind—and with his mind's propensity to wander whenever his feet were traveling—reminiscences of his early professional days and the circumstances in which he had formed his first ideas about photography now came back to him. If the camera had taught him anything, it was the here and now, an indwelling of a personal presence tied to the fact of the moment, and the feasibility of obtaining *proofs*, successful photographs, which would also attest to the photographer's presence. The complex relation of the record left by photography to the factual had preoccupied Tallini from the very beginning of his career. "Don't you ever wonder what it really is we're doing here," he had asked a fellow newsman in a bar in Saragossa. They had just pulled back from a fire-fight along the Ebro and were deep into a bottle of Rioja. "We're making all this into fact, aren't we? Turning every detail into fact, all indubitable facts. Don't you think that perhaps sometimes we record scenes and catch things that would best be forgotten, and that will escape becoming facts if we turn away from them, if we don't collect those moments? Like the killing we make available as fact, very different from words that can only talk *about* it. That's only part of it, though. As photographers, we can actually *proof* a moment of our existence, of our experiencing the fact, whatever it may be, a burning town, a face, the instant of impact of the bullet and the last gesture of the fellow who stopped it."

Tallini's inner agitation betrayed the depth touched by the experience caught in such images. In photographing professionally, he found that his private experience was bound to fundamental questions, and he was accountable for what would, without his intercession, remain mere possibility, possible moments of possible lives. It was given to him to bring them into actuality, into the realm of facts. Being there, such was the nature of the fact-maker. "The falling tree in the forest may crash with or without noise, but it becomes factual only by the human observer there. And if I'm a photographer, I can produce *proof* far superior to other descriptions, which only represent the fact in language, but representation is not a matter of fact. And please don't bring in painting, that's totally beside the point here. What painter has ever presented facts? Nor does he represent them, if he's worth his salt. The artist annihilates facts, as has been conclusively shown with the *objet trouvé*, for instance. No kind of realism ends up with a fact on the canvas, and no kind of abstraction either. They're nothing compared to my proof of fact. They lack instantaneity, and that is what is caught in the silver salt emulsion, because the fact is a matter of light."

The documentation on film of arrested moments in real lives—this slice through a conscious whole—had to signify a considerable expansion of an individual's self-consciousness.

It also induced a puzzled wonderment about the bullet-struck soldier's privacy and the ethics of eternalizing his final second, freezing it into an icon of sudden death. For it generalized an abrupt lethal act by violent and impersonal agents at the expense of one singular and private experience. Was this fact, now widely circulated and revived with every viewing of the image, comparable to any other fact in more than its mere capture on the emulsion? Or was there a special quality here, not in the successful adjustment of a mechanism to a light phenomenon, but in the nature of the event?

Such considerations had led Tallini to an early rejection of fact per se, of a fact sensed as universal, as everyone's everyday naïve perception. He raged at the tyrannical aspect of the closed state of factual existence ensconced in the contemporary mind, and he proposed a *quality* of fact, however generally disregarded, that comes to contradict that closure with the intuition of a categorical distinction. Upon his return from the East, he would insist that all facts are not factual in the same manner, as personal experience had shown, so that even if quantitatively they all amounted to the same factuality, qualitatively they differed "in their existence in the moment of their development, when still open on all sides, unrestricted in their meaning, still able to be experienced in a dynamic response." This entails, on the part of the observer, a receptivity far beyond the quantitative certitudes of facts universally received as ground of action.

These speculations had preoccupied him in his younger years. They did not spring out of a theoretical bent, but from his practice of photography. Tallini's experience behind a camera in war-ravaged Spain had led to critical reflections that were reinvested into his craft and formed his professional style as well as his thinking. Beyond the gradual purification of fact in general, he elaborated on "the natural fact, a functional datum *given in front*" that was radically different from an artificial system contrived by human ingenuity. Tallini's drift seemed to imply that only by literalizing this artifact in a work of art could the crushing reign of the factitious be redeemed and transcended.

Later the political had intruded, the practicalities of life had dimmed the light-image and distanced the imageable. With the work on the living saints, there had been a recovery of his speculative mode with the shift to the imaginable. But after India, this had presented problems of its own, manifest in a despair at the quality of work available and a consequent impatience with associates and the shallow range of their pre-occupations. And then, for no clear reason, with the cave idea came this explosive opening. Within the security of a self-motivated immanence, he had thought in terms of *leading* his life and, somehow, even his destiny. Suddenly, that feeling had been displaced; some other agent was guiding him. Its objective was as yet ill-defined save for the responsibility he felt to answer the appeal of the other, intimated, but not yet reachable as presence. Ancestral entities in search of representation were beckoning, and it never occurred to him to refuse the assignment.

◗ ◖ ◖ ◗ ◗ ◖

Back at the Trocadéro, the traffic of the multiple intersections slowed his progress. Liberated by his flight from Ladsnik, and with the rest of the afternoon all his, he drew up a mental list of things to be done before he could leave for Spain, and found it surprisingly short. He had to get the Ferrari, of course, but beyond that and a few phone calls and some appointments to be cancelled, he didn't see much that would keep him here for more than a day or so. Now that he had a destination and was in touch with guidance, however impersonal and undefined, the Paris treadmill of social functions and business palavers struck him as a regression to a past, distant and defunct.

His experience in India had shown him a possible life that was not just one thing after another, but change, metamorphosis: the spontaneous new beginnings of a life of initiation. Clarity was still lacking as to the cave people's role in his life, yet this afternoon's experience confirmed his intuition.

Although what they conveyed was hardly more than a feeling —all trace of which, furthermore, had vanished by now—it yet was a feeling that was not only *about* something new but *was itself* radically new. Though as yet unable to say what it was, he could conceive it as functioning like an organ of perception, like the eye sees or the hand apprehends. It was a subtle thing, no doubt, and apparently not at his command. Tallini decided he would pursue this feeling-idea with his cameras, the same tools he used to pursue more concrete subjects, and the only means he knew. He would bring back from Spain some footage that would knock Ladsnik's socks off.

Tallini's enthusiasm mounted with the dizzying rhythm of cars zipping past him. There he stood, pondering the potential of his endeavor to situate photography at a crossroads of science and philosophy, where he deemed that all relevant action took place. What validated the medium for him was its *proof of fact*, with the proof being scientific, but the fact philosophical. It had hitherto been evident to him that a totality of photographic facts would clearly show what was the case at the shutter's moment. But now the opening to the elusive cave residents threatened to demolish all categories. He had to admit to himself that, as things stood, the subject that possessed him was singularly maladapted to his photographic purpose. Then it occurred to him that once he had peopled the caves, it would no longer be *his* purpose that mattered, but *theirs*. His job would simply be to determine the basic elements among which the camera would move, and then to feel with the cave people—or perhaps *for* them—that atmosphere of just sky, stone, and vegetation, in a certain light. And the animal world, of course, to the extent it was represented in those Andalusian hills. With a good lens and lots of patience, the perfect light would come for that sort of thing. He would conjure up a world, *their* world, through the lens's eye. He would find the most propitious atmosphere and turn the camera over to them!

Absorbed in his excitement, he stepped off the curb; a cab swerved around him, its driver hurling an insult, weighty with Russian accent. Tallini barely noticed. Welling up in him was the photographer's creative fervor for *being there,* at the right moment and with the right light. That was the trick, being there as innocuously as possible, making oneself disappear. *An absence of presence.* Then seeing what the camera sees, when *they* are behind it!

Despite such soaring visions and the influence of his readings in epistemology and general philosophy, he meant his inquiries to remain entirely practical. Their particularity lay in his understanding that the photographic capture of the image was insufficient in itself; his intent was to supplement it by valorizing the *being there* of the photographer. Tallini by and large confronted life instinctively and freely based his arguments on feelings he never pretended to have examined or understood. But now, as he crossed the Pont de l'Alma, he stopped to look down at the waters of the Seine and felt a serious need for introspection. What was it that was happening? First the compelling interest in the cave subject, and then, today, this fleeting contact—ephemeral when objectively considered, yet fraught with inner suggestions of permanence. Otherwise, why this directive to travel, which was tantamount to a rendezvous? And what about the unaccountable familiarity of the first call on his attention, right in the midst of that swank madhouse? What has a past must have a future, and his font of intuition and feeling at this juncture seemed more secure than all the facts uncovered in his studies, facts inherently meaningless because they were presented without regard to a qualitative canon evaluating each case in point. His vision of the caves' profound reality and of a contact with their first human inhabitants looked to facts not for confirmation, but rather for the sense of amazement they conferred on the existence of the evidence as such. *Thinking the fact,* with all the insecurities caused by such a breach in the solid rampart of objectivism, presented itself now as a real necessity.

All information, any indications pertaining to the first gropings of human consciousness, would have to be rethought through this filter of familiarity he had been given in front and all at once. A newfound thinking faculty itself now begged for closer examination. The idea of a living font of knowledge seemed preposterous at first, yet after some reflection, he concluded that this *knowing in front* had been his procedure since the beginning of his thinking life; he simply had not noticed because he had never paid attention to the questions. Where do such questions come from? Is it perhaps a general state of affairs that the essence is provided first, before any particulars can be known? He was by no means certain, but he considered that the essence must be given, a gift, since no particular attributes are available that could ferret it out. As long as the essence remains unknown, how would one determine the facts to gather round it?

And so it happened that Tallini, now walking briskly toward the Latin Quarter, noticed the low November clouds reveal a tattered patch of sky, and the blue of it filled him with an abstract longing difficult to situate. Then the clouds broke apart with a gust of wind, allowing the cerulean patch to grow, as a weakened sun peeked through and filled everything with marvel. Even in the center of Paris, nature is full of signs, and for Tallini, *this* sign was powerful. Living in him was a bohemian on the verge of being set free, though for the moment, the lures of society still carried the day and kept him pacified. Yet at times like these, conventions wore thin, and nagging doubts trailed him. Every one of his moves seemed to compromise the intuitive mind that was granting him access to this new world. There had been compromise before in his life, and he had always weighed it carefully and usually found it amenable to inoffensive rationalizations. Now things were different: far more was at stake—his immediate future, the nature of his next film, and perhaps the very course of his life, all because he had asked himself new questions and something ancient was answering.

☽ ◑ ○ ◐ ◑ ☾

Tallini had slackened his pace over these reflections, breaking his resolute stride. He found himself heading toward

Arvan's store—indeed irresistibly drawn—as was often the case when he walked through this *quartier,* the very heart of ancient Lutèce. His thoughts had simply taken over, and his feet had brought him to where he now stood, transfixed. Though blind as a rule to the seductions of Parisian shop windows, he never failed to come to a halt before Arvan's display. Within, disposed with the same French flair that elsewhere arranged high fashion, lay glittering geodes, halved and polished, revealing miniature crystallized caverns. Sumptuous feathers and an enormous turtle shell lay in one corner. Among fabulous vertebrate specimens, a python's jaw, aggressively agape, showed the articulations of mandibles and winglike pterygoid process. An accompanying schematic model explained the cranial mechanics permitting the reptile to swallow whole a prey of considerable magnitude. Surrounded by big conch trumpets, the many-chambered spiral of a fine Jurassic nautilus invited meditation on the Golden Mean. There were assortments of insects trapped in chunks of ancient amber, carved fragments of ivory, sandy starfish, a big black ammonite whose very name harked the beholder back to the Pharaonic ram-headed deity. The twisting of this mollusk evoked the coiling whorls of those particular horns, a perfect pair of which were displayed next to the fossil.

To Tallini, however, the most prodigious objects in the collection were those silent tokens of vanished human life that formed the core of the dealer's inventory. As he now stood lost in thought before Michel Arvan's latest acquisitions, those relics of young *Homo faber* glowed with special meaning. Had he not, less than an hour ago, experienced what could only be interpreted as contact with these early craftsmen? Had they not solicited his attention with a sign of familiarity, and had they not signaled specific instructions? Up to now, these objects of their fabrication had served as herms on his backward travels against the currents of history, and the earliest signs of manufacture were also the last markers of a mind homologous to his own. He had been resigned to finding beyond them no more than an informational desert, with stone reduced to sand, a desert in which he could at best hope for traces subtle enough to have escaped all previous explorers. Without artifacts, the only tool to forge a link amid the dangers of this arid passage would be a daring intuition. And that intuition had now arrived.

Arvan, a reputable dealer in what his trade called "ancientries," had recently let him handle some specimens kept in special cabinets in the back of the store, objects Tallini regarded with awe. His contacts with these early testimonials had been like long drafts at the last watering hole before the crossing he intended. Touching them, he felt fortified with ample reserves. More dangerous, however, than starvation or dehydration, and demanding complex prophylactic measures —about which he had learned in India—were the fata morganas of a brain able to produce, even in the most desolate ecology, a feast of phantasms. Past voyagers, intrepid but short on the disciplines of the imaginary, had become snared here and there amid the treacherous dunes, tied to the hitching-posts of their own projected selves! There they remain, reveling in an opulent flow of theory, settled in total forgetfulness of aim and purpose. *These* pitfalls are difficult to guard against or to prepare for, but by the grace of his recent evanescent encounter, Tallini felt uniquely protected. His privileged access to the cave people—which he accepted with humility, without claim to merit—would enable him to distinguish truth from counterfeit; the feeling of connectedness and familiarity would be his trusted compass for this adventure and his sole orientation on the road to the presence beyond.

None of the pieces in the window bespoke such prehistorical primacy, however, and so he let his gaze come to rest on a group of flint knives—lethal edges flaked with masterful delicacy—specialty of the Dordogne's stone knappers. Nearby lay an important specimen of a fist hatchet shaped to fill a man's large grasp—he flexed his hand involuntarily to sense its fit. These were mature achievements of Paleolithic sophistication, and while they addressed only indirectly the object of Tallini's interest, they did stimulate consideration of early aims and purposes. In short, they presented themselves to Tallini as a communicative medium, a language to be read by the contemplation of its signs.

Wherever stone has been worked, no matter how little, the presence of a hand is manifest and a gesture can be gauged, a gesture that negates the acceptance of pure necessity through a modification of the given. Eyes shut, he had weighed in his hand the stones that Arvan recommended, appraising their mass and the feel of their surface. He had noticed some items, highly valued by the shopkeeper, that looked hardly worked at all, and questioned Arvan about them. "Archeoliths," Arvan had replied, "that's what I call them. First because they're always the oldest, and second because they express the principle so clearly." Tallini was holding one of those specimens in his hand at the time, and the dealer had reached for it. "*Mais voyons*, you're holding it upside down! You'll never get to know it *that* way." He raised it to the light: "Almost nothing, it could be *any* rock, except for this here, see? Almost nothing, but look how he shapes it just about perfectly to its cutting function, do you see it? By this slightest of shavings! It's the *principle* that's attained here, the modification is just enough to distinguish it as artifact, as a product of human fingers."

Michel Arvan was an esthete. Held between his thin tobacco-stained index and his thumb, with the rest of his manicured hand cupped around it, setting it off, the humble chert became precious. He was also a businessman, however, and knowing the Italian's interest, spared no effort to broaden his prospective customer's acquaintance with the topic, to the point of entertaining him with tales about singing stones, oracle stones, speaking stones ". . . such as the one beneath the throne at Westminster which raised its voice only to name the king who was to be chosen. If a certain stone uttered prophecy, Socrates tells us, the ancients would take it as the truth."

Tallini recalled the tour he was given the day Arvan, who had noticed him in his store before, stepped up and introduced himself. They had strolled around this temple of curiosities, stopping here and there, while the host kept up his commentary. "Here's a specimen of rare *ceraunias*, the so-called thunderstone. The ancient Greeks found them in conquered soils and named them after their thunder, *keraunos*, you see?" He pointed to the catalog he was holding, where the characteristics of the stone and its history were laid out. "Legend had it that these stones had fallen from the sky and all-powerful virtues were attributed to them. They were worn as amulets, like this one." They both stood admiring the incandescent celestial stone blackened with the patina of the ages, resting before them in its velvet case.

"It's true that all stone is of inconceivably remote origin," the dealer went on, pausing to offer Tallini a brandy and a cigar, "but of all of them that have come down to us, even more or less eroded or incomplete, the most valuable are those known in our trade as face-stones. Some of them merely show a number of contours that appear like stone sculptured in very low relief, almost photographic representations of men and women, barely modeled—perhaps even more engraved than modeled—into various attitudes, some dancelike, some in poses, all very serious and oddly noble. Even taking into account the abrasion of time, these simulacra or imagos or eidolons, or whatever you choose to call them, are indubitably *there*. Those who claim otherwise simply have not seen a good specimen. Like this one."

To illustrate his point, Arvan removed a rock from his private collection and permitted Tallini to examine it. "Priceless," he continued. "This fascination with rock fragments is as old as human perception. Superficially, man may have changed, but *this* remains, this intuition of a mysterious presence in rocks, in stones, a presence hinted at by their distinctive shapes. Scientific investigation doesn't even begin to break the spell. The so-called irrationality persists: the more we examine rocks and stones, the more unfathomable they become."

Tallini had garnered much information from Arvan on his several visits, but nothing had affected him as deeply as the dealer's small face-stone collection. Holding one of these objects in his palm, he distinctly felt the stone had passed through many hands, through many centuries; privy to many songs in many tongues, privy to much *speaking* in tongues, and certainly the focus of contemplative adoration. He also became convinced there was more to these stones than could ever be elicited by such delicate appraisals as were offered by Monsieur Arvan. Not that the dealer failed to show the utmost respect for these relics: "Such face-stones were the most highly prized and warred over," he explained, while Tallini clearly made out a venerable, bearded, laurel-crowned profile on the contours of a piece of quartz almost polished from handling. "They became trophy stones, fetish rocks, totem stones. Along with the clan gods and the firestone of the next hearth's spark, they were transported from cave to cave, across vast ice sheets to Europe, over land-bridges long sunk beneath the sea."

And migrating steadily toward Spain, thought Tallini. He was keeping his eyes on the stone.

"But you're not looking hard enough! Look harder, deeper, you'll see entire tableaux! Layers of images, a mineral microcosm! It's a well-known tendency in all humans, this recognition of themselves in natural phenomena. And please don't think that anthropomorphizations of this sort belong to the vision of a primitive mentality alone, or to a Narcissus in the mineral mirror. Look intently at a tree or at a rock, look long enough and eventually stone-skinned faces surface. And faces in the clouds, who hasn't seen them? This faculty seems to be deeply ingrained. Of course the solid modern mind and its logical reasoning try to make short shrift of such fortuitous light effects, but I say that what meets the unreasoning eye, the *pre*reasoning eye, must be a reality in itself, more pure perhaps than the one we produce by theoretical means—and which, by the way, we contradict every generation or so. That's why we must regain the stone-gazer's eye, the simple alert state of prehistoric mind, the newly awakened dream-heavy soul. Then apply this spring eye to widen, to open up that reality of ours, constrained as it is. . . ."

Though Tallini had managed to maintain to a high degree the elusive quality of beginner's mind, he had come to the stones with a highly trained and sophisticated eye. He was by no means surprised to see pictures in the stone; he saw images everywhere, just as Arvan had said. He saw them at will, to the extent that such sightings had practically determined his profession. The dealer was right, of course: along with the other senses, with hearing in particular, the modern eye had been abused and become habituated to the worst insults. It had become inured to the sensory challenge of every moment, and met it with automatisms. It was to some extent because the visual event did slip by in largely undifferentiated moments that he had begun to arrest it and had begun thinking about the *quality* of its occurrences rather than merely about things comprising the factual event. That put him among the experts rather than the beginners. But in his own mind, the image of the true viewing of the stone included the context of the stone being viewed, the hand that held it, clumsy still, and rough; it included the individual observing his stone, and his surroundings, the cave, the protected environment that would make possible such leisurely and unguarded pursuits. The vision of the beginning could no more be isolated from the environment of the beginning than from the mind of the beginning.

Still gazing into Arvan's window, Tallini was now both frustrated and exalted by the sense of connectedness he felt "coming down": frustrated by the relative uncommunicativeness of the tactile sense; exalted by the recognition of the other and the familiarity of the unknown. He understood that the tactile sense is a feeling unto itself and not the feeling of another, an intransitive feeling not easy to encompass. Its physical manifestation is an unlocalized touch, like an inner presence. Why the contact through this obscure and polyvalent sense? Why did he not have visions or hear voices? Why touch? But perhaps sight was too superficially tactual to make contact with the ancient tribe. Hawks and falcons that command vast spaces have themselves developed into a winged eye, and they touch at great distances and with surgical precision. The early cave dwellers, on the other hand, would have devised an eye for closeness, for form rather than detail. They specialized the inward look, developed the reflexive, the relation with what is closest, the self. The eye that was their breakthrough is an eye that draws distinctions not out of sharpness of detail but at the bidding of the mind's idea of difference, a negation of sameness, an individualization that would permit relations and proportions—in a word, the unfolding of the new brain.

Perhaps that was why the first human beings moved inside. They had not begun inside the cave, those first ones, but had gone inside, acting out in physical moves the need for interiority that would lead them to self-consciousness, to self-reflection. For this travail, they needed shelter within the earth. But what made them begin to look for it, or when did they begin to recognize it for what it was? There must have been someone who *first* . . . then there would have been beings who moved *inside* to live. They may have displaced other beings as a direct result of having domesticated fire, although the events Tallini aimed for probably belonged to an even earlier time. What made them move inside? He saw it as a *mission* whose purpose was to establish the matrix of the human mind. *Mind* did not satisfy him, but he considered *soul* and *spirit* equally inadequate for such action as already adumbrated an intentionality. The time is ripe for a turn whenever newly accessible experience can no longer be inscribed by means of the tools currently given. But though this new tool is defined today as the perfection of the cortex, Tallini carefully avoided positing this as the cause of the cave man mission.

Deep in the caves' hidden recesses, the traces of this gestative activity must have been inscribed in a variety of ways into the rock, on the walls—traces that could be read. Without insight into their function, however, there could be no interpretation, no evaluation of the finds beyond the aesthetic. In historical retrospect, it seems plain that this turn must have been access to a linguistic universe, but Tallini took great care to avoid anachronistic impulses that might have enlightened these instinctive beings with an insight into their own purpose. Only under conditions of extreme circumspection, if at all, could quality of facts be induced.

On early visits to Arvan's, Tallini had practiced holding archeoliths in the palm of his hand, thinking that whatever mystery they might contain would not remain mysterious were it visible to the naked or even the instrumented eye. It seemed natural that the sense of contact with the Stone Age would involve contact with stone. So he made it a rule, which he applied during the sessions with Arvan, that the first encounter with a stone was blind contact in the palm of his hand, checking the fit of the grasp, the natural positioning of the fingers—in a word, the *feel* of the stone in the human hand. Tallini was convinced that simply to pick up a stone with the intent of working it, the hand would have to have been structurally the hand of today, and capable of judging the properties of stone. The grasp, then and now, would have been homologous, sharing an origin in the creative mind, the mind of distinction and negation. "In the early worked stone," Arvan told Tallini, "in the archeolith, the principle is that the stone is *worked; that* is the statement. A kind of eolithic minimalism."

Tallini had ventured the thought that stone itself had been the cave people's medium, a constant preoccupation, as soon as they became aware of something *to be done.* He found out that the dealer had precise ideas about this past society: "They were constantly seeking the right kind of rock for their various purposes, or perhaps for certain shapes or hardness —think of the variety available. Everyone collecting stone, studying it, examining it. Certainly there were specialists: grinders, flakers, polishers, sharpeners, knappers. That's how I see it—a regular industry."

Tallini didn't want to contradict the expert, but this wasn't quite how he envisioned the scene. He said that they stared at the stars at night and at stones in the day, and he asserted this as if evident. He even proposed that they looked themselves deeply into both stars and stones as into mineral *grimoires* of heaven and earth. "What were these caves, after all? Is it not conceivable that after emerging from them, those troglodytes found themselves under the starlit celestial vault as if in a larger cave, but capable, after their experience of interiority, to extrapolate yet a further outside? Could it not be like those miniatures where the sky is vaulted over a paradise—Adam and Eve in naked modesty—outside of which the four winds blow, the angelic temperaments color with trumpets, the deities repose on clouds?"

Trying to comprehend how they had come to start working stone in the first place, he wondered what had been the relation of the worked stone—and the particular stone's manipulation—to the general idea of working stone. How did either come about, and how were the stones affected by their shaping? With this heightened value, what did they become? And what did it do to the worker, and to the tribe? It seemed reasonable to assume that in Stone Age society there would have been a general handling of stones, perhaps not as neatly Cartesian as Arvan would have it, but surely a throwing, and therefore a gathering, a sorting of stones, and a knocking of them together for sound, for rhythm, with much accidental chipping and breaking.

None of this, of course, addressed the history of worked stone; there Monsieur Arvan was his guide, for what was a matter of evolution to Tallini was history of art to Michel Arvan. Both history and evolution have direction, however, whereas random activity, with its lack of rules, is not even play. Tallini's improvisational experience as a musician had taught him about necessity. For such random activity was indeed heavy with hidden possibilities and covert patterns. A rudimentary social structure such as a Stone Age group with random stone activities would be the most likely setting for the breakthrough in worked stone, and thus evidence of a "new" necessity.

"Speculations, grandiose speculations," Arvan would say whenever Tallini tentatively aired such notions. "One must remain practical, my friend. Isn't it enough that they left us this incomparable heritage? And I do believe that utility was

24

a driving force, though it doesn't seem to enter into your equation at all! I find it more compelling than a *cosmic* necessity. Don't you believe there were those who considered a stone solely as the prosthetic weapon of the hand, strictly, you might say, in terms of survival? There was even a traffic in such stones valued for their potential form. That adze over there, for example: it had to be perceived as dormant in the stone, isn't it so? What kind of mind divines the red-beaked Horus waiting in the black granite block? An alabaster virgin inside the quarry's rough-hewn? Michelangelo himself described the sculptures struggling to be liberated under his chisel. Matter, which is to say stone, was no obstacle for these early stone shapers because they had well served their Paleolithic apprenticeship. All due to the opposable thumb, of course, a manipulating hand—tool of tools."

Ah, the hand, the prodigal hand, as yet untrammeled by conventions. Tallini had obtained an overview of its antecedents in zoological texts, but he felt that in such linear developments only half the story was told. Following it through the Hominidae, there was no avoiding the synapse where linearity short-circuited and the process exploded, with effects no longer proportioned to cause. For the hand, formed and organized for the capacity of working stone, had to be led by a mind that could project the idea. And what could link the mind to the hand in the consciousness of an idea if not a language, or at least a *name* to distinguish particularity?

Tallini tried hard to feel himself into that universe of undifferentiated stone and random activity, where cave man, *his* cave man now, aeons ago was still an inseparable part of the universe, a universe of stone. This being, he reasoned, this creature, issued from the developing life of the world, was no infrahuman primate. Not humanoid at all—neither apelike man nor manlike ape—but man, *cave* man, equipped with the power of speech, reason, opposable thumbs, focused vision, and the spark divine. A dweller of caves, he could consider settling down, once having domesticated fire. By its safety and its light the Stone Age flowered, an interglacial renaissance of freezings and thawings, of silence and of speech. Lord of stalactite chambers, garbed in fur and skins, the cave-being mastered his medium by firelight, working the stone to the disclosure of its secrets. Such, in Tallini's mind, was the history of stone, and Arvan was its interpreter.

"Working the stone, yes," said Arvan, "but also keeping it as found, neither tool nor weapon, but just object, a possession; such collections are sometimes found in caves, and I hold them to be the beginning of capital. But I also tend to think there was always some utility to them, perhaps a reflective quality among others, although your theory of night sky and stone as protocabalistic speculums might go a bit far." And when Tallini suggested there had been mind and voice to match the hand, the antiquary said he was evoking "the kind of mind to which stone poses a mirror."

And after a pensive silence, long by Arvan's standards, "The history of stone has many chapters, some of them still barely understood, others completely esoteric. Take my friend Gaston—a thinking man, philosopher, scientist, but above all, poet. 'Arvan,' he told me, 'the age of chipped stone is the age of tormented stone, whereas the age of polished stone is the age of caressed stone. Yes, Arvan, and the mystery goes even deeper. The savage smashes the flint, he doesn't work it. The man who works the flint loves the flint, and one doesn't love stones any differently than one loves women.' "

Despite their eloquence, the dealer's definitions rarely satisfied Tallini entirely, yet they usually managed a contribution to his thinking, oblique though it might have been. How could anyone have satisfied Tallini's hankering after a particular lived moment and a specific individualization: a first differentiation, the instant when an accidental chipping is recognized as *special*, and a distinction is drawn within the hitherto indifferent mineral universe.

They talked for a long time on that occasion, and a thoroughly fascinated Tallini reluctantly took his leave. On the way out of the shop, almost at the door, a ray of late sun striking a showcase arrested his passage. Displayed within was a resplendent pearl shining from the folds of Arvan's gray velvet sea "like Venus-Astarte herself," Tallini mused, and the nacreous afterimage lingered on.

A passerby on the narrow sidewalk almost jostled Tallini into Arvan's window, breaking his contemplation. At any other time, he wouldn't have hesitated to enter the shop, but the prospect at this moment made him aware of the radical change effected by the event at the CINEDOC party. He knew it would be out of the question to confide any of this to the dealer; it was much too fragile a matter to be exposed to possible sarcasm, however veiled and diplomatic. Yet he realized he would be unable to speak about caves and cave people without taking this new factor into account. It had become the most important element of the subject now within his reach, carrying a potential for information that far surpassed anything implements and artifacts could offer. With some regret, he considered the possibility that in this single afternoon he might well have outgrown Arvan and his knowledgeable approach. But the pang of melancholy went, and he opted for the comforts of a good café. One of his favorites was located down the street from the antiquary, on a corner by the river. Run by an Alsatian, it was frequented by writers and intellectuals, among them a number of foreigners.

Tallini bought a newspaper at the kiosk, swung himself through the revolving door, and was greeted by savory fumes of knackwurst, a specialty served at any time of day or night with a side dish of sauerkraut, reputed to be the best in town. Sitting down amid the bustle, satisfied he had finished at the library once and for all, Tallini reflected fatalistically that, in any case, the initiative lay in the hands of the cave people, who were not to be tracked down in books on prehistoric studies, where their absence could be ascertained on every page. They were bound to be strangers to conceptual terminologies ordered by rules of grammar and syntax, just as surely as they would not have found a place at that table of journalists across the room, whose words he could not hear but whose gestures spoke volumes. He vaguely knew two or three of them, reporters on matters political, criminal, and social, who overtaxed the language in those overlapping domains. Could this really be the culmination of an immemorial striving toward consciousness and its communication? What a lamentable dissipation of a supremely specialized energy revealed by the primordial word of the beginning!

"Impossibile!" The word had slipped out, and the waiter looked around, nervously flicking a white napkin. Tallini cleared his throat, ordered a *petit noir,* and opened the paper, staring at the type without reading. The first words in the caves must have been of unimaginable abstraction and inclusivity, and the *first* word a complete sentence containing in itself the entire linguistic universe, actual and possible. This essential quality of initiation, always a oneness containing all, is an intuition that would have any one word of a language reveal the tongue in its essence. But the first word contains a language not yet deployed, as yet unknown, unspoken. The pressure of everything linguistic, of wordness—in the beginning, word has no language into which to channel itself—dams up in layers of meaning structured into abstractions. *"Abstrutture,"* he said, not loudly enough this time to be overheard. Suddenly he felt very pleased with himself for twice having changed his afternoon plans. Once for going to the CINEDOC reception, and once for deserting it. Had it not been for Ladsnik's invitation, he would probably be sitting in the Bibliothèque at this moment.

He mentally passed in review the several books he had on reserve, now abandoned and betrayed. There was Obermaier's study on human fossils in Spain, Cartailhac's *Les mains rouges et noires de la grotte de Garges,* and particularly Pellicer's *Estratigrafía Prehistorica de la Cueva de Nerja.* This last concerned a relatively new find that was becoming one of his prime objectives, a book from which he had already culled over a hundred pages of notes. Notwithstanding the authoritative flair with which these works were composed, Tallini kept finding their subjects empty silhouettes begging for content, for a topography that would offer coordinates for the projection of these early silent cave entities onto the barren plane of the mind. He had slaved over these books until they sapped

28

his energies and threatened to subject his own intuitions and speculations to the strict intellectuality that reigned in those proceedings.

But now these futile cogitations faded from his brain, for among the effluences of *Chez l'Alsacien*'s vaporous kitchen, he was surprised again by the tactile feeling of something poised to come down, and as he turned his attention toward it, he discovered it had *already* been there—a pseudo déjà vu, because there was nothing to be seen. Neither was there imagination, because *unimaginable,* a notion an Indian guru had taught him to conceive as a polarity of the imaginable rather than its limit. Being thus, deprived of all content, it presented to experience a mere shell of its possibilities. Immersed in the sensation, Tallini became convinced that such tactile feeling depended on point of view and could be modified by a different setting. He simply *had* to get to the Spanish hills to test this assumption.

TWO

THE LIGHT-MACHINE

"**P**iero!"

His reaction, after the first shock of hearing his name, was one of annoyance, café encounters being a sure interruption of one's train of thought. But it was Benji Gauthier looking down at him, and seeing Benji was always a pleasure. Furthermore, his friend's intrusion didn't seem to affect the feeling of contact in the least. Tallini motioned for him to sit. They had been meeting for years in just such fortuitous café encounters. Their acquaintance dated back to the Spanish war, when Benji's articles in support of the Republican cause had been highly visible in the French press. Tallini had stayed with the Republican forces until the fall of Barcelona, then covered the retreat into France of the defeated troops and civilian refugees, reaching Paris with some heartrending documentation and a reputation of his own as combat photographer. That was when he began to frequent the café where Benji had been a regular for years.

Tallini was in a somber mood during those few months that would separate the Spanish prelude from the first moves of the broader struggle to come. Only with Benji did he allow himself to voice his pessimism concerning the future of the continent. Benji was a great believer in the might of France and England, and the defending power of the Maginot line. And then there were the Soviets, archenemies of the Nazis. Even after the Nazi-Soviet pact, Benji maintained that Stalin was only buying time and would attack when the moment was right. Hitler would be fighting on two fronts; he couldn't be that stupid! But Tallini had seen German planes in remorseless action, and he had seen the opportunistic political intrigues of the communists in war-torn Spain. He was still smarting, furthermore, from the indifference displayed by the French republic toward the Spanish antifascist struggle, and it had left him with nagging doubts about the French nation's resolve. Such topics had been explored whenever the two men met while the Paris of 1939 was preparing to celebrate the 150th anniversary of the Revolution. Both were spending that summer there, Tallini because he had secured a contract for a photoreportage of the festivities, and Benji because he rarely left town in any season and had a predilection for Paris in the summer.

During the intervening twenty years, Tallini had been absent from Paris several times for long periods, while Benji had hardly budged. Beyond his pleasure in discourse, there was something reserved about Benji, and rather little was known about him. No occasion ever arose that would have moved Tallini to inquire where his friend lived, or how. Benji wrote articles on current affairs for mildly leftist journals with small distribution, and it was always easy to know what he was working on, as he freely discussed his ideas with whoever sat at his table. Nowadays he was involved in the public discussion concerning the role of technology and science in the grave events of the two world wars and their possibilities for the future. This literary activity, although highly esteemed by his peers, could hardly have sufficed to keep body and soul together in the Paris of the 1950s. It was assumed he had some support abroad, perhaps from the United States. His French was perfect, and he looked like any aging Parisian intellectual of modest means, although he was said to be a Carpathian Jew who came to France in the 1920s and, with the help of mysterious contacts and counterfeit identification, had managed to survive in Paris through the Occupation.

For Tallini, a meeting with Benji was always of interest, even if he tended to monopolize conversation as a forum for his pet theory, something he called *"la syntactique."* For as long as they had known each other, Tallini had heard him speak about this idea, yet he still had little more than a vague notion of what it was. Although Benji mentioned it at least once in every conversation, he could not be persuaded to define it. "Every last term cannot be defined. For me, *la syntactique* is a last term," he would say in his somewhat weighty central European manner. He was often witty, sometimes profound, but never transparent to Tallini, who, whenever *syntactique* was mentioned, suspected his friend's opaque diction to be intentional and of highly conscious construction. Tallini took it for what it basically had to be: a logical structure into which Benji attempted to fit his world. The ways and means of the fit emerged only in context, and the man doubtless had his reasons for shielding from the beam of clarity the inevitable concatenation that formed the *syntactique.* Tallini was prepared to leave the matter unresolved.

But Benji could also be an attentive listener, provided he thought it worth his while, as he mostly did with Tallini. The latter would present his latest preoccupation, and Benji enjoyed the variety. To him the game was the renewed challenge of bringing his friend back to *la syntactique,* which he rarely failed to do, if ever so subtly. Tallini was patient, letting Benji speak at length whenever he felt so moved. It was a trade-off, for Tallini expected equal time. In a group of acquaintances, a subject introduced by the wider company more often than not fell short of Benji's approval, and he would turn away and sigh in resignation at the subject's worthlessness: *"Vaut pas la peine qu'on s'en occupe, ce sujet."* Then he would leave or else impose his own topic by managing to subsume, sometimes after long and intricate meanderings, *any* subject in terms of his *syntactique,* thereby making the point that *no* subject encompasses its deepest signification unless subsumed by *la syntactique.*

It was difficult to tell whether *la syntactique* involved a system of nature, a theory of language, or a cosmological structure. Whatever his subject, those who had followed him for some time felt that at its core *syntactique* was a theory of necessary combinatory order. Benji was polyglot and clever with words, always alert to their interlinguistic relations. His ideas were usually couched in a good-humored turn of phrase, and in company that looked for relaxation rather than instruction, he would easily capture the floor and direct the discussion. If someone wanted lighter fare, he was always free to move. At *Chez l'Alsacien*, everyone was sure to know at least one person at every other table. The café's success with the literary and journalistic crowd was rooted as much in this unengaged intimacy with its undercurrent of literary, political, and social attitudes as in the favorable ratio of knackwurst to sauerkraut served.

● ◐ ○ ◑ ◑ ◐

Benji had seen several of Tallini's enthusiasms come and go, but none led to more controversy between the two friends than had the project of his "light-machine." Tallini had been working on it for some time, but only brought it up with Benji after achieving what he believed to be a first small success. Unfortunately, the assessment turned out to have been too optimistic. Benji's initial reaction, furthermore, could hardly have come as a surprise, considering his distaste for anything mechanical: "What are you doing, playing with machines? Don't we have enough machines in the world as it is, and haven't we recently had an ample demonstration of where machines and technology can lead us?"

Tallini tried to explain *his* wasn't that kind of machine, that he was merely aiming at a qualitative enhancement of light. "It's light itself I'm after. Pure seeing," he said. He protested that his efforts were scientific and philosophical in equal amounts; he thought he could produce light of a superior kind that might be highly beneficial to humankind. Wasn't there evidence already that certain colors had specific effects not only on plants and lower animal life but even on higher mammals and, most important of all, on human beings? Science had gone wrong, he claimed, when it abandoned the idea of quality. His own experiments were not within the quantitative spectrum, but concerned with qualitative light enhancement that could mean a radical expansion of human perception. Wasn't it well known that sight is to a great extent an acquired faculty? And couldn't it be that humankind got stuck with a received, an atavistic vision of the world? And as the pineal gland is a degenerated third eye, couldn't there still be unknown nonvisual photoreceptors in humans that would be sensitive to a more refined and qualitative light phenomenon?

Benji had listened patiently. "I don't know enough about the technical aspects of the subject to judge these refinements you are after," he said, "but one thing I know for certain: you may want to do something purely scientific, but if you get results, a technician will step in sooner or later, with an application that can be exploited for money or for power. You will in time lose all control over your machine and your scientific ideals. Technology will go where *it* wants; it has an agenda of its own. It is not based on human aims but strictly on itself. It grows out of itself, and its developments in turn stimulate scientific thinking, so they form a closed circuit totally out of touch with anything human. So how can it be concerned with what is beneficial to humanity?

"You speak of qualitative improvement, and I'm happy to hear you haven't forgotten those qualitative facts you used to talk so much about. Certainly *they* would play a part in those more elevated human concerns such as art and spirituality and ethical problems. How could science care about these, when its essence is a disregard of the qualitative, of sensibility, feeling, emotion, all of which is necessarily subjective? Or have you, by chance, gotten hold of another science, one that has abandoned objectivity and fits your qualitative facts? Then your machine would rather belong in some gallery of the Rue du Faubourg St.-Honoré, where I see contraptions of all kinds peddled as works of art."

Tallini was incapable of laying out the substance of his research in a logical or even comprehensible sequence of terms. But he did express his disagreement with the notion of a *speed* of light and its consequent limit. "It's a limit of our minds," he maintained. There was no "limited" speed of light, and therefore no speed at all! Whether produced in a Big Bang or by divine will, a *Fiat Lux* existed and could be experienced by a corresponding *Vide Lumen* that allowed the former to be known and studied. Nor was that creative light-moment the onetime miracle of some putative beginning, but an ever and constantly recurring event at every point of space and time. Better, *Fiat Lux* was the point from which both space and time emanated, continuously created without beginning or end at every subsequent point of space and time in an expanding, limitless universe.

That, at least, was the interpretation Benji's more rigorous mind had constructed of the bits and pieces laboriously brought forth by his friend. In fact, Tallini's ideas were expressed in a mixed jargon of physics, electronics, and photography, none of them subjects to arouse Benji's sympathy. In general, talk of machines provoked him, and he didn't mince words with his friend. He had remained active in the postwar discussions among European intellectuals about the technological efficiency manifested in mass destruction and the use made of nuclear fission. The Nuremberg trials were still fresh in everyone's memory, and it was clear that only the misappropriation of modern technical thinking could have achieved these ghastly results. He reminded Tallini of this, and it was perhaps not accidental that he was working on an essay about the influence of science and technology on contemporary ethical, artistic, and spiritual expression.

Tallini was profoundly shocked by Benji's interpretation of his endeavor, but it did not dissuade him from his project, which he felt to be beyond reproach. He was inured to opposition and derision and simply avoided bringing up the subject. Benji, on the other hand, although refraining from reference to the machine, made a point of freely venting his thoughts on science and technology whenever an occasion arose. Surprisingly—and to Tallini's credit, he thought—his friend was showing a growing interest in his ideas on the topic. He did, however, remark on one particularity: Tallini's speech problem, a slight impediment and one of the more salient changes

Benji noted when Tallini reappeared in Paris after the war, seemed particularly pronounced in those discussions, as it was with the topic of the light-machine as well.

They had not seen each other for six years during the war. Their last prewar Paris summer and the celebrations of the Revolution had been followed by a winter of suspense, which became known as *la drôle de guerre.* Life for Benji had continued on its usual course, but Tallini was often out of town on assignments. He was documenting the effects of the waiting game on the nations that bordered the Nazi state and on the Allied garrisons that faced it. The German attack in the spring of 1940 found him with a unit of the British Expeditionary Force. He stayed with them through their retreat to Dunkirk and was evacuated to England along with them. But he did manage to see Benji one more time before leaving the Continent to its Occupation.

Realizing, a mere four days into the German attack, that no serious obstacle remained between the German panzers and the capital once the defenses of Sedan had been breached, Tallini overcame a nightmare of traffic and fuel shortage to get to *Chez l'Alsacien* in hopes of finding Benji. Tallini urged him to leave the city by any means possible and to go south. But no news from Sedan had been reported by the Paris papers, and the city was quiet in its customary routines. "In any case," Benji had said, "the French and the British surely have some tanks of their own, and even with a breach at the front, it doesn't mean Paris will fall and the war be lost." He brought up World War I, when the city was twice threatened and twice saved. "When their capital is in danger, the *poilus* know how to fight!" Benji was touched by Tallini's concern for his safety, but thought his friend unnecessarily alarmed. He resolutely refused to consider leaving Paris—his books, his work, his routine. It had been a great relief for Tallini to find him safe and sound after the hostilities. They resumed their café get-togethers, their friendship strengthened.

One afternoon, Tallini arranged a meeting at the café with an acquaintance, an engineer, who had expressed interest in his light-machine and might want to have a go at its construction. The engineer had reached the stage where more precise details, even measurements, had to be produced for him to evaluate its feasibility. A problem had apparently arisen, due mainly to a paranoid secretiveness Tallini had begun to exhibit ever since Benji's rejection, a disposition poles apart from the cooperative attitude a prospective partner had right and reason to expect.

Tallini asked Benji to forget his prejudice for this occasion and to attend the meeting, or more precisely, to be present at the moment of introductions. All three would chat for a short while, time for Benji to size up the man. Tallini needed the security of a second opinion, and here he would obtain a highly regarded judgment. Incisive evaluation of his fellow man was one of Benji's noted faculties. In addition, he had a fine nose for foolishness and a great impatience in the absence of individuality, talent, and basic literacy. After taking an instant measure of this person, he was to retire to another table, beyond earshot, having communicated his verdict by a few parting words in a prearranged code. Such was the plan, typically Talliniesque in its detailed layout.

Benji agreed to a truce, sensing an opportunity to satisfy the curiosity the light-machine had, little by little, aroused in him. He was himself hoping for a second opinion, in the form of a qualified stranger's unbiased reaction to Tallini's mystery machine—a *first* opinion, to be exact, seeing that his own, with its lack of expertise, counted for naught and had wisely been left unconsolidated. It would be an occasion to obtain a measure of insight into Tallini's invention. Furthermore, he felt that if anyone was entitled to clarifications on this matter, he should be the first.

Benji had believed all along there was a body of ideas in his friend, ideas that simply hadn't yet ripened, which explained why words came to him with such difficulty. This lack of maturity in Tallini's thinking allowed his mind to entertain this unfortunate machine obsession. For Benji, a large part of intellectual life resided in discovering early traces of such yet-to-ripen ideas, which are like buds to be tended into flowering. He usually pursued them in their written form, in books and reviews. However, in his relation with Tallini, he felt he had definitely played a maieutic role. Could it be that this bud was now opening? If so, he certainly meant to be present. Ever on the scent of ideas, Benji was pragmatic. He had seen too many fortunes made with apparent nonsense to let *anything* slip by, even a long shot like this. For all he knew, Tallini might be the next Edison. There was little to lose, and if nothing else, the occasion offered an attractive psychological dividend. A fork exists where madness and genius part ways, yet they do remain, if not brothers, at least cousins. He had observed the workings of Tallini's mind, had tried to infer the state of his soul, and had thereby become interested, and sometimes concerned, wondering whether this man, although not yet within sight of such a bifurcation, was perhaps heading for it. Yet the un-self-consciously poietic nature of a wandering dreamer might escape the choice. At least such was Benji's wager.

So he took a hard line toward Tallini's proposition that he size up the engineer, ironizing outrageously, refusing all subterfuge and deceit. He declared it an ethically self-defeating scheme that would start the partnership off on the wrong footing and chided an embarrassed Tallini for envisioning a scientific collaboration on the level of a manipulative business mentality. He did this kindly, with tongue in cheek, while ensuring his own presence at the discussion. Not only would he be delighted to attend, he *insisted* on being present and introduced as a friend and supporter, legal adviser, biographer perhaps, or any other function he could fulfill, as long as his competence had a basis in truth. (The ethical argument was of the essence, incidentally bringing to light he had at one time read law at the Faculté de Droit in Lyon.) He could at least be helpful with the more philosophical aspects, especially in case of eventual publication. After all, from what he had gathered, this matter concerned the mechanics of light, didn't it, and therefore had to encompass both physics and philosophy. And if he *was* to promise his services in evaluating the moral and intellectual character of someone (and here he played cautiously on anxieties Tallini did not yet recognize himself) who could after all be an inquisitive intruder, or even a thief in the night, he preferred to have time for a thorough observation. Such people could be consummate actors; they were professionals. With his usual moral thoroughness, he seized the occasion to warn his friend of the pitfalls of snap judgments.

Tallini agreed, and together they welcomed the bearded and bespectacled middle-aged gentleman, whose punctuality earned him merits with Benji from the start. Introducing himself as an assistant professor at the University of Louvain, a specialist in medieval philosophy and technology and a practical physicist and experimental tinkerer in his spare time, he admitted, perhaps for Benji's benefit, to a near-metaphysical conception of the mechanical. All of which was somewhat removed from the "engineer" heralded by Tallini, whose raised eyebrows signaled surprise at this biographical offering. Tallini's reaction was not lost on Benji and led him to wonder about the depth and nature of the relationship. Were they always so wrapped up in technical talk that these simple facts had never surfaced?

Tallini was at first defensive, as if facing an unsympathetic stranger; then, a moment later, he was affable and forthcoming on matters the two men had manifestly discussed in detail on earlier occasions. If any common ground underlay this conversation, it was largely lost on Benji, to whose consternation the strange introductory prelude turned out to be but the first of a devastating series of equivocations and retractions and a fundamental ambiguity that played itself out in Tallini's hands, literally on top of the marble table. But not before both parties came to agree that the meeting itself was based on a misunderstanding, as became apparent when the professor from Louvain, hardly seated, asked (perhaps in a simple reflex to Tallini's visible nervousness) brusque questions about the material he had come here to see, the documentation he was to be shown today. "Shown? Today? Impossible, a regrettable *malentendu*," Tallini countered, unflustered, though with voice slightly on edge. He *couldn't* have brought these things to the meeting, for the simple reason he didn't have them with him in Paris. He reaffirmed the existence of a small model and of photographs of a larger model that had been unfortunately lost in a fire last year. He had rough blueprints, and though he wasn't himself an engineer or draftsman, the drawings were clear enough. Unfortunately, however, everything was in Milan; he wouldn't dream of traveling with such documents. With both arms in a dramatic gesture, he repeated, "Unfortunately, *peccato*, all in Milano, via Brera, by the museum. You know Milano?"

The professor seemed puzzled and insisted he had been led to believe . . . but Tallini cut him short. He had everything in his head; he would draw a sketch. Benji signaled a waiter and asked for pencil and paper. It was one of *l'Alsacien*'s endearing features to distribute sheets of cheap newsprint and diminutive pencils on demand. The prospective partners were facing each other over the table, and Benji considered them in profile. Tallini began to sketch a polyhedron in cross section, and Benji observed him closely, looking at him as if for the first time. Was his prudence, the wariness so characteristic of him recently, evaporating for some reason here before Benji's very eyes? And why a sudden openness for the benefit of this unlikely professor? Was it a sham, invented for his own or for Benji's benefit? All along, he had behaved like a self-contained event, like a play without a stage. Now suddenly the performer was becoming an actor, addressing the house from a proscenium before the curtain rises.

Benji had rationalized his friend's incursion into the scientific as an understanding refined through long experience with the photographic light image. For a less active mind, such inroads might be no more than a natural and legitimate step; however, it had vitally transformed Tallini's imagination. Sometimes such openings at first offer no more than panoramas of abstraction, needing time to gain a concrete parameter.

Tallini began to commit to paper an appropriate metaphor with a force that made the lead tear through the flimsy newsprint. The proficiency of his draftsmanship, astounding to Benji, was undeterred by an accompanying stream of words in two styles. Most predominantly, there was a running commentary detailing the progress of the drawing—affable, helpful to one who had to grasp the image upside down and hidden behind Tallini's free hand, which covered the upper part of the sketch under pretext of holding the sheet in place. This commentary was intermittently sprinkled with questions, sharp darts thrust from behind a curtain of sociability, chronological queries apparently irrelevant to the matter at hand, yet aimed at placing the professor's actions at certain crucial times of the recent past. Bent over his paper, Tallini intimated that the enclosure he was drawing should be seen as dodecahedral and lined with twenty-four smooth surfaces, reflectors of sorts, set at a wide angle, two to each plane face. Did he complete his studies at Louvain? And when did he matriculate? And what year was it, exactly?

Asking, he raised his head a trifle, just enough for his upturned pupils to clear the bushy eyebrows and achieve the shortest path between two points. They looked hard at one another for a moment—a challenge in that gaze!—and before the answer situated the professor at his university during the Occupation years, Tallini was back to the paper, his hand working with dexterity. Those hands were indeed a marked component of his generally imposing presence, not only because he used them with Mediterranean expressiveness, but because they were, somewhat incongruously, the huge and heavy hands of a stonemason. They stood out from his general appearance, which was marked by his homeland and in certain meditative moments recalled those busts of Roman dignitaries whose empty eyes stare into the past while their perfectly typical features live in an eternal present. Even before realizing the refinements they hid, Benji had been so impressed by those hands that he had once inquired about traditional professions in the family, if there had been sculptors perhaps, builders in stone, or some related occupations. Tallini was not aware of such a background, but admitted, without giving further details, to a special feeling for quarries.

Tallini apprised his audience—a spellbound Benji, a puzzled professor—that the reflectors were to be thin layers of a highly polished stone, a mineral akin to mica he said he could readily obtain. A thin ray of light would be introduced into the enclosure to mark the point of *Fiat Lux* that would multiply into a strictly limited spatial universe. The reflectors were angled and arranged so the geometry of light would evolve close to the walls of the enclosure, creating a hollow sphere of luminosity around a central space where one could locate something, perhaps place someone, *un soggetto,* let us say, or . . . Tallini hesitated, with a searching look and a wrinkled forehead, as if he had never before wondered what it might well be that one would place at the center of such manufactured light activity. At this point Benji interjected, helpfully, *"Un osservatore, per avventura?"*

Tallini's eyes brightened, he straightened up, put the pencil down. Of course, of course, how could he have missed him? An observer! There was awe in his voice for this appearance of what had been inaccessible, though just on the tip of the tongue. Now that he could make it roll forth and fit it into his structure, he was moved to tears, or at least made it seem so. Totally sidetracked, he savored the word and addressed Benji as if they were alone, as if his friend's shift from mute witness to inventive participant had entirely invalidated their prearranged roles. The professor cleared his throat, put off by the Italian interjections, feeling left out and vaguely insulted, wondering whether he was being had. Tallini, shameless, performed extravagantly, producing another, ironical self, one new to Benji. Grandiloquent, he pretended his heart was warmed by such precision of terminology.

But the man from Louvain was not finished. He mustered an unexpected sense of humor, and asked why one would want to keep the *osservatore* (crassly imitating the intonation he had just heard) in a box. That brought Tallini back to his drawing and his senses. With a few bold strokes he finished the sketch. He slid the sheet of newsprint toward his vis-à-vis, giving it a half turn to let him view it right side up, yet keeping hold of it at the two upper corners. This gave Benji the occasion to contemplate as fists those dukes that had intrigued him ever since their very first meeting: their strong handshake, their gestural expressiveness, their elegance when delicately raising a glass to someone's health, and just now their deftness in executing a complex design. Here, on the cool marble table, they were exhibiting an antithetical will of both offering and retaining. Benji stared at the drama of ambivalence performed beneath these large bony surfaces, metacarpals rippling in indecision and knuckles white with contrariety. Perhaps some caution was warranted when so much energy was pent up in so much . . . so much mistrust, it occurred to Benji, mistrust combined with his manifest desire to transmit whatever it was he wanted the world to know about the apparatus. He was not handing over the paper, but merely letting the professor glimpse it. Another moment of torture, and he pulled back the sheet, folded it neatly twice, and stuck it in his inside pocket.

Well before Tallini had finished the drawing, Benji knew he wouldn't let it go, that he would never hand it over to a stranger. Not primarily because the fellow had revealed dubious political leanings, but because the genesis of the drawing had radically altered its creator. Benji was convinced of this, yet he was unable to pin down the nature of the change. The thought crossed his mind that the alteration might have occurred earlier and had been reenacted here, manifestly for him, as he was the only one capable of deciphering, beyond the Gordian knot of unassorted strings of conversation, beyond or beneath the language of this meeting, a pantomime played for his benefit. He alone—and surely not the "engineer"—could have read the silent message of the gestures. That there had been a change, "a synthesis that signified a fundamental difference," was confirmed by Tallini after the professor from Louvain had withdrawn with the same tactful punctuality so pleasing to Benji in his arrival.

Indeed, had he been asked to make the report that was the whole forgotten point of his coming, Benji would have had to confess to perfect neutrality. Beyond the impeccable arrival and departure, he had retained no distinct impressions of the man. Nevertheless, his timing was a gift that Benji found germane to his own maturing relationship with Tallini. To *these* ends the stranger was so perfectly and innocently adapted that any questions of character or usefulness vanished. Whether in tacit agreement with this assessment or in distracted self-absorption, Tallini, true to form, dispensed with all explanation or justification of the small drama he had unwittingly produced. Louvain had come and gone and left them to a brief tête-à-tête. Benji, who had no questions his friend would be able to answer, appreciated the advantage of letting the matter rest. Tallini said a few cryptic words concerning the synthesis that had come about while drawing "this idea." He never thereafter spoke of a "machine."

Benji didn't bother to interpret the paraphrase. He had felt only too well what took place, and knew it had precious little to do with what either of them might have projected. He also knew it was the end of the light-machine. "Tallini's discovery of the metaphor" is what he called the process he had witnessed. Between the concrete photograph—the proof —and the abstraction of light, Tallini had been looking for a technical mediation. With the concourse of circumstances, the dynamics of the situation, and the inner tensions that lend the triad its power, these incommensurable dispositions that make the moment converted commonplace to the exceptional. "He is born to philosophy," Benji thought as he listened to his friend struggle to denounce the "materialization of the idea" as an "unworthy crutch and perhaps a miserable fraud." Benji felt he had played his part successfully, allowing Tallini's "synthesis" whatever its momentary form, and thereby allowing the transcendence of the light-machine. That evening, they separated with the unspoken understanding of their newly-won closeness.

◗ ◖ ◯ ◯ ◐ ◐

"What sort of things are you reading these days at the Nationale?" As the waiter brought Tallini's coffee and took

Benji's order, Tallini gained a moment's delay for his answer. Benji had been laudatory about the studious habits he had recently acquired. It was hardly in Tallini's nature to dissemble, but if he was going to admit his change of heart about bookish knowledge, he had to come forth with a reason, and again, he couldn't think of any but the true one. Should he be candid about the whole matter? There was really no need to beat around the bush with Benji, not after what they had gone through together and notably not after the session with that guy from Louvain. Or was there? In any case, he welcomed the opportunity to talk, and Benji was the only one he could talk to about such things. So he began by explaining how those cave explorations were fine as far as they went, but for him, the main thing was missing, namely, the presence of early humans in the caves. No sense doing something about the habitat without bringing in the inhabitants. But how? He had some ideas of his own, but he didn't quite know how.

His hesitation measured the inevitable distance of every spoken word from its truth, something he had come to expect and had learned to evaluate. (Tallini was no longer a man of fiction and machines.) He knew action fails to the extent that truth is absent, and this conviction underlay his mistrust of speech. Yet there is meaning even in the lie, and that meaning is the truth of the lie. But an approach to truth must ever be less than absolute—Tallini had experienced as much—and a speaker of truth is advised only by a private honor system of the soul, which grades judgments of relativity that cannot be expressed in degrees. In turn, these subjective gradations themselves vary according to a number of levels at which an act can be potentiated. But Tallini was undaunted by truth's perpetual compromise. It was the effort that counted, and as far as it pertained to the cave people, he knew he hadn't even tried. How could he explain to Benji the truth of the contact he had made, with what words, here in this sauerkraut atmosphere? But does the atmosphere affect the telling?

Certainly Benji would receive only words and not their inessential context. Then again, what determines the limits of a context? And in this particular case another problem loomed behind Tallini's concern, one of which Benji had been a part: the apocalyptic collapse of the light-machine. It had been only two years, and there would be no way the sense of repetition could be averted and no way it could be denied. While he himself had dismissed the Louvain caper long ago, it had to be alive in Benji's mind, though it was hard to know exactly in what manner. Not unfavorably, to be sure. But how would Benji weather what certainly must appear to him as repetition, unless he understood the difference? Still, even if Benji hadn't forgotten the machine incident, he must also know the episode had, in an almost covert manner, made them grow closer. There was now an implicit understanding of continuity, almost a sense of working together.

Although he trusted Benji, Tallini wished to be circumspect. He explained he was investigating the state of those early people. He wouldn't say *mental* state exactly; there yet would hardly be a mind as we think of it. But there must have been a receptivity to language, mental pictures, a *wordness* of some kind. What is that state into which language falls? What was there before? These were the questions demanding clarity, but all he could find were descriptions of sites, bones, artifacts, tools. These were interesting, of course, but they had little to do with what he really wanted.

Further, Tallini wondered whether the ideas in those books just filled his head with misconceptions rather than contributing to the search. They could even eventually block any direct information he might receive, especially if he was to go into the field to shoot some footage. He told Benji that his academic research might be counterproductive, an impediment to a style, to a way of being for which he had already developed a special feeling unlike anything he found in those weighty tomes.

But Benji was perceptive. "You wouldn't by any chance care to elaborate on this information you might get *directly?*" Benji's heavy eyelids were half closed as usual, as if to dam behind them the clarity of mind he parsimoniously dispensed. Tallini stirred his coffee persistently. He had become a point of intersection between two powerful lines of force. Benji's glance, providing the first coordinate, would be cold, were it not for the genuine interest it conveyed, directed to the human rather than the personal. The second line of force came from an unspecified darkness, a powerful stream of sentience that came to Tallini—as real as Benji's presence—like an intuitive, emotional, knowing feeling. This force came from the cave people. Both forces now were strong, with Tallini the locus of intersection. A little whirlpool was stirred up in the coffee cup, and he felt pulled into the turbulence, engulfed in darkness, chaos. But Benji's gaze flashed against the obscurity, the eye's ration of fire; the logic shone brightly and brought to the fore the chaotic and dark emotion of blind sentience. Again Tallini felt them very close, the early ones. Were they attracted by Benji's eyes? Did they long to see what he saw? Did they yearn to draw attention? Did they crave description?

Tallini spoke briefly of his joy and satisfaction with Benji's response. He felt certain that Benji would understand, and told him so. "Something has opened up, a radical change. But it just happened, just a few hours ago, at a ridiculous party. No, it has nothing to do with anyone at the party; it could have happened anywhere, I think. Let's say that I'm involved—no, it's more—I'm in contact with another state of being, my own, but with others also, like ancestors, the first ones. I beg you to be patient; I'm simply incapable of finding words for the event as yet. It is the moment of the real becoming of man, not in the generality but specifically at that early interglacial moment when the words came, or even more precisely, when the word came." Tallini stopped and had a sip of coffee, stirred cold. He had wanted to take a step, but it seemed no more than a stumble.

Benji's sauerkraut arrived. "If I had known what we were going to get into here," he said dryly, "I would have ordered something lighter." He tucked his napkin into his collar and arranged it carefully over his shirt front. "Call it a breakthrough—you're in touch with a source of some kind. Why shouldn't it happen? Perhaps you know now what I consider a worthwhile subject. You can't find the words because there are none for you as yet. Before you can formulate something —that is, string it out in words—you have to have thought it as a whole. Otherwise, we'd all be barking like dogs instead of saying anything coherent. And when I say 'words,' I'm speaking loosely, as we do all the time. I don't mean the audible or visible component, the voice, the writing—that's just one part, the practical part, the terminological. Important for us mortals but not for contacts such as you cultivate. Now, it takes time to say something, but it doesn't take time to think it. If it did, you would already have thought it, *capito?* I don't mean mulling it over, triturating it. I mean to think it as a whole, there's no time there, it's the moment. That's where such contact situates itself. It's an observation of that wordless thinking, which would take a completely different form, of course, a non-form rather. There's no knowing what the senses would evoke under such provocation. Not necessarily a representation, if you know what I mean. Representation and the whole conceptual baggage to the devil! It's a different world, and I don't see why we shouldn't call it a transcendence. What else would it be? The way you live the moment in the act, in the gesture, so you can think it, with the same liveliness, living thinking. Now once you get hold of that, once you observe it, you find out lots of things that never have time to come into words." Whereupon Benji attacked the knackwurst with determination.

Tallini was afraid he might have revealed too much. What did Benji say? Did it pertain to the experience he, Tallini, had tried and so miserably failed to describe? Had some small part of it been received by Benji? What did Benji make of it? What did he *really* say? Had his own openness, his revelation, his confession, been received with respect? He was ready to get up and leave, but was kept there by the insistence of the tactile feeling, the contact with the cave people, stronger than ever. He felt they wanted him to persist.

As if he was aware of his companion's crisis of doubt, Benji looked up from his plate. "I am really very interested," he said. "I hope you realize. *Very* interested, but life must go on." He then apologized for dividing his attention between intellectual and gastronomic necessities, and bid Tallini to continue in the certainty that he was listening to every word.

Reassured, Tallini explained he had no doubt his intense concentration on the cave people these past weeks caused this feeling-experience to occur, although the preparation may have already begun while filming in India, when he had seriously started to practice hatha yoga. At such meditative times when his attention was focused, he had perhaps known the glimmer of a similar feeling. But that was nothing compared to what had been happening this afternoon, happening right here in the café even while they were talking. It wasn't constant, it seemed to come and go, quite beyond his command. But of one thing he was convinced: the contact was as certain as any other, a familiarity as sure as the table at which they sat. But, he stressed, it was "no more than pure contact," without substance or definition, an unsituated contact based on feeling, a thinking new to him.

Tallini recalled what Benji had said about representing it —namely that it couldn't work. To hell with representation! He liked that. The creative gesture just didn't square with a representing that surely would have to present once again what had been presented before. That was, after all, a large part of his profession, and he knew the limits of the procedure as well as anyone. After this contact with the cave people, of course, he was devoted to fighting representation in a nonphotographic context. No, he wouldn't let his experience of them become an occasion for representation. It was like a certain moment that is always present, must be present, but there had to be a first time for it to be present, and it was that originality which was making itself felt, but not by representation.

Typically Tallini, Benji thought. Superficially incoherent but with a deep logic all his own. He wiped his mouth on his napkin and took a sip of Riesling. "This familiarity you mention," he remarked, "it surely must be a recognition of sorts, don't you think? The memory of something interior, intrinsic, evocative, as the only possibility of contact, something that conjures up the very same consciousness of it *in yourself*. The possibility of memory is always subsequent. But in your quest, the original is the only one that counts, and the question remains: is there a remembrance here too?"

Tallini had indeed asked himself where it might all come from if not from memory, be it but the memory of words. "One furnishes self-consciousness," he replied, "and it will make the contact, put one in relation, and therefore push one into representation. Refuse the representation, and the relation and contact are gone; despite all efforts, it is doomed and one crashes down to the logical, and everything starts all over. No, I don't think it can be guided, it's something that must happen: it's an *improvisation!*"

The term had come forth unexpectedly, the concept of improvisation never having crossed his mind in connection with the cave people. He did, however, happen to know more than a little about it, thanks to a passionate involvement in his student days with a band that played tangos and jazz, two forms of popular music in which the art has survived. Now through his perception of the cave people, he felt the full meaning of improvisation, for they were improvisers by necessity and the original agents of beginner's mind. The contact with them had not only held steady; it had strengthened its grip on him as he uttered the word *improvisation*, a term that validated the notion of originality.

"Has to be improvisation; all the rest is rationalizing," Benji responded. "Needs a careful investigation of the nature of improvisation, though, which is an impossible task to impose on the improviser, who can do nothing but improvise. If he stops to investigate, if he thinks about the improvisation, he has already become another, and he has, as you say so well, crashed into the logical, the determined.

"Call the other a critic if you must, and today the critic is liable to say, 'Hey, I want to improvise too!' Fine, I say, but don't waste your life. If you're a critic, you'll probably never improvise anyway. You might not even be allowed to improvise and keep your job, so rather stay a critic. Improvisers are born, I say. They usually improvise from the beginning—and you can take that beginning back to the single cell—only the substance of the improvisation changes with their development. Now the ideal conduct for improvisers would appear to be something like a ride on the tip of an arrow into the unknown, when in fact it is more like a stumbling forward, inventing one precarious foothold after another."

Benji stopped to pour himself another glass of Riesling. "The improviser can never know what he is doing, where he is going," he continued, "because it would close off the unknown, the improvisational future. He must remain entirely in the moment, where the form is being built, unstable from moment to moment, in disequilibrium, a process ever unfinished. What he is doing reveals its meaning only in the future, but it has to be acted out in a past that did not as yet possess the sense of it. The improviser juggles with a future perfect, but as soon as he realizes the implications of what he will have done, that meaningful present moment in relation to a future and equally meaningful moment, he must adjust it in yet another improvisation, or he will crash.

"There is a sense here of the future determining the present. On what basis the adjustment, you ask? That is another problem, and probably the main one. It involves a certain fittingness of the improvisation, a suitableness to the particular context. Some people speak of *vraisemblance*, and I remember a mathematics professor of mine who spoke of idoneity. There's a call for improvisation in his discipline as well, no doubt about it, although the royal domain of improvisation, the prototype, is music. Typically, improvisation is verbal, and I mean both speaking and writing. As to the archetype, the gesture, it is pure creativity, the fiat out of nothing.

"The crashing into the logical, as you put it so vividly," Benji continued, "is more particularly the crashing into memory and self-consciousness and, most important, into a concept ready to establish an objective relation. And there you have it: a representation. Now you are no longer stumbling forward, you know the road and have your feet firmly planted on it. You are walking in known territory; you are walking in the past. You look around and feel present, but even the purest perception is already past.

"Think of the circuitry perception goes through! It takes time. All of which does impose certain considerations, don't you think? First of all, there can be no method, can there? But you wouldn't say that improvisation obeys no rules at all, that it submits to no law, would you? I know this illusionary point of view is currently in vogue, and very skillfully practiced, too, but it's nothing if not an effect of closure in certain artistic disciplines. It's a stewing in one's own juices, I tell you, and it leads nowhere, although it can be a very lucrative point of view, and there soon will be no other one left. But the creative focus is precisely the struggle between the purity of the improvisation and the necessity of the law, a law I call *la syntactique*."

"Am I improvising?" Tallini asked himself aloud, and Benji could not be blamed for feeling questioned. And before Tallini managed to reformulate his inquiry about the "basis of the adjustment," so artfully converted by Benji, as usual, to his own terms, the latter answered the purely rhetorical question. "I can only hope you are, and I believe you are. I think you're the arrowhead of this vector. But just because you are imaging it, by the necessity of the law, doesn't mean you have to crash; nor does it make the contact any the less real. To the contrary, it gives you a way to the real itself, if you handle the situation. Where do you think the self-consciousness comes from that makes the contact, if not from similarity with your representation, that early man you speak of, those original cave people, or whatever you want to call this point of initiation.

"We all must contain this possibility of originality. It must be within our experience, and it is only a matter of bringing it to our attention, this self-consciousness. Somehow your attention was drawn to it, but the unknown you were really stumbling into was the original, the primordial in yourself. That familiarity you feel is similarity without concept.

52

The true mystery lies in the appearance of this particular context as a site of breakthrough, of transcendence. Some kind of predisposition, no doubt, and a matter of timing, this job showing up at the right point of maturity. Pure hypothesis on my part. I don't wish to theorize the subject, but there are' signs. Yes, it is important because of the signals and the significations. I have had some experiences, very different, of course, but nonetheless . . .''

But the question of his own improvisation had stayed with Tallini. In fact, he had never considered its possibilities outside musical practice. It took Benji to grasp the concept and open it up. He was certain Benji had not had the advantage of musical practice, yet he exhibited a real feeling for the art. What he said was quite valid, albeit somewhat theoretical. What does improvising feel like to one who exerts it in language or directly in life, to one who does not possess the musical prototype? The improvisational consciousness Tallini explored in music has no counterpart in the plastic arts and in no way corresponds to the aleatory practices of contemporary painting. In such arbitrary representations it is not the handheld brush that is improvisational in the moment, it is the eye that commits the creative gesture *after* the painting is complete, and it frequently does so only after repeated viewing. But in true musical improvisation, it is not the ear that attempts the creative act, it is the music made. Construed in its entirety in the moment of becoming, the creative gesture need not be found in the result. In fact, it is *lost* in the result. This is how Tallini thought about it, while the tactile feeling was strongly coming down as if to validate his understanding.

Benji, meanwhile, had launched into one of his soliloquies that were always in danger of losing the thread of the topic altogether. Tallini managed to cut in and bring things back to improvisation, which he felt relevant to his work and the experience thereof. "Musical improvisation is a dying art, except in certain corners of popular music. And even there it has become corrupted, either by the influence of the aleatory in painting or by academization. But it still potentially exists in music in a way it never could exist in painting."

What interested Tallini now was the extent to which Benji's point of view reflected a lack of experience in musical improvisation. He laid out for his friend how in improvisation the ear does not create the musical form the way the eye conforms the accidental into a work. Here Benji picked up, willingly admitting his deficiencies for the musical, "But not for the tonal, mind you, for there is tone in language, where I pride myself on an ear of some finesse. I know the musical repertoire but unfortunately never practiced. And I'm familiar with the principles, but can't read music. Not much of an ear, simply don't have an ear for any tone save that of language. If truth be known, I find music damn distracting.

"But beyond all that, I can understand what you say, and I think I can grasp it, although without feeling it. As to the accidental in the work of art, its evidence is everywhere. Any accidental conformation can become a work, through repetition of an a posteriori rule of creation. Of course, by then the improvisation is dead, and with it the art."

Out of consideration for his friend's sensibilities, Tallini proposed that Benji's *syntactique*, like a harmonic-melodic structure in music, might be the proper guide for a *non*musical, and therefore presumably linguistic, improvisation. An amusing notion, Benji thought, *nicht schlecht*. "But it sounds too much as if *la syntactique* was superimposed on a medium, which it is not, of course. It is rather the soul of the medium itself; it is what makes it what it is, what makes it become what it becomes. The way every language has its soul, or its spirit, if you prefer, that which flavors the world it unfolds. *La syntactique* is what *all* mother tongues have in common, and the problem of translation is precisely that only the mother tongue reveals its soul. It's relatively rare to possess two mother tongues, one to comprehend the data, another to present the version. Without this double insight on a single idea, the translation will be shallow, as most of them are. In the marketplace, of course, you can interpret any language with another and render the sense in a general way.

54

This is good enough for most descriptions and for getting your business done. Here an interpreter suffices, and one single mother tongue. But translating means to carry the soul of one language over into another, a difficult task. That is why poetry, a self-representation of the spirit of a mother tongue, just doesn't translate. Like its soul, each tongue has its unique poetry: the tongue's self-transcendence."

◗ ◖ ◯ ◯ ◐ ◗

This was not the first time Benji Gauthier had expressed his views about the mother tongue. Tallini gathered that he regarded its formation as a primordial inscription of essential understandings that imbue words with lifelong meanings. According to Benji, the mother tongue in this formative process established the moment of coincidence for the ultimate linguistic complementarity of word and term: the integration of the poietic idea with the comprehending concept. Tallini was greatly attracted by these psychogenetics, which made at least as much sense to him as did anything else he had read about the origin and constitution of language. What he intuited—though certainly never formulated—was the concordance of this primitive creation of the human mind, repeated in every toddling phenotype, with the beginner's mind he favored: the mind of living thinking. Representation by photographic fact had allowed him the freedom to partake in the undistractedly perceptual premise of beginner's mind.

Now Tallini seemed to divine the working principles of his own thinking, of the improvising mind, and this recognition of himself through the language of the other was a step in self-perception, in self-awareness, and ultimately in a cognitive observation of himself. This movement toward self, spurred by the other but in essence an act of self-confirmation, turned into a quest for the other's understanding through a *communication* of self. Can there ever be understanding of self in the absence of the other? Did Benji understand? The implications of this question hovered over their exchange, and Benji's answer was as direct as the question. "For me to know you, you must know me." He thought that knowing the other was tantamount to interpreting a newness and integrating it for future recognitions, shared in communication. "But reception of the new is not a unilateral disposition," he continued, "because it is conditioned as well by the other's presentation. What distinguishes the new would go uncomprehended were the presentation not in some way or other indebted to the old held in common. Reception is therefore conditioned by the other as well as by the self.

"And please not to forget," Benji further admonished, his tone distinctly triumphal, "that all of this occurs in language, where all of us share a terminology. Also keep in mind that in principle, a language of terms knows no communication problems because every disagreement or misunderstanding can be settled by reference books, grammars, and dictionaries. The mathematical language is of course a prime example of this, as are the other formal terminologies our logic may invent. Clearly such systems are recipients of the old we hold in common and not the improvisational newness never encountered before.

"What profound trust we place in such terminological structures coming out of ourselves, what confidence of their correspondence to a valid world abroad! We're never disappointed when the world considered is the old and already known. But the new belongs to the transpersonal faculty of the linguistic self, and the word, its medium, is blessed with a solid foundation in the term held in common. This state of affairs reduces the dangers encountered in the process of self-transcendence, an alienation resulting from a distortion, or even a loss of self. No one wants to denigrate the splendid visions of the mystic's transcendental consciousness, but unless a shared terminology maintains common ground with the other, the mystic self remains stuck and fails to transcend its form in order to make significant change. Able to evoke the image, but not to shift the point of view in conscious reflexivity. Am I making myself clear?"

Benji paused. "We often fail to appreciate fully the problem-solving potential of terminology, which itself remains by definition within the old, within what is known in common, the objective part of language. But of course, as I said, it's complemented by the individuality of the word and a subjectivity flexible enough to introduce the new and make language an open system. And that is never an isolated system; it's always an understanding, a knowing of the other."

Although a multitude of notions had gathered in Tallini's head, he refrained from speaking because he knew from experience that any proposition he might make at this point would only confuse what had been gained. As it stood, Tallini had listened—and Benji did not speak particularly slowly—with a fair understanding of topic and context, with neutral attention, and above all, he had responded to Benji's ideas about the language of terms. Long ago, he had read that the ancient Egyptians had evolved a demotic script for this kind of practical linguistic material, while hieroglyphs, as the term suggests, were reserved for what a latter-day conception of their cosmogonic and cosmological intuitions would come to call "the sacred." At the time, it struck him that these hieroglyphs, intending levels of relatively abstract thinking, in fact represented the details, in a picture writing, of concrete objectivity. The demotic, to the contrary, empowered to refer to just such and only such concreta, to all appearances consisted of a set of thoroughly conventional abstract signs, blameless of any representation. During his library research he had run across some books on Egyptian monuments, and their inscriptions had revived these observations. When he brought up the subject, Benji turned out to have had a more than casual acquaintance with what he referred to as the "Pharaonic glyph."

"A creation of genius, my friend! And what you say is amusing indeed, just because it is so Pharaonic, this kind of cross-referencing. And you are *almost* correct, so please allow me an adjustment. There does remain in the demotic a link backward in that it retains the *gesture* of the hieroglyph. It therefore remains tied to its hieroglyphic origin by what must be an ultimate etymological contact. Evoke the hieroglyphic image by the abstract demotic gesture and inscribe it by physical means into the muscles and the nervous system! Can you imagine *inventing* that? The proposition is a veritable occult practice of the divine glyph through its gesture, *manu scriptus*, without any consideration for an outside reality, without reference to the environmental phenomenology. It elicits the inscription through a conventional linearity of signs with clear cursive intentions. And this inscription—acted by the body, not thought by the mind—filters down into the general population, to the extent that people *write!* Which they do with a vengeance, a driven bureaucracy of scribes. Since we got to know the Greeks first, we call the Pharaonics uninspired, impervious to change, empirical—*merely* empirical—and *fantastically* repetitious. But how else do you practice?

"Your interest in the Pharaonic glyph doesn't surprise me a bit, by the way, not with your interest in caves. As for myself, I went through Gardiner's *Grammar* for all the wrong reasons, but I won't burden you with *that* story. Eventually you might wonder about the cave drawings, the direct precursors of the glyphs. That was the long practice, the Paleolithic apprenticeship in the caves, and the perfect mastery of line achieved for us to witness. By the time humans could live out in the open, they had everything named and classified, the whole phenomenology. And appeared on the world stage with their writing fully developed, like a bolt out of nowhere. A monument, every species a letter in an endless alphabet. And what were they talking about in those constructions? The Pharaonic called their hieroglyphs 'staffs to lean upon.' *Who* did the leaning? Good question! 'Experts' say 'the gods,' a feeble translation, believe me. The sign—the ideogram—is like a small flag, a banner or pennon of sorts, cloth wound on a pole, the experts say. It's supposed to be an emblem of divinity, but that's simplistic, as it leaves us with a symbol of an emblem of a god. By the time it reaches our words, we're four times removed from what we are talking about."

Benji paused and somewhat deferentially inquired if "this sort of etymological fantasizing" was of any interest whatsoever. Tallini begged him to continue.

"Fortunately the ideogram is frequently spelled out by sound signs, so we know the three consonants that compose it, *NTR*. When that flag is combined with another sign that looks like a bag of linen and carries a meaning of *cloth*, as well as *thing*, we get meanings which have retained these three consonants to this day: *natron*, a hydrated sodium carbonate; *nitre*, sodium and potassium nitrate, a fertilizer; and *nitrogen*, a component of all proteins and nucleic acids. For terminological purposes, this should help the etymology of *NTR*, don't you think?

"Then there is the intuitive reading that's not in the books but certainly relates to that fertilizing substance. It's chemistry to us, but it was still a natural effect to them, the effect of *natura vegetans*, a nature where we find once again our three consonants. Well, *that* is what's leaning on the hieroglyphic staffs, leaning on them for support in the communication of meaning. Not the meaning of the marketplace, as we have seen, and for certain not the meanings of your salons. And on the other hand, we have a method to make this understanding accessible, not through the consciousness of mind but through the consciousness of body, by a cursive that contains all the gestures of empirical and pragmatic objectivity. And why do the books say they are 'gods' who use the glyphs? That's the most pertinent question of all, and the most revealing, when you think it through. Obviously, because that is what makes the most sense to the contemporary mind, in the context where the symbol appears."

Yes, Tallini enjoyed Benji's forays into such distant territories, but he had also learned that, as a rule, they were at their best when left uninterrupted. Far too often, having jumped in with a hasty formulation, he had thrown Benji off track, inadvertently scuttling the topic altogether. Beyond the show of a disabused world-weariness bordering on cynicism and a discursive style that was, far from egotism, rather like the unraveling of a cocoon spun over years of solitary cogitation, Benji was a serious thinker, practicing a communicative poiesis. Tallini, for his part, when temporarily distracted, might let his thoughts assume a mien of their own; lost in

Benji's terms and syntax, he might even have his moments of vacancy. Yet he needed to hear someone who could respond to his lived experience, to an adventure he felt incapable of articulating by himself. And Benji had his own demands, which he sensed might be met by Tallini's explorations. But whereas the latter's needs were evident, Benji strove to keep his own well under cover. Nonetheless, Tallini detected a yearning behind the intellectual bonhomie. In such cross-currents of experience and expression, of action and discourse, the complementarities were played out.

Benji had spoken about the mother tongue before, and Tallini had come to take it as a reminder that in their exchanges neither one was using his respective mother tongue. Although Tallini's French was spiced *al italiano*, his command of the language was perfectly adequate. He had learned it in his childhood, as his mother had been educated at a *pensionnat* run by French nuns, and she had carried away from the experience a snobbish predilection for the language. Thus she persisted in addressing her son in French. He spoke rather well, and volubly, about politics or photography, but he was now feeling the futility of attempting to express the "coming down" he had felt, even in his mother tongue.

In the touch of the cave people, were they not extending themselves in a struggle for recognition, and had he not responded with an extension of himself? If he was to look closely, would he not see himself held incommunicado by a language that simply did not cover this particular contingency? For it seemed to him that as soon as he attached language to the tactile feeling about the cave people, the presence turned to its polar opposite, leaving him with words to designate the *absence*. And yet it was this sentient experience of contact with an origin that was the sole and singular thing he cared to communicate.

Tallini suddenly longed for fresh air and, even more so, for silence. Their meetings had a way of ending abruptly, and more often than not, it was Tallini who moved them toward a close. After some time around Benji, self-reflection could become a pressing need. Nor, as a rule, was their parting of the ways accompanied by undue talk. The intensity of discourse had stood in contrast to the relaxed and dispersed congregation of the café and might have left a casual observer at a loss to explain the apparent coolness of these adieux. Farewells did not extend beyond a word or two; nor were there arrangements made or even hopes expressed for a possible future get-together. Momentarily blessed with omniscient insight into these two psyches and their interplay, the imaginary observer would have fathomed, at deep levels, their shared desire for further exchange and therefore a reticence to speak of it. Each placed trust in the other, unvoiced but manifest in every exchange. They were committed to an undefined process, a mutually beneficial complementation. The rule that lent the game its seriousness was the rule to keep the game alive, both in presence and in absence. Thus conditioned, departures were disarmed, and fluency guaranteed the reunions. No explanations would be needed the next time. The discussion would resume not where it had left off but where, by then, they would have individually brought it.

That night they left together. After they had each negotiated the revolving door, they silently shook hands and walked off in opposite directions.

THREE

TRAVELS IN TIME AND SPACE

His head reeling with ideas, Tallini intended to return to his hotel room by the shortest way possible. There—prone and staring at the ceiling, his favorite reflective position—he would sort out the events of the day. Reaching the Place St.-Michel and about to walk up the boulevard, he stopped and turned for no clear purpose, perhaps only for a parting glance at Benji's stooped silhouette. His friend was no longer visible, but Tallini's eye was caught by a light effect across the river. The sun had already set on the city, but a flash of luminosity played back and forth for a second between the twin towers of Notre-Dame, as if protesting their surrender to the dusk. On a whim, he changed his course and crossed the street toward the Île, but by the time he leaned against the parapet, the monument was brightly floodlit. Had he seen a last glimmer of daylight caught in the celebrated luster of the limestone, or was it a first flash of the artificial illumination that each evening rescued the cathedral from the dark? No matter, here she stood fully lit before his gaze, calming his brain. Kneeling inside this enormous hollow cross, untold multitudes had prayed and meditated. For them the question of origin and destination was settled once and for all. They would look upon his preoccupations as folly, and there were times when he came close to feeling they might be right. But the world of faith, like that of nature, is a spontaneous gift, neither chosen nor bargained for. Unlike nature, however, faith is not *necessarily* given, and it had not been given to Tallini. What had been given to him was the passion of discovery.

How badly he had stumbled in trying to convey to Benji the opening he was experiencing! He shook his head and bit his lip in embarrassment and anger at himself. But how could he convey the meaningfulness of this contact with himself and yet with another, the ultimate ancestor? What had Benji said? "You can't find the words because there are none for you as yet." But there, across the river, on the cathedral's façade, Adam and Eve, in their fallen state, answer all queries about the origin of man and woman. Their words came from Adam's naming of all living things, a language he certainly taught Eve, his very next paradisal adventure.

This biblical origin of language had figured in one of Benji's monologues, and Tallini remembered it clearly. Benji had seemed to put much stock in what he called Adam's masterwork, the translation of divine will into names. Tallini was surprised by his friend's intensity as he spoke eloquently of Adam, made of dust, alone and speechless, but with the breath of life in his nostrils, a living soul called upon to name the beasts of the earth, fashioned of the selfsame dust.

Benji drew Tallini's attention to an earlier production, of both "man" and the "beasts of the earth after his kind," on the last working day of that first creative week. To Tallini's amazement he even quoted chapter and verse. "Note that the creative work stands in distinct relationship to language. There is the command of *letting it be*, which we might conceive as what is to be created, then the creative action of *making*, and finally the linguistic act of *naming*, which is like a prefiguration of Adam's later task. Not to be forgotten also is the prefiguration of Adam himself; surely you remember: 'Let us make man in our image, after our likeness.' *That* Adam of the early aeon was made androgynous, both singular and plural, and has given rise to much speculation, though I think that at this level of abstraction, duality within oneness remains the most becoming image for this peculiar creation.

In contrast, Adam the namer—who may, for all we know, have had to name himself, as no one else seems to have done it for him—the linguistic Adam has gained a clayey consistency and lost femininity as well as plurality.

"Note that although he is several times addressed by his maker, he still has not pronounced a single syllable. He will first speak when naming the various entities of nature. For this naming parade, only the animal kingdom is specified in the text, formed 'out of the ground,' but the creatures come with a context that is vegetal, mineral, and elemental, the beast with the field and the fowl with the air, and by the time his day is done, it is nature, complete in all its detail, that Adam will have named."

What Benji said was manifestly the result of a deeper reading of the text and not an extemporaneous invention. Tallini felt ambivalent. On the one hand, he appreciated Benji's poetic and imaginative approach; on the other, he wondered if any solid footing was possible on grounds of such mythical material. His doubts, which he voiced carefully, could hardly have come as a surprise to Benji, who proposed that in the absence of a consciousness able to report on the experience, such solidity of footing may after all not be what is required for a true understanding of the origin of language.

"We witness the event, we observe it in every newborn child. We obtain abundant linguistic data empirically when we observe babbling infants, but theories built on this information merely confirm an inherent mystery. Nothing is lost by examining a traditional text, mysterious one way, mystical the other, and I suspect that something might be gained. Mind you, I'm by no means attempting a textual interpretation, nor do I take the text as divine revelation and truth absolute. But I do find it of interest to fabulate, if you will, on such an original, such a remote expression, to see what may come forth on a subject that remains as obscure and controversial today as it must have been in that antiquity. It's a point of beginning, justified by the evidence that language, back then, and still now, is considered a fundamental and real fact of human life, perhaps *the* determining fact, yet remains without clear explanation, and therefore mythical, mystical. Then as now, nothing can really be structured without in some way or other coming to terms with the linguistic problem."

Tallini sighed, took a last look at the monument to faith, and crossed the quay. Now that the day was over, he thought perhaps he had been too harsh in his judgment of what the Bibliothèque had to offer. Conversations with Benji, always stimulating, tended, after the fact, to leave him with a sense of dissatisfaction and with a slight anxiety that there might have been misunderstandings. Now he felt uncertain about what had been said and what had been achieved. That was the advantage of books—there was a security in print, black on the white page. Even if not understood at first, books could be consulted again and again; they remained unchanged with every reading. With Benji, this was out of the question. How many times had Tallini asked him for elucidation, only to be presented with a brand-new argument the relevance of which would demand other questions ever more remote from the original topic? Books, furthermore, were published, accepted, read by experts. Perhaps he was wrong to dismiss them too lightly. Nevertheless, by now he was convinced that all the world's libraries would never contribute one iota to the cognitive feeling just transmitted to him by the early ones, and that this contact alone could yield what he was trying to establish.

He caught himself and wondered what had happened to that marvelous bohemian mood set off just hours earlier by a scrap of azure sky. He knew the answer as soon as he thought about it: he had lost contact with the cave people; he was alone, nothing was coming down from them. How had it happened? He remembered their presence was strong when Benji had arrived, and it stayed strong for a while. He had not noticed it go, and not until now did he feel the absence. Try as he might to reestablish the contact by an upward-directed concentration while he continued his walk back to the hotel, the cave people remained absent, silent. But once aware of the cause of his gloom, Tallini pulled himself together and cheered up. He had no doubt they would be back. In the meantime, he reminded himself that he had been going to the library not to gain knowledge but to acquire terminology. This in turn revealed to him the subtle and beneficial influence of Benji's ideas, and reconciled him with his friend. By the time he reached his hotel he was quite worn out, both physically from all the walking and emotionally from the sum of the events of this exceptional day.

● ◑ ◯ ◐ ◑ ●

The next forty-eight hours saw Tallini at his most efficient. He was intent on getting out of Paris just as soon as possible. On the third morning after his marching orders had come down from the cave people, the Ferrari, freshly washed and shining, was being loaded with suitcases and photographic equipment. He had dropped by at the café the night before, but Benji was not there. And despite all his activity, he had received a brief sign from the cave people—while buying some shirts in a crowded department store—that they were still in touch.

As he went to the desk to check out, the morning mail was being sorted, and the clerk handed him a letter. It was from Rome, from his mother. He stuck it in his coat pocket, settled his bill, tipped the porter who wished him a bon voyage, and launched the Ferrari into the ordeal of Paris traffic. Once he reached the autoroute, the trip became exhilarating, and with every kilometer he was shedding more of the burden success had heaped upon him in the capital. He knew he had gone through considerable changes since his interest in the Paleolithic began. His mentality, his consciousness had been profoundly altered by the feverish pace of his thinking and reading, a process that culminated in the radical event of contact at the Ladsnik party.

Conversion cannot be dismissed as a description of Tallini's state despite the term's inference of a *faith* gained or exchanged. He did, at extreme but fleeting moments, envision his actions as a symbolic compact with his anonymous forebears: awareness of *their* mission in counterpoint to a mission of his own. The quality of his attention to this theme already far exceeded the demands of the documentary he was vaguely projecting. Through a power that multiplied his energies and capabilities, *they* were reaching out for representation, and *he* had come within reach. He was beginning to accept the notion of a hidden, even esoteric agent of this theoretical complex that had already uncovered so much, albeit *in abstracto*. He felt confident that his recently acquired sensitivity would assist him as he did practical fieldwork aimed toward some measure of *confirmation*. Again, the sacramental implications of this word were germane to the psychology of his discovery, though the question as to what exactly was to be confirmed remained in abeyance. This he would find out at the living sites that had inscribed the past. His practice of beginner's mind was doubly effective in that it precluded all interference of received ideas and, by keeping him from realizing his proximity to purely mythical constructs, spared him the crippling reaction of an ingrained positivism.

He drove for several hours before pulling off the highway for a bite to eat. At the restaurant he remembered his mother's letter and opened it without curiosity or pleasure. Their relationship had never been particularly close. She didn't approve of his profession, of his politics, or of the life he led. She had had "higher expectations" for him. He sometimes stayed with her overnight when in Rome on business. She wrote at Christmas and on his birthday. That the present letter arrived out of season was its only interest to him. It turned out to consist of a few lines explaining that within the pages of a Bible kept in the room he occupied when staying over she had found a note in his handwriting, and she was herewith forwarding it to him. He saw immediately that the note dated from his last visit, and read it attentively.

Realizing most of the material gathered so far useless for my purposes. None of it takes into consideration the inner state of the entities of the earliest traces. Convinced that much evidence has not been picked up, has been overlooked as unessential. Stone

Age man is not so much man living in the Stone Age, as it is stone turned into man by the effect of the age, the post-Adamic. The rock is the basic stratum, the bottom of the pit that ends the Fall. The entity works its way back to the light and breaks through, a point comes when the entity separates from the stone, by seeing the rock as separate.

◗ ◖ ◯ ◯ ◐ ◕

After lunch, as he drove into the afternoon, the letter came back to his mind. He was somewhat surprised that his mother had bothered to send his scribblings to him. Convinced she could not have made head or tail of it, he would have thought she would simply throw it out. He never did feel he knew her very well, and whenever she spoke to him, she seemed to be addressing someone he had never met. She didn't know him, not like Marpa, the warm Sicilian peasant woman who had been his governess for the first six years of his life and whom he dearly loved. As for the distance between him and his mother, it lay partly in an instance of discovery when he perceived her for the first time as a person, with her particular ways and failings, and no longer as an almost unapproachable figure of authority and wisdom. This happened in his seventh year, shortly after Marpa was let go. His mother learned from an indiscreet and treacherous housemaid that with his five-year-old playmate, Renata, he had been indulging in what his mother called "a little game of *touche-pipi*." Whatever the accuracy of this call, and despite the near-criminal implications with which she charged that term as she reprimanded him, it never for a moment displaced the facts of the incident as they applied to *him*, which was the only manner in which he was able to feel and know anything about them. It was a first conscious emotional experience, a first probe out of infancy. It overreached childhood, landing him in an adult world, a world he had hardly known existed.

In importance, this experience was surpassed only by an-

68

other around the same time, with which it shared certain emotional and existential characteristics: the discovery of music and, with it, a budding notion of freedom. Although young Piero had taken piano lessons for some time, his true opening to music came only when his mother, in consolation for Marpa's departure, bought him a piano-accordion. In her choice—imposed over the objections of Monsieur Radoux, *professeur de piano*, who disdained this *instrument de café-concert*—the full pedagogic potential of the instrument could not have weighed in the least. Lacking any experience in either the practice or theory of music, she was therefore unable to appreciate how her fortuitous gift furthered in her son a means of self-discovery. For while he was taught how to *play* the instrument, its physical constitution and, in particular, the disposition of bass notes on its left hand—the side responsible for breathing the bellows—provoked a *thinking* as well, which in retrospect he was able to identify as an early investigation of a natural system.

This was a first wonderment at a logic given in front: the laws of harmony. For the peculiarities of the instrument now forced him to master a left-hand behavior quite unlike the right, whereas Radoux had taught him at the piano, correctly so, to minimize any functional differentiation between the two hands. Learning the piano, indeed, involves training both hands at a par in a mirror-imaged ambidexterity within one single system, and eliminating any technical stylization on the basis of left and right. The action at the piano, lying in a fixed horizontal plane, is essentially the same for both hands. The accordion, as he found out, couldn't be more different. The right hand plays a piano keyboard and can be observed by the player; the left blindly plays an arrangement of buttons. But the most significant difference between right and left—and in this the thoroughly schizophrenic accordion is perhaps unique—lies in the disposition of their notes. It is achieved for the right hand according to a diatonic principle (a linear scalar order from low notes to high) and for the left, a harmonic principle, the cycle of fifths, a system based on the subdivisions of the vibrating string.

Every time the boy picked up his instrument, this system speeded his assimilation of the basic principles of modulation through the twelve tonalities according to the cycle of fifths, a theme on which he soon began to improvise. Much later, when the historic convulsions of his time had long since interrupted the leisurely pursuits of childhood and adolescence, Tallini's interest in the laws of harmony and the wonderful cycle of fifths persisted. He came to consider how the disposition of the right hand is an arbitrarily imposed principle, pitch being no more than a single element's relative situation at a certain point of the keyboard. It does not infer an inner musical constitution. On the left hand, however, the cycle of fifths presents the emblem of the harmonic principle, the *ratio* of music. Homologous in nature to the overtones produced by the vibrating string, it exhibits these relationships within, as well as between, the twelve tonal families. In brief, it opens the path to the center of musical theory. Its practice offers the inexhaustible voyage around the harmonic clock face, passing through the mysterious six o'clock enharmonic change, while the twelve tonalities—with C at high noon—grace the dodecalogical sites of the temporal cycle.

Made entirely on his own, his discovery of this jewel and the peregrinations it afforded, proved to be an essential key to the art of improvisation. The heady potential of inventive openness and spontaneity translated into a new sense of liberation. It was in this state the boy had made that other major seventh-year discovery, in which his mother's authority was suddenly convicted, by the proof of his own experience, of grave inconsistency, and possibly of lies. Once the principle had fallen, the lesson was rapidly generalized. Unable as yet to verbalize his rejection of his mother's evaluation—expressed with her Francophone realism—of his experience with the newly discovered opposite sex, he briefly considered that she was unaware of its true nature, just as Professor Radoux had seemed unaware of the importance of the cycle of fifths. The boy's refusal to accept her judgment was his first willed opposition to automatic assimilation. He stubbornly clung to the experience as he had lived it, in terms that were sensory and emotional, and refused a false verbal interpretation. This refusal had a liberating function akin to the laws of harmony in the arrangement of the accordion's basses. And again, this new possibility of mental insubordination—which had expressed itself musically in improvisational creativity once the cycle of fifths had been understood—now figured among a small but lengthening list of changes in his mental makeup that he was making by himself, which notably added to the interest and enjoyment of his daily life.

The events themselves were less important than the early self-reflection they stimulated. Some facts are of the essence and need to be brought to light. In this adventure with Renata, he had inadvertently entered terra incognita, and his comportment had been subjectively spontaneous, not to say instinctive. This circumstance cloaked the experience under innocence, in the most radical sense of the term. The maid's report could scarcely represent what was true in *his* world. In fact, the affair had lasted for weeks, had known a courtship of sorts, followed a development, created attachments, served needs. That it should have led to a physical exploration of one sort or another had in retrospect always seemed to him a matter of evidence and utter normalcy—just plain horse sense.

Although not yet self-reflective, this mental disposition was essentially already his own *during* the experience. It deemed his mother's scandal as unfair and unwarranted. For if the nature of his discovery and its natural consequences were known to her, why then hadn't he been warned, as he had been of all the other things that were not to be done, all the actions that were not to be taken. Furthermore, in all those others, the fault, as well as the reasons for the prohibition, if not transparent in themselves, were always easily and straightforwardly explained. This particular case was unusual in that the nature of the transgression and the wisdom of the interdiction were totally absent. Considering the gravity of his mother's somber demeanor, it was equally remarkable that no public punishment ensued. Usually the maid, the cook, and even Professor Radoux would all chime in with coordinated disapproval and appropriate moral comments. This time there was general silence, with only a sneer from the young chambermaid, a cynic down to the etymon. The little girl stopped coming to play, and musical rather than sexual explorations took over his life and quickly made him forget his sorrow and embarrassment.

His two discoveries were linked fundamentally and in several ways. Marpa's departure, for instance, encouraged—perhaps promoted—them equally. With her discipline gone, the concentrated regular daily hour at the piano soon degenerated into an impatient fifteen minutes here and there, just enough so he did not have to lie when questioned. The piano's loss turned out to be the accordion's gain. The cycle of fifths, along with his penchant for tango and valse musette, decided his preference. Marpa, for better or worse, would have tempered his enthusiasm and imposed perseverance at the more demanding piano, which incorporates the cycle of fifths as well, although not physically marked on the keyboard. Marpa's constant presence was comforting but restraining. Once she was gone, his exploratory drive took two directions: one in separating, in discovering a difference, the other in joining, in uniting twelve sounds that had been twelve distinct individuals into one progression according to a pattern, with degrees of relatedness.

But Marpa would have disapproved. Endless hours wasted on an instrument that was played in brothels and on street corners with a tin cup at one's feet? Had she stayed, she might have prevented the discovery. Her departure had been unplanned, forced by a serious economic depression that dictated a narrowed household, with only the cook and the aforementioned housemaid, a German girl who worked au pair. She was very young yet already buxom, and steaming with peasant heat. She exuded health and a faint barnyard scent. Soon after Marpa's departure, the au pair allowed a bit of play at bedtime, when young Piero would attack her with a pillow and they would end up rolling on the bed. This little pleasantry seemed to amuse her greatly, and she would often try to hug him close while he fought her off. For him it was a novel change from the solemnity Marpa displayed when she tucked him into bed, a simple religiosity she evoked at the prospect of slumber and dreams.

One day the girl suddenly removed herself—for reasons presumably beyond the boy's innocent comprehension—to a dignified adult aloofness. Only much later did the true nature of their evening entertainment become clear to Tallini, as did her later treachery. In the Renata episode, to which the German girl was only (to be etymologically precise) a prelude, his innocence was unimpeachable. Upon revelation of the complementary difference between himself and Renata, there was a moment's hesitation in view of the logistics of completely unknown, virgin territory. There had been no previous input from the powers that be, who had built up his world of perception and feeling. The entire experiential field of the other, and of its difference, had never come up in words, or at least not so he could have understood it. And yet, when the incident occurred and was what it was, the other and her difference were manifest in his experience of it; he found the silence of his elders inexplicable.

But this had not been a time for reflection and explanation. It was a time for action. It was perhaps his first consciousness of intuitive decision, a self-conscious action, this experiment in pure innocence of the mechanics of sex—inventing it, improvising, and performing what can only be called an impotent sex act. Its shortcomings were no qualitative degradation of an experience significant, along with the cycle of fifths, beyond all others so far in his short career.

● ◐ ○ ◑ ◑ ◐

Tallini's destination was a small fishing village not yet disturbed by tourism and chosen for its proximity to a widely publicized find, so far largely unexplored, but said to involve a large cave containing Paleolithic evidence. Tallini had read about it at the Paris library, and the prospect of visiting this site elated him. Behind the wheel of the Ferrari, his mind, in its freeway meditation, was thoroughly without care. In the past, some of his more daring ideas had come to him in just such vacuity.

At the moment Tallini was thinking about grottoes. *Caves* they are called in English, but in Mediterranean languages they are grottoes. Aladdin, for instance, might have been hard put to discover treasures in a cave rather than in his legendary grotto. And whereas the cave predominantly expresses the unfurnished empty darkness of an underworld, the grotto tends to be a site of chthonic marvels and initiatory mysteries, a locus of light, either from the radiant sparkle of jewels or from the clarity of hidden teachings. The distinction between cave and grotto is one of darkness and light: the grotto is a diurnal cave, the cave a nocturnal grotto. A pragmatic reconciliation into a total habitat can combine grotto and cave in a hypothetical quaternary imagination that reduces the universe to make it fit inside the earth. Alterations of this abode—inscriptions, markings, paintings on walls and ceiling—all become expressions of cosmic directives. The identity of being and rock resulting from such immediate perception of a limited totality was a theme Tallini had been exploring and had begun to formulate in that note his mother had found.

It was the middle of the night when he reached his destination, but the town was wide awake. Fishing along this coast was a nocturnal enterprise, and half the town—even the children, wildly at play despite the hour—waited up for the boats to return. The thickly whitewashed Andalusian façades, meringued in the flickering glow of the gas lamps, lent the scene a carnivalesque atmosphere. He had heard much nostalgic reminiscing about their daylight dazzle back then when he observed how a cruel sun could hide dive bombers that turned children's playful shouts to fearful screams. His arrival excited much attention, and here and there, on the wrought-iron balconies jutting over the cobbled street, figures could be made out in the late shadows, some girls, some women. A crowd, mostly youngsters, gathered in respectful silence around the Ferrari, while Tallini took his luggage and equipment into the *posada* and registered at the bar, where the owner was still serving a table of midnight diners. Then he went to park the car on the plaza, returned to the hotel, and went directly to bed.

Next morning, he spent little time admiring the seascape from his window. His attention was entirely drawn inland. He had gotten up early and taken a brisk walk before breakfast. From the upper part of the village one could see limestone cliffs in a harsh, gnarled environment that looked surprisingly inaccessible. Somewhere up there the cave had been found, and all his instincts told him of treasures awaiting him, their real discoverer.

The owner of the hotel, Giorgio, was Italian, a propitious omen to Tallini, echoing as it did the sense of familiarity that weighed so heavily, in the abstract, with the success of meeting the unknown mind. From Giorgio he learned that very little of the countryside had yet been explored. Local people avoided the hills; there were superstitions, talk about disappearances, and so forth. Furthermore, the recently found cave of Paleolithic remnants, one of the attractions of this site, was not open to the public; a permit had to be secured from the authorities. No, Giorgio didn't know how long it would take for such a permit to be issued. Only official commissions ever came for the caves, and they were accompanied by people from Madrid. But if it had to go through the local authorities . . . Giorgio's shrugging shoulders and raised eyebrows were less than encouraging, but the gesture was so Neapolitan as to counteract Tallini's annoyance at the news.

Tallini dreaded all contact with the authorities and decided not to spoil his first days with these formalities. Giorgio could arrange for a guide to accompany him on daily excursions into the hills. The guide would probably arrive within the hour; in the meantime Tallini should have a leisurely breakfast on the terrace. No? He didn't like to eat outside? The coffee got cold too fast? Very well, inside then. Giorgio led Tallini to a corner table, where he could watch both the sea and the activity at the bar.

The guide entirely spoiled the first excursion with his persistent questions concerning Tallini's person and proposed activities. He made scant pretense that the local authorities were the true source of his curiosity. In turn he was quite useless as a source of topographic, historical, or simply practical information, either because he lacked command of the facts or, more likely, because he had recognized Tallini for the bonanza he was, and figured that the less he told, the longer he would be needed. In this, however, he had miscalculated. That very evening, upon returning to the hotel, Tallini, deciding he would have to be alone in that wilderness, paid him a week's wages and let him go. The man objected he was the official guide for these environs and that foreigners were not to walk the hills unaccompanied. But Tallini spoke very good Spanish, knew the Andalusian temperament, and was not easily intimidated.

Howling winds working at the roof's ridge of layered tiles roused a dreaming Tallini, and he was surprised to find he immediately recognized their particular noise. This was definitely a sirocco blowing in from the Sahara whose grinding rumble he had first heard long ago, while under fire bringing images of death into focus, and fearful the gritty wind would pit his lens.

Indeed, when he gave up trying to sleep and decided to go downstairs in the little dawn light to see how things looked inland, he encountered Giorgio, who advised him to get his car under cover right away before the sand ruined its finish. Giorgio gave him directions to a garage. "This is no day to go into the hills," he told him. "You won't be able to see a thing with the dust in the air up there."

Tallini had trouble finding the place and then had to bargain over the price, surrounded by palm trees bending in the gale. Then he worked his way back to the hotel against the stinging gusts that continued to intensify.

Although relieved to be at Giorgio's, with hot coffee and

fresh rolls, he was very much annoyed that the day was shot. "Tomorrow," the innkeeper said. "It will probably subside by tomorrow, but sandstorms *are* frequent this time of year."

There was nothing for it but to stay in his room, where he passed the time reading, dozing when the uproar ebbed, practicing asanas, and writing a letter to Benji. After apologizing for having left Paris without saying goodbye, he described yesterday's first excursion into the hills where, despite the awful guide he now was rid of, he felt quite heartened:

> *It would be difficult to find a more suitable landscape as background or a more agreeable environment in which to function. The hills are absolutely charged with a presence, but a presence from another world. There is no doubt this was a site of considerable activity in the early Paleolithic, you can feel it in every rock. Have not yet found any artifacts, although it is said in the village that many such things were discovered before the war. This region of Spain was fiercely Loyalist, and a subtle oppression still prevails.*

Tallini's third day at Giorgio's began with an encounter. Entering the breakfast alcove, he noticed with a trace of annoyed surprise that his table was occupied. Thinking of it as *his* table after occupying it for two breakfasts stemmed partly from a strong possessive instinct and partly from his experience that hotel guests almost never sit inside when they can sit on a terrace overlooking the sea. The half-dozen tourists at Giorgio's *posada* confirmed his postulate. But on this third day someone proved him wrong, someone he encountered first by signs of absence: a book left open on the table, a shoulder bag on the chair. He looked around, but he was alone in the alcove. On the terrace, two tables were occupied, and at the railing, a woman was contemplating the sea. Tallini looked down at the book: *Opuscules* was the heading of the left page, *De l'esprit géométrique* the right—*Dio mio*, the Pascal of the *Pléiades* collection! Just then, Giorgio brought him a cappuccino, and with a little jerk of his head toward the terrace said, *"Francese."* As he passed the terrace door he called out, *"Mademoiselle . . . café . . . servi."*

There were only four tables in the alcove, set close together, and wherever Tallini sat, it would be at arm's length from the new guest as she came from the terrace. He looked up just enough to bow his head in greeting—a subtle greeting by Italian standards—and noted she wore glasses and bluejeans and was in her early twenties. And while the young woman—indifferent to look at, he decided—began sipping her coffee, he rose ever so slightly from his chair, leaned over toward her table and addressed her profile even before she had turned her head in his direction. *"Scusi, signorina, ma . . .* what is your definition of the point?"

Whatever he may have expected from this approach, it certainly wasn't the clever rebuke she offered about reaching conclusions on evidence literally windblown from the terrace every time the front door was opened, a *courant d'air* that must have gotten between the pages and muddled his detective work. Actually, she was reading the *Entretien avec M. de Saci*, a few pages away, because of an interest in the phenomenon of *conversion*. Right now she was on her way to the beach, however, and couldn't take time to argue the point abstractly, perhaps as a metaphysical expression of origin; even less to demonstrate it as a phantom on a flat surface, which would take quadrilled paper, a drawing instrument, a straight edge, a compass, none of which she had brought along for her swim. But if his need was urgent, perhaps she could evoke a definition for him right on the spot, provisionally, *ça va sans dire*. Saying this with a disarming mimic gesture of discovery, she then indicated a right-angle corner of the table, where one could observe the vanishing vertex of a pyramid indefinitely decreasing along its dimensions. And as he manifestly had not had occasion to acquaint himself with the slow, hard, and inflexible views of a geometric spirit, she ventured to hope that at least he was able to exercise the flexibility of its complement, *l'esprit de finesse*, that would by the movement of the outside make him know what is happening in the inside, and thus read her overwhelming desire to lie, alone, on the beach, and to leave any arduous thinking for a later occasion. And so she finished her cappuccino, picked up Pascal, shouldered her bag, and with the sweetest of smiles, was gone.

But not quite yet. Not before Tallini noticed, in her gait, as she made her way toward the door, a certain irregularity, an almost imperceptible unevenness, a way of putting down the left foot that made the right shoulder rise a little. In a word, as he observed her leaving the breakfast room, he became aware of a slight limp, a trifling matter, almost nothing, yet a faint disability nevertheless.

FOUR

IN THE BOULDER

Walking out of the village toward the hills, Tallini tried to put the encounter with the young woman out of his mind, feeling the sunny morning endangered by the vaguely Parisian aftertaste it had left. The redeeming difference was that something had been *said* at the breakfast table, and probably said relatively well. Verbal fluency was a talent he plainly didn't possess, and it impressed him whenever he encountered it. He was growing more aware that his own difficulty arose when he tried to formulate what he was actively *thinking*, what therefore was, in his mind, presently happening. The flow of social language was quite different from anything Tallini understood by "thinking," and when he tried to bring that thinking into language, he fell into a thinking style which was mildly aphasic. Only when formulating, as he would say, what was "coming down now," would he break through to an inner search for effective language. Whatever "came down" was *less* than language, for it didn't include the terminology he would then be at great pains to bring up, term by term, like heavy building blocks. But these generally turned out to be not staunch nouns but verbs, often in such indefinite forms as participles and gerunds with predicative tendencies or, worse, isolated conjunctions—in short, a style strikingly at odds with the ideal of distinction and clarity.

With the cave project, however, a new element had begun to influence his verbal expression. He felt for the first time that something needed to be said, not so much to communicate with others as to be said for its own sake. If indeed Tallini had arrived at a sense of the power of the word through the pathologies of its banalization, he now became aware as well of the endangered state of the speech venture altogether. The ideas this brought to mind were new to *him*—that is, they afforded him the experience of *thinking new:* "Thinking new what is coming down now." Not thinking *about* something new; that would be blatant self-contradiction, as he would have to choose a "new" to think about, and then it would no longer be new in the thinking. No, thinking new was thinking the new itself, shooting it *live,* in the parlance of his trade, and any further talk about it would be thinking *about* it. It would be the film in the can, taken out again and again. Tallini was interested in origin, in incipience, in beginning, in everything that implied newness. But now he had also become aware of the responsibility of realizing the speech venture itself, in that the cave project had brought him to concentrate on speech, and, by extrapolation, on language in general.

He walked through a desolate countryside of rock and gnarled wild olives escaped from cultivation ages ago and abandoned to their destiny on the rough and reddish sunscorched slopes bordering the road. The fall rains had been inadequate and the dust whipped up by yesterday's winds still hung in the air. His step was somewhat heavy at first, reflecting the burden of his thoughts. However, by the time he reached the foothills, his pace lightened in anticipation of a day in the hills by himself. He had come here to have a metamorphic riddle solved *in situ.* To allow an entry for the unexpected, his experience had taught him not to fix his topic rigidly but to work around and about it in that subtle state of balance between absence and presence that had at times proved conducive to the descending light.

And so this morning, he asked himself the essential question—what had it been for *them,* the first ones, and how would *he* be able to remember? Some sort of memory was a crucial part of his mission, but it would have to be a far deeper recall than that of the mind and less diffused than any genetic anamnesis. This recollection would have to hark back to the bones, ever present in the intent of his mission. Bones had been found in these hills, bones that could be studied, even dated. Except for some marks on the rock walls—signs that could hardly be called images—not much could have survived from the time he was attempting to contact, a time before anything but domesticated fire and such simple tools as stones or fallen branches that even higher animals are wont to use. But the bones and the rocks had lasted as a double link to the past, and there was little doubt in his mind that they would lead him to some discovery. He had been struck by the great similarity between bones and stones, both so charged with past, both housing consciousness of the mineral, and both functionally related in their supportive, structuring role within the living being and within the planet. But what could have taken the place of a *past* in those first ones who scratched the rocks and left the bones, those who were new to the world and for whom the world was new? And what was the extent of the newness within a context of what must have been as old as the universe?

He knew such questions were merely formulations that served to keep his mind on, or near, the subject. Sometimes the flimsy elaborations that entertained his open mind seemed superfluous, a hindrance even. Had he not experienced answers "coming down" at the most unexpected moments, when no questions were asked, when the mind was totally occupied elsewhere and with the most banal matters? These events, though not frequent, were utterly significant to him, yet he greeted them with suspicion and even a tinge of moral indignation—mistrusting what comes too easily, a residue of his background's bourgeois ethic. Although he tested these answers at least as broadly and thoroughly as others more circumspectly acquired, he had never been disappointed by them. None had ever been deposed, and he had come to recognize them as the small miracles they were, calling them "data in front" or "given in front." They were answers preceding the questions, knowledge before and in the absence of method. They had remained as valid as other conclusions he may have worked on for years, some of them for his entire intellectual life. It also seemed as if data given in front, pure invention to the enlightened mind, despite discontinuity—or perhaps because of it, he couldn't decide—more often than not brought forth new ideas that set in motion new processes, as if on grounds of newness itself.

As further corroboration of such arbitrary and purely intuitive data, he reminded himself of the times he had awakened from sound sleep with solutions to technical problems obtained in the absence of his rational self. Somewhere along such experiential evidence lay the path by which a contemporary mind could reach those beings whose entire experience had been not the use but the *initiation* of that very mind. This had to be given; it couldn't be figured out. But would it be given to a mind jealous of the verbal facility of a bespectacled, bluejeaned French lady, to one preoccupied with where he could get a Ferrari serviced in this wilderness? Though it seemed outrageous, experience was whispering that it might well be given in the midst of such distractions.

But how had it been for the first ones, patently absent to the event until *after*, those who in the moment of the data had *no past at all?* Certainly that first flicker of thinking had come down in a similar manner. There must have been a moment of becoming when there had been nothing before but distinct *elemental* perception, when the eye still contacted the sheer *fire* of the Great Flame. Before conceptual speech, before the distinction of color-form—a distinction that already necessitates *naming*—there would have been something more than just nothing. Not a thing *seen*, assuredly, but a something, an anything perhaps, a generality of thingness, an empty but glorious form, and through this there must have been a relation to something, to anything that was already there, since to be comprehensible to any degree, what is new can never be entirely new, but must be tied to a context by some common quality, be it but the simplest one of being, of existence, of extension.

This anchor has been an intuitive acquisition as far back

as the record goes: a first place to stand, the primordial hillock in the void. The beginning lies in the act of negation in the midst of nothingness, the sole positivity in the gesture of the act. The common quality of oldness here is a chaos for which the new is an absence, a lack. The new is but a lesser oldness, and that lack is shared by all. This shared quality, which in the old is any quality whatsoever among many, in the new is very special in that it is the only part of the new that is old. As to the sharing, it is of the widest, the most general and generous kind: whatever can be new in the old will sooner or later be thus perceived.

But what was already there? And how to perceive what is new in the moment when perception turns to thinking, what is new, but also what is old? What remains *purely perceptive,* elemental in thinking, and what is absolutely beyond perceptual reach in the idea? A reply here can exist only in the most radical sense of folding the question back onto itself again and again as one would close a fan, pleating the multiplied image into a single sheet: closing the spectrum between a primitive/ original perception and the unimaged idea. A formal and logical answer was the last thing Tallini's self-interrogation solicited. He was merely—though importantly—arranging his mind to keep it present, although ready to fold at the slightest sign of the moment of coming down, always uncaused and unexpected. This relation with the old, furthermore, is not the only bridge to the new, *originality* being another, readily distinguished from the artificial "novelty" that will be trite and hackneyed by tomorrow.

Up to this time, Tallini's ontological stance had made him defer the vexing problem of a possible *artistic* transcendence, a pertinent question, but one that brought on a strange reticence quite contrary in style to his usual, almost brashly confident beginner's mind. He appeared to have construed the work of art as a uniquely intimidating object. Though it did not exactly stop him in his tracks, it did demand some nimble mindwork for its circumvention, as he didn't feel equipped to meet it head-on. His profession, itself only recently embraced by the aesthetic establishment—on grounds he actually found difficult to reconcile with artistic creation as he envisioned it—swept him along into a domain in which he functioned yet somehow felt betrayed. So he had been "in the arts" all along? And speaking prose as well, *sans doute!* He thought he knew what he was doing without needing aesthetic commentary and multiple decipherments. He was, after all, a photographer, which, to his mind, entailed the production of the most precise *image* of a moment incontrovertibly lived by someone, and by someone, moreover, who is a *photographer.*

For Tallini, such a one was the master of the devout recording of light-events, from first stalking and capturing an instant to confining it to the flat surface that images inhabit once they have been tamed. The awareness of the light-moment and the attention brought to it render with the greatest precision imaginable the visual effects of fire on earth, light and shade in their total extension. This polarization—arithmetic that reaches duality by splitting oneness—demands a spectrum of grays between *black and white* when presenting sheer unadorned *being* in planar form. Perception of the three-dimensional original, on the other hand, is pathological without its color; nature is inscribable only through the spectrum. With bidimensionality, in contrast, the color-form on the plane is flattened into a découpage that undercuts the depth of the image. In the plane, Tallini found all colors recapitulated in the perfect polarity of black and white and the infinite gradations of their interaction. To distinguish planar areas by their color rather than by their limits with other areas, in his mind amounted to an almost anachronistic misunderstanding of two-dimensional abstraction. As the surface of a thing, this plane is misconceived, its true being veiled, unless—and the condition is demanding—it become a unique object, a *work of art.*

The essential irrelevance of color-form to the plane is clear from the fact that it contributes nothing whatsoever to the most exhaustive geometric investigations. Live color, natural color, is a temporal, cyclical phenomenon characterizing the state of natural structures. Typically, the whiteness of the root, untouched by light, sustains the green of vegetative synthesis, which by a gradual reddening (*"toute chose rougit en vieillissant,"* says the Philosopher) is burnt to the blackness of putrefaction, a new absence of light to nourish a new whiteness. Tallini thought of the absence of light containing the germ of creativity in nature as germane to the abstraction of the plane sustaining the infinitely shaded black-and-white inscription. He had heard of Goethe's theories, and it made sense to him that colors originated from both light and darkness, just as the form of the black-and-white image arose in chiaroscuro, a term in itself expressive of the dual agency. Photographic color was misplaced realism to him, a distraction of the inherent analytic faculty of the lens in its service to the *camera obscura.* Instead of an experience of depth in formal differentiations by subtle qualities of gray, color led to valuing superficial concerns, because color has no meaning within the timelessness of pure planar extension. Not to mention the unavoidable garishness bound to ensue from arrangements of color in disregard of their natural signification. As for the abstraction that sustains the flat image, he considered black-and-white photography to correspond to a more profound realism, not by a mimicry of surface coloration but by upholding the principle, Goethean rather than Newtonian, of color generated in nature through the opposition and interaction of light *and* dark.

And so for Tallini hiking through this Andalusian terrain, the lack of mediating vegetation pointed up the primordial extremes of relentless light and still unawakened earthly darkness.

◑ ◐ ○ ○ ◑ ◐

Camera obscura! A chance event in his early childhood had influenced Tallini's relationship to the camera. He had encountered it shortly after seeing for the first time a performance by a famous prestidigitator, who made a profound impression on him by pulling all manner of things, including two doves and a rabbit, from a big black box that had been assembled on stage in full view of the audience. When shortly thereafter little Piero was given a cheap box camera, it was as if he had received that black box of tricks in miniature. Moreover, the pompous and very authoritative master of ceremonies had introduced the magician as a great artiste, another first for Tallini, who had never before been in the presence of that legendary species.

It goes without saying that he corrected these misapprehensions; yet it may well be that these early events instilled some enduring attitudes toward his craft. For instance, he never allowed a total eclipse of the amazing aura that had seized his interest from the beginning and continued, in his mind, to surround the process of photography. Furthermore, after his infantile concept of "the artist" had provoked a fit of hilarity around the family table, he became somewhat irrationally suspicious of art and artists altogether, and even maintained that photography knew no common measure with artistic creativity at all. How could a purely mechanical manipulation of a technical apparatus pretend to artistic creativity? To him, art was the closest mimicry of the becoming of something original, inexistent before a poietic gesture made it come alive out of elemental raw materials: the words of a mother tongue, a palette of colored earths or pulverized minerals, a block of stone, or tones of various pitch. From the artist's hands, a creation could come into being and be kept alive by the continued receptivity of a changing world. The prestidigitator's trickery had been a parody of this creativity, a mere sleight of hand, but photography never pretended to creative feats. Its joy resided in the moment of choosing the image, in the shutter's click thereupon, and in making a straight print from a perfect negative. Its magic lay in the preservation of moments as evanescent as time itself. This instantaneous recording, albeit performed with varying degrees of skill, vision, intelligence, and taste, even in its highest reaches lacks the basic prerequisite of art: creation of the absolutely new, of what never was before. The photographic image, to the contrary, preserves what *has* existed and would otherwise be lost.

Tallini felt this capture of the visual moment as a significant achievement in itself and a contribution to humankind's evolving vision. Its exclusion from the artistic realm, far from being a devaluation, would rather have been a healthy safeguard against the general banalization of the arts, vulnerable to unscrupulous commercialism and an ignorant and malleable public. Others evidently disagreed. The effete minds of professional critics and theorists of the arts were taking it along the same path of spineless hype that provided a largely illiterate public with instant and hollow culture, and both critics and dealers with a profitable racket. The press photographer he had assisted at the age of eighteen saw his work housed in museums and books written about it.

Tallini's career had moved in another direction. His decision to cover the Spanish civil war had been entirely political, certainly not "artistic," and possibly not even photojournalistic, although it led directly to a career in film. Here he had come in touch with writers and artists, but their aims in art, when not commercial, had struck him as so muddleheaded that they forced him to evolve his own ideas. But now the adventure had clearly gone far beyond the photographic such as he envisioned it, and he had begun to wonder about what he had so inadvertently accessed. Might it be a new dimension in the recording of a present moment, or perhaps even a new moment by a more conscious definition of the present? And could it be, removed from the contemporary present so deeply rooted in the past, the newness and, in the most literal sense, the *originality* of art?

Tallini stopped to wipe his face. He was in a sweat, less from physical exertion than from these ruminations that always ended in self-contradictory impasses. What was he doing, mulling all this over once again? The cave idea had introduced an unknown into his work, exploding it in the process. It had landed him far beyond a mere search for images. To begin with, he ceased altogether to think in terms of a "searching," which was quite useless in this domain. However the search may have metamorphosed—into a waiting, an expectation, a meditation perhaps, or a prayer, some would say—it always related to origin and the creation of the new.

So why was he delving into the old? He had ceased any *effort* of discovery precisely because a search can only turn up the old. Whether direct or indirect, there had to be a complement to searching, perhaps the uncovering of *something* within an examined object (something present but hitherto hidden) or else the searching *for* something. In both cases a concept, a description of some kind, however vague or sketchy, must necessarily precede the search. Were this not so, one would be looking at random, with no hope of recognizing when, if, and even what one had found. Whenever it is the result of a search, of a method of finding, the find corresponds to some expectation that in turn modifies the nature of the find. It's a loop, a vicious circle for anyone to see, at least anyone who cares to look.

Tallini cared. He spent most of his days within and around such loops, and was impressed by their temporal implications. They showed a persistence of the old within the becoming of the new that would seem to jeopardize all pretense of originality. But the part of the new that is already old —the part setting up the new and making it comprehensible —can be eliminated by blocking the act's futurity, simply by excluding a search.

He suddenly felt exhausted by his mind's incessant repetitions. A huge boulder by his path offered an inviting patch of shade. Lying down flat on the hard-baked reddish ground, having stopped his forward movement, he could see only sky and rock.

Things were precarious for him, and he felt both envy and contempt for others who seemed to know what to do at any given time, as if no alternatives existed. This difficulty had revealed itself in his youth, when his photographic interest offered him an answer, makeshift perhaps, but even at that preferable to a question never asked at all. Years later, his mother told him that when he was barely out of infancy, she at times found him crying in real bilingual anguish: *"M'amie, ma cosa devo fare!"* His elders may have interpreted this lament as a regrettable lack of imagination, countering it with toys, games, and other distractions. For him, however, the question had quite a different tenor. It was easy enough to find something to do, but how was one to know it was the thing that *needed* to be done. The Italian, with a *dovere* driving the doing, is closer to "what *should* I do," even "what *must* I do?"

A childish deontological plaint, it may have fathered, many years later, a certitude that every consciousness inserts a unique doing into the event. In the plant kingdom, the expression is specialized and finds with natural inevitability its adequacy of response to the otherness surrounding it: with the physical evidence of rooting, of synthesizing, of the huge font of cellular wisdom, the plant's gesture is imprisoned in perfection. At a distinctly other level, representing a very first *un*rootedness, animal instinct, though still holding a large stake in the natural, already sketches traces of emotional and passional gestures preparing the breach of the inevitable: differentiated reactions, tactics, a faint assertion of the random, of the individual, a general decline in natural evidentness. With the coming of the cerebral cortex, at last, all evidentness disappears from action; for self-consciousness, natural gestures are no longer *obvious* and none can be universally discerned, save the most basic vegetative forces of continuity and reproduction. Henceforth, the canon of doing may be imposed by whim, determined by number, or legislated in a variety of ways, but in no event is it adopted by a natural conviction based on the inevitable. Thus the question of *doing* is born.

◑ ◐ ○ ○ ◑ ◕

To keep within the boulder's thinning strip of shade, Tallini now had to sit up against the rock, its shape bending his head, neck, and shoulders forward toward his raised knees. His mind—his soul, perhaps—was greatly stimulated by the memory of that childhood query which had remained *new* throughout his life. He felt strangely at ease in the awkward jackknifed position that wedged his upper body against the boulder's overhang. Thinking about the realms of nature had been especially rewarding in the shade of this granite block. He had made the trip before, but this particular transport had excelled in its double theme of motion and action, and he briefly marveled, once again, at the folly that will interpret rocket-propelled space exploration as an opposition to inertia, a self-distancing from the dark mineral heart of gravity. The thought of it made him laugh. He was taken aback by the sound, like an animal call, a dog gone wild, perhaps, like the olive trees. If they, why not he? "Where there be need, the remedy flourishes," to paraphrase the poet.

The continued motion through the realms of nature, through the space created by an opposition to inertia toward autonomy and lightness—a flight from the center of categorical heaviness—is already active in the pull of the plant toward the antipodal source of light, toward a pulverization at the brightest of centers. Next, there is a continuing motion of the heart, emotion expressed in physical action: a gesture. These connections were well known to him, but that motion continued by the fact of inertia he felt powerfully in the close quarters he occupied between rock and hard clay. He was forced into a cramped position by the sun's climb toward perpendicularity. Almost immobilized yet psychically alert, he felt himself responsive to the attraction of the solar pole and unusually aware of its force.

It is said that kneeling in prayer is an abdication of physical movement in the horizontal plane in favor of a static verticality. Roots nourish the soul's rising and give it a hold, and he was striking roots in an ever closer, intimate contact with earth and rock under the protection of the boulder. By raising his eyebrows and rolling his eyes upward, he was able to augment the spare components of his field of vision, almost geometric in their simplicity: a patch of sky defined by the edge of the overhang and the close horizon of the hill; a texture of rubble and shrub and an occasional block of stone like a fist in the landscape. Now these were circumstances conducive to a lexicon quite distinct from what might be elaborated on a Paris boulevard. What was different was the *space* available to words, which allowed them to reach their full stature in measured timing, launched at a quiet pace, in a noble state, yes, with patience. It was far removed from the treadmill mind.

Now the poietic component—usually differentiated from the mind as *soul*, or, with Greek precision, as *psyche*—was breathing more freely than ever, out of this awkwardly positioned body. Yet how self-contained he felt in the refuge of this wilderness! The back of his head pressed against the rock, occipital bone lodged in a depression that couldn't have been more perfect if cast in plaster, the nape of the neck supported by a smooth bulge polished during aeons of subtle erosions, his trunk encased in a rock face that conformed in all details to the lineaments of his back and shoulders. He now felt settled as if in the arms of a trusted friend, no longer opposing the will of his own form. The rock had received him as if custom-carved; now it rearranged its surfaces for his slightest move, as if to cushion him on air. If here and there a spot of hardness remained, it was only meant to keep him aware of a physical presence, however accommodating. The rock's nudging conveyed an eagerness to reclaim its own.

Rock-consciousness—strength, stability, support, basis, refuge—all the possible contexts where *rock* could appear, were transfigured in his contact with the mineral, yet it was present as the old within the transcendently new. This "old," which through its familiarity allows recognition, is the setup for the new, it is the basis on which the new is comprehensible. When Adam was presented with all species of beasts for their naming, he had been living among them in the Garden for some time. To name them, he certainly had to recognize them, and why shouldn't he? They had been created somewhat earlier than he, were gallivanting all around him, free as he himself, and he had had ample opportunity to make acquaintance. Suddenly, almost on a whim, he was empowered to name them, to think about them from an absolutely new perspective, the linguistic. These beasts would never be the same *to him* again. The naming made them new, but only to *him*. The basis of their naming, whatever had to be known to make the naming possible, remained unchanged. Were this not so, the naming would have missed its object, as an arrow misses its target. And so, as they were created, they accompanied their namer in his mythical descent. He landed where one lands when one falls: on red sunbaked earth such as this, on the ground, perhaps next to a boulder, and in the relative dark—coming from the brightness of paradise, the eyes not yet adjusted—he looked for cover against the rock, in its oldness, the old allowing the new.

● ◐ ○ ◑ ◐ ●

Noon had come and gone, and the day, beginning its decline, shrank the remaining shade of the overhang. The moment came when the bright-eyed cyclops stared full into the boulder's face and all shadows disappeared, save for the spot Tallini's body cast on the rock, its image tamed by the surface. The light was almost unbearable in its mounting pressure; all around, it harmoniously wed the mineral in a gaudy festival of shimmer and reflection, sparkling inventions that danced around him who casts the only shadow on this stage. As far as his vision reached, all was conquered by light, and the full force of the sun concentrated on what resistance remained, on *him*. His body, his persona, they had become the blind obstacle to the flattening intensity that had silhouetted him on the wall. He, his self, was but the pretext for this cutout to which he corresponded precisely, into which he fit perfectly, by which he was identified: he played his part of darkness on the flat rock wall. All volumetric functions, intellectual, linguistic, or intuitive, relaxed. Gone was the bulk, burnt out of him, leaving an abstract resistance that opposed the energy for the sake of its manifestation. With a soundless sigh he marked his relief at the vanishing mass as it melted from his being, gravity no longer vertically pulling toward a central point but expanding its force horizontally over his shadowed shape on the boulder's shell. The sun contradicted by his ambit, gravity annulled by his vanished mass, energy from above and force from below, both met in Tallini's shadow to fuel his two-dimensional adventure.

Retrospectively, Tallini was to think of the shadow moment in the rock surface as a transitory phase, with the cut-out a threshold in a gateway to a world of negated volume. And yet, in the lived experience of this instant, he moved through two distinct stages. In the first, the shadow on the rock face, although merely introductory to the essential event, was nonetheless a moment of uncommon stability. Never had he felt so perfectly adjusted, so assured in his place, so immediately connected and certain of his shape, ascertainable at any point of its bounds. For a transitory, evanescent moment he encompassed himself within perfectly attainable but equally untranscendable limits. Gone, in this domain, were the three-dimensional textures that demanded progressive adjustments involving judgment, hence choice, and therefore, eventually, error. In the shadow of the plane, to the contrary, the voluptuous calm of certitude reigned in an uninstructed and fully unconscious communion with a unitary environment, identical at every point of contact.

In the second stage of the transition, however, all self-assurance vanished from Tallini's recollection. The very idea of reminiscence seemed misplaced; he felt as if he was in a state of partial anesthesia that had affected his personality, his self, his ego. It was as if the loss of perspective had suddenly struck him with the full consequence of leaving a world-in-the-round. For the spatial diminution was paralleled by a reduction of consciousness. Whereas he had relished the control of extension and mobility, he suddenly experienced his spaceless quarters as an uncanny loss of individuality. The sole existent quality was a flatness common to all, which rendered illusive any notion of personal value or importance. Even his paradigmatic shadow was undergoing an oppressive equalization. Multiplicity of planes, an attribute of volume, was now only a fantasy engendered by a solipsistic existence in an expanse that knew neither above nor below, thereby precluding a face-to-face meeting between its denizens. All one could ever know of another was the thinnest membrane of its limits. Without the experience of a vis-à-vis, furthermore, a mirror image could not be formed, with the resulting lack of a consciousness of self as plane.

The moment of the threshold was fleeting, yet the ineffable transition through the plane afforded him as a shadow phantom a grasp of its limitations—a condition unattainable in a conscious volume where bidimensionality is mere surface and its expression pure fantasy. Tallini glimpsed both sides of the partitioning threshold, and both were volumes between which the planar moment held him bidimensionally as the arithmetic mean term (Two) between the spatial extremes of concrete (Three) and abstract (One). A momentum originating in positive volume turned his shadow into a gateway to negation. The two volumes were to each other as inside to out, two sides of an identical volume, two aspects of the same; one was the other, but reciprocally inside out. Where the one was multidimensionally expansive, the other was introspectively puncticular, and it was the latter that now opened to Tallini, once the shadow yielded access and the bidimensional phantom lost its relevance in a plenum of mineral volume. With a deep breath of liberation, Tallini regained awareness of himself. In a transport of amazement, he experienced his inorganic consciousness.

The reversal of his three-dimensional existence was now complete. The sojourn in the plane had been a purgatory of volume, of bodily matter, of all he had known about himself by seeing and touching. What *now* had taken form was everything that had *then* been formless, while the material reality of his existence had become as elusive as had formerly been the notion of his self, his ego, his personality, his thoughts, feelings, and emotions—the vague sum total of his life experience. In this new existence, his body, the perceiver, was an idea he could call to mind at will, whereas his hitherto intangible self was now clearly exhibited before him, and this in the form of a grain of salt. He was contemplating the speck of mineral that defined him far more precisely than his body ever could. It was predimensional, puncticular, as was this entire world he had slipped into, a world where part and whole coexisted without differentiation. Encoded and inscribed, the grain of salt had captured every emotionally suffered experience of his life, and with this understanding came salty tears that drew him back to himself, into this center of his being. And once the scission that had been keeping him apart from himself was mended, he realized he had not *found* this salt of his here but had carried it in his bones, accumulated over a lifetime. This salt had been in his body; it had circulated in his blood and had been precipitated into his bones by cellular experiences. Only now that he inhabited this mineral world could he encompass it and through it grasp the logic of his destiny.

Instruction and understanding were instantaneous as dualization ceased. He was this salt, his salt, as if he had never been a body of flesh. And yet he was made aware that only the cellular can experience, while the mineral can only record. That was the first lesson. The salt was the sum total of the past, but a past that went far beyond any one bodily manifestation. This past, which he now knowingly inhabited, went back all the way to its mineral fount, back beyond the existence of a fiber-and-tissue world. He lived the exceptional insight granted by this return to the primal inorganic cause, this rock from which the speck that was he had dropped, like a seed ripe with origin, its affinitive constitution beginning a random wandering that would encompass his temporal existence. But such an entirety of past—not just one, but *all* his pasts—contains the full potential of future as well. And so he had been given to inhabit this rarest of abodes, the seat of temporal wholeness, which is the permanent present of the salt.

No sooner was this stability acquired than a movement revealed itself inside the salt where he had settled. He saw it was the process of inscription, the multitude of minute adjustments constantly recording into the stable whole. For an emotional inscription was rarely settled all at once—nor once and for all—by a simple code or legend. Between the macroscopic cellular experience and the microscopic mineral inscription a transformation took place much like his dimensional translation through the flatness on the rock surface. It was a dismemberment of the experience, which revealed the essential complexity of even the slightest emotional transport. The resultant elements apparently had been related in nature to specific organs or functional organizations—such as heart and lungs and the circulatory system, or the kidneys, liver, and small intestines in their function of individualization and assimilation—and had consequently initiated the inscriptive process by choosing a mineral structure in the vicinity of such organs or in some way connected to these organic functions. Eventually such elements had to be released from these regional undertakings and brought to a gathering center that was the body's single most massive mineral structure: the thighbone, or femur. The revelation of the function of this structural component and its symbolic status as locus of all stability and permanence was itself a highly emotional experience, and touched on the mysterious alternation of appearance and disappearance.

These inscriptions differed greatly in their complexity and importance. Some could be compared to rapid jottings not likely ever to be revisited, but others were of vast complexity and would be referred to time and again, every reference modifying the original entry and amplifying its importance to the constitution of the whole. He was led to believe that some archaic markings—sometimes long-forgotten graffiti, residues of early glimmers of consciousness—had recently generated ample glosses. All this graphic activity, however, was merely the elaboration of a final network sustaining the conformation of the whole and guaranteeing its stability by continuous minuscule adjustments and changes. Essential significances had been extracted from inscribable experiences and were being carried forward in the structure of the salt, forming that web of relations to which he was now being introduced. He was made to understand that, whereas this elaboration was a natural process consolidating the saline element's crystalline structure—a kind of inorganic process of digesting the subtler influences of the experiencing organism

97

of which the mineral was a part—the pathway along which the inscribing emotions traveled was contingent on initiatives taken, whether consciously or unconsciously, by that living organism. And thus it was in the nature of these determinations that the ultimate instruction of the boulder would reside.

Until that moment, no voice proffered the information that was reaching Tallini about the principal function of the mineral milieu. All these notions were exuding anonymously from his environment, and Tallini sensed an eagerness on the part of his surroundings to convey their significance: rock, hitherto considered dead and useless, was being accorded tardy recognition. But oddly, one single voice was now gathering, a strong and grave voice he could hear clearly, as if it were speaking nearby, although it contained an echo of vast and distant empty spaces. It was speaking a language he had never heard yet understood perfectly, inviting him to travel the network he himself had created and would have to traverse time and again until he could face its many bifurcations in total indifference.

"Yes, yes," the muffled boom intoned, "your emotional inscriptions have guaranteed your future. They will form your next body, which will further inscribe and form the countless ones thereafter, and we, the Spirit of the Mineral addressing you, will gladly serve, as you are part of us and we are part of you. Without such future, your nature, though it may be of light, would slip back into the darkness that hid the light for aeons. As long as this nature lives in your body of emotions, it must experience through them to form your future, for there is no staying still in the vortex of what your shallow vision calls 'time' and uses as a measure, as if it were but another one of your dimensions. But we whose roots reach back before your time and your perspective, we shall sustain your future and offer our marrow to your ceaseless scribblings until your diffused and contradictory present precipitates into the Whole, just as our great dispersion once crystallized into an Origin."

The voice fell silent. With its compelling tone, its gravity, and the paradoxical intimations of immediate presence and unfathomable distance, it had fascinated Tallini's sensory capacities to the point of eliminating all perception but the auditory. Now, in the hush still vibrating from the majestic utterance, sight returned to him, and to his amazement, he looked out over an immense prospect that could only be called a landscape of dichotomies. As far as he could see, and all around him, space was created by a network of bifurcations, emanating right at his feet. If he were to take a step from where he stood, it would have to be in one of two directions, and he could see that just a short way down either path, another choice would have to be made, and so forth to all infinity, as far as he could tell.

As he was contemplating this sight in a state of troubled irresolution, the voice returned, this time in a more jovial, almost familiar mode. "Go ahead, take the first step. There is no standing still. But already you are paralyzed by the choice, weighing the advantages of the one against the other, although you clearly know nothing about where either one will lead in the end. All you know is that after this choice, there will be another, and another, and how are you to know what your future choices might be? You are like the chess player calculating the moves to come but beset by the incertitude of his opponent's responses. Note that in your case, the opponent is no other than yourself. Yet you may take one path or the other and know as little about what *you* will do as the chess player does about his opponent. But you yourself have created this divergence in a choice that must have caused you a tear or two, if only in your heart. You don't recognize the occasion, of course. It may have been surrounded by dramatic commotion, by all the elements that make up human considerations and that probably influenced your decision most— all the personal concerns of like and dislike, hopes and fears, of advantage and disadvantage, good and bad and right and wrong—and all measured by your shortsighted human morality and the pitiful understanding you call knowledge. But all this has been worked away in that great refinery of inscriptions, the mighty thighbone, as you have already been informed, because in this mineral domain, which is the intraterrestrial workshop of most basic energetic tasks, all the particularities of the occasion are irrelevant. They belong to a state of flesh and blood that has no existence here, where only the final results are registered.

"Each juncture you see before you is an ultimate effect of an experience inscribed in a certain act, a step, a decision taken. Each bifurcation is a fork of either/or, showing that every positive act has its negative, a path not taken, yet remaining as potentiality. That path includes all the other possibilities that might have been, no matter what they were or if they were better or worse. As the network clearly shows, choice is effective not only by what is chosen but equally by what is not. This choice, made in ignorance, will influence every other all through the network. And if individual mortal life is short, life as a whole is infinitely long, and you will in one form or another encounter the same choices to be made again and again along your path. You have come to this spot to hear what I now tell you."

The voice swelled and seemed to be joined by others, by a multitude of others in unison. "What I am telling you is this: eliminate the network of dichotomies by not choosing. *Do not choose.* If you stop your mind from choosing, you will feel the magnet of affinity that forms these bifurcations, two poles, negative and positive. In yourself you will find these poles as well. Remember the law of opposites; observe the crossing. Trust this affinity, and do not choose." And the chorus in unison took up the chant, *"Do not choose, DO NOT CHOOSE . . ."* as Tallini, his mind a perfect blank, took a step into nothingness.

FIVE

DESCENT TO BLUE SILENCE

Tallini found himself precisely where he had been all along, immobilized beneath the boulder's overhang. There had been no transition, no shift of consciousness. No crossing back through that mysterious membrane separating the two worlds, inside from out. The same patch of sky, squeezed between overhang and hill. A sirocco, exhausted by its sea voyage, was now barely wafting the slowly shaping clouds into view. Southern desert beasts in fleecelike rags conflated into veiled human forms, only to dissolve into pure texture before disappearing behind the overhang. Tallini had seen such a texture before; it was akin to the boulder's inner atmosphere. He accepted this recognition without surprise or disbelief, without mental comment, the dynamics of his thinking unmotivated by analysis of his perception. What ambition, save a weatherman's, would not be misplaced in wanting to measure clouds, to weigh them with the mind? For the pure play of a disinterested observation, they must remain, collectively, "clouds," unless patterned to namable forms of earthly objects mimicked as they pass through the sky. In that case, clearly, no individualization exists in the *observed*, only in the *observer*. For this reason, the observer must be known to himself before the observation can be understood. Tallini, in his idle contemplation, was concerned not with the phenomenon of condensed water droplets suspended in the atmosphere but with observing his own thinking procedure, the kaleidoscopic transmutations of his fantastically metamorphosing mind. It has been some years since the world relinquished its material construction to become a swarming process of electronic clouds. It has been even longer since the sun rose and set unchallenged. Yet one trusts that a chair will safely hold one's body, while the circulation of the earth is lived only through its long-range temporal effects, and never as the movement of which one is an integral part.

What dawned now on Tallini's cloud-observing reflection was that cloud, boulder, or whatever else might be observed is always *past*, and the observer's point of view is a window on what *was*. These are bygone clouds and circuits, and as long as they are objects of observation, they remain perception, thought, and memory. To lend them presence, Tallini sensed he must transcend perception. Observing the observer's observation would include the perception in his present thinking. The ascertaining instance of observing, through a window's perspective, a retrospected outside, constrains the observer to identify momentarily with what has passed; it demands a re-cognition that makes unavoidable the already seen, the already thought. Instead of living the spontaneous present, the observer runs the risk of thinking—or more aptly, re-thinking—such ready-made structures in the instant of perception. There is necessarily always a sense of the previously experienced in the perception, be it only perception per se. The recognition is always old and, through the constraint that frames the window, always reductive.

For Tallini, the situation held some vaguely photographic implications, and he felt the hazard of a squandered presence was best countervailed by dropping shutters once the perception had been acquired. A curtained window brings the magic show to an abrupt ending and is thereby most likely to induce the observer to turn to inner spaces. Continuing into an open future belongs to spontaneous, improvised presence only; it is not within reach of the past. Though originally open in its own experiential present, the past—now observed as its own by the present—is closure, and can be made available to futurity only in present experiencing. Tallini sensed the potential at the juncture of horizontal present and vertical past. He was the conscious observer at this intersection and experienced the present in the observation of the past, *his own past*. The past that was proof of his presence.

Under the boulder's overhang, Tallini avoided assailing these notions on temporality with his reasoning powers. He limited himself to meditating such things as a sort of counterpoint to the clouds drifting by. With this opening experience of past recognitions, of all the past that has gone into the immediate happening present, conserved for the present moment—with all this, he knew, cogitation would play havoc. His was a vastly expanded *vision*, although the window had not changed dimensions and the view remained the same while changing: clouds. The airy phantoms, slowly pushed by the southerly breeze across the skylight of that vision, sent a temporal message by their mutating shapes. They might enter one side of the frame as a trumpeting elephant and leave the other as a group of dancers. These are not forms, they are aggregates of blind obedience moved by an affinitive principle in a pattern of randomness. The cloud obeys the same necessity as does the puncticular boulder, and depends on the same freedom of chance. Necessity offers security and is old in its every moment; freedom offers the hazards of the unknown and remains forever new.

Tallini rubbed his right forearm, which had gone to sleep. The contemplation of clouds had led to a high degree of abstraction from the phenomenal world, and the arm's numbness was a symptom of a far more general languor. Persisting in his meditation, he reduced his awareness to the metabolic processes managed by the most primitive of vertebrate brains. Instead of calling the higher mind-components to attention, he let the remaining spark of consciousness fully invest the early processes pioneered by his reptilian ancestors. The gesture of attending to the insensate forearm, therefore, was dictated by his organism as a whole. His sight dissolved into a blur of light and dark, but a sudden powerful olfactory capacity almost choked him with the acrid boulder's sulfurous scent. The soil around it—by climatic action unlocked from the plutonic rock, its fiery soul relinquished—lay prone, a near inodorous dust. Picking up a sea tang even at this distance, he sniffed the air for unknown presences, for others who might contest this spot of earth he had inhabited forever and would inhabit forevermore, given that he was inhabiting it *now*. The territory was *his;* he would defend it to the last against any aggressor. A belligerent baring of claws and fangs might be called upon to that purpose, in a first gambit of intimidation.

Beyond just staying alive, he was aware of the urge, the necessity to show one's *being there* as such, as oneself, different from everything else around, to make oneself known. Here was the first step toward status, influence, power. There were special gestures for all encounters, from simple greetings to overt hostilities. A fight didn't have to be to the death, but could be a ritual dance to show off one's advantages to a potential mate. It counted in the contest for food and the satisfaction of all other hungers as well. Always, success lay in the art of presenting oneself advantageously. Then there were the terrible tempests that could not be managed in any way, blind irresistible tensions that drove one rashly, wantonly into destruction and. . . .

A shudder pulled Tallini out of this rudimentary, brute self-expression, and as his consciousness broadened, the world around him lost the hard cast of objectivity as sole dictate of its existence. Breaking the tyrannical equilibrium of stasis, as an organism as yet unframed by past and future, he began to perceive a world however vaguely modeled from previous experience, an inner landscape he would have to adjust to the image reflected back at him. He felt a sense of release from the cold-blooded depths of the primitive brain as he established himself on this freer level of mirrored awareness.

Save for the absence of a verbal language, a certain conformance to his earlier cloud-mind here became apparent. Indeed, elephants and desert beasts and dancers existed only by the grace of these *terms*, and the means of naming possible existences were as yet unavailable to the limbic extension of consciousness in which he momentarily resided. Yet unnamed models of previous encounters existed and were proposed to the senses, compared and modified, in an exchange that closely resembled a generalized cloud-game. He understood the game better as his experience transcended a lower awareness level. No longer did he struggle to assert himself within a frozen exteriority. He felt engaged in an exchange, and what he perceived could to some extent now be adapted to his experience. Liberated from the constraint of a world imposed upon him, he was able to focus on preferences in configuration and coloring: a choice, where earlier there was but sheer necessity. What was beyond understanding could temporarily be left out, and what was readily recognized helped to consolidate earlier acquisitions and augmented his security.

At this apperceptive stage of consciousness, which brought past experience to bear on the present revealed by the senses, Tallini was still one step removed from his fully awakened faculties. But soon the prospect of the impending descent to the village, by inserting an element of futurity, reestablished his access to a normal human level.

He had a powerful prevision of a solitary return to his room, an imperative need to avoid any encounters. His mind mapped a path of back lanes and shortcuts that would steer clear of the village's main street to get him to the hotel's side entrance. This anticipation demonstrated a high degree of autonomy from metabolic *idées fixes* or emotions that tend to deviate the best-laid plans. Thus, for example, though his stomach was growling with hunger for Giorgio's *lasagne* after a day in the open air without a bite since breakfast, he knew perfectly well that the conditions for digesting the day's events were silent privacy and preservation of his present mood. He had no doubt that the higher purpose would prevail. A fulcrum of this potential was the fully self-reflective capacity of observing himself as actor within his experiential environment.

◗ ◖ ○ ○ ◑ ◑

He moved his body slowly to prevent any excess exertion from involving a brain he was determined to keep as idle as possible. Cogitation would come; it couldn't be helped. But if the experience was to be short-circuited by logical intrusions or banalized by rational argument or small talk, it would be lost to the moment, and perhaps forever. His aim was to keep intact the peculiar state of mind communicated by the boulder and to counter the "thinking about" by reinforcing the experience of presence. He brushed himself clean of dust, stretched his arms and legs, and with a last look at the boulder, set out for the village. Although his descent led him over the same path his morning climb had taken, the experience was as different as night from day. In the morning, he had made his way uphill through a landscape in extremis, overburdened with top-heavy hunks of rock whose hard indifference exhibited a grandeur totally misplaced amid the moribund vegetation attempted by the near-barren soil. He heard not a whisper, not a breath, his own body providing the only life sound. A step away from arid desert.

The evening walk turned out to be quite the opposite. From the first downward stride, the mere dynamics of descent contrasted with the uphill effort. After the sedentary afternoon, the shock and spring of each step caught Tallini up in the rhythm of the exercise. With metabolism adjusting to gait, energizing blood and breath, walking struck him as a splendidly inventive compliance with the demands of gravity. Receiving in return all the vigor he dispensed, he was elated by this process of energy conversion, by its prodigality, its disregard of purpose. He was tumbling down ten times faster than he had climbed, yet experiencing a thousand times more. It was the energetic conversion that drove him, not the law of falling bodies. His arms swinging, his enormous hands scooping the air, he let himself fall, step by step, feeling the resistance of the ground driving a power through the soles of his feet and into his newly invigorated muscles. His head was humming with circulation, not thought: a Dionysian drive. The Great Pan lives and all is greatly alive! His eyes were on the path, yet he perceived the nature about him as a panoramic vision unbound from the mere sense of sight. Where in the morning there had been little to see, now wonders were brought to life as Tallini moved along with an extraordinary sense of being drawn toward a center, feeling the ease of a fall into the denseness of matter.

Now the velocity of his descent bestowed an air of fantasy upon the landscape. His surroundings seemed to flow by, whereas he, divorced from his rushing body, was immobile, a boulder-trained witness to the passing scene. The observer was amazed by a moving landscape no longer the static, dehydrated skeleton that he had, on the way up, so summarily dismissed as unworthy of attention. With an ontology all their own, the rocks were relating to each other; they were organized into groups, into families of rock, neighborhoods, domains, a sandstone nation with overtones of fairy tales. As he moved, parallactic shifts lent intention, volition, even personality to the landscape, which suddenly anthropomorphized at his gaze. He could make out stately patriarchs in hoary beards, a grieving woman in widow's weeds, infants cavorting in the dust—all personalized by sharply chiseled profiles and shadow-sinewed lineaments. In that very moment, the tactile feeling of the cave people came down, and he knew that what he was seeing, they had seen before him, long ago.

On all counts this triumphant realization should have at long last confirmed a pragmatic basis for the overlap of the two minds, present and primitive. But it somehow was hedged with admonition, and perhaps contained a first true teaching, where hitherto mere confirmation had always held sway. The instruction was unclear to Tallini but evidently directed toward the rules of the game. Was he playing a game? Was he improvising? Or had he fallen into cogitation? Where was the boulder now? It was outside; and he was definitely outside the boulder. The spell was fading, and with it the contact with the other of the cave, with the mind of origin.

The lesson had been lived, however, and the anthropomorphism vanquished. An increased awareness remained and accompanied him the rest of the way down. Exclusive of all mimesis, a different kind of resemblance now lent features all their own to the rocks, a mineral countenance that acknowledged a likeness, a similar cleaving and eroding within the contextual environment. Yet their individuality was not to be denied. The common origin—the original block, the mountain, the earth—had been a long hardening, practiced through fire, dried by air, quenched in water, then solidified, providing a place to stand, a primordial hillock forming a condensation that was in turn, within this particular gravitational field, matrix to further metallic compaction.

Tallini reached the bottom of the hill. On the road, his pace eased. The cave people were in touch again, tacitly contemplative of their success. Tallini was returning to the even emptiness of mind he had vowed to maintain until back in his room. His resolution was somewhat jumbled by the vigorous descent. If there had been losses, there would also be gains. The fading of the boulder experience into memory would have to be measured against a new relational insight into the mind of origin. Identification had been his effort so far, but the interlude of anthropomorphic mimesis had forced him to consider differences, free differences, unsubordinated to identity. What might have been of utmost importance to the original mind may be quite futile to the present, be it even beginner's mind. In the short span between ascent and descent, the world had changed, and an evident state of affairs on the way up had proved mere simulacrum by evening. Where in the morning he had seen cacti, flat flanks gangrened, their verdure prematurely conquered by the brown of the soil toward which they were inexorably slumping, now there were proud opuntias, temporarily wrapped in a mantle of inert cells in order to diminish exposure to the desiccative passion of solar rays. During this destructive phase of the solar cycle, it is natural wisdom for these desert dwellers to take the cloth of mendicancy and protect the invisible germ of buds that wait only for rain to dot the hills with flowering reds, yellows, and purples. Greenery returns, and the sun no longer burns, it nourishes.

Tallini was invaded by the power of the dry earth's energy reserves, its waning vitality in the absence of water, its potential for blossoming. In this empathy, and with the new presence emanating from the landscape, he discerned the dissolution of rock by wind and water and the unlocking of its energy, not yet as fertile soil, but as an inorganic structure that provides form for processes of future living organisms. After the elemental fusion of a totality alchemists still plot to sunder, the process that takes the rigid mineral crystal to a flexible cell is a first substantive transcendence. Flexibility is the first new finding outside the boulder.

The way Tallini was seeing this life-cycle process as a whole precluded the banality of its phenomenal phases, momentarily overcoming linear time. The subtly and inexplicably altered landscape seemed to be attempting to draw him away from himself. Under this attraction, Tallini felt displaced, freed from gravity. As this privileged position proved illusionary, he discovered other centers with his every move, redrawing an ever-changing periphery. He awakened to the movement within this horizon, an immobility observing itself, aware of its own change. Every rock formation, every single stone was different in each dynamic moment. Multiple perspectives of the single event combined into a flow not unlike a sign language, or perhaps some kind of silent music. These similes occurred to Tallini before he thought of camera and film, though that might be considered more appropriate to a *cinéaste*'s imagination. Yet linguistic and musical notions accompanied this particular unfolding by an association built on inner recurrence, on a subjective repetition. Film, in this case, was not evoked; it would have to have been thought for.

The strength of his resolve, the steadiness of his projected will, the faith in a conviction unexpectedly gained in the descent—such was his frame of mind that as he was perceiving things, he saw how they really were and how they worked.

Was to see them this clearly to master them, to make them happen his way? Be that as it may, he managed to reach the hotel's side entrance without having met a soul, unlikely as that was in this animated village toward day's end. For a heady moment he felt he had denuded destiny. All conceptual veils fallen away from her, reality stood naked before him, unnamed but observed. The side door opened onto a corridor leading directly to the stairway, avoiding the dining room and bar. Giorgio was busy in the kitchen, and no guests were about. Tallini slipped into his room unnoticed, locking the door behind him with a sigh of relief. He had dreaded having to talk to anyone, as it surely would have destroyed his very special state of being, and he seemed to have no words at his disposal.

The room was elegantly bare. A wooden table and chair made locally—the sort of thing one was beginning to see at antiquarians on the Rue du Bac—were pressed into service for no better reason than ready availability, lending them the stamp of necessity that makes for subtle decoration. White-washed walls, a bed, a Moroccan rug on a tile floor. A minimal bathroom and not much else, except a light so blue as to turn the room to sapphire. Burlap curtains covered the glass wall facing south, toward Africa. The cloth, roughly anilined with chemical ultramarine, resisted the assault of light by the unrelenting fire of the flawless sky and by its reflection from the becalmed sea below. A resinous blue bathed the room, a blue that remembered its cool origin even in the harshest noon glare—almost a cathedral indigo. It conquered everything in the room, yielding only to the white walls that shone through in a dull cerulean. The red floor tiles were dimmed to an indistinct mauve.

From the Great Indian Desert of Rajasthan, Tallini was familiar with this cooling effect in the absence of air-blowing machinery. Entering a tent for darshan, he had begun to shiver with the sudden drop in temperature and the chilled stillness filling an incensed domain long vowed to meditation. But in this secular hotel room, it was a strictly etymological nonchalance that played the mystic coolness to its diamond edge. It pleased the ancient entities, whose touch he was receiving ever more distinctly, as contact, or as presence.

So by all evidence, the *sensorial* process, in the newness of sentience and feeling, had to be primordial. It therefore wouldn't have occurred to Tallini to assume a posture beyond awareness of the sensory moment. Such contact was bound to be a primary, original mark of self-conscious spirit in reflective observation of its own sensory being. The room retained a cobalt cast even as the half-light faded and Tallini turned on the little desk lamp. He sat down slowly, carefully. The boulder experience was intact; he would fully unfold it in this blue grotto.

In this state of vacuity, he became aware of the importance of what must now occur to him. This self-observation struck with a boomerang effect that brought him the sense of involvement in a participatory rite. As he began to take some notes, one elbow on the table, left cheekbone resting on his fist, a tear ran down over his upper lip, where the tongue carefully probed it, drawing a distinction: it is a salty, not a bitter tear. This differentiation caused him an emotion akin to joy, a calm inner jubilation that seemed to resound in the hollows of his bones. There was, in the literal sense, an *impression* of the larger bones of his body, a pressure, primarily on the thighbones that bore the weight of his seated body like the foundation of a building. It was as if the ideas he wanted to inscribe with a stylus on the flat surface of a page had by some mysterious adaptation conformed to the marrow of his bones and were there effecting their inscription in the round. He was also certain that the other, the original observer of the primitive mind, was equally filled with joy at the event, inscribing it as well.

The connection resided in this common experience, the inscription bound all parts in a linkup, or better, a *linkback* to the original. Inscriptions intended for the flat page were being inscribed into the volume of the bones. In the sapphire room, errant reflections suggested tracings of an electronic order, but the only perceptible form lay in the distinction drawn in the salt. A part of him still occupied the boulder, his own osseous contribution to a mineral realm becoming conscious in him. Soon this abstract minerality melted away, and he found himself once again outside, the mineral core inside his body. He was looking at volume rather than inhabiting it: inside out, on a secondary level. On the paper-strewn tabletop—a letter, notes, landscape sketches—he calmly extended his free hand toward a thick green felt-tipped pen and brought it to a blank sheet to document the transition.

For a long time, Tallini sat at the table, pen in hand, meditating on his contact with the mind of origin, its difference and similitude with his own. If creatively improvised newness—the tool of transcendence—was an experience held in common with the early people, it seemed equally certain that the being informed by that newness was bound to differ at distinct mental stages. For the mind of origin, for which *everything* is new, newness must have been the simple and primeval awareness of being present here and now.

He had visited this strange consciousness of being present, which one might assume would pervade every living instant. It was the marvel of simply being there, a feeling so basic as to go unnoticed. A feeling, nevertheless, potentially new in every moment that is lived, thus making every moment newly improvised. It is said that when one is alone in extremity—and specifically in the instant of death—this feeling is renewed in the total and transcendent experience that not only represents a spatially and temporally exalted awareness of the instant but includes an entire life of presences. Tallini concluded that the consciousness of being present here and now, as transcendental experience of improvised newness, was necessary to the mind of origin, but it was no longer effective in the contemporary moment.

Out of meditation, Tallini, as the artisan he was, turned to practical thoughts about an old concern now affected by what had just been coming down: the question of doing, of what could be creatively undertaken, Benji's *"sujet qui vaut la peine qu'on s'en occupe,"* as well as his own *"Ma cosa devo fare?"* Yes, he would have to discuss this with Benji. Perhaps he would write to him again. But the hand that held the green felt-tip remained unmoved and unmoving. His hand would wait until it moved of its own accord to form the phrase by which he hoped to hold fast to the moment of transition from one stability to another, from silent self-awareness to the voiced certainty: "Everything speaks."

After another long meditative moment, he added some sentences meant to express how the world of the boulder had by no means simply been an illusion, how its qualitative reality easily held its ground against a world of abstracted discourse, constraining in its very intent. Though there had been no words in the boulder, he wrote, there had been *idea*, and in it a kind of aphonic thinking that could sustain his absence and also enable him to return. After all, he now possessed a password, given in front by his contact: "Everything speaks." And he felt that with the inscription, return had become integral to the experience.

He stared at the phrase he had written, trying to encompass the idea. No words in the boulder, true; but there was an arrangement of signs nonetheless, complex in its detail though simple in the overriding principle controlling the system, establishing the whole: an organization in polarity, the binary opposition of the complementary duality within oneness. Could this activity not participate in language, and was it not readable, theoretically, from its first conjunction to its last multiplication? Based on choice without preference, every bifurcation/conjunction in this extended duality/oneness was complete spontaneity, total improvisation. At each juncture of the process the situation was new. Never before had there been so much precedence as in that present moment. From all that has been conserved, what configuration would appear to associate in the newest invention?

Now Tallini perceived that alone *the self*, stripped to the bare bone, creates and interprets the unprecedented as he had experienced it in an environment of maximum precedence, and if he could recognize this fact in all its qualitative being, it was because he had himself designed it as the past of a given present. He was therefore himself intimately involved in the knitting of this substratum within which his own frame of osseous structure evolved. This is what he felt his note to Benji had expressed. Without rereading it, he addressed an envelope, placed the note inside, sealed the envelope, and went to bed.

Once again, the night was anything but restful. His physical agitation reflected a soul caught in the storm wont to accompany stages of major transitions. His mind had been destabilized by the eccentricities of his experience, and the imbalance had persisted through the descent from the hills and into the blue room. With consciousness dimmed into half sleep, he spent the night between snatches of dreams and bits of feverish thinking, waking and dozing, tossing and turning, until a benevolent dawn brought relief with the thought of Giorgio's coffee. Unkempt and unwashed, he made his way down to the foyer for the day's first espresso.

Giorgio usually opened the kitchen around six, but he seemed to be late this morning. The young French woman, herself in quest of an early cup, was sitting on a divan in the foyer. He bid her good morning and with these ready-made words he stepped outside the blue mineral silence: *"Bien le bonjour, mademoiselle."*

SIX

BENJI'S FEVER

Benji got out of bed with a headache, and even the morning *noir* at the corner bar didn't help. He walked around the block once and encountered the garbage collection truck, which did nothing to elevate his mood. Back at the apartment, he sat at his desk and shuffled through some papers. A top priority was the unfinished critique of technological science, whose deadline was approaching. He simply *had* to wrap it up today! But his mind was elsewhere. He was thinking of his friend Tallini, who would most certainly have left for Spain by now. It wouldn't be uncharacteristic of him to leave town abruptly, in which case he usually wrote a word soon thereafter. Benji fully expected to hear from him in the near future.

A strange journey, this trajectory from the young combat photographer obsessed with facts to the successful cinematographer touched by the East and in contact with transcendental entities! Yet even in the early days in Spain, he could scarcely have been called a hard-boiled realist—not with the qualitative modification of facts he was touting! Still, Benji thought a certain scientific positivism was not to be disregarded in his friend's reliance on instrumentation, the camera, and the insistence on the "proof" it was purported to furnish. In those days, Benji sometimes thought of him as a *scientiste raté*. But by now he recognized in his friend's "qualitative facts" an expression of two contradictory faculties of mind, oxymoroned by his budding philosophical consideration.

Tallini was undoubtedly dedicated to living reality as experienced in every moment, although such a project valorized a qualitative subjectivity with little bearing on the reasoning mind. But it was equally evident he could never be satisfied with life as a pure flow of feelings, and that he considered a rational accounting of himself and to himself as an equally important necessity of human existence. His camera thus came to play the part of an alter ego, liberating him to experience freely and openly the quality of the event in its emotional immediacy, while the instrument retained the instant —in the well-named *instantané*—which at a future date could serve to recreate at leisure a rationalized past without compromising the original intuitive action.

Not that the Tallini of yore would have recognized such an analysis as a description of his purpose. Surely his behavior did not carry out a conscious plan. At any rate, much had changed since those days, most importantly through the flap over the light-machine, which was a considerable step in Tallini's development. Benji had hoped it would mark the end of his flirtation with science and machinery. After the Louvain session, his friend had avoided the subject. But Benji figured that at the very least, the event had caused him to exchange the concrete particular for an equally concrete universal: Tallini had discovered the whole world to be a light-machine!

This new orientation no doubt had played its part in his work with the master yogis. The change had been humanizing, a shift from nature and its laws to individuality and creative mind. Benji was amused as he remembered suggesting an "observer" for the center of his friend's projected light show, and the latter's surprise at the discovery of this human "illumination." With the sojourn in India, his interest in natural and factual phenomena had been replaced by a fascination for the past. Both exhibited common traits, however. In both, Tallini was concerned with *light,* and in both he was thinking of extremes, of limits. For the extreme of nature, his scrutiny settled on a cosmic light that is the limit of time, space, and mass. As to his research into the past, it introduced a different temporal extreme. Though not on a universal scale, time here also found its limit in light: in the individual light of mind, of reason.

At their last encounter, all this was topped off by the intriguing revelation of some sort of direct contact superseding any documentation accumulated by academic research. Of course the questions asked by Tallini were hardly the kind to be treated by scientific inquiry. It seemed as if his friend's pursuit was aimed at a state of mind immediately preceding its opening to language, so this essential humanizing step could itself be experienced. And if Benji had understood correctly, Tallini seemed to base this gambit on a privileged connection with entities who had *been there.* If at first this conceit had seemed preposterous to Benji, it was at the moment much less so, due perhaps to his slightly feverish state. For in fact this truly historic event—this beginning of history, as no history can exist before a mind to register its happenings—was as much the common heritage of humankind as any other historical moment, and in principle, at least, was therefore accessible to the historians of all later times. More specifically, it was accessible to one who was privy to a witnessed account of the event.

Benji was jotting down some notes on these topics he hoped to discuss with his friend at their next meeting, when his writing hand attracted his attention. That hand was itself exhibiting quite a bit of know-how: fingers and wrist jointed on delicate hinges moving in perfect coordination. Certainly he was not consciously controlling these minute gestures. He had discussed with pianists the extraordinary feats their fingers performed, and they confirmed that the last thing they did was to control, command, or even observe what their hands were doing. Their minds might be in the sounds, or even in images quite unrelated to their performance, but certainly never in the fingers. Most would go so far as to maintain that were they to think about what their fingers were doing, they would be incapable of performing. This was an acquired know-how of the body, but it seemed to Benji quite similar to an inborn faculty such as breathing, for instance, considering that the music made was carried by air. The instrument receiving the hands' gesture is truly an extension of the body, molding the sound according to the fingers' action. The music itself completes the circle, returning to the ear as the air does to the lungs. In both cases there is a self-contained practice of the body that incorporates outside and inside into an uninterrupted cycle. The objectivity in both cases—air and music—is recycled by the body, allowing the next breath, the next phrase. In either case, the perfectly integrated whole defies any separation of subject and object.

Thus Benji's reflections led him to speculate on a perfect state of unity and balance between subject and object, innate in a pre-self-conscious humanity and perpetuated in the arts by an acquired technique. It must have been the coalition of emerging mind and developing hand that eventually broke up this near-paradisal state of perfection. In fingers and opposable thumb, the mind must have divined a tool's prototype and created a distance by this intuition, which step by step would construe an objectivity. This was the hand that could grasp a stick for a purpose, making a first conscious use of an outside world, in this case to extend the reach of the arm or to pick up a stone to throw and reach even further. And soon other uses are found for that stick, as a lever, perhaps, to pry up a larger stone. This need not be accompanied by much thinking or theory, and yet there was here an incipient technology, a technique that preceded any science. Benji had envisioned technology as deriving from science, but now he saw how body know-how came first, and that it was already *tekhnê*.

He opened the technology folder, but feeling hot and thirsty, he went to the kitchen for a glass of water. That headache was still bothersome, and he definitely didn't feel his usual self. He considered returning to bed, but thinking about Tallini's early people and their earliest tools brought to mind the antiquarian his friend often talked about, whose shop of prehistoric artifacts Benji had never visited. There he would be able not only to consult an expert but to obtain further insight into Tallini's endeavor and perhaps into Tallini himself. On the way he could pick up his mail. Perhaps there would be news from Spain.

118

● ◐ ○ ◑ ◐ ●

Arvan was in his showroom arranging a display of arrow-heads when Benji entered and introduced himself. Tallini had mentioned his friend to the dealer, who welcomed him cordially. Benji spoke briefly of his work on the irresponsible developments of technology and how, perhaps influenced by Tallini's fascination with the Paleolithic, he had begun to wonder about the very beginnings of tool and weapon making.

"Ah, yes, the early history," the antiquarian's face lit up. "For nearly two million years of the great Ice Ages, man's principal medium was stone. He trained his hand on it, and every movement of that hand either left its mark on the mind or had its roots in it. In retrospect, the very seed of technology can be said to reside in the stone. Chipping stones and flaking flint nodules provided the working edge and point needed for the functions performed by teeth and jaws. Pounding, scraping, cutting, grinding—all this was made possible with the advent of *Homo erectus*, whose bipedality liberated the upper limbs from the chore of locomotion."

"As well as freeing the hands for gesticulation, the germ of language," Benji interjected, "and for counting."

"Indeed. Despite narrow jaws and heavy jowls, the power of speech is growing in the creature. And with the *armed* hand, he has developed techno-organic extensions of his body. The bow is a good example of such extracorporeal limbs, an extensile arm, deadly at a distance when fitted with one of these aerodynamic arrowheads." Arvan handed a prized example to Benji. "A deceptively simple invention, it incorporated many of the faculties developed during man's long arboreal stage with its perfection of the grasping prehensile tool, focused sighting, and calculation of the springing leap. Indeed, we first see the bow in those sophisticated prehistoric rock paintings where hunters are always running with tremendous bounds or kneeling with bows flexed and arrows flying. These were the first practitioners of projectile predation that left the hunter well out of range and uninjured by the hunted. With its tautly strung gut and bent wood, it provided the capacity to shoot farther and faster than a man can throw: the first high-tech weapon. And it introduced the disassociation from death that comes with remote-control killing. Yes, it was cleverly conceived for multiplying the arm's strength by precisely orchestrating those eighty-eight muscles required for its performance."

"So there we have a stretched string," Benji interpolated with some animation, "simultaneously introducing the laws of harmony, proportionate sound, hence music *and* geometry, for the bow is almost a musical instrument in itself. Stop the bow string halfway and you have a note an octave higher. And the human ear is innately attuned to recognize that—it's man's quintessential hallmark."

"Quite so," Arvan replied. "It's also a fire-raising instrument, the twisted string round a twirling stick that creates friction, most useful to early man for mastering his first great tool. Indeed, still close at that time to his eternal origin, the human being was an exalted creature, highest in the animal kingdom. But he was already locked into the bow's evolution, which was destined, or should I say doomed, to culminate in the gun, and ultimately in the shoulder-borne surface-to-air missile. Don't laugh! The entire gamut of murder machines, as well as the most marvelous of human creations, have their genesis in stone. That should intrigue you, Monsieur Gauthier. From what I've heard about you, and from what I can judge for myself, you're a man of *ideas,* and I gather you haven't come to look at primeval souvenirs. Quite different from Piero, who couldn't wait to get hold of an eolith and then feel in his hand everything he wanted to know about it, as if he had some karmic affinity with its maker. But strange as it may seem, when it comes to worked stone, your approach may be more akin to that of our Stone Age forefathers."

"You intrigue me, Monsieur Arvan," said Benji. "Please do go on."

"With chipping and flaking, we're no longer dealing with an idle curiosity about pebbles underfoot, to be thrown at the nearest target—a propensity we haven't lost to this day, by the way. No, we are examining a purpose behind the seeking and shaping of a stone whose form already lends itself to a specific use, a connecting of cause and effect, an *idea*. Perhaps this is the first idea for which we have physical evidence because that's what worked stone is: the fossilized intelligence of its worker. That's why such slightly worked stones are called eoliths, quite literally 'stones of the dawn.' They are the first trace of logical thinking at the dawn of civilization. And as your own interest is less in the artifact itself than in the idea behind it, so the early knapper was not driven by the creation of a tool but by the idea of its use. And here, my dear sir, is a parallel that will confirm your worst suspicions. Just as in modern times huge technological innovations derive from requirements of warfare, so the bones of early flint-flakers are often found near those of now extinct animals, slain with the most primitive of tools. The dawning of the mind's reflection, evidenced in the stone, shows a predatory nature from the start. We haven't come very far since. At least our killer instinct never seems to die."

"As Goethe put it, 'Mankind moves forward, but Man remains ever the same,' " Benji remarked. "It's disheartening that the first tools were themselves lethal weapons, but you must admit that for a carnivore mankind was very deficiently outfitted. The newfound hand with its fully opposable thumb added dexterity, but it hardly made up for the absence of claws."

"An interesting point, this carnivorous nature of man," Arvan agreed. "Fortunately for his survival, he possessed the means to invent murderous tools: a cerebral cortex. But here enters another twist that goes a long way to explain humanity's disastrous history. Lacking fangs, horns, and claws, the natural instruments for dealing death, he also lacks the instinctive taboo that tends to deter predatory animals from attacking their own kind unto the death. Mechanical weapons are uninhibited killers.

"And there are further ramifications to this human status of inadequately endowed predator. When the mechanization of death by slaughterhouse technology dispensed him from hunting for food, the predatory instinct found satisfaction in taking aim at nature's other resources. Man's technical skills make the whole world his prey."

"Nor did our most holy text in any way deter him from this enterprise," Benji joined in. "It rather encouraged him to have 'dominion over every living thing that moveth upon the earth,' if I remember correctly."

"Ah, yes, the Good Book of Abrahamic religions! Not particularly inspiring of respect for life, it must be said. And who knows, perhaps this reckless license from such an unimpeachable source played its part in the sixteenth century, when Bacon, discovering the power of a renascent rationality, conceived applying it to the exploitation of nature. But we are speaking only of our own neck of the woods. Have you traveled, Monsieur Gauthier? Do you know the East?"

Benji admitted to sedentary habits that kept him close to home, excepting some displacements in Europe, forced by circumstances. But of course he was familiar with Oriental literature.

"Then you must be acquainted with another kind of technique, as basic to the lives of Orientals as ours to us. By the way, I've noticed that our friend Tallini brought back an awareness of this from his visit to India. I'm speaking of inward-directed techniques of living, such as the various yogas of Hinduism, the Buddhist techniques of the mind, or the Chinese meditation-in-motion of t'ai chi. I know that at first sight, these techniques may seem like different endeavors, but they are attempted solutions to the same problems: how to live within nature, to be autonomous in an unpredictable environment, and therefore, in the end, to achieve a certain mastery over material existence. They differ in that Western technique, directed outwardly in an effort to dominate the world, tends to neglect an inner life, whereas the Eastern approach is precisely the reverse, an inward-directedness that tends to neglect the outside world in an effort to dominate the self. It stands to reason that each one could learn something from the other, don't you think?"

Benji found the conversation stimulating, and he brought up the remarkably early scientific activity of the Chinese in the invention of gunpowder and the printing press, which preceded the Europeans by quite a few centuries—inventions that did not lead to techniques of warfare nor to an "Age of the Digest," mass-producing tabloid wisdom.

"Indeed," the dealer resumed, "we absolutely cannot interpret Chinese inward-directedness as a lack of inventiveness or practical incapacity. To the two inventions you mentioned we could add a lesser-known example, though even more significant because it concerns number: their most ancient anticipation of our most recent arithmetic application. Five thousand years ago, the basic arithmetic module of binary calculation was invented by Fu-Hi, an ancient Chinese emperor. Rediscovered by Leibniz, it has now proved indispensable to cybernetics. Now you will note that, taken together, this trio of inventions—gunpowder, the printing press, and binary computation—technologically evolved, almost defines the course of our present culture. But in China, none of these inventions were submitted to technological development, and this know-how was used as such, for fireworks, art prints, and, if anything, some benign accounting."

Benji added that this Chinese conservatism and a mistrust of labor-saving devices can already be found in early Taoist literature, in which it is said the user of machines in time will turn his own heart into a machine, and with such a machine heart, he will have lost ingenuousness and therewith the certitude of spirit alone compatible with the true Tao.

"Clearly," Arvan continued, "the ancient Chinese approach to technique avoided harming the environment and might, for all we know, have been beneficial to the inner being of those people. By renouncing mechanization, which replaces the illusion of progress with a faith in production, they preserved their artisans, always an essential part of creative cultures. It has been said that mechanized civilization is the agony of the world, and we in the West are about to prove it. We have violated nature and fouled our nest and allowed our inner being to lose its cosmic connection, presuming we still believe in such.

"Yes, I admit to a deep skepticism concerning the survival of *Homo sapiens*. Sustained by the concept of evolution, the notion of the infinite perfectibility of humankind is a splendid one. However, we're dealing today with creatures of infinite needs and desires that can be satiated by nothing but the only progress they can any longer conceive: perpetual technological innovations."

Benji turned thoughtful. "It seems the point has been reached where matter can no longer be violated for the selfish sake of man, but must be understood as an expression of spirit, and that its manipulation must be an offering to spirit."

"The dream of alchemists, dear sir, but further than ever from realization in our day. And more's the pity. Mankind got off to such a glorious start. But if we continue on this path, we'll all be back to chipping flint in some not-too-distant future. And it will take us quite a while to produce a masterpiece like this one ever again."

So saying, he removed a flint object from a showcase and held it up to the light. "This is one of my prize artifacts, a Solutrean 'laurel-leaf' blade with both pointed tips intact. A spectacular specimen of a Paleolithic master lapidary's technique. Large, yes, about thirteen inches long, and look how incredibly thin it is, about a quarter of an inch thick—it's almost translucent. You can clearly see the way he worked both sides, carefully calibrating the center ridge to create these attenuated ripples, yet leaving such flat scars that the blade feels almost smooth. Obviously, no one today could duplicate the manufacture of these delicate stone leaves, tapered to the keenest cutting edges known before the invention of steel. This piece, radiocarbon-dated at approximately 18,700 B.C., when much of northern Europe lay under a deep sheet of ice, is still as razor-sharp as the day it was flaked. No built-in obsolescence here! It's just perfect for trimming a beard like mine." Adjusting a mirror on the counter, he proceeded to demonstrate its efficacy, much to Benji's delight.

● ◐ ○ ○ ◑ ●

By the time he got back home, Benji was shivering and sweating all at once. "A little early for a Paris *grippe*," he muttered, and proceeded to prepare a grog for himself, with rum, lemon, and a bottle of Burgundy instead of water. Josephine, his devoted cleaning woman, would be coming the next day. She would go to the pharmacy and then cook up a little broth that could put life back into a dead man. Until then, he'd stay in bed and sip the grog, which was already improving his mood, if not his fever. It felt luxurious to lie there in the middle of the day, a dizzy buzz having replaced his headache, and think about nothing. But as soon as he thought about thinking nothing, ideas streamed in.

Could one really say that technology started with some Neanderthal using a tree branch as a lever to move a boulder? And didn't apes already use sticks to reach what they wanted? No, one had to be reasonable. The use of the lever would not have even a marginal effect on the world where this tool was used, and certainly none on the cosmos in general. But it would be beneficial to its inventor, who could gain stature within his Neanderthal clan, and it might make his fortune.

But this was all nonsense he was thinking, twaddle it was. When it came to gauging the effect of technology on man and his environment, a primitive lever could hardly be compared to unleashed atomic energy. It was a different order of things. The lever effect was hardly noticeable, while atomic power was capable of eliminating intelligent life on earth, perhaps from the cosmos, so there would be no one left to *think* that cosmos, and nothing would remain but a dumb universe, turning upon itself for all eternity.

Benji shuddered, and no longer knew if it was the Paris flu or the thought of such man-made futility. This thought had rarely left him since the power of nuclear fission became generally known. A cosmos rendered meaningless by the "progress" of mankind struck terror in his soul. But other instances of mass destruction short of such absolute annihilation had come to the fore. Instead of a one-time blow that would end it all, there were death camps, organized starvation, displacements of large populations, all leading to the indiscriminate death of vast numbers of humans. What they all had in common was the need of technical and bureaucratic know-how implemented by blind machinery.

He was trying to put these ideas out of his head, hoping to get some rest, when he noticed a distinct change in his room. It wasn't quite his room anymore; it was smaller. The walls were no longer papered with those yellow Art Nouveau flowers he so enjoyed; they were composed of rough stone. The ceiling was definitely vaulted, and there were ornate columns rising from the floor. It looked like a crypt he once visited in Aix, and his room now gave him the same feeling of overrestoration.

A stirring in the corner attracted his glance and he noticed a shadow where the door should have been. There was no door, but a familiar-looking man was standing there. He looked like the waiter who served him his morning coffee, but turned out to be Tallini, yet not quite Tallini—a mixture of both. This semblance of Tallini was dressed in light summer pants and a long shirt, both of the same coarse striped material. The pants, much too short, showed his bare ankles and sandaled feet. He also wore a cap with a visor. The get-up was very unlike Tallini, and yet it was Tallini's voice he heard: "I hate to see you in bed in the middle of the day," the fake Tallini said without further greeting. "The town's changed a lot since you last saw it, and you should know what's going on."

Benji climbed out of bed, fully dressed. They left the room through an opening in the wall, and then began to ascend a terribly narrow corkscrew staircase, the Tallini figure leading the way. The staircase led to a landing where another aperture had been smashed through the outside wall. The bogus Tallini was looking through this hole, and, when Benji reached the landing, he turned around. "I don't believe there's anyone left," he said, "but I see the moving van has arrived."

126

Benji looked out. The site, totally unfamiliar to him, defied description. There was an ambiguous quality to the scene's every detail. Thus it was unclear whether the perspective of the esplanade was receding into space or backward in time. Or did this diminishing line of counterthrusting arches fade off into symbols of a myth? Then again, the arcades' tapering façade didn't *look* like anything, but rather *sounded* like a harp's overtones stretching a glissando toward a tragic dénouement.

There was, however, the real moving van the Tallini figure had mentioned. Parked in the dark shadows cast by a warehouse across the street, its rear doors were wide open, and Benji could see it was empty. There was a mystery and a melancholy to the street that left him deeply troubled. He had no doubt the portentous van was waiting for him, and he realized he was indeed ready to go.

Then he noticed the shadow of a human form falling on the sunlit esplanade directly behind the warehouse. So there *was* life in the town! "Look, there must be someone standing there!" he said to the Tallini figure, who peered out, then pulled back with a short, mocking laugh: "It's a tailor's mannequin left behind. Don't you see the shadow doesn't move? There was a clothing shop on the other side of the plaza; they didn't have room for it in their cart."

Benji kept looking at the shadow, hoping for it to move, hoping as if his own life depended on finding another living being in the town.

And then it happened. On the left side of the street framed by the jagged opening, a young girl appeared, running in the sunshine and driving a hoop's zero before her with a short stick. This flash of life had an astounding effect on Benji. A feeling of exaltation seized him, along with the certitude that in the train of this innocent child a vast swell of humanity would soon come marching, bedecked with garlands and bouquets, returning the gift of mankind to the deserted metropolis and filling the esplanade with rousing hymns to life and liberty.

"I knew there was life," Benji shouted in great excitement. "Hey, little girl, come over here, wait for me." But the child continued rolling the big ring across the plaza and disappeared behind the warehouse. Again he heard the fake Tallini's cynical laugh. "Oh, it's the hoop girl. She can't hear you, she's deaf. She was abandoned as an infant, but survived, I don't know how. She recently invented the wheel. Comes every day to play with the mannequin."

Suddenly Benji lost all interest in the deserted town. In a flash of anger, he swung around and in a sharp but controlled voice, his face distorted with hate, hissed at this ridiculous figure who now seemed to be wearing pajamas and had shed all resemblance to Tallini: "You're a sham, a miserable counterfeit." He fairly pushed the words through his teeth. "She didn't invent the wheel, she merely found this hoop somewhere around an old rotten barrel, that's all. To invent the wheel is not just to find a round object, you stupid fellow. To invent the wheel is to conceive the idea of the axis, an invisible axis, thus discovering the reality of ideas, of a world you can't see and can't touch but is as real as all the objects that clutter *your* real world, and perhaps even more real. And it is only because of this idea that an axle will some day make the wheel into a useful object."

At that moment, he no longer remembered why he was so angry at the other, who just stood there, looking at him sadly and, despite his odd attire, dignified. Benji was now ashamed of his inexplicable outburst, but the man before him was very calm and seemed not in the least upset at being insulted. "Don't vent your anger at me, just because your city has died. At least I died with it, whereas you slept through it all."

At those words, Benji sat bolt upright in bed, drenched in sweat. Josephine was standing in the doorway.

"Mon Dieu, mais Monsieur est souffrant. En voilà une histoire!" And she hurried to the bed to take his pulse.

SEVEN

RECOGNIZING HEPHYSTA

In light of their Pascalian exchange a day earlier, Tallini's greeting to the young Frenchwoman was unpardonably trite. Seeing him so disheveled, however, she was unlikely to take it seriously. *"Salut,"* she said, sizing him up, "you look like you really need Giorgio's coffee."

With stunning effect, the movement of her head had exposed her profile to a shaft of early sunlight from the foyer's only window. To his *own* dismay, Tallini realized he did not have his camera, now cruelly missing from the image-hunting hand. At such predatory moments, appearance is supreme and the human being disappears, its shimmering torso to be set in a silver emulsion after the hunter's triumph of cunning and calculating aim. The weapon would not be Amor's bow and arrow, but the cheap hocus-pocus of a black box hidden in the hand. Neither is the heart the target, nor, deeper, the soul; the image is the game, the most exterior aspect. An image, furthermore, valued entirely for its light components rather than for the feelings or memories it might later provoke. Beyond the light effect, all else about the moment evanesces.

Like any lovesick lover: Is she here every morning at this time? Will she be here tomorrow? Will the weather hold, the light be the same . . . and will I get the shot? A ruthless possessiveness not of her being, not even of *her* photograph—in this instance almost anyone would do—but of the light-event, the light-moment, unique. Now, having lived the shadow experience of adequation to the plane, he realized the distortion (down to film speed and evaluated exposure) derailing the communion, so that if he persisted, he would lose the moment for *her*, without gaining it for her *image*. Changed not only in the figurative sense of Benji's "metaphor" but by the bare bones of the boulder, Tallini now could generalize the countless moments of a life of either/ors and if/thens, of missing one's own for the gain of the other, the other missed for the gain of one's own: *"M'amie, ma cosa devo fare?"*

"You here . . . now, but . . ." he stammered, suddenly disconcerted.

"I could say the same. We'll just have to make the best of it."

This meeting seemed to be off on the same ill-fated footing as the last. Tallini tried to pull himself together, to break with the automatism that produced the banal greeting and his subsequent chagrin.

"Please don't misunderstand me, mademoiselle. I am surprised, at this early hour, that's all; and of course a bit embarrassed, *gêné* . . ." and he brought his open palms close to his face, his fingers pointing to the unshaven jowls. He then looked down at his wrinkled attire and shrugged, "A long story, mademoiselle. A long night."

This casual looking and pointing at himself instantly brought him back to the being who had emerged from the boulder, a self in touch with the mind of origin. While that which calls itself "I" when it speaks mimics the mind in physical behavior, it is the self in touch that is looking at itself. When Tallini pointed to his body, he felt no sense of identity, only an echo of another sort of "looking at himself," a self-observation thus entering the realm of possibilities. What he actually pointed to—the stubble on the jaws, to be precise, the crumpled shirt and pants—evoked but a sense of alienation that stopped just short of questioning what kind of an unkempt clod could be sporting this attire. A second later, having cleared both photographic and physiological hurdles, he found himself in the self just recognized, the self in touch, found himself suddenly and simply *there*. He was present in the presence of another who was unknown to him in all the ways that were particularly hers, in all her individual and personal specificity. Yet she was by no means inaccessible, for he shared with her the broadest human generalities of consciousness, culture, and language, the collectively known, the old that gives the new a ground for assimilation.

Yesterday's preoccupation with coincidences in time and place was active as well, and now fully realized. This present encounter was an incredibly unlikely circumstance that had to result from innumerable moves at once necessary and contingent, referable and random. Facing the woman in Giorgio's foyer made the link by contiguity more compelling. The context suddenly ceased to be a mere backdrop, a setting to a play, and he felt it drawing around them both to reveal relations, a symbiosis pulling the scene together into a whole. The previous isolation of the main players now appeared utterly naïve. In contrast, Tallini perceived the convergence of event and context as evident. Better, the context had become an integral part of the event. And the idea of context itself had changed. The fake perspectives of the stage's enclosing backdrop opened up to lively vistas and expanded to horizons of potentially unlimited worlds. The universe of this event was no longer confined to the foyer, to the bar, or even to the hotel or to this particular locale on this particular beach. The context, in fact, was as infinite as the precedents of the event, his life and hers, with their genealogies and their every bifurcation, every yes/no, all the way back . . . to what? It seemed to him that every single fiber woven into this event shared a common origin. And what was now coming from the cave mind had had a hand in the weaving.

Looking at her, awed by this comprehension, Tallini sensed a sea change. No longer was he trying to fill a silence inherent to the situation, a silence that, if given a chance, could itself well reveal the moment's perfect medium. Free of the search for words, free of motives and drives, neither measuring advantages nor weighing chances, he simply stood there, freely present and available to her presence, a contemplative observer overwhelmed by the universal relatedness sustaining the entire situation.

He was also aware that a fitting response to what was happening to him might be in order, but for now this was beyond him. He was simply looking and seeing. He faced her, so to speak, purely. This purity compelled an absence that denoted openness rather than void, and through such openness he was receiving an impression of wholeness. Not that he perceived the entire scene expanding beyond sensory means. To the contrary, as a whole, it lodged in his perception of a minute detail, a strange speck of light in the tableau.

Earlier, while he had been evaluating the light that was modeling her portrait, she had moved her body slightly, out of the thin ray of sunlight whose effect had so enticed him, and which was now playing uselessly behind her. As this luminosity that aureoled her form was in large part hidden by it, the narrow vestibule remained dissolved in dim diffusion. In this setting, *en contraluz* such that her features were barely recognizable, Tallini discerned a spark igniting the pupil of her eye, out of reach of any beam that could have struck the reflecting surface of her iris. To his open receptivity this smallest lucent detail illuminated the entire situation. For he intuited that the light was not reflected, but was an inner light emitted, and in this he realized the significance of the event in its entirety. An elusive grasp, indeed, in a flurry of living thinking. As he attempted to hold it to an understanding, it congealed into thought and broke the spell. He was left with the bare fact that what he was looking at was looking back at him.

"No need to be embarrassed on my account." Her tone was milder. "Perhaps you will sit down and tell me all about it." And mildly chiding him for his formality *("mademoiselle-ci, mademoiselle-là")*, she told him her given name—or at least, attempted to do so. But Tallini was still caught up in his experience. The optical phenomenon vanished even before he had consciously registered it. Only a disappearing afterimage rescued the fading intuition and allowed its memorization as thought. There had been an emotional surge, however, concomitant with the mysterious flash and just as unexpected.

In his younger years, Tallini had known his share of emotional turbulence and misery. Only during his stay in India had he encountered the disciplines that attempt to examine and control this tyrannical aspect of the human makeup. Gurus and lamas he came to know presented him with a variety of methods, and all agreed on the necessity of dominating the emotional vagaries that cluster around the ego to sully all clarity of thinking and perception. He also had come in touch with notions for redeeming emotional complexes, once they were brought under strict control. He was never able, however, to draw any coherent conclusions about such positive use of emotions, and the possibility sounded remote, considering the arduous groundwork required. But the emotion accompanying the present experience of the inner light now called this sharply to consciousness, much as an odor can evoke with great accuracy a long-forgotten scene or a particular frame of mind. Could it be that the sporadic efforts he had invested in these control techniques since his return from the East—to be frank, he couldn't credit them, so far, with any notable improvements in his daily life and conduct —were enabling him to recognize something exceptional in the emotion that had accompanied the observation of the inner light?

This was no everyday feeling arising from the blindly ego-oriented well of instinctive sensibility, set off by some arbitrary memory association and thrusting its energy from a lower plexus toward heart and head, flooding everything with its dreamy self-flattering experience of "I" and "me." It was not. It lay deeper and ran calm and secure and purposeful, inscribing the event in its very happening into a permanent medium, with a simultaneity that shut out all circuitry. It did not seem to be an inscription of objective content (what content in the sparkle of an eye?) but of the quality of the experience. This quality, in turn, precluded dismissing the observation as accidental effect, as an optical illusion, the quirk of an optic nerve caused by all that glare in the hills. Such rationalizations were swept aside by the force of the emotional surge, strong enough to leave in its wake a trace of tears. Nor did it escape him that this was the second time in one day and night he had been thus overwhelmed. There had been the salty tear in the blue room only hours earlier, brought forth by the boomerang feeling of a return to origin, to rest, to absolution. And just as then, the surge seemed not to radiate from the solar plexus but rather to rise through the skeleton and leave its imprint in the larger bones of his body. What seemed to travel through his frame was that inner light and the possibility that in his state of attentive passivity he had been able to receive it, interpret it, and retain it in the marrow of his bones.

Aware, in his silent immobility, that the seconds were passing and the young woman looked puzzled, Tallini approached, took her hand, and touched it fleetingly to his lips, then reached for a chair and sat facing her. The enchantment dissolved. The woman in close-up, no longer perceived through that momentary openness, now impressed him as a being both mysterious and plain. Under ordinary circumstances, he might not have registered the slightest interest in her. It is well known that interest is not readily aroused without some measure of the unusual. The unexpected, the undefined—they pique our interest. But there was no ambiguity in her. She was undistinguished, though her features were sharply expressed.

In the extraordinary present circumstances, however, Tallini's reactions to the woman were not only part of the constellation that illuminated his discovery but were shining a bright light on its progress. Understanding that plainness, which was new to him, and the mystery, which was old, she came into focus as she looked up at him from the divan and, in a voice perhaps a trifle high-pitched for the hushed morning hour, diagnosed his need for Giorgio's brew. Now, in her proximity, he thought about the plainness that accompanied the mystery. Where had he met it before? Was it in that landscape, where the earth was seared pure and plain as an uncolored drawing? Or in the bistro, where one may take one's beverage neat—plain, in a word? In his mundane haunts, where purity of plainness was rarer than rare—seldom remarked and usually devalued to homeliness—Tallini had either never encountered or never noticed it. Twenty-four hours earlier, still blunted by Paris, he had failed to notice. How could he have missed it?

Her attempt at conversation faltered as Tallini remained taciturn, still assimilating his enhanced perceptions. Perception evolves through the observer's experience, and the extravagance of the boulder episode had allowed Tallini access to a different level. So his perceptive system, in transcending itself, incorporated the difference, assimilated the new. Was it this newness that allowed for these perceptive incidents and their inscription? Whatever the reasons, "he saw with brand-new eyes" and was aware of a wider horizon of communication. Ejected from the cold boulder of silence by the act of addressing the woman, he could beam his attention in her direction with his new insight. If the shadow passage on the boulder's face and the sojourn in its spaceless volume had shaken a blind trust in reality's strict weave, her unambiguous responses reassured him of still being in touch and functioning normally. He sensed no subterfuge, no evasive maneuver—a novelty for him, surrounded by intrigue as he usually was.

Tallini appreciated the value of plain speech and thought she might eventually offer plain answers to plain questions. Somewhere between Benji's philosophizing and the salon's inanities lay a possibility of plain speech, with her, by the look of her, and by the way she said her name: "Hephysta!" That was what he heard, but it was by no means what she had said. Nor did he hear it when she said it, but later, as she began to rise from the divan. Giorgio had just arrived and was opening the kitchen. The divan was low and her body out of balance because she had turned toward him, not moving her legs. An awkward twist of the hip revealed a certain stiffness and constraint; her slowness resided in that hip, which seemed carried with effort and perhaps with pain. He remembered noticing her limp at their first encounter and jumped up as soon as he saw her move, gallantly offering his arm. And perhaps, as he hovered above her, now bending down to take her hand, his closeness might have accentuated her difficulty. Nevertheless, the irregularity was disconcerting in such a healthy young body. But maybe the body had come to this globe in a haphazard manner, thrown into its world, perhaps in a rage over some profoundly atavistic disobedience, some archetypal revolt. By the nature of the fall, she was injured on arrival. The hip had no part in her plainness but was a sign of an enigma as old as the ages. Hephysta! The name had come down from the cave mind with force, and, for the first time, with a touch of authority.

Giorgio called to them, and they went over to the bar, where breakfast would be served. So far, few words had been said—about the beach, about the weather—and though he knew this small talk had to be made, Tallini hated it because it usurped time from what eventually would have to be said. No longer the inarticulate mumble of the salon, his verbal parsimony now was rooted in a sense of value and care. A conversation about the weather might not vary much here or there, but the qualitative range available to such a simple subject could encompass a vastness perhaps less accessible to intellectual abstractions. The true context here was the entente revealed to his new-eyed glance, in which weather comments, to his mind, were affording an adroit approach toward a region of unvarnished dialogue.

Over breakfast, they began exchanging cautious questions and cautiously concise answers (Milan and films for him, Toulouse and teaching for her) while all the time he was intent on telling her what he had to say, which would have to include his understanding of the plainness of her being and the possibilities it held for him. For her part, she couldn't wait to know what he had had in mind with that definition of the point.

As it turned out, she didn't have long to wait, for he thought it might be best to get it behind him as soon as he could, and so he brought it up himself. "About yesterday

136

morning. . . ." She was waiting, but as he tried, from the position of his "new" today, to recollect a yesterday immeasurably remote, he found grave difficulties in evoking the mood of "*Scusi, ma.* . . ." His normal sense of time had been invaded by a discontinuity evident in a defective sense of linearity as well as in uncertain logical connections to this particular yesterday he was trying to evoke, which remained but tenuously related now to his less-than-a-day-later, yet timeless, present.

The struggle to revivify what had been the definition of the point—its counterproductivity would become clear to him only days later—was quickly displaced by the shining newness that had come to his life overnight. New was the dimensional abstraction of the passage in the plane, which had afforded him a perfect sense of fit in an environment, a perfect relation of self and other; and new was a second degree of dimensional abstraction, his point-defined microscopic experience of a volume world turned outside in. He had not lost the boulder's profound instruction in abstraction. His qualitative reorientation amid concrete facts made a mere phrase of "the reality of the outer world." Now these words were but another arrangement of grammatical elements open to rearrangements, such as "the world of the outer reality," which was not the same, of course, but not entirely different either. A fundamental principle of order lends legitimacy to both, and both can be pretexts for thinking. The freedom of thinking either, of thinking them both, of evaluating the relative informative energy of each results in an increased autonomy of the thinker and greater independence from the given, which allows not only its closer scrutiny but an alternative to something passively received, a faculty of rearranging the event.

This was happening with Hephysta at this very moment, beginning with her naming, when apparently unimpeachable information had been dismissed out of hand and replaced on the subjective strength of some superior insight, *beyond evidence.* His recognition of her earthly plainness coupled with her fiery spirit—so searing yesterday, and still smoldering today under the early morning sun—was confirmed by the lame hip and had, by inspired association, called forth a new name.

"The definition of the point," Tallini went on, with some semblance of composure, "it was an error to bring it up. An error yesterday, induced not only by a sea breeze, as you have pointed out, but by a desire, clumsy, I admit, but also sincere, I swear, a desire for acquaintance—as we say in Milano: '*La conoscenza, la posso fare?*' It is an error today for reasons that in part are obscure to me but are certainly connected with developments in my work over the last twenty-four hours, which account for my appearance, for which I apologize. But it is an error today also because we have talked enough about the past, and here I bring it up, this unfortunate patch in our past, *mea culpa.*"

"The only past we have, so far."

"I thought you might be curious and I wanted to explain, but I can't. I have lost touch, something I do not fully comprehend. *Mais . . . passons.* The question itself was an error, I'm just finding out. I should have asked, What is the *point* of definition? Definition limits; and whatever definition you offer, there is another you have left out. Verbal, connotative, denotative, rhetorical, demonstrative—there is no end to it, and one is no better than the other. Believe me, mademoiselle, I have studied the question in some detail. There is said to be the *definiens,* and there is said to be the *definiendum.* One is supposed to define the other, but usually they get mixed up together to some extent, and only repeat themselves and each other. Tautologies, circularities—the world is full of them. I mean the world of language, of course. I have a good friend in Paris, Benji, you must meet him. You go to Paris sometimes? Never? I can't blame you. Overdefined, a city of limitations. People are defining themselves with everything they say— themselves, not the other, as they believe. And everyone in his own language. Have you ever noticed how *everything speaks?* But tell me, mademoiselle . . ."

"Sidonie," she insisted.

138

He did not intend to yield on this matter. The name he had given her had come down from the cave mind and Tallini trusted it. Besides, now that he had recognized her, he felt himself far better qualified than her parents to name her. After all, the ineptitude of creators for naming their own creations is well documented. He remembered that Benji had reflected on the deity's need of man to denominate the animals once they had been given form. Was this part of the cave-mind heritage, a naming before the caves, an atavism from the time outside?

"Ah, you see, you are defining. You are defining, and what kind of definition might that be, the definition by name? A nominal definition, perhaps, to answer my own question. Such definitions define the word, define it as being your name. But what does it tell me about you? Let me share a secret with you: I *have* a name for you, I have it on the tip of my tongue, which is where names land when they slip from one's brain. Give me time, it will come forth." (*La commedia*, he knew she was Hephysta, but how could he tell her?) "For the moment, I will call you mademoiselle; it suits you, but of course it is not a name, there are millions of mademoiselles, but there is only one. . . ."

He caught himself in time. What was going on? She must think him quite incoherent and presumptuous. He felt he hadn't spoken in ages, and now, suddenly, he was saying something—though on the surface of it, he was saying very little. Yet the mere liquidity of the flow kept contact alive; moreover, it gave him time to gather his faculties. The oscillation and its mental activity, dissembled by his chatter, might land him further than he was willing to go. If he crossed the threshold he would likely leave behind a solid edifice: the *known*, to which he now clung, on the edge of panic.

The moment's briefest hesitation coincided with a sudden and fleeting interpellation from the cave people; as usual, this intercession only revealed what had been there all along but had as yet not entered self-awareness: their own involvement. Had it been triggered by some unanswered question?

139

And why did he need a logic for these events anyway? Had he not witnessed—nay, *lived*—the process of chance and necessity, yes and no, into an equilibrium that determines perception's best guess?

The quirks of the mind are unpredictable, and a most casual and disinterested throw of the dice can come up a winner. He had read that few inventions were due primarily to straightforward diligence and rational application. Chance enters with a guess, an error, a playful act, or an instant of total distraction from the work in progress. It is not the steady aim that strikes the bull's-eye. The marksman hits the target in a relaxed gesture circumscribing the theoretically impossible center, as inaccessible as the motionless line through the axis of the rotating wheel. He cannot know the ultimate instant of the shot, which is always unexpected, as is the answer to a question yet unaware of itself.

"Only one you, and only one I," he finished lamely, distracted now, the current from the early mind coming down hard. The tactile feeling was becoming more pervasive, encouraging, reaching into his imagination to show what was meant. "Only one you, and only one I." The phrase seemed to echo back and forth between them, between him and the current.

What had to happen so that there was only one of a kind, each with a name all its own? The current hesitates; it does not remember. How was it before names, among the unnamed? How did the nameless find their difference? It does not know; it has no memory; it does not receive questions; it only passes what is and what remains. The unnamed are beyond, free, outside, at the beginning of the current. When the current was young, the unnamed were few, but they were *all* the unnamed, and for that time they were many. While the current was still running slow, time was very long for the few. Then the many became more, and faster, splitting up and joining together, like everything else outside. Everything was outside before time became short. But in the long time, the time of no memory, everything was outside with the unnamed. Outside of what? The current does not understand questions. There are answers only where there are no questions. It has no memory. For answers without questions, one must be outside. Outside is where they were before they went inside. How was it before? But it *is* before, and there is no inside, even the parts of the whole are outside of the whole.

This echo was absorbing Tallini's attention, and Sidonie, herself distracted by the beckoning sun now bathing the veranda in ocherous warmth, availed herself of his absentmindedness—which she had begun to accept as part of the man —to suggest they move outside. Following her through the sliding door, still lost in his thoughts, he stepped from the bar's cool penumbra into the radiance of the day. The sun struck him full face. The gold light surprised a wide-open iris, admitting a flow of incandescent energy. Pupils ablaze, Tallini lowered his eyelids and entrapped the sun-bolt racing on two

In the evening, by the lake, all come together, some standing, some flying, some swimming, some running on fours. Things are much like other things, nothing is very different from anything else. Everything breathes, multiplies, devours, nourishes some other, the other nourishes others in turn. The other is very much the same, only different in ways, how it moves, some on fours, some on twos, some in air, some in water, all are tied, connected, some more here, some more there. Fearless on two legs is the same as fearless on four. What flies as an eye is the same as the eye and is bound to what sees with the eye. What devours the dead is the same as what makes the dead into earth. All is secure, what must happen, happens. The other who is most alike comes closest, for touching, for playing, for fighting, for loving. All is dream, all is echo. All is outside, the breath is outside, in the wind, in the waves back and forth by the shore. The eye is outside, flying, then dropping like a stone. The blood is outside, flowing and making live; then resting, dead; then flowing again. And there are no names, only the sameness of many. The same gather with the same. It is good to gather, there is more blood in the gathering, more flow, and although the gathering is of the same, there are some who are different, they are bigger with the flow. They gathered to touch the sameness together, that closest sameness that makes them all the same. They practice together, the stretching, always the stretching, of limbs, of hand. The hand is perfect, but it must be stretched, then rounded, stretched, rounded, stretched. The practice of the hand, it went on all the time, it was like the hunger, all the time. And the stretching, the stretching to other places, then coming back. Moving, flowing. . . .

141

converging brain tracts to its decussate encounter. Having by its electric violence flushed visual debris from the optic nerve, the fireball, surrounded by darkness, irradiated all the colors at the edge of light and dark to produce its three-dimensional picture show.

Blinded by so much luminosity, his step across the threshold evoked a synthesis of the cave people's agelong travail toward light. The flash of this irrational association allegorized his movement and suggested the possibility of quite another approach to the early mind. Immersed for a living moment in a world where configurations usurp the voices of ideas, his gesture—the step over the threshold—is transfigured. And suddenly he was acting as the agent of a ritual gesture first performed by Paleolithic beings and repeated ever since in numberless expressive forms: the giant step from darkness to light.

The moment had ended long before he reached the edge of the terrace overlooking the sea, but he construed this episode immediately as evidence of his closeness to the cave mind now receding further and further. Only a glimpse, but it was more than ever before. The episode was destabilizing; however, it represented yet another wave in the increasing oscillation, and he had time—while Hephysta arranged the deck chairs for the best view of the beach, where some fishermen were spreading nets—to wonder whether to attribute his condition to a further development of the contact with the cave people. He was quick to reject that hypothesis, as the ancient mind's tactile feeling always transmitted a familiarity that offered shelter, a refuge from the obscure complexities of the unknown.

In some way he always recognized himself or some aspect of himself in the cave mind. He did not consider that such contact might have been the preparatory training for a potential now declaring its actuality. It may have predisposed him to the extraordinary, but it had not prepared him for the actual oscillation as it tore at preconceptions, mocked certitudes, rode roughshod over evidence—until he let go, realizing no acquired conduct would stand the test of this encounter.

No longer would he curse his speech for lack of profundity or even of coherence. The fact of articulating sounds, of emitting audible forms to be received by an ear organized to analyze vibrations and to decode them in a mind other than his own—the general connectedness this process demonstrated—suddenly revealed a miracle of such magnitude that the process in itself redeemed any deficiencies in execution. This amazement at the obvious was an apprehension in the full sense of the term, both an intellectual grasp and an emotional dread, as he experienced the anxieties of diminished control and attention, his certitude unsubstantiated by his flimsy propositions. He was at a loss to find adequate language. In this turmoil, at the inchoate moment of discovering the other beyond the evidence of his design, might not the mysterious bond between them break and Hephysta vanish as suddenly as she had appeared?

He needn't have worried. For the recipient of this eccentric courtship, the event was anything but routine. Unaccustomed as she was to male pursuit and sensitized by its neglects, yet refined, on the other hand, by the solitudes of this disregard and—through scholarship, literature, the arts—thus richly instructed, Sidonie had a perception all her own. Despite the uncertainty this encounter provoked, she felt ebullient and excited about its unusual, perhaps unique nature. Although such divergences had only infrequently modified her path of life, she scarcely required fiction or philosophy to know that Italian filmmakers rarely notice plain women. On this occasion, no ready conduct came to mind, lest it be one of some prudence.

"Monsieur Pierrot," she said, as soon as they were settled at a table, "I'm glad we abandoned geometry to your inaccessible yesterday, but for a lesson in the logic of nomination, today is still somewhat young. And you may call me whatever you please, as long as you will permit me to have this first cup of coffee peacefully, while it is still hot. In the meantime, do tell me about your work."

Hadn't she heard him? Didn't she understand that this was precisely what he didn't want—his experience of this present reduced to a reference to the past? He had patiently borne with the necessity of their introductory exchange, which he figured to be polite. And he had attempted an apology for past foolishness, a gross misjudgment, with which his present thinking refused to comply. He saw a chasm, with yesterday's past on the other side. Clearly he possessed the power to bring that past across the divide, to make it appear and act in the present. He thought his incapacity to do that now, with the definition of the point, was perhaps an aberration caused by fatigue. Beneath this rationalization, other feelings were brewing, obscure but vitally exciting. The idea came to him that he could, by a certain willed immobility of mind, by banishing thoughts as well as the language which remembers them, choose to leave that past event on the other side. This conscious willing would be a new power. He sensed the freedom of it and, in contrast, the slavery of the unchecked flow from past into present and on into future. Was it not enough that uncontrollable atavisms in one's present impose their options on one's future?

His face pale with fatigue, he made an effort to mirror her airy mood, remarking how her charming tonic accent graced the last vowel of his name, making him feel, *"comment dire . . . ? Presque funambulesque!"* But this was his last concession; he had to let himself be carried where he wanted to go.

"It is a struggle, every possible moment," he heard himself say, "to realize the opportunities presented when they are given. Most of the time we pass one another without seeing or hearing, without feeling, without paying attention. I speak for myself, of course, but from experience, *nulladimeno*. It is my case, this failure of attention. For some reason or other, one becomes wrapped up in oneself, and as a result, encounters only phantoms, shadows; one gets caught in an enclosure of sorts, a loneliness one has constructed for oneself, and it doesn't matter how many friends one has.

"Yes, it is my case, mademoiselle, I never understood it until recently, but it is my case. Perhaps yours is different, although I feel you yourself are not quite satisfied with this shallowness, this lack of focus and awareness, and also not fooled by such surface contact as it offers. I have experience in surfaces, and not only geometrically speaking; but such abstractions are totally absent, or at least they should be, when it comes to our relation with the other.

"But my concern is elsewhere, with what I am discovering—and I hope you will understand the difficulty in relaying this. It is *new*, so you must be patient. What I am discovering is the nature of the contact with the other, which is not destined—yes, I believe that is the best word—not *destined* for the personality of the other at all, not for the *person* as one usually thinks, and abysmal failures are the result of such misdirections. Therefore—and I'm sure you'll understand—this attempt aims at something that appears to be there before you, and yet . . . it gets lost in some vaporous conglomeration.

"I am not being critical of the other, believe me, because the other is not different from myself. Of course, one is always more tolerant of oneself, when one really ought to be more severe. That is human nature. But I'm speaking of the real aim of this contact with the other. I see it goes beyond the person—it's transpersonal. It doesn't refer to the person, doesn't refer at all. Ideally, that is. Although in fact we always differentiate in what we are faced with—the other—and we limit ourself to this differentiation, this content, all mapped out, when in fact, there is nothing very solid there at all. The limitation, the definition again. One's contact is not with another personality, or at least that is not the aim.

"This may seem quite incoherent, and I apologize if I'm spoiling your morning espresso for you. I have spent a sleepless night after an incredible day and am not quite myself. Although I am actually in the process of becoming myself, literally, and it's a process I cannot interrupt—for love or money I cannot.

"Money is always problematic, and now . . . but this word *love* came up accidentally, an idiom, *une tournure*, so to speak, and as you say, it being early for logic, perhaps it is early for love. Then again, perhaps it is never too early for such a universal topic, especially as it entered the conversation on the sly, not through me so much as through the language itself. I hope you understand. But precisely because I do not refer to personalities, we can look at the topic dispassionately, or better, with equanimity, without being moved or even threatened by attachments or any negative outcomes, *n'est-ce pas?* But this might introduce a certain ambiguity, for if I say 'dispassionately,' I certainly don't mean 'without compassion.' I remember, when studying Latin as a boy, my confusion with the word *altus*. This same thing exists in my native language as well, of course, but I had never noticed it there. How can the same word refer both to height and to depth? A naïve question, a little boy's view of the facts.

"Ah, the facts, they are another story. Now I say to the contrary that we can be dispassionately compassionate, so if we speak dispassionately of love, we speak not with a lack of compassion—how could we speak of the one without the other?—but with equanimity. I don't mean to treat these things abstractly, dryly, in the manner of some dissertation. No, it is with great pleasure, with living joy that I consider these things, and I may point out that when they address themselves, too strictly perhaps, to a limited personality, they frequently lead to sorrow, not to joyfulness as they should. But if this wider horizon that has opened is to unfold, that other is required to call these things forth.

"So you see we need the other to reach our wider horizons in a real sense, not as abstractions. I say *need*, but that might imply dependencies, so I will replace the *need*, but not by *desire* so much as by *love*. Here's where compassion also is necessary, so we do not use the other for our selfish purposes. Perhaps you have heard all this before, as I must have heard it many times. I believe this is all common knowledge, plain good sense, and it doesn't matter if the content is old, as long as the experience of it is new. But perhaps I am getting carried away. You haven't touched your espresso all this time. . . ."

She had been looking at him, wide-eyed. He seemed to have grown taller in the open, and his words carried farther in the fresh air. She had become aware of a difference since they left the bar, even before he had begun to speak. There was something heroic about him, something vaguely tragic, prophetic, with that drawn face and those wide gestures. It struck her that he actually seemed to be made of earth, just like the Bible said. She thought the waves below the terrace, the waves that were breaking with high tide, also had a bearing on his condition. And then there was this fiery something, unaccounted for by his Mediterranean heritage alone, something she thought might entail a possible danger to himself, and to her.

Actually, she felt him to be very much in tune with the natural elements, although she had never had such a feeling about anyone before. She had taken her espresso along from the bar; the cup was still half full. When he stopped talking, she turned away and drank it down in one gulp. Toying with the cup in her hand, she seemed to be searching the grounds for a reply. One thing was clear. Despite all appearances, his intensity was not directed at her at all. It was aimed beyond her person, through her to another, even if the other was an impersonal horizon, an abstraction of sorts.

Sometimes, at parties, Sidonie had been frustrated by people who made her endure palaver unsupported by their errant minds and restless eyes. But never had she heard this inconsiderate use of an interlocutor so openly admitted. Never had she witnessed a demonstration of the proceedings within the very discourse that purported its application. But it was also clear to her that *this* occasion was fundamentally different, and because she was unable to rationalize the difference, to pin it down, she fixed on what seemed to her his self-contradiction.

Brought up to engage an argument for far lesser peccadilloes, she set to stiffen her critique. She thought he was valorizing the encounter, yet at the same time cheating it of its object by situating that object in an unspecified beyond. She demanded clarification in simple and concise ideas, having been trained to that effect. By this process, she obliterated her intuitive feeling, which was close to the truth and could have provided a crucial clue to the encounter: that he was made of earth, that his words were carried by the winds, that he was moving in waves, at high tide, and that somehow he was aflame, burning. Through her self-referral, a drop of poison penetrated her defenses, causing her to become self-conscious. Then she saw herself as flawed, her ordinary looks —a face without a single striking feature—inevitably accounting for her lack of magnetism. He, on the other hand, was touched precisely by these circumstances, and the energy they thus managed to generate by this opposition put both of them at ease. For her there was a sense of having found her ground; for him, the confirmation that indeed she was Hephysta.

"It sounds to me," she ventured, "as if you were postulating a certain refinement, a purity of feeling, perhaps, in these terms that convey goodness itself, saintly, one might say. I appreciate that these qualities must be shared, and I conceive the inconveniences of such an arrangement as well. I am not insensitive to the idea of love without attachment, particularly if it is to relate to this peace of mind with which your ethical propaedeutics would have it cohabit, this ideal of undisturbed evenness of mind, of temper, of composure. But from what I know of love, you'd better stay away from the one if you cherish the other. The reaction is not necessarily reversible, and that may be a matter to consider—that one should have acquired perfect equanimity before ever falling in love.

"Am I to take this as a teaching, a threat, or a statement of policy, Monsieur Pierrot? And why should anyone care for such a lover, whose joy—I presume we are here speaking of *joie* and not *jouissance*, not even *jouissance de l'esprit*—why should anyone care for a lover whose joy lies beyond, resides, *et c'est bien le cas de le dire, mon pauvre Monsieur Pierrot*, in some *metaphysical* beyond. And you will note that in this case—exposed by *me*, at this moment, it must be *my* case, *non?*—in *this* case, I was saying, the linguistic representation fits the facts marvelously, don't you think? And what next, *caro fratello?*"

That facile manner once again! Is it possible to express anything when it comes out so smoothly? Isn't language an effort, a work? For Tallini, she was speaking from memory but not by heart, with bits and pieces put together from what he had said—what *had* he said? he couldn't remember—and from what she knew, what she had learned. Instead of letting the language speak, she overwhelmed it with her presence. But it was by no means *l'eau qui coule* of the salon. There was substance, tightly controlled by mind, a bit hard, perhaps, and cool, if not cold. He was used to all that from Benji, who epitomized an acquired Gallic *ratio* for survival ("when in Rome, beat the Romans at their game"). When the language speaks, one has a choice: to take a chance at voicing the intuition in live thinking, or to join the trivial plane of the salon. She was somewhere in between. If only she'd clear out that elegant rubble and discover the value of the plainness he had seen!

She didn't improvise, which was a shame, but at least she was in touch with music, studied voice, was taking lessons. She had a feeling about songs, about words and tone. He commanded her to sing, immediately, to sing what she was about to say. She blushed a little but was amused. She said it didn't work that way, especially in the morning, and outdoors. Too much competition from those waves. And anyway, they were no longer alone; other guests were on the terrace now, having coffee, feeling the sunshine, listening to the waves. This banter fortified the polarity and spread a shared conviction that a step had been taken. Sidonie surmised that his extraordinary state of mind had to do with whatever had brought him to Spain, and so she persisted, "You still haven't told me about your work."

"I am thinking about time." She couldn't be sure he meant it as an answer to her query, but he had aimed at nothing less. "About the importance of what is first in time, although I know this to be a fictitious formulation. But what can we do when we can't live what we know? Of course, as soon as you think about it you can see that beginnings are quite impossible, strictly speaking. Except for the *Fiat Lux*—letting the light be there—no pure beginning seems possible because it is always already a beginning within light, a birth into light, not an appearance out of nothing, like the light out of darkness.

"Strange, is it not, to think light can come out of darkness? Like something coming from nothing. And yet. . . . But darkness coming from light is easier to see, isn't it? Because it would seem that it amounts simply to extinguishing the light, to eliminating something that is there. But that is problematic also, because, after all, the darkness could be there, and eliminating it would amount to light, if you know what I mean. Forgive me, mademoiselle, I don't know why I'm getting into all this, but it is just what's coming to mind, so I permit myself—selfishly, I know—to go on. But this something coming from nothing, it is difficult, but it seems unavoidable. After the *Fiat Lux*, there is always already something in process at every beginning, what with the light being there; a context, and that context determines what follows. But beside these inevitable limitations, such a beginning is freedom, and from there on, every next step is a step into constraints, and we are going from light to darkness."

"Your work. . . ."

"But I'm telling you! What else can I do with words? Later there may be pictures, but for the moment, words are all I have."

A sudden sharpness in his voice did not escape her, and again she sensed peril, a danger to her familiar conduct of mind, to received truths and beliefs that had gone largely unexamined. She felt her life—built on all this, like every other—could somehow be threatened by what she was hearing. It was not fire that had sounded the alarm this time, but the keen edge of his retort cutting into the fabric of her confidence. She glimpsed not only that strange love of his, whose fervency would so coldly bypass her person, but an empty construct as well, too remote for *her* words. She may have divined that this sharpness had been honed on someone like

Benji, but she couldn't have known how much obfuscation and diversion it had already cut through.

Tallini felt equipped to handle *his* Hephysta's sidetracks although they differed from Benji's in nature: they were female, they were *lunar*. Where Benji pretended to adhere scrupulously to a topic, all the while distorting it beyond recognition through analysis and reference, she would unconsciously adapt it to her own train of thought, her personal interests, or her visual response to language. The result could banish any conversation to the most distant and irrelevant avenues. Though an egalitarian by conviction, Tallini knew enough about the sexes not to disregard the fact that men and women use their heads in subtly distinctive ways. Experience had taught him to watch out for what he sensed here: the lunar sidetrack, as he called it.

"What I mean," he continued more calmly, noting the effect of his *brusquerie* in her expression, "is that eventually I hope to have some film on whatever I am living and experiencing, and until I can show it to you, I have to try to communicate it by speaking, which is not easy for me at times, at least on this subject. The film will be the concrete result of what is now still rather formless, nothing more than an invisible and inaudible presence somewhere in what I will call my mind, not just the brain. In this I follow the ideas of the Parisian friend I already mentioned, who doesn't believe the mind is in the head at all. He thinks there is a lot more involvement than just thoughts and mentation, and sometimes when he speaks of the mind, he will also speak of the heart. So I must give some credit to Benji when I speak as I do, some credit for the ideas—he has a historical sense I lack, and a vast education for which I never had time. Not that I haven't thought about these matters myself, of course, and I may differ with him on various points, particularly since my experience with the cave people began—that is, since I became interested in shooting some footage on the caves and their inhabitants." The topic was unavoidable in the long run, but he would speak about this work on his own terms.

"Ah, yes, Giorgio mentioned you went into the hills to explore caves and I was interested. . . ."

"No, no, Giorgio doesn't understand about the cave people. I have never spoken to him about anything. Only to Benji. And now I am speaking about it to you, which I do not find easy, precisely."

"I'm really quite sorry; I won't interrupt again. Tell me what you think about the heart."

"What Benji talks about is an evolution of heart and mind together, guided by a perpetual, unchanging spirit. I am not using his words exactly—perhaps he never spoke of spirit, perhaps he spoke of being, or essence. I don't recall, and the term is unimportant. But we came to talk about the possibility of something unchanged in all this evolution and I believe spirit is as good as any other term here, don't you think?

"But maybe you feel we don't need such a constant? In that case, we may forget about it. It makes no difference to the historic argument as Benji presented it. It only becomes necessary, in my experience of thinking about this, when you try to get to the beginning of things, to find a point of origin. According to my friend—somewhat of an expert on ancient civilizations, I might add—well, according to him, the evolutionary process of the heart stands at a very high point in ancient Egypt, which means it is not yet obscured by the later development of mind in the West, in Greece. I remember what he said: 'The mind leaves the heart, takes the road to Hellas, and makes history.' He has such a way of putting things, Benji has."

At the thought of his friend, Tallini became pensive and fell silent. He had written a few words to him during the night; the letter was in his pocket for mailing. The woman fell silent, intimidated and annoyed at herself for having been, as she saw it, cowed; and annoyed at him, too. Each to his and her thoughts, they listened together to the waves. Tallini remembered Benji's talk about breaking through, the breaking away of the Western mind, leaving the heart and establishing itself in the neocortex. When the Western heart is not roving Occidental byways—so Benji elaborated—to find periodic resting places in early Christianity, in medieval cathedrals, in Pythagorean echo chambers, or even in occasional heresies, it remains in Egypt, cultivating its own knowledge, a wisdom of the heart.

All this had penetrated Tallini's consciousness as aesthetic form. He felt the sense of it, stimulating, exciting even, yet now he was having trouble as he tried to speak about it. It seemed to him that his words and phrases were missing their mark, conveying nothing close to the feeling he had retained from what Benji had said. And as he trudged through a description of the Eastern heart and mind—which had never been submitted to a radical split akin to the West's and thus had suffered only a partial distancing in transient episodes of alienation—Sidonie abandoned the effort to follow him, focusing instead on his depth of feeling. As far as she could tell—and what mattered, indeed, was not what he might have said but rather what she made of it—it was an exposé of these two contrasting mentalities, a dirge of the mind sundered from the heart in search of a freedom tragically grounded in fictitious epistemology, and therefore an illusion. It was also a lament at this mind's ruthless overwhelming, by technical know-how, of all potential alternatives in a world now characterized by the dominance of brute force.

"There are affinities like that," she ventured, intending more than just to break her silence, "an affinity for the mind, not necessarily evil, and an affinity for the heart, not always kind. But I have the strange feeling, Monsieur Pierrot, that you want neither one nor the other. It is that 'spirit' you were talking about, that 'being,' that 'essence'—you don't quite know which one it is. But it seems to be everything mind and heart are not. I believe that's where your passion lies, and your attention, and on both counts, *tant pis pour moi*. But I'll take my chances, which seem to me to be fair, to say the least, despite appearances. You are an interesting man, Monsieur Pierrot. Too bad you're falling asleep."

He sat up with a start; he had indeed been nodding off: "Oh, please do forgive me. Yes, I'm dead tired, and have to get some sleep soon, but I've heard every word you said, believe me, heard it and taken it to heart. And it is most inconsiderate of me to make you spend a sunny morning this way. I shall go to my room in a moment, and we can meet again tonight for supper. But before I go, I want first to say that perhaps I may have seemed unduly somber just now. I did adopt some of my friend's pessimism, after considerable deliberation of my own, I assure you, but I lack his sense of humor and his elegance. It is a pity.

"Perhaps you are shocked at these views and think them reactionary, or perhaps you're disturbed by what sounds to you like some kind of religiosity, a manner of "baba cool," as the young people say in Paris, and you would be mistaken on both points. I know one becomes more conservative with age, but I've kept such decay within very decent limits, I assure you. And although I consider modern mankind a disaster, a veritable plague, I do understand this particular expression of mind—still expanding in the world, you must admit—represents a necessary experiment mankind cannot escape, doesn't have the right to escape.

"In our time, with all that faces us, man is like the perplexed Arjuna in the Gîta, another of Benji's studies I've profited from. Our Western experience is yet another attempt at a definition of mankind. Does it sound outlandish that there should have been many attempts preceding the present one—I've heard it argued the division of a cell is already such an attempt—and that they have failed by necessity, by the necessity of evolution? Innumerable failed attempts at a definition of mankind through its experience, each attempt a failure—from the very first splitting of the very first cell— and each brings the knowledge of the failure, which becomes inscribed and thereby included in the next attempt, the new becoming assimilated in each subsequent endeavor. It has become clear to me that failure is the hallmark of evolution. Were the idea of mankind actualized and accomplished, its experience would be fully inscribed, and humans would disappear, not by extinction, but by transcendence."

She noticed the difference between this and what had come earlier. The part about love and compassion, almost fluent for all its meanders, had been presented with ease, she thought. A tale spun out of himself, no question about it. The later part, involving the Parisian friend, sounded altogether different, stiffer, self-conscious. For this she threw back at him, silently and unawares, the very same criticism he had earlier leveled at her, about knowing by memory and knowing by heart. Only she conceived it in terms of a literary critique of unassimilated material, a distance from the subject, the lackluster secondhand. She thought he might be far better off were he to forget about his friend and follow his own road more securely.

What she was unaware of, what he had withheld from her, was the larger context of the cave people, who had been close to Tallini for almost twenty-four hours, although they had played their game of fading in and out. As always, he was unable to tell when or where the feeling faded, just as he never could tell precisely when or where it returned. For when it did, it did so with a feeling of having been there all the time. Suddenly he would know the cave mind was back, and therefore realize it had been absent, a realization that somehow harmonized with the intuitive certitude that it had been there all along.

At first this had been somewhat bothersome. It was akin to those aporetic propositions about origin he tried to suppress but that came up as if by themselves, always leaving the mind restless and defeated. But he soon understood that what appeared on a verbal level as a logical conundrum, at an experiential level dovetailed with the experience itself, and in its nonoppositional quality in the face of a yes and no—a being and not being—seemed to encompass an important part of the experience as such. *What* the experience was, this he did not seriously question. Ever so much closer at hand was the quest of *how* it was. The "how" could be contacted by presence; it was the "how" that got the photograph. The "what" had to be given in front; he couldn't make it up, unlike those painters he had known, some of whom spent hours setting up a still life, and forty-five minutes to throw the painting together. Sometimes quite a good painting at that, which was hardly the point. Or was it part of the point, the *geometric point*—what *was* its definition . . . ? The relative excellence of the painting might have been a matter *she* would have raised. What was he going to do about her? He simply had to get some rest. His mind was dimming.

He stood up quite suddenly and pulled an envelope out of his jacket pocket. "If you're going to the beach, you'll pass the post office, and I would very much appreciate your mailing this letter. I must retire for the day, but perhaps we can meet here tonight, for supper, *vers huit heures?*"

He handed her the letter. It was addressed in a thick green handwriting. She moved her head slightly in silent assent. "Tonight we'll talk about affinity," he yawned, apologized, and made his way toward the stairs. Only after he had disappeared did she reflect on what never seemed to have occurred to him: that she might be otherwise occupied tonight around eight o'clock. She wouldn't be, of course. She had every intention of being at the rendezvous, but that wasn't the issue. What counted was that she reflected on the matter, just as he would have expected her to do. Then she mailed the letter and went to the beach.

EIGHT

IN A GARDEN

Tallini may have been dozing off on the terrace, but back in the blue room he felt his exhaustion fall away and all at once was wide awake, in a light, airy mood. The past twenty-four hours seemed like a mirage, with events running together in a labyrinthine fresco he needed to unravel. Everything that had happened, as well as the sites of the events, all seemed related in some inevitable yet undecipherable manner. Events were not joined by any causal link or rational principles but by the mere fact that they had been experienced by him, as if the experiencing itself had attracted hitherto unrelated objects and places to each other with invisible lines of force to form a whole whose meaning transcended anything that could be gathered from its parts. The boulder, the landscape, the path leading to it and away from it, the room and its blueness, Hephysta, the bar, the terrace—all had become related in a way he was now touching in his thinking, but without words, for he had no words in mind. A new sense had been injected into these components, into this objectivity, a new life, as if he was engaged in an artistic creation, shaping a world to his idea.

Recently, a complex of thinking utterly devoid of words would intermittently arouse his anxieties. Sometimes the isolation of being incommunicado would panic him headlong into speech, leaving the mute thinking process in shambles, and the experience never failed to disappoint him. This time, however, he felt indifference toward communication, as one might feel about a childish pursuit outgrown overnight. This wordlessness was a valuable tool for staying in touch with the totality of the day's experience, a synthesis beyond representation. He could not attain this realization while fully occupied by his thinking attention. Rather, it was achieved by an indifference that quelled all distractions. To be beholden to terminology would dilute what his wordless thinking was accomplishing effortlessly. In similar conditions in the past—though none ever approached this present sense of completeness, of unity—he feared that without adequate terminology, the experience would remain unreal. Now the indifference to communication had brought about the contrary: if he spoke of the experience, the reality it possessed in thinking would vanish forever.

Tallini had slid from his chair and was sitting cross-legged on a pillow, leaning against the wall. His eyes were closed and every trace of tension had vanished from his features. He was facing the blue curtains of the window, and through his closed eyelids, the world was a blue globe rising. As it rose, all the heaviness of his body flowed downward, spreading out below. The globe was rising into an ever lighter blue, while the heaviness of his body was sinking toward darker shades, until a golden whiteness spread above and a somber indigo sustained him from below. Then above and below disappeared altogether, and he found himself outside, in a garden, in nature. Before he could wonder where he might be, he knew he was in the present. Not the present he had so often thought about and discussed many times with Benji, that unfathomable juncture between past and future. *This* present had no common measure with past and future; it didn't even belong to a domain of temporality. Neither did it have to do with instantaneity, being full of motion; nor was it fugitive, or ungraspable. It simply didn't belong to the same system as past and future. It didn't belong to any system at all. That, in fact, was its main, perhaps only, attribute.

If he looked downward, toward the darker blue, he saw quite clearly the constraints of a past determining a future in a strict system of cause and effect, so that by means of assiduous effort, all futures would eventually be able to retrace their past. Such a system was like the base of an equilateral triangle formed by a vector that points directly from past to future. But when he raised his eyes and looked about him, he found himself and his verdant surroundings on the apex of that triangle, whose rising equal sides retracted, meeting at the single point that was a present unconnected to the system below. Nothing here comes from anywhere in the past, nor does it go anywhere in the future. Everything is new at every moment and lasts in a present of constant change. This seemed to him perfectly natural, perfectly transparent.

He was puzzled only by what was occurring below, the enormous complexities of an infinity of causes in every single effect, and reciprocally, the indefinite effects of any single cause. He was appalled by the illusionary logic of lives planned on a past impossible to circumscribe yet projected into a future equally impossible to calculate, appalled at the misery and catastrophic consequences of automatic compliance to this unfounded mechanism. Its mutually unfulfillable necessities stood clearly revealed. The past needed a future to become past; the future will need a past from which to be projected. But the present is absolutely self-contained, independent of past and future, autonomous, responsible only to itself, to its own awareness. It did not come from past nor will it go to future. It is a beginning and an end in itself. The past depended on a future looking back, and the future will depend on a past looking forward. But the present is in itself and looks only at itself. It alone lives in absolute freedom and continuous creativity.

What a beautiful garden! Was it so beautiful in itself, or was it because, in its presentness, it could not be compared to any other that one might have seen before or might still hope to encounter? It was incomparable, being the sole one. The observer's enjoyment of its nature was also greatly enhanced by the absence of feelings and emotions liable to interfere with his straightforward approach to its detail. Its nontemporal *now*, furthermore, was resonating in a nonspatial *here*. Together they were establishing true presence. And as this atemporal present was relieved of all duration, so was this nonspatiality relieved of all extension. The abundant vegetation was growing no more over there than it was over here, where it grows right through the observer.

Within himself, he located the stomachic taproot with its food-searching rootlets of appetite, and he could follow the process of ingestion through the chylaceous sap of the circulatory lifeline. Though long freed of all mineral umbilicality, he carried within him the consciousness of this vegetation that still clung to the earth and was still tributary to the chthonian seed. Through his interiorization of what continues to experience itself objectively, he possessed the means of recognition of the object, the conscious means of his vegetative entity and its assimilative, circulatory, and respiratory functions.

He needed but approach a particular detail of greenery, a twig, by fixing his attention upon it—physical displacement does not factor into this universe's ambit of presence—in order to establish it as the inborn, the ingrown vegetative principle of which his present circumstance made him so intimately aware. Being, it came to him, must be the very best way of knowing. To *be* the plant must be to *know* it. This experiential evidence was neither a commonplace nor was it metaphysical. It was new to him, and it had always been there. It was given in front, beyond cognizing, yet it did not come down from the cave people, though it brought the cave people into his thinking. Everything was here and now, with no above nor anything around, no horizon. It was not nothingness, but openness, a sense of possibility with a dreamy link to an echo of elsewhere, of past normalcy.

And now the cave people exerted a gravitational pull, a constraint he experienced as the suffering of his present state. The pull resolved into a backward movement, and not having been ushered in by a turn of his own volition, it resulted in a blind backward motion in which he had no say and which he did not control. His gaze remained moving in the present, but the backward pull created distance and time, fixing his gaze into the past. He was on the verge of backing out of the present, being pulled blindly into what had been. This was quite different from the boomerang effect when an autonomous expression folded back to its original self, toward origin, in a moment salty with tears. The cave people were in the past now, pulling him back to a moment *that had no past.* Is the beginning, then, a very special present, a present that is *unique?* Now they did not reach him by touch; now they pulled at him and caused not joyfulness but sorrow. This oscillation was no linkback to origin; it was a track into the bygone, fixed and rigid like a rail, a direct line to the known, the thought, the spoken in all its pasts, simple and composed, perfect and imperfect. It is impermanent memory.

By some quirk of fate, an experience remained uninscribed, through inattention or perhaps emotional incapacity. There are innumerable rationalizations for the failure of experiential inscription—and few voices in recognition of its creative possibilities. Because of such failures, experience must and will be repeated, again and again; therefore life is a redundance of opportunities, a glory of experience. Without it, there would be nothing that *matters,* nothing that becomes concrete, that takes on color. And by the agency of the human skeleton, experience in its totality will be inscribed concretely in the mineral. With deep emotion Tallini registered in the marrow of his bones the universal possibility.

◗ ◖ ◯ ◯ ◖ ◗

His attention, renewed by this intuition, returned to the twig, and it responded willingly. He remained well aware that although sensory perception gave him the twig in minute detail, it furnished but a superficial understanding of the living entity. What was new—because the vegetative principle was inborn in his own physicality—was the depth of his realization of the plant. Yet intuition told him he was not to invade this interior plant space, that it must come forth by itself and reveal itself to him through its relation with his own interiority, the site of recognition. Out of an ideal universality not yet fully experienced, particulars express themselves, and the experience of the particular will be an inscription toward a universal.

He felt the fervor and commitment of a calling, a sentiment familiar to him. It was like the mission of the cave people, who moved inside for the purpose of "establishing the matrix of the human mind." He might have characterized their travail in different terms, now that those who moved inside were beckoning to him—outside, yet cognizant of *their* interiorization. The move, however, was and remained heroic, mythical, beyond words, out of memory's reach. He carried it inscribed in his frame. Their primordial innocence of any *within* confined separation to physicality, and these material distinctions themselves were softened by a blameless hetaerism of unselfish individuality. Minimal separation between individuals precluded the need for a medium of communication. The very notion of choice did not exist. Necessities of life were equal and identical for each, so that concordance was natural and evident in every act, and every act a proper gesture at the proper time. As everything to be experienced was identical for everyone and manifest to each, there could have been no newness, only a constant confirmation of the status quo, with inscription thus doubly precluded in the absence of interiority. Their world was evident in every detail, so no question could arise. Therefore, the shift, the move they made, did not result from their confabulations. Nor could they have discovered prior to the move an interiority consequently occupied by the group—as if there were empty space in the absence of an occupying volume! And yet, in a universe unquestioned, an answer must have come to one of them, opening the world to inquiry, revealing the evident as taken for granted and introducing a minimal imbalance into perfect equilibrium. In a word, initiating a fluctuation. There must have been someone who first. . . .

Although his attention was ostensibly fixed on the twig, Tallini was not thinking only about the plant. Could this be what Benji meant when he spoke of association? For Tallini, this split attention was part of thinking, the part that made for improvisation in music. How strange, he mused, was the not infrequent occurrence of great musical talent without improvisational gifts! Whatever its merit, it missed the better part of the art. Benji would describe improvisation in terms of a decentered thinking that was often inconceivable to nonimprovisational minds—highly intellectualized minds in particular—and therefore subject to a gamut of misinterpretations. He thought he detected, in minds from which all concern with improvisation had been eliminated, a fundamental incapacity for a kind of freedom that was most essentially human. "Such nonparticipation," he maintained, "spells forfeiture of what is a uniquely human privilege. No animal improvises, no plant, no stone. The improviser must be aware of his improvising gesture at every continuous step of the improvisation. It is in the qualitative *nature* of this awareness that distinction resides. This is evidently not a concentrative effort, not a conceptual gathering as would be needed, for instance, in the case of a *reading*."

Tallini once told Benji that musicians characterize the nonimprovisational mind as reading: "He doesn't improvise, he only reads." Or, perhaps, "He has to *read*." He explained that, unlike reading, improvisation does not gather in its own moments; the gathering occurs between those moments. It is a preparation consisting of all that is known, all that has been cognized, experienced, remembered, learned, and lived. Ideally, none of this is ever present in any detail at the time of improvisation. It exists as a totality, however, as the improviser, the individual, whatever makes him *whole*. "What makes him whole molds the flowing process," as Benji had interpreted his friend's description. "It is in such terms that language can be defined, and it is true that language is the paradigm of human unity. Not a unification by arrangements, concessions, laws, or even force, but a unity that springs from its own medium—this, always ideally, is within the reach of language alone."

Might he, by living thinking, raise this twig to an improvisation that rested on the unity of his entire experience in observing, learning, living? With this bold question, Tallini heard himself in deep breath. Cross-legged on his pillow, he had let his meditation slip into an uncertain zone between sleeping and waking, a fertile region, according to his Indian guru, when cultivated by a disciplined consciousness. Then it can result in "conscious sleep," as he called it, used by most practitioners for the advantages of repose without the break in consciousness normally occurring in sleep. Two hours of conscious sleep were said to replace a whole night of the fitful and cluttered slumber that has become the lot of humankind. But for the Rajasthani holy man who taught the practice under a tent in the desert, this was only a first step, merely an early dividend on this particular path to self-knowledge where conscious sleep figured as a prime meditation.

He was Tallini's best encounter, this Rajput who had read law at Oxford. Before implementing his father's wish that he should practice in Jaipur, he had asked for a year of travel in that Mother India he knew so little. While visiting some relatives in Pondicherry, he was introduced into Sri Aurobindo's circle, where he first heard of conscious sleep—and perhaps even of consciousness. Be that as it may, he returned to Jaipur a sadhu, soon attracted a following, and eventually moved into the desert to live an ideal of permanent consciousness. The higher aim was a return from conscious sleep with some gain beyond efficient repose.

The guru had been evasive concerning any specific achievements, but it was clear that maintaining consciousness was not a goal in itself; it was but the *possibility* of a spiritual undertaking. With the evocation of the possible, the rajah, in private darshan with Tallini, would employ the tone and gestures of Indian gentlemen who read ontology at British universities. "What was this capacity of the possible to afford a phenomenon, a being?" he asked. "For the possible is the region where the event is not only enabled but also impeded in the drive toward actualization. The possible may just as well not happen at all."

Transfixed less by that gamut of possibilities than by the magnetic eyes and perfect teatime manner, Tallini was treated to analyses that allowed what might or could happen, without disallowing what had in fact happened, is happening, and will happen, given time. Such encounters were not common for the sadhu, for Westerners were rare in this desert, but he had been cum laude, after all, and had greatly enjoyed his stay in Europe. He spoke mostly to passing nomads or to peasants and beggars from the surrounding villages. More rarely, sahibs came from Nagaur and Phalodi and, on holy days, even from Ajmer or Jodhpur. From what Tallini could gather, he spoke to them all in the simplest way about everyday occurrences, feelings, and emotions, gave no advice, performed no healings or miracles, but exemplified a way of life that consisted primarily in staying awake to a conscious contact. Tallini learned that this contact could be experienced, but only with patience and after rigorous practice of meditation. Because the Italian sahib was only passing through "like so many people in the desert," there would not be time for such instruction.

What struck Tallini was the certitude emanating from this dhoti-clad person, making it appear that he incontrovertibly experienced whatever he said, living it at the very moment he articulated the ideas. Tallini felt in this encounter an entirely new definition of presence. The guru maintained he was building his life on experiences that had their origin in conscious sleep and were then recalled by a meditational discipline into the waking state of ordinary life. What was impressive was the man's experiencing of his own ideas to a depth of self-understanding that was apparent—evidenced in tone, expression, gesture—yet unfathomable to Tallini. Tallini became aware that the transmission of this autoreceptivity was in itself a teaching, certainly the most valuable he received during the brief time he spent in the holy man's presence. What guruji was saying became unimportant; the speaking itself was what communicated.

There were clear but distant resonances here of what Tallini already knew about language from his discussions with Benji. What was most striking, however, was the difference with which he received it. Where did this difference reside? By his understanding of himself and by his gift of expressing this faculty, of acting it out, guruji had drawn Tallini's attention to a distinction not only between the two of them—there, in each other's presence—but between each consciousness and every other, and between each consciousness and its world. By effectuating an extreme difference in their shared reception, he led Tallini to realize a distance, made him sense it distinctly, if only for that brief moment, and not only to *think* it occasionally, in the midst, perhaps, of some snarled misunderstanding. That distance measured a chasm between them, invoked by their unequal evaluation of the terminology they shared. There, under the tent, Tallini had watched and listened as the terminology broke open, the words like so many birds in volume and on wings of air, pigeons homing, living as life itself.

Tallini heard his own chuckle—ghostly in the quality of distance it brought to his waking ear, yet indubitably *his* as it reverberated in his diaphragm—and felt the slide toward wakefulness. At this point of release from the practice, the exercise of abstention, terminology became relevant again, by a strict avoidance of fixing upon it. Terms gathered at a far remove from their center of gravity tend to crumble under wakeful scrutiny into meaningless articulations. An overall intuition is recommended instead, the subtle grasp of an entity by inference undetermined and therefore difficult to characterize. Tallini had heard it variously alluded to as atman, the soul, or breath of the self, perceptible, according to some *chelas*, to the rarified and immaculate awareness inside conscious sleep, and a lingering moment in the exit, like an afterglow in the recapitulation of a mood. It could also be referred to as the carrier of life experience, the inheritor of all past that has been particularly experienced. Then again, in terms more immediately sensorial, a point of light or the sustained aural phenomenon that makes *shabda*, the cosmic sound-word, available. In fine, such indeterminations, atomistic or ethereal, do not immediately propose hard and fast terminology.

It is remarkable that these various types of intuition, whether auditive or not, lend themselves to a description based on a *hearing*. The surging word depends on the directedness of this hearing, on a proper hearing gesture. This word does not originate in sound, but being heard, it is nevertheless perceived as such. The nature of this word, a variable that would name each particular episode for retention and future accessibility, remained a stumbling block for Tallini until his guru entertained him with the inordinate length of words in the archaic dialect spoken in the region. Tallini, who in his rather superficial assimilation of scraps of the surrounding language blithely structured translations according to his own mother tongue and its organization, thought he had isolated certain repetitive phrases. He was subsequently amazed to discover they were single words of many syllables, incommensurate with the six- or seven-letter average word of European languages. This was a distinctly different conceptual horizon, his teacher pointed out in his lilting but perfect Indian English. The old man connected the giant words of his people's tongue with an indifference toward the analytic mind. For them, clearly, speaking of "word" translated into speaking of "language."

So far Tallini had to admit total failure at this reentry stage of the exercise. He would be immediately flooded by terminology, which blunted and effaced the border experience. In a much too sudden shift he would find himself wide awake, mentally alert, and physically refreshed. Conscious sleep would be forgotten until the next attempt. The affirmation that only the single word is fit to mark the single instant containing its total episode—this was a proposition that could perhaps be ascertained in certain older languages, but hardly in the efficient analytic ones of today.

This time there was a chuckle, and it was enough to bring Tallini to a question he couldn't recall—better, that he couldn't *call*—but which formed in him as a twig of verdure living on chlorophyll, just as he was living on blood. In this liquidity, in this circulation, the symbiosis allowed a feeling that could be experienced to the exclusion of all mind beyond. Within the *ex*clusivity of the plant kingdom, nevertheless, a generous commensalism is offered to all sentient beings. But only the human divines the concreteness available in this emotionless and thoughtless world, an inner, organic comprehension whose grasp is far more certain than anything intellect can offer. The seed's mineral unity is maintained in vegetation from seed to seed. Interjected into that major cycle, the development from seed to fruit, a colorful subtheme in multiplicity, is an embellishment by its lush formal inventiveness. Functionally, it provides the space where mineral dissolves and circulates. The liquid mineral thus partakes in the experience of all organisms from seed to fruit and gathers a part of this experience for inscription into its solid core of superior permanence.

From the point of view of *in*clusivity, however, the mind's capacities are without compare. To include the mind is tantamount to including inclusion. The inclusion/exclusion complementation of subject and object, mental trickery to logic, is nevertheless amply demonstrated in the living fact: the vegetative system is embedded in every human, and the single vegetative seed contains humankind in its entirety. The symbiotic accord achieved by the worlds of humankind and vegetation is foreign to the animal and mineral worlds, both of which have their own commonalities: through the emotions and through the mineral seed. This age-old conceit of two seed lines in humankind—one vegetal, one mineral— takes on an added gloss from such thinking.

But Tallini's living thinking was no mere cogitation. Thus instead of a passive luster he turned these ideas into the light of action. He communed with the twig, and for an immemorial instant, with the vegetative in its totality. Its metamorphic qualities reflected in his own mobility/immobility, frozen into instant and infinite change. He had never heard of the mineral and the vegetal as the double seed of humankind, nor did he hear of it now, and yet it brought him back to that paradise of garden, where the seed that goes to fruit parts from the mineral seed that stays seed in what is, compared to an organic world, a mineral realm of relative permanence. The organism that comes to exist on this permanence is itself marked with permanence. Here the permanence of the living fairly equals that of the inert. Whatever the impermanence of later and more complex forms, the bearers of a first photosynthesis are still present in their original form and function, indispensible. That permanence is presence; it is a closeness of the living to the rock, to its mineral content.

Every organism, having fed on this mineral permanence, is marked by it; it is the old in it. The new is life, and with life a first touch of impermanence. Life travels a path of liberation away from the relative permanence of the rock, yet it pays its way in impermanence, accepting death as traveling companion. On the level of the algae, there is as yet hardly any death, and the relative permanence of the form seems assured. On its scaffolding the turmoil is played out of forming, deforming, unforming, reforming—the constant taking apart and coming back together in an activity whose roots leave marks deep in the mineral core. In their revolutionary dedication to a light the mineral has never seen, the first tentative algae broke the mineral unity, introducing multiplicity and multiplication. It is a phase of the cosmic doing/undoing: the liquifying of the mineral seed and its consequent corruption in order to nourish the new color green.

Thus begins a superphase of undoing that will detail a world. Already contained in that undoing, however, is the proximate doing, a directedness toward the vegetal seed, the next reunion. This new oneness again contains an undoing, once more the liquification that will detail the life of the species in its expression from seed to fruit. This is the full world of vegetation and of everything that carries seed. Within this grand spectacle of undoing, the next oneness is already adumbrated: humankind.

Was *that* the vision that brought about the chuckle, or was it the other way around? Tallini didn't know. But he was certain that something had been retained, not in words but in an impression, an atmosphere he could revisit and perhaps in time assimilate. Everything would be different, of course. Nevertheless, he knew something had been achieved. He was wide awake now, and filled with a vague desire to note down some aspects of his experience, whatever could be put in words. He felt it would help him in evolving a script for that documentary he was contemplating. Whatever it was, he decided to put it into a letter to Benji.

NINE

INTERLUDES

Tallini spent several hours at the small rustic table that served as his desk, struggling with words to express his adventure in the hills. Certain that the few pages his labor produced would never survive a rereading, he stuffed them unread into an envelope addressed to Benji. Arising from his chair, Tallini suddenly felt totally drained. He must have dragged himself to the bed, although he remembered nothing of the sort when he awoke in the dark, fully clothed. His watch showed three o'clock.

The first thing that came to his mind was the missed supper date with Hephysta. Figuring he could catch up with her at the early morning espresso, he undressed and slipped under the sheets for a bit more shut-eye. The next thing he knew, it was past ten o'clock in the morning, and, as the curtains hadn't been drawn, the room was a riot of white light. He decided to skip breakfast and to remain in the room until lunch, resting and meditating on his adventure and what it might mean to his endeavor. That would be the best way of keeping the boulder experience alive as long as possible. All the same, he was looking forward to lunch and an encounter with Hephysta.

When the time came, however, she was nowhere to be seen. He lingered over his food, but she didn't appear. When Giorgio brought him his second cup of coffee, Tallini casually inquired whether the young French lady had shown up for lunch yet. She was gone. Took the seven o'clock bus down the coast. No message. She'd be back in three days, on Thursday. Or perhaps Friday. She said she'd call. "You didn't know she was going? You were expecting her? *Peccato! Ah, le donne. . . .*" Giorgio himself was married to a dull woman with funds and ambition. The hotel was in *her* name. The two men, of the same age, had hit it off immediately, and Giorgio took vicarious pleasure in what he interpreted to be his new friend's budding romance. He assumed he was witnessing the first act of a play—drama or comedy, one never knew at this stage—one more performance to add to innumerable others enacted in his lobby and dining room. He was resigned to having forfeited his own part once and for all. To him Tallini's style personified freedom and the adventurous life.

Yet he felt Tallini was very different from the others, that he had something to say, had seen things, done things. He kept a respectful distance; it was a sentiment akin to shyness that kept him away, although shyness could never otherwise be called one of his traits. Tallini would actually have welcomed more ample occasions to exercise his mother tongue over a glass of wine. The wife was ever present, however, and Tallini attributed Giorgio's remoteness to *her.* But in fact, it was Tallini's own inner intensity that intimidated Giorgio. The innkeeper could know nothing of Tallini's obsession with an ancestry not of the blood but of the mind. Nonetheless, in his own perceptive way, Giorgio divined in his compatriot an epic performance quite incommensurable with what he had been offered so far by the haphazard troupes that peopled his tourist seasons. No, Tallini was not one's average tourist. And Giorgio felt respect for such superior destinies, for anything that broke the mold of average living.

Tallini had counted on seeing Hephysta to straighten out their unfortunate mix-up and perhaps, at the beach, to focus exclusively on their acquaintance. Now, lunching alone, he understandably found himself somewhat at loose ends. Whereas her absence had changed his plan, the beach idea persisted, although not on the town beach proper—the shore

172

observable from Giorgio's terrace—which only the villagers seemed to use, and which Tallini had never frequented. The foreigners sought out more isolated spots.

Nevertheless, late one night up in his room, he had seen the little town beach in another way, as if it were another shore, the inverse of this sun-drenched site: a moonless midnight shore. Working on his notes, he heard a shout carried over the water, piercing the darkness of sea and sky that engulfed him as he opened wide the window. A chilly breeze from the offing was its only material touch, the rest a colorless void to the eye. The call was followed by another moments later, unmistakably in answer to the first. In the medium of this impenetrable dark, the human voice took on an eeric directness that shattered the useless straining of his gaze into black nothingness.

Tallini lowered his eyelids, mimicking that moment's gesture. It was an instant that belonged to his first days in the village, before the boulder experience, and therefore already somewhat distant. Between then and now, his new experience was bound to have modified earlier conditions he was attempting to revisit. The boulder, forceful new mover of his mental world, had taught him the common limit between extremes, an integument shared by opposites. Now, sitting on the terrace with his eyes closed, surrendered to lightless surroundings, his eyelids captured a segment of darkness that fit the inner void to a forming interiority. Between an empty open self and a tenebrous world, his closed eyelids flattened what the Jaipur guruji had called "the frontal plane" into a limit for both self and world, their common surface. This plane plays the role of separative juncture, a surface in a field of darkness between the extremes of inside and out.

Tallini was now inhabiting this surface between the edge of darkness-as-volume and the opposite edge of darkness-as-space. Volume was an extreme of outermost being-there, and space a pure inner openness. Neither can exist without the other, and they are bound by the frontal plane, a dimension inconceivable to either one. The volume in this bedarkened occasion was not a vision but an expansive sound, and only a misguided effort of perception would intend a darkness incapable, for sheer ambient obscurity, of proving its own presence. By shutting out this impotent mass, Tallini shifted his attention from sight to hearing, with vision receding into the flatness of the eyelids expanded to the frontal screen. That sound had possessed him then, its outer volume smoothly shaped, by ear, into inner tonal space. Now he attempted to image auditory and optic nerves, tracking the aural configuration as it shared in an energetic circuitry equally accessible to the eye. Imagination easily adapts sound-forms for transit through the optic centers, thereby creating a reverse energetic flow, a countersight conditioned by sound to travel, against prevailing currents, from nerve to retina, to be dispersed on the lens, screened on the frontal plane, and projected in color, through the iris of the eye, into a world.

Tallini's meditation on that sonant midnight hour was disturbed by a noisy tourist couple seating themselves nearby for lunch. Eyes opened wide and ears filled with the commotion, he nevertheless recalled how struck he had been by the acoustics the blind shouts evoked, as if at night this great landlocked sea, tricontinentally corraled, were not wide open to the sky as by day, but restricted in its elevation by dusky vaults to a confinement aurally interpreted in these cloistered calls and hollow echoes. It created an effect of proximity, as if in a shrunken universe distance had abandoned its standards.

There had welled up in him a feeling of intimacy with these unknown fishermen in their rowboats, who were taking advantage of calm waters and by sound situating themselves in relation to others. He had pulled up a chair and remained seated by the open window for some time, intermittently nodding off in a zone between wakefulness and sleep, between insight and dream, until, with the earliest dawn, some fishing boats returned, hauled onto the beach far below his room by their crews wading in, yelling at the dark-garbed women come to meet the catch. Their heads were draped in heavy, coarsely knit black shawls to protect them from the sand-laden wind. The merest sliver of moon gave just enough light for the eye

174

to break through, to make out their billowing silhouettes and barely distinguish them from an indistinct background of sea, sand, and air—black figures defined on charcoal gray.

Tallini was aware that his mind's memory, turned colorful and detailed, was no more than visual fiction, as it was not by image that the scene had revealed itself but by that closed and proximate universe of sound whose waves transmitted the event with remarkable truth and detail. Even facial expressions, too distant to view whatever the visibility, and feelings were conveyed by tone and in total disregard of any visual context.

● ◐ ○ ◑ ◐ ●

The tourists at the next table were chattering, clattering dishes and silverware, thoroughly disturbing Tallini. Suddenly, he longed for an open sky and the silent solitude of the hills. The disappointment of having missed Hephysta lingered and marred the moment far more radically than the neighboring tourists, mere scapegoats for his irritation, ever could. Contemplating his present situation as from a distance, he saw himself childishly spoiling a beautiful day because of this contretemps. A brisk climb into the open spaces would put this mood to rest, he told himself, whereas the confinement of his room might exacerbate it further. After all, where better to write to Benji than in the boulder's shade?

With the thought of the boulder came a longing akin to homesickness, which energized him into action. Within minutes he was on his way. But far from allaying his mood, the day was to bring further disappointment. He took to the path with the feathered gait of a lover, but in fact, his destination was *a rock*, and the quality of this factual—though enigmatic —mineral entity had not remained frozen like so much silica in the landscape. Could he have overlooked the possibility that what he was counting on finding did not exist readymade, that its raw material required a binding agent, just as it had two days before? Whatever the boulder might have represented forty-eight hours earlier was now past, and he was navigating not by stars but by memory. Was he aware of contradicting, in this willful impulse, blind and unthinking, what he had acquired and so carefully protected in his reentry, and had intended for meditation and assimilation in the seclusion of his room? He was the very picture of forgetfulness, out of touch with the guidance of the early ones, their touch in abeyance. Did he but remember the cave people who had brought him this far, this close to himself, to them? Without this living governance, his outing to the hills was scarcely distinguishable from a tourist's day, with its simple enjoyments.

It goes without saying that under these conditions, what he found when he reached his goal was a rock, cool as rocks are in their essence, even while the sun is tanning their hide. Whatever it was he personified, it was equally unsuccessful in warming the dead stone he was courting. Would he ever stoop to admit that for a shocking moment he was surprised the boulder did not recognize him?

But Tallini was not easily defeated. He took out his writing pad and settled himself against the rocky contours. A comfortable position eluded him, however. For a long time, he shifted back and forth, moving this way and that, searching for the precise spot where he had sat when the rock was so incredibly hospitable, to his body first, and then to his mind. It was in vain. He might as well have tried to feel at ease on a bed of nails. Every irregularity was like a stone spike through his shirt. When he caught himself doodling on his pad, he conceded that he had, at least for now, nothing to say. It would have been more honest to admit he had momentarily forgotten what he had to say. Still, the realization that he would not have to write to Benji after all came as some relief. When he stood up and started to walk around, he realized, with a start, that he hadn't even brought along his camera. He suddenly found himself feeling utterly at a loss. He turned on his heels, picked up the musette bag he had left at the boulder, trudged back down to the village, and then went over to the beach to watch the sunset. Tomorrow would surely prove to be more fruitful.

The next morning, he let himself loiter over breakfast with an extra espresso. Where had he been this past day? How long had it lasted, this empty state of depression? He remembered the noisy tourists and, after that, his inane flurry of activity. How had it happened? No matter, it was over. He had thought he knew what the mind wanted: repetition, to follow once again the path into the hills for another try at finding the trace of the boulder world. It had been a wrong tack, an aberration, and it had brought on a sort of malady, a state of mental feverishness. But it was finished now. He just sat there, letting his mind wander, hardly watching its meanders, and leaving his body right where it was.

What had been interrupted was his recollection of the nocturnal beach. Now he was irresistibly drawn back to the fishermen's night by a need to live a deeper understanding of such ordinary everyday events as he had registered then. It was as if a signification, missed in the past, had once more become available, this time recognized as the rarest of occasions: the second chance. It was like a sudden involvement with another life, another manner and sense of being, an unexpected fit into another world. He would have wanted those sounds of silence for his own.

He sat there, deep in thought, until he could feel his body heavy with inertia, so it took a distinct effort to pick himself up. Then he walked onto the terrace and, leaning against the railing, looked down at the beach. How innocent it looked in the clear morning! The wind now blowing softly along the coast was of a different purpose from the one that arose so darkly in that fisherman's dawn. *This* wind was shimmering with sunlight and felt neither cool nor warm to the skin, tempered as it was by vegetation, having blown over wheat fields and lingered among heliotropes tall as cornstalks. The night's desert wind had come, however, from a different source, from a site of searing radiation, where shade is at a premium and dusk is a revival. All warmth had been lost in the long contact with the sea during the crossing, and it arrived with a disagreeably chilly bite and blowing sand gathered over vast mineral expanses. It was an elemental brute force that stung the beach of the returning sailors, the kind of wind locals identify by name and blame for heaviness in limb and soul.

He had heard a plaint clearly arising from that shadow world—which also struck him as the more real. The sounds, the figments of past recalled by the ear, by the heart, here on the terrace and within sight of the daylight beach—those sounds synesthetically floated precise images of the night-time event as it lived in him. Its extraordinary lucidity may have lain in the spherical nature of the aural medium, its expansion into volume and reception, as three-dimensional tone, far less defined and far more diffuse than the colored spot, the point, fused by the intersecting beams of binocular vision. A visual entity is immediately a named object, while sound, in its qualitative range from noise to musical tone to the melodies of nature, tends to invite a lingering in the medium as such. Sound is a release, furthermore, from the penetrating exploration of vision, whose reflexive circuit between visual perception and conceptual term is brief and precise, its process sure and geometric: crosshairs engendering a point, two linearities, left and right meeting in a three-dimensional outside focus and a two-dimensional frontal plane where all conceptualities can inscribe themselves. Benji had called the mind flat, with its rationality hostage to surface in its need to code and fix calculations and language.

Didn't this pertain, in contrast, to his discovery of the night-sound volume? And wasn't it all related—this came to him now, why not earlier?—to the contact he was attempting with the people of origin he could never quite reach, even when feeling he was living in their presence? There could be signs they were closer than he thought, closer also than he could see, but always close enough to be heard, close enough to share the sounds of their being. That's what had happened with the people on the beach, in the sandy gale, as the boats came in. It was a state contingent on the sound that provided data in the round, inaccessible by linear means, yet able to furnish the optic screen with a conceptualized plane image.

The sounds from the beach meant volumes, tones, pitches, shouts, and melodies, all bound in the forthrightness of what cannot be overheard. Hearing them—or being heard by them, which seemed to him like much the same process—was entirely contingent on his being one of them. Tallini, in retrospect, concluded that, for a moment, he had been.

Until the boulder brought it alive—by some intuitive correlations of space and form—the beach night had lain fallow in his mind, unattended yet not forgotten. However, linked with the adventure in the hills, it reflected the same aspect of instruction so manifest in the latter. He considered it an experience with a teaching built in, not for any further good or profit, but for the sake of the experience in itself, which wanted to be known, to be thought.

He didn't attempt to explain this to himself any further, no longer feeling licensed, in fact, to delve in any depth into these events in search of explanations, even when they were of everyday life. Since leaving Paris and the Bibliothèque Nationale, he had glimpsed the futility, the evasions, of that sort of explanatory endeavor. His attitude remained free of all Pyrrhonism, needless to say: absolute doubt had no share in Tallini's follies. But he had long observed Benji's healthy skepticism and the strong affirmation it harbored. He had been by himself shaping a more mature sensibility into a critique of his own perceptions, feelings, and actions, in the process weathering such potentially disabling realizations as might inhere to an experience unique to himself, unlivable by anyone else and therefore uncommunicable and finally incomprehensible to anyone else. Seized with awe—as well as touched by some anxiety—at the responsibility entailed in such a solitary project, he had refused himself the shallow consolation that everyone else was equally saddled with his own unique destiny.

Far from being fazed by the patent banality of this sort of insight, he had come to sympathize with Monsieur Jourdain, Molière's social climber who sought refinement and in the process discovered himself speaking prose. Would the good

179

burgher have seemed less of a fool had he discerned not quite so much, had he stopped short, in syntax as well as in wondering experience? In other words, had he not, in order to marvel, been obliged to focus on the particular, instead of remaining in the dazzlement of an earlier generality?

Benji would have argued that in a speaker's ontology, prose is a late detail, and by the time such detail lords it over speech as it does over vision, the experience has long since diffused into something beyond simply speaking, something more than the intransitive state of speaking, of being a speaker. Monsieur Jourdain's wonderment might have gained a dimension of profundity, and perhaps silenced his deriders, had he been capable of surprise at an *earlier* condition, at a prior logical stage, namely, at the *being* that is essential to being a speaker, indeed at speaking itself. In his natural state of joviality, Monsieur Jourdain was known to be good company, and in daily life he was a perspicacious and successful tradesman. He was a resounding failure only as a man of the world, a role he bought for himself and performed as if in caricature of himself. What consumed him and drove him into ridicule and eventually destroyed him was the desire to become, by education and refinement, other than he was. But how would he know who he is, what he is, how he is, Tallini mused.

The autodidacts of literature had long aroused his interest and even his sympathy—Bouvard and Pécuchet, for example, copycats by nature, yet willfully bent on creativity. They join Jourdain, exposed in comic failure on a sardonic pillory. Tallini, with his light-machine and other foibles, was sensitive to the genre. He recalled how, at the time of his preoccupation with that fanciful mechanism, Benji had delicately elaborated on the difference between dilettantism and natural talent, asserting that creative effectiveness at times accompanies a combination of the two.

"It's a combination to be found in inventors, in scientists," he had said. "And it's rampant in the arts, in painting, at least since the turn of the century. Gauguin, van Gogh,

Modigliani, Soutine, even Cézanne—all talented dilettanti. One need only compare their life experiences to those of the professionals of the painting salons, who live on government commissions, have fat bank accounts and decorations, and are always to be found at social events that are monuments to their vanity and nothing more. Not much left of their production, except what with hundred-year hindsight looks rather as if it belonged with Jourdain and his pals. That's because time has reversed the roles, turned things around, as it eventually does with everything. Dilettantism is at the heart of modern art, the explosion of a vast reservoir of natural talent that had been successfully suppressed by nineteenth-century professionalism. Its cultural time arrived, but late. That particular compression of talent went a long way, but has exhausted itself and is just about done with. It was inevitable the talent would run out, but the dilettantism continues on its own, and that's what the pillory is for."

Benji had also ventured that a gullible public ("led around by the nose on a very long leash, always far behind"), having barely assimilated the idea of an avant-garde *("requiescat in pace")*, now takes the travesties of giftless puffers for the cutting edge, when in fact they are buying a new professionalism already ensconced in business and university. He felt that in such a climate, even untalented dilettanti were hard to find, and he chided the new contraprofessionalism for traveling the easy, effortless, ever-popular road: an indistinct and crowded caravan of minor personalities, with its dearth of ideas, of style, not to speak of taste, all with the same frenzy of self-glorification, mired in the ever-present social slush.

"The avant-garde has to turn rearguard," he had declared. "Not retro, which merely recreates the past in the present, but a battalion that covers the main body's hindmost by guaranteeing the space toward the rear, marching away from the main body and visiting the past where it resides. The farther you can go back, the further you can go forward.

"The past must become like a tree's root system: the deeper the root, the greater the crown. It's in the finer rootlets you might find the dilettanti of the future, doing the job for which no one else has time. As to the new professionals, the contraprofessionals, they'll turn society into a desert," he had concluded, "while artists, individual creators, have moved elsewhere—or more likely, they have stayed where they have always been, obscurely working the new."

Tallini pulled up one of the wrought-iron chairs. Ordinarily, he would have considered such idle reminiscing a scandalous waste of time. At the moment, however, he was quite willing to allow this apparent inactivity, his indolence reinforced by the disappointment that Hephysta, scarcely found, proved missing. Having planned on going to the beach with her, he had found nothing around to enliven his spirit in her absence. He had been caught off guard, and his vexation revealed a hitherto unexamined dependency. In contrast, his present passivity could be attributed to no such constraint; it was voluntary, autonomous, and informed. As such, it was immune to the kind of soulless activity that had savaged him to the brink of depression during the last forty-eight hours.

His unsuccessful excursion was chastening in light of the quality of experience he knew to be available in those hills. Yet he suspected the boulder of having set standards that would not soon be surpassed or even equaled. And no, *that* boulder could not easily be found again, not now, not with his attention drawn to its existence and its possibilities. The key to his experience lay in the aleatory genesis of the event, its free circumstantiality, unhampered and unprepared—such was the open sesame to the boulder's interior. There could be no repeats, no replays, no return engagement of this show.

But now he was able to review the episode as a whole and to compare the two approaches: the initial success and the subsequent failure. The difference of his approach stood out. In the first encounter, he had never *thought* about the boulder at all. Its shadow was what occupied him, because of its usefulness. The boulder itself had been an object of absolute indifference, and he would have been at a loss to describe the thing against whose bulk he leaned and in whose shadow he rested. It had definitely been the shade that concerned him, and it was the shadow that absorbed him, once he had the sun full face, once all the shade had been consumed. The only shadow had become his own, and, up to a point, he was able to view this happening. He had observed the shade's diminishing progression until it was no more. When it ceased to be, the boulder must have taken over. But the boulder was not within his field of vision. His back was turned to it, and another, a more subtle sense, must have guided their relation. Whatever his visual interpretations after the fact, they had to be a degradation, a reduction of this subtle link.

The revisiting mind is set in a frame all its own, ornate with reminiscence, nostalgia, and a belief in repetition. Tallini hadn't stopped thinking of the boulder. Thus his return was a reflection in every way, and he had arrived brimming with thoughts, questions, and speculations. His folly was clear to him now. There had been no quest on his part when the boulder presented itself unheralded, giving itself by itself. Therefore it was received as such, as given in front: "Received as given in front," he muttered. It had been accepted by no effort of his own, and he could claim no credit for any action in the experience. In fact, his contribution would have to be cast in an altogether negative mood—as having been *un*observant, *in*attentive, *un*conscious—although the experience itself had been as positive as can be. He had done his best in his last letter to impress upon Benji the sense of reality he had felt in this basic circuitry into which he had been transported.

"*Transported*, Ostheim, just imagine!" Benji had stopped by at the gallery of a close friend from his Vienna days, a dealer in master etchings and lithographs, at one time curator of the Munich Pinakothek. When Benji wanted some exchange on a special subject, von Ostheim was the one with whom he felt at ease. He was also the only one fit for the intellectual complexities presented by a case such as Tallini's.

"Took him a while to find the word," Benji went on, "but when he did, he made a giant step. Speaks of a load of preconceptions with which he's been contemplating the world so far. Everything's different. 'Everything speaks,' he wrote to me. Never for a moment the thought that he might be a dreamer. No, this thing has become more real to him than our world is to us."

Von Ostheim had never met Tallini. He was past eighty in a life of disasters and had always been of a retiring nature, never keen on new acquaintances. While his memory was perfect for subjects that had always interested him, his attention slackened easily in those that had not. Were he to be absolutely frank, which he certainly wanted to be, he would have to say that, well, Benji was a dear friend and a fine conversationalist, so it didn't much matter what he talked about, as it always came down to the same conclusion anyway. But this friend of his, this Tallini, only from what he knew— through Benji, of course—na ja, how should he say, a little *meshuga, nicht?*

"And whatever you might think, Gustav"—Benji used the first name rarely, only when he wanted to be impressive, and here he was leaning forward until he was so close to his friend's face that the man could feel his breath—"he's right to persist, he has a destiny, he always had that certain something, *musisch, weißt'e?*"

Von Ostheim pulled back a bit. Not only from Benji's eyes, which were too fiery for his comfort, but symbolically from the whole affair, which sounded much too adventurous for his taste. Having just been entertained with Tallini's latest message in Benji's interpretation, it seemed to him that the interpreter was beginning to resemble the description he gave of the distant friend "touched by some deity perhaps, not the maddening kind, the tragic, but a muse that smooths the way for what we cannot understand. Not like the nine sisters who turn the vision into art, poetry, dance, or science, but a muse that cleans up the vision itself. A new muse I am inventing, one that removes the scales from the eyes of mankind, Ostheim, what shall we name her?"

184

Von Ostheim told him to find his own designation for her. He felt he didn't have the wit for the clever answer that was wanted, and certainly didn't intend to make an ass of himself. But Benji had already skipped elsewhere. "I wonder what such a removal does for the patient? Would it be like a cataract operation performed on the spirit-mind's eye? But such a procedure on a natural eye is a restoration of a vision that once was. In that case, what vision is it that our muse restores? Are we born with a scaleless spiritual eye for the clear perception of an evident reality, and are scales then deposited with the very first visual experience, continuing to collect through the very act of everyday perception, like the coating in the water kettle with every pot of coffee?

"But perhaps humankind as such is afflicted from birth with this visual obstruction—or is it rather an impediment of visualization? Whatever we call such a hindrance, restoration in this case must be to an anterior state that is prehuman, in other words, the paradisal state of Adam and Eve perceiving the evidence of a natural state. What else?

"Now it's quite true that their Creator had already injected Himself into that nature He had just created. He planted a garden, which takes a lot of rearranging of the natural phenomenon, including some consideration for the soil, which must have been rather clayey, judging by the use to which it was put. But seriously, isn't there some significance to be read into the idea that our earliest ancestors' first perception was neither a forest nor a jungle, but a garden?"

Von Ostheim wanted to know more about the boulder experience. Was it a dream, a fantasy, a hallucination, or did the fellow really expect his friend to believe he had in some way sojourned in a rock? Benji chortled. "For heaven's sake, Ostheim, bridle that literalism of yours! Can't you conceive that on occasion the senses outdo themselves? Aided by a certain passivity or inactivity of mind, fingertips can feel what they aren't touching, ears hear what has no sound, eyes see through usually impenetrable surfaces. And remember that thinking itself can have a sensory capacity.

"Now we know the man's obsessed, strangely haunted by

the earliest experiences of the human mind. He mimics that early mind, he gets into it, he has contact with it, from what I understand—he speaks of tactile feelings coming down. His mind might wander in an early eolithic space where stone is a pervasive presence, and given the intense concentration with which he is able to focus, these projections can be very strong. He has a talent, no doubt about it, a *daemon* that can lift him to great heights."

Ostheim ventured that he could just as quickly be hurled down into mindless depths by such a genie. Certainly there was something unbalanced in all this.

"It's a fine line, Ostheim, but I'll bet on him. Note that in his letter, he is anxious for me to know this was real, not a dream, not a fantasy, not imaginary, but actually lived. He insists on this point. He's concerned about my understanding all this, which of course I do, and he should know it. I find his concern on this point somewhat naïve, as I would hardly expect him to waste my time or his on fantasies. The interest of his experience lies entirely with that perception of it as reality, as neither dream nor hallucination. Then again, I *know* the man, and you don't. So whereas I know he's as sane as you and I, *you* can't be expected to swallow whole something so outlandish.

"How do I understand it? Well first of all, there's the fascinating fact, often mentioned, of the unfailing sense we have for what belongs to our everyday world and therefore is 'real,' and what is merely imagined. But our everyday world is different for each one of us, with a different threshold between reality and imagination. Perhaps some of us see the imaginary in places where others see the real world, and—most importantly—vice versa. Going back in time, we can assume the given 'real world' changes with the centuries, and certainly with the millennia. You'll admit that the real world must have looked different at the time when the earth was still considered to be flat and no gravitation was needed to stand safely on its ground. That general difference had to influence specific details. The more so for those earliest of eolithic times when sense perception was still being tested and prac-

186

ticed with the attention of a new consciousness, and the feel of reality was perhaps still uncertain of its thresholds.

"As I said, there is a sensory potential in thinking, bound to be in greater evidence in a young mind, in an incipient mind. Not to speak of a *first* mind. A first realization must have been a consciousness both of perception, equivalent to a self-consciousness, a new grasp of what was being seen, heard, felt, and of a someone who grasps. Surely the mind finds its earliest reflexivity in perception, and sounds were first isolated into words in just such thought-perceptions, with their conceptual potential. As always, Ostheim, I'm interpreting a few passably incoherent paragraphs the man sent me, but I'm pretty certain I'm reading them correctly."

Ostheim wondered whether such disorder in a man's head was not a form of insanity rather than a creative chaos.

"It's the cross he has to bear, I tell you. The terms don't come easily when the concepts are new. The words are too far removed from a terminology as yet. He is with the words, away from the terms, but he floats in a perception that is voiceless, surd. The word is not yet heard, so the term can't be pronounced. He labors over it sometimes, for the sake of communication. It's truly painful to watch. I've been trying all along to feed him what I think he can use. But now he's out of my reach, he's on his own. And he'll do all right. I know the hills will loosen his tongue.

"You ask why he's doing all this to himself? My dear Ostheim, if I knew that. . . . Here I can only conjecture. Again, there are as many perceptions of the world as there are perceivers, and who knows how he lives his experience. But I can tell you he is committed to it, totally committed; he doesn't hold back. But he wants certitude, he wants to know how his experience is founded. It's the question of what there is to do, and it comes in the wake of the question of what there is. All this from a conviction—acquired or inborn, I don't know— that a reason must exist for him to be where he appears, a reason that alone can determine his action at any particular moment. Hardly a new idea—it goes all the way back to Egypt, where it is depicted in the papyri and on the temple walls and has been called 'the proper gesture.' The gesture that does perfect justice to the moment. And how do you know the moment? By the experience of the stars, and by the thinking of principles—a far closer translation for those *neters* that pedantic professionals of the Pharaonic hypothesis call gods. We may no longer believe in astrology, nor do we represent cosmic and natural laws by the living forms that surround us, but we still interpret the phenomenon, and think and record its laws in symbols. But what is special about Tallini is that he precludes these objective movers. Unlike those hordes of believers who in one way or another ask such questions, he lacks the naïveté to accept an unknown entity that could wield such power over him."

TEN

SUSPENSION

Tallini had been making his way on the now familiar path, but proceeding quite uncharacteristically without the slightest consciousness of the surroundings. His very gait—irresolute, automatic—betrayed a lack of purpose. The day before, he had wandered fruitlessly in the hills, resulting only in a healthy muscular fatigue that let him finally get a good night's sleep. But this morning, over his early coffee, Giorgio had reminded him that Sidonie might be back that day and she would call to confirm. His step reflected the somber state of mind into which, for reasons unclear to him, he was cast by this information. Though the days since the boulder and his missed appointment were filled with a sense of loss, it was not of loss on her account. The sensation of absence was intransitive, not of something or someone, not of anything apart from him, of anything that was not he himself. The loss was reflexive, but he did not know what the reflection might mirror.

In the early quiet of the parched countryside, the only sounds he heard were in the movements of his body, his steps, his quickening pulse. On the dusty path leading into the hills, his muffled footfall mimicked soft mallets on low-tuned kettledrums; his deeper breaths, expanded by the climb, played counterpoint. Underlying all rhythmic experience throbs the essential rhythm, the most personal beat, the heart, which always persists. The shift from this ever-present—hence old

—rhythm to the pulse of the incoming abstracted touch, the grasp of the new, is sudden in its discontinuity, but also soothing, because the old, the heart's rhythm, "always already there," continues. The old within the new—Tallini would soon take it for granted again, as he had to that day, to that moment.

Meditating on this, he kept his eyes lowered, his gaze following the path just ahead. Not by the grace of civil engineering was this path blazed and maintained but through a pedestrian usage just heavy enough to keep the sparse vegetation at bay. He had never encountered anyone on it, and yet the dusty trail remained alive, perhaps too deeply carved into the landscape ever to disappear. Almost invisible in rocky passages, it reappeared where the ground was offered to its dusty meanders. This soil, trod to sand and kicked up in dust, was unfit for rooting. A common mind and will had paced it to get from one place to another. To what purpose, he wondered. For human companionship, for family or friends? Or was it for commerce, a single-lane traffic of merchandise? He had heard of *contrabandistas* in the region, with pickup points all along the coast. Was it a passageway for illicit dealings? Drug smuggling would explain the absence of beasts of burden on a route of swift couriers. Or perhaps it was only the benign trace of a shepherd's steps to and from his house in the village to his flock in the hills. Repetition, to and fro every day, morning and night.

It came to him then that this path had been created through a repetitious act, had a precise aim, a set end for a set beginning: a classic case of cause and effect. Whatever aim had formed this path, he suddenly realized, it was not his. He had struggled a good part of his life on paths not his, but that was over now. He declared it was over at that very moment, and to prove his point, he stepped aside then and there to clear his own trail through the stinging cacti and esparto of this savage landscape. Thus, in such an instant, he could change everything by striking his own walk, no longer blindly following the trodden way. To ensure a break as radical as possible,

190

he changed direction, making a quarter turn straight into the hills.

What happened was to be expected. The hill, whose easy contour he had been following, now steepened. Worse, it changed character as he progressed, turning mountainous. To climb straight up was soon a daunting undertaking, and he was obliged to zigzag, which constrained his free choice, and so, obdurate, he headed for the greatest verticality. His brooding mood evaporated as the challenge claimed his full attention and energies. He began scrambling along an increasingly precipitous face of scattered stone rubble, turning his ankles; rocks cut into his shoes, which proved much too thin-soled for this exercise. Soon he found himself negotiating particularly difficult passages almost on hands and knees.

From time to time he thought he spotted outcrops that might offer stable supports and temporary resting points. Upon approach, however, they turned out to be freestanding boulders of considerable mass, their equilibrium so precarious that it seemed the merest touch would start them rolling, risking a rock slide. Finding his footing became a purely intuitive endeavor. There was no calculating which rock would hold or which would go bouncing down the slope, setting additional debris in motion. He had been looking neither left nor right, but when a sizable rock whizzed past him as it thundered downward, he followed it with a glance as it vanished below. Much further down, in a different depth of field, miniaturized by distance, he could see almond groves in dazzling sunlight encircling a peaceful whitewashed, red-roofed hamlet, a languid Andalusian microcosm.

The sensation of having long ago undergone this instant abruptly seized him. Fear gripped him, rising from his solar plexus to oppress his breathing. Paralysis halted his progress and blocked retreat. He despaired at his great danger in this unreachable isolation. Inner panic raced his blood and immobilized his muscles, triggering a childhood flashback.

He had been visiting relatives when he was seven or eight years old. With a cousin and her friends, he was playing in a large abandoned stone quarry. The excavation had left terraces that made for exciting climbing. So absorbed was he in his amusement that he never noticed the others leave. Inexperienced and unguided, the novice mountaineer suddenly found himself on a narrow ledge, unable to continue and without sufficient foothold to turn around. As he looked down, he realized he was perched at considerable height. He froze, terrified. He pressed his body against the stone wall, but it felt as if the rock were pushing back against him, pushing him into the chasm. For the first time in his life, he felt the presence of mortal danger.

Tallini quickly recognized that the earlier event matched his predicament on this Spanish slope. It was as if a part of him had not changed since the early incident. In the quarry, at the moment of panic, when he was on the verge of moving in a way that might have thrown him off balance, there had come what the retrospective adult characterized as a sense of deliverance into an unsuspected world, a world composed of sound. It had been as if ethereal strings sustained quivering notes behind a children's chorus rising in formless harmony. The sound was beautifully modulated, but yielded neither unison nor any kind of chord or cluster of tones. A sound that was not heard, he realized now as he relived it, for the sound was around him again—an organic sound, the sound of his own entire organism. It obliterated time. It was, he now knew, quite simply the sound of life within him, vanquishing time not through the moment but through eternity: a truly transcendent experience. Whereas the moment, theoretically at least, hovers within reach of the human sensorium, eternity remains by its very indefinition out of bounds to anything sentient. Life alone is exempted from the ban. Life, mediating between being and eternity. Thus Tallini's reading.

Such insights did not belong to the unthinking instant of the sound. Realizations came afterward, when he pondered what had happened and, in particular, its link to his mysterious passage through the boulder. But within the sound, the present incident was tied immediately, without reflection or cogitation, to the quarry of his childhood. Then too the sound had transfixed and immobilized him on his precarious toe-hold, saving him from panic. There he remained, absent to himself, weeping profusely but without an audible cry or sob or any bodily reaction that might have endangered his balance, until his companions finally noticed him and summoned the firemen. As the rescuers told it, the child was radiant as they helped him down the ladder, though tears were running down his cheeks.

Tallini's current predicament on the face of the mountain clearly called for quite different conduct. It called for precisely the opposite; to save himself he had to move. The proper gesture now was not to rest immobilized but to break the paralysis that had overtaken him when his knee had slipped against an unstable stone, triggering a small-scale avalanche over the edge just beneath him. Flat on his belly, face down, he grabbed instinctively at anything he could grasp as he heard the slide of debris below him. There he lay, a rock in one hand, some gravel in the other, his body pressed to the ground, convinced any further move would take him down. It seemed as if one of earth's more stable elements was in revolt, in this stage of rock's travail from single mass to dust, to ever smaller and more volatile elements. Nothing could stop this incessant and total activity, and yet he clung to it for safety. The ground on which he depended was movement itself. It was a chilling thought: the longer he remained immobile, the more difficult and more perilous would be any further move. At this tense moment, the sound overpowered him, and an inchoate recognition became identification.

The child on the ledge had needed help to escape, but the man alone on the unstable slope was forced to confront the danger. For the youngster, the "sound"—the life within him, still tentative and malleable, still mostly potential—evoked a world so distinct as to evaporate the familiar one into the difference. It made him at that moment immortal. To the boy, that new world was broader, freer, a possession newly gained. To the man it was a renunciation of the old. The fool as child, the man as fool. Tallini saw himself twice immobilized, first by the charm of innocence that opens every door, and next by the apprehension of death. Both were needed to serve the present Tallini in his attempt to survive them both. He didn't know whether sweat or tears were drenching his body, but he was exuding moisture and dispensing heat. He knew what incredible muscular feats this energy of life can perform when threatened. An incident flashed through his mind, told him by Benji, about a woman who had lifted several times her body weight in the panic of saving her child. Benji! He promised himself that if he got through this alive, he would take the next plane to Paris to see his friend, to tell him all that had happened, to hear his thoughts about it. In the meantime, muscularity was hardly what was wanting here; what was needed was its mover, who had defaulted at a time of crisis, and was now failing to appear at the inquiry.

All at once, court, judges, advocates, accusers, defenders, spectators, all assembled within the silent voices of the cave people, their touch now in the inner ear. Always haphazard and uncommitted, their contact this time felt complemented by a steadier element that was sharing the life-flow coursing through him. There could be no doubt, the cave people were within a sound that was taking over, a new mover. A question sounded in the lower range of adult voices: "Whooo?" Then from the amphitheater, the unbroken soprano of the children's choir: "Heeeee!" Who is he who may disappear over a precipice, and who is he who hears the sound, the first sound ever heard, the sound of life? The sound rose from below, from a void, and although it was a sound of life, which had always meant fullness for him, it was also a sound of emptiness. And whereas this emptiness of life in the sound was infinitely consoling—trustworthy, he might say—the fullness of life had always demanded a guarded approach to its seductions, its pitfalls, yes, its treacheries. As a child there had been nothing inside the sound, nothing to remember. But this time he had held on to the void, the emptiness, as space inside him, abandoning himself to the sound that was a ground of nothingness. It not only sustained him but lifted him to his feet as the sound rose inside him, the sound of life out of the open void. Light as a feather, he was on his feet, and not a pebble rolled. Lightly and securely he put one foot in front of the other, and before long he reached solid rock, a sliver of the earth's crust set on edge. As Tallini rounded it, a valley came into view, its warm slopes planted to vines that gesticulated at him comically, like friendly gnomes abandoned after having been nurtured for their benign fruit. But they were alive and would long be so.

● ◐ ○ ◯ ◑ ◉

"The hum of life," Benji declared, visibly affected by Tallini's account of the sound and his experience on the mountain, but also attempting to keep matters within reason. "The hum of energy is noticeable when degraded to any degree, into electricity, for instance."

Tallini had flown to Paris and was now sitting with Benji in a cozy bar on the Rue Daguerre. He had just laid out in a few words his adventure of the day before. Benji was immediately struck by the authoritative tone and soon would spot his friend's newfound fluency as well. Tallini explained how the feeling of identity was contained in a sound and was registered through the sense of hearing, which in this case proved to be very precise, unmistakable, and narrowly selective.

Benji suggested a similarity in the olfactory: "You know, the way certain smells can convey, over decades, a perfect accuracy of recollection. In this case, precision is not formal, as it is for the eye, which specializes in color-form; it is atmospheric, and at its purest and most accurate, inaccessible to image or word." Warming to his subject, he elaborated on the abstract fantasies of the olfactory, which builds its castles of air. He recalled the pervasive odor of a certain leek and chervil soup, simmering on a country stove, an aromatic vapor more evocative of a nation than of a recipe. He went on to recount legends of that miraculously perfumed odor that wafts through the palace like incense, signaling successful *conjunctio*. Tallini was at an impasse. How to describe a sound in words when the sound is heard because *there are no words?* How could life be described without language? He would state the facts, then, and leave the rest alone.

Benji noticed that his friend seemed unwilling to push his narrative to the event's conclusion, felicitous as it must have been. This temporizing might cheat them both of any account at all; first, because a search for words is in its essence a reductive exercise and cannot yield the truth of the experience; second, because the evening was progressing and soon—should he find the search too difficult—Tallini might abruptly look at his watch, offer a "Ciao," and be gone. Benji ordered another Calvados for both of them, offering some pleasantries about *Feuerwasser* and how it dissolves the tongue. Then he encouraged his friend to speak, and to stay immediate and direct, close to the experience. He wanted closeness to the feeling, to the sound.

Might he have done well to acknowledge the impossibility of the task? He didn't do that, but in one way or other, to his mind, *all* their conversations had as their background one aspect or another of linguistic impossibility. It was a constant preoccupation with Benji, and he intended the *syntactique* as vehicle for this impossibility. "Where there's transcendence, there is impossibility . . . If there were not this impossibility, there couldn't be a transcendence . . . Transcendence is the impossible; that's why impossiblity is the essence of transcendence. . . ." He turned it round and round, large reflective pauses between his phrases, as he stared at the Calvados he was twirling in his glass. He was thinking that Tallini might not yet fully understand the freedom this impossibility could procure, the looseness it allowed, all of which was essential for negotiating this transcending tightrope act. Experience and language, two worlds, two laws. Impossibility was part of the bargain, and had to be experienced to be known. That couldn't be pointed out, and so he said instead he wanted to hear whatever presented itself.

Relating the rescue would be no problem, Tallini thought. He might leave out the sound—the center of the experience—and concentrate only on the energy, which did the physical trick, after all. He'd call it his *own* energy to remain simple and understandable, but he would know better in his heart. Benji wouldn't get the *closest* narrative—far from it. The childhood event in the quarry would have to be omitted. It was much too speculative and outside the realm of words altogether, entirely a matter of sound that just did not dovetail into words. And yet, both times, in the quarry and on the slope, he had experienced the same elevation—no, that wasn't the term—the same *suspension*. What he had experienced as a child, and had lived again in those hills, was founded on the mineral realm, the lithosphere—on rock, and also the boulder before, when the mineral ceased to be just ground and had dissolved into an environment, its volume becoming space. How significant to him! But in what words could he make it significant to another? And again, how could he describe what had instructed him when he left the beaten track, with regard to being, doing, risking? How could he convey his state of special awareness where each step's progress gives rise to an exact correlation with its means?

"A path laid down in walking" came to him, a phrase he had heard or read, although it had remained relatively meaningless until those minutes on the slope, at the fork of choice between moving or falling, when he had the paralyzing conviction that to move would be to fall. He had left the beaten path to lay down his own, and this had led to an impossible choice between yes and no. Thus he would narrate the challenge of laying down a path whose next step was impossible.

But when the time came to tell his story, all inhibitions fell by the wayside. His account was dramatically detailed, although it certainly was not an exact version. Benji spurred him on with questions. He wanted to hear more about this suspension. Tallini explained it as "upward, an elevation, an aspiration that holds you from above." In the quarry, this had kept him upright far more reliably than his shaky legs could have by themselves. And though the sound seemed to come from below, the suspension was related to it as positive is to negative. This is how he remembered it now; and it was just what he had felt at the vertical crag.

197

And there was something else. After he had escaped from the steep face and rounded the slope above the valley, he had stood contemplating the entire panorama, noting the features of the terrain as would a topographer—the color-coded alternations of raw nature and cultivation, the silhouettes of whitewashed farmhouses clustered on ancestral soil, the subtly curving band of the sea far beyond, like a buffer between land and horizon, mediating earth and air. "I could readily perceive all this, but I also detected less visible presences. Not that I saw them, but they were there. And when I looked, I absorbed more and more. Across the ravine, Iberian afterimages emerged from the ancient palimpsest of this valley. It wasn't mere light play on the contours of the rocks, but lively sculptural forms and forms behind these forms, all set into motion, like cinematographic flashes. I saw their attitudes, their gestures and masks, even a speeding rush of Moorish troops, so vivid, marauders from across the Mediterranean. And everything I saw I could identify in its particular phase of becoming whatever it was, and I did so with increasing ease. Veils, robes, and banners fluttering in the strong mineral light brought these presences forth from the outcrops, and they seemed to pose in sociable groups. Others, perhaps of a different species, distinguished themselves from the same backdrop and simply stood, facing me. A kind of Paleolithic *tableau vivant*. I could make out the minutest details—their skins, furs, and adornments—and they appeared to be living right where they were, just standing there, but clearly beckoning. And wherever I scanned the circumference of my visual field, I spotted signaling signs of life."

With this, Tallini believed he had given the bare facts, although realizing his recital never approximated the essential experience. Benji thought he had done much more than that, however, and told him so. "There are so many misconceptions about communication in language," he said. "As you know, I consider language as twofold: terms and words. That structure isn't peculiar to language, of course. Most fundamental concepts must be considered as dualities within oneness. We've talked about it off and on, but perhaps this is your moment to test the concept. It's sure to be invaluable in the territory in which you are maneuvering. You're looking for your bearings, and this will come to you in language, but language at its ultimate capacity, language as such. You'd be sadly frustrated without it, I'd say. The problem with words is not that they are powerless or worn out. How could they possibly be so, when at every moment there are a multitude of sentient souls who hear them for the first time? No, words are as vital today as they've ever been, if we treat them for what they are, and that means they're never absent from the company of their terms—at least to begin with, until we have a solid grasp of the sense of language, of a language of origin."

"Yes, that's what I'm trying to find, exactly what I'm seeking," Tallini interjected.

"Ah, but it won't come by search and effort, believe me, only by experience. Experience that goes to the very core of the matter, of course, the bones, where it may store its substance. On that score, your experience in the hills qualifies with honors, I'm sure. But problems remain in your linguistic exposition. Such experiences can exist outside of language, of course—in the animal, in the leaf, even in the nucleus of the mineral. How, you ask? In the animal, there is an emotional contact, pure and simple, without words or meaning, that manifests in its cries, its speech. In the plant, which lives that stupendous chlorophyl adventure, there is intimate knowledge of sunlight. As to the mineral, well, after what you've told me and written me about your acquaintance with that world in the hills, we needn't dwell on the mineral.

"But these experiences outside language are very slow to unfold—extremely slow in simpler organisms—compared to the practice of words through the use of terminology. We're speaking of millions of years for them to register in the more inert strata. It's important to realize how inscription is also attained, though more slowly, just by experiencing existence, without involving terminology. Before language, this occurs without thinking. But there's also a "thinking" without terms *after* language, a sort of overcoming of terminology. That can only come later, of course, once language has been healed and correctly positioned. What the hand was to your cave people, this language will be to present-day man. It will afford an occasion for transcendence."

"The most important thing for me," Tallini pointed out, "and sometimes I've even thought about it as a mission, is to make myself understood."

"No," said Benji, "that's a basic misconception that burdens almost everyone. In fact, your best course lies in verbal expression itself, expression without ulterior motives, so to speak. That's where your true responsibility lies. The word comes to you in the experiential act that calls for language. The speaker is coupled with the experience—that's what makes the call. And the words are—or are meant to be, but of course rarely actually are nowadays—the experience in expression. Note that the wordly attention's commitment is entirely to the language thus created, and not at all to a communication of something to a third party. Here expressive linguistic material can never be found by searching nor by drawing it from some kind of a reserve, a bag of terms, a language pool. You must let the word come to you, as it is, and not from a ready-made lexicon. In order to achieve this pure reception, which is your task 'in' any expression, you only register the term, notwithstanding the fact that you express yourself in the word that comes to you. And expressing yourself in words is all you're responsible for. All the rest of the baggage—the spelling, the grammar, the syntax—it all gets carried by the term.

"But term and word are always in touch; it's impossible to lose one by neglecting or favoring the other. So it's in the *reception* that everything—or nothing—happens, and the first step in the expression is correct reception of the word, which is through the term. Terms are quite empty, mere shells or molds. Words are always full of meaning, charged with meaning, but formless and wide open. But the word received for expression must be spared the content already possessed by the receiver, which he might try to fit into it.

"As much as possible, you want to keep the configuration, often nebulous, in which it comes to you, and you want it to retain the context, the situation in which it speaks. In order to keep the word uncontaminated, as it were, you must receive only its term, and the term is all form and no content, absolutely devoid of meaning, while meaning is all the word has. Remember, you are the first reception, before you pass it on. After all our talks, you should realize why it's important not to infuse with meaning what comes with immediacy, as this infusion could only be your specific meaning. That's all there is at that moment. After reception, that meaning will have changed, because the word will have appeared—I almost said 'suffered'—in a new context. Each time a word comes to us, its context differs, hence there will be variation, however small, in the meaning. This differentiation doesn't yet occur in the act of reception, and therefore you can't receive a word for what it is, without reducing it to your understanding. Nor can you disregard the meaning of a word—meaning is all it is, wordly meaning. Such an empty reception can only be accomplished by the term, which has an existence of its own, and needs no meaning. By thus receiving the *term*, you won't reduce the word's meaning to your own, which is all you have at that moment."

"You seem to imply that the term is form and not content," Tallini ventured. "Could it not appear then as a visual object?"

"Yes," Benji responded, "you can see terms on paper, you can handle them with the page, you can record them, you can inscribe them in matter. Not so for words, which have but one thing: meaning, nothing else, not even sense. All the rest belongs to terminology. I do want to insist on my main point: when language comes to you, as first receiver, it comes as terms. There are ample rules for the constitution and usage of terms: dictionaries, grammars, and the laws of syntax, which enable a *syntactique,* an arrangement, a pattern—first of letters, but eventually also a pattern of thinking. All this must be accomplished by terminology and in the absence of words. Only after technicalities of terminology are resolved is the word invited to join the term in celebration of language. Once grounded in the term, it can express itself fruitfully, ripening

201

in the process. The term is the apparent, and the word doesn't ripen before the *appearance* of language. You have a two-tier language, and the term is the apparent level, it is visible, or can readily be made so. The word is never visible as such, but it is audible, although here again, it is easily confused with its term. Keep in mind, the term is always perfectly known; there can never be disagreement on terms. That means you need contribute nothing of yourself in their reception. The occasion is selfless, but that's another lesson."

They sat in silence for a little while. Then Benji brought up the boulder experience, which he was eager to pursue. "You did give me some indications in your letter, but it was difficult to make out. . . . "

"Very difficult to talk about," Tallini fell in. "Like being pulled into the center of the mineral mass, it was. Not all at once, mind you, but by stages. I've been giving it a lot of thought ever since, and it really was like losing one's dimensions, first losing the volume, ending up flat in the surface of the stone. Sounds ridiculous, doesn't it?"

"Not really. After all, human consciousness didn't start in three dimensions. It hasn't been so very long since we mastered the third, in fact. Just look at painting, at the Sienese gold ground. A totally un-self-conscious absence of three-dimensionality. Certainly not because they didn't have the ability, the know-how, for such a representation. That's a naïve argument. There is no creative concept that can't find its technique, as would soon enough become evident with Giotto and the Florentines. But in the meantime, the Sienese —who merely reflect the psyche of their time—are perfectly satisfied with two dimensions because they are as yet incapable of living, of feeling, and thus of expressing space, a third dimension. They still lack a sense of existence in volume. Your experience might have been far more comprehensible to them than it could ever be in today's polydimensional climate. Their psyche still being two-dimensional, they really didn't have a consciousness of their own selves that could have put them in relation to a world.

"Some authors have traced the modern idea of space to the first awareness of landscape, and even specifically to Petrarch's experience on a mountaintop in southern France, which he described in a letter. It's well worth reading for his emotional agitation at this discovery. Hard for us even to conceive what it is he discovered, it's so evident to us, as if it were inborn. But medieval man was not ready as yet to abstract dimensional quality from his quantitative perceptions, the quality that could open him up for space, for land and landscape, and lend him a consciousness of himself, the ability to situate himself. For him, heaven and earth met in his very soul and not at the horizon. And this space, which was conquered less than seven hundred years ago, but has served us so well since the Renaissance, is now itself under attack from all sides—art, science, cosmology. That's part of the turmoil of our time, finding the ability, the art, to live and express a new dimensionality beyond the third."

"So if I understand you correctly," Tallini responded, "experiences like mine with the boulder would have been rather common in the thirteenth century?"

"I wouldn't really know that, of course. But I'd wager they would have been less traumatic than they are to a mind totally imbued with volume, as are yours and mine. But tell me more about the experience, how it evolved."

"Well, I could say that I felt at the time as if I had stood perpendicular to the ground at one moment, and then suddenly collapsed like the vertical leg of a right angle, by ninety degrees. It felt as if the gravitational force pulling toward the center of the earth suddenly became directed horizontally and all the downward weight transformed into surface tension. What can I say? It's not easy to explain."

"But surely existence in the plane must have been rather comfortable, in a sense, much less complicated, both emotionally and sensorially."

"The first thing that struck me was the sense of contour. That's what I call what's left of the senses. In three dimensions, when you think about it, no principle of contact is given between objects or people. Most things don't really fit one with another, and the contact has to be individually evolved, by gesture, by trial and error, by language, or some other approach. You can only appreciate the complexity of this situation once you have experienced two-dimensional contact, the sense of contour. Volume can't be composed as can the jigsaw puzzle of the plane; in space, there are insurmountable imperfections in fitting. In the surface, all these complications are gone. Only contour remains, and it exists in most intimate contact. Nothing interferes with the edge running all around in perfect fit, in total contiguity with a uniform environment. Yes, I'd say it's a tremendous simplification. But what is most remarkable is the fit, the way you are perfectly adjusted to your environment."

"You certainly gain in identity what you lose in capabilities," Benji added. "The advantage of that perfect fit is that you know exactly who you are; the disadvantage, that you are very little."

"Quite true, and there is also a definite reduction in self-consciousness accompanying the spatial diminution. With flatness the only quality, there's no vis-à-vis, only contiguity. Without the other at a personal distance, consciousness of self is lost as well. Nor is there observation as a whole, only a sense of neighboring, a one-sided cognizance. But what are we talking about? It's a purely hypothetical state if one hasn't experienced it. Why is it of such interest to you?"

Benji did not reply immediately. He was still marveling at Tallini's ease of expression and his newfound self-assurance. Then, after a while, "Well, I'll tell you. First because it is something that happened to you, and *you* are an object of my concern. Then, of course, there's your literalizing of a historical mentality that is a stage of human consciousness. It's fascinating in itself, but admittedly such archeology is not my prime interest. What *is* is the existence of a precedent for our own situation, because we are today ourselves in a position where we will have to find a mountain to climb in order to obtain a new vista from its summit. Anything we can learn from that precedent is bound to be helpful to us.

204

"The problem is where to find this elevation from which we shall espy the next dimension. But just like Petrarch, we are already living in it, and it will just take the adequate coign of vantage—let's call it 'an idoneous mountaintop'—to open not only our eyes, but our feelings as well, open them to a new world.

"Note how our case differs from the medieval at the threshold of the modern: our next dimension has already been expressed in the ideologies of mathematics, physics, and cosmology, and still we are unable to live the new world. The formulas for matter and space-time are there in front of us, nineteenth-century epistemology lies in shambles, but we live and think like good burghers of a century ago. Why, it's as if at the time of Petrarch's climb, the laws of perspective had already been worked out and America discovered, and yet people were still living in a flat world. Which, of course, a lot of them were even a century later, and some perhaps still are today. In fact, these earlier states of consciousness continue to exist in all of us, which is why you were able to make the contact you made with the two-dimensional."

"But don't forget," Tallini interjected, "that state turned out to be intermediary to yet another reduction, this one to a point at the center of the boulder—truly one-dimensional and yet a volume, a negative volume, if compared to the three-dimensional one, and. . . ."

"Yes, I gathered something of the sort from your letter, but before we get away from the surface, try to tell me what it was that struck you most forcefully and immediately in that strange environment, what was most distinctly different from your previous state."

"Oh yes, this I can tell you precisely. It was the simplification of life at all levels, as you've already guessed. What disappears are all these various adjustments that have to be made in volume and yet are impossible to achieve to any degree of perfection, this illusion of distance created by the depth of field—all this is gone, along with the distortions of perspective. Then there is the shell of separation that envelops and defends every individual volume from intrusion or

205

even contact. That also vanishes to leave the planar entity with a simple and unequivocal principle of action."

"And thereby liberates it from all personal ethical decisions," Benji concluded. "I can see how in the absence of perspective and distance, and with the impossibility of facing and apprehending the other as an entity, but only as a common limit, the sole activity in the clan of two-dimensional beings would reside in this contour-contact. The only possible action, the only influence on the environment is exercised in that common limit, and the result of this transaction is always perfect agreement, the perfect fit you mention. Not that one can in any way distinguish between two-dimensional entity and environment. But if we had to define flatness, we might say that the essence of the flat entity lies in the limit of its action.

"In case you're wondering why I'm so fascinated by all this, let me tell you that I've been working on my technology essay, and there, of course, I have much to do with principled action, with the morality of our doings—that is to say, with ethics. And here one has to go back and try to find out how it happened that man's actions became so unbridled they are threatening the entire human enterprise. Well, it does seem that going back in time is also a going back in space, a retracing of dimensional expansion. And this retracing can furnish information about the transition from one dimensional state to the other and therefore may help us with our own problems of transition from a third to a fourth dimension."

At this point a waiter came over to inquire if they were having supper; if not, he would gladly move their *consommations* to another table in the rear. Benji replied that they were on their way out, whereupon Tallini settled the bill. "I made a reservation at the *Closerie des Lilas*," said Benji. "Hope you don't have other plans. You won't believe the *tripes à la mode de Caen*. And an excellent little Fleurie to go with it. Are you game?"

As they strolled along the animated street, Tallini admitted it was great to be in Paris with his friend and to be able to talk things over. But he also didn't hide how glad he was not

206

to be long absent from the Spanish hills, as he intended to return that very evening. He mentioned the sense of safety he had acquired in those hills and how on the flight to Paris he had been gripped by an anxiety of never getting back. Benji let him speak. He sensed that much had happened to his friend, even since this boulder incident, and as long as Tallini was so delightfully talkative, Benji would restrain himself as best he could. Once they were installed in the restaurant, and had drunk a first glass of Fleurie to each other's health, Tallini began to relate the final phase of the boulder experience. Although he didn't mention the mineral voice he had heard, he described as best he could the network of dichotomies with which he was presented and the ultimate path—unchosen and yet taken—he had trod. And he asked Benji for some thoughts on this imagery he felt he had lived.

"Let me see if I understand you correctly," Benji replied. "You seem to have been faced with two sets of destinies of essentially identical binary opposition. That is, the alternatives were perfectly equivalent to you, as you knew nothing about them except their polarity, which in some way made them opposites of one another. If one was yes, the other was no, if one was right, the other was left, save that, prior to any action of yours, neither one was left or right or yes or no or anything else. And yet you had to proceed, and only with your passage would each juncture gain its characterization, namely, that one path would be taken and the other not. Along this process, a web of action will be traced and relations determined from juncture to juncture. The process necessarily leaves a part of itself at each fork of either/or—an imprint, a mere trace—yet it indelibly stamps the juncture with a choice. Because willed or unwilled, action is always choosing among alternatives. The process eventually exhausts all possible either/ors that apply to its particular existence, and I presume it fades away, its entire career now lying in the net of relations established by the totality of all its dichotomies.

"But note that the necessary refusal of one possibility at each juncture is not the mere discarding of a 'could be,' whose effects might be tied to a psychopathology of regrets, the

207

'could have been.' It goes without saying that nothing of the sort was in play in the situation you describe. No, the preclusive refusal is creative, and by refusing actualization, negation in itself is suggestive of a wealth of possible existence—free, unfettered by prescribed or predictable structures, forms, and functions, and open to nonlinear improvisational space, a space of creative imagination. But tell me, how did this adventure end?"

There was a long silence from Tallini. "I don't know," he finally murmured. "I really don't know. I sometimes think it didn't end at all, and that I am still traveling on that network." And to himself, under his breath, "Not choosing."

Then he got up. "Thank you," he said. "You give me much to think about. My plane is at midnight, I must be on my way. But I'll be in touch. Thank you . . . and *ciao.*"

ELEVEN

THE SOURCE

Despite his late return, Tallini was up and on his way into the hills early the next morning. His talk with Benji had filled him with new energies, and he decided to push further inland than he had gone so far. He was making his way through an undulating terrain of knolls and boulders when his trail abruptly gave onto a small plateau, oddly flat in this landscape. Protected by encircling hills, this natural stage was startlingly level and surprisingly colorful. Amid the shades of brown, the vegetation's green and gray brought forth a vital glow. He found himself standing in a verdant arena contained within a specific radius. At a short distance, all was gray rock and boulders again, up to the crest of the hills. Hardly luxuriant, and seemingly rooted to the very stone, the plant life had become denser and greener until it reached this secluded corner. Here the heraldic colors of the plants were flying on so many emerald banners and the light enmeshed in this synthesis exhaled a stomatal humidity, a moisture of plant life Tallini eagerly sniffed. He was tasting the serous lightness of the air and riding the volatile complement of fire it was carrying to his blood.

A small stream issued forth amid the rocks, as if trickling right out of their stone hearts, pencil thin yet sufficient to soak the ground under his feet. Exhilarated, Tallini listened to its murmuring patter among the boulders, the delicate silver lisp of sounds dispersing whatever echoes of Paris might have persisted in his inner ear. The stillness of the site magnified the rich tonal variety in its flow. Before, he had noticed his footsteps, his breathing, his heartbeat, each event marked by periodicity and by repetition. Now it struck him that he had heeded only half of what those signs of life presented. He had observed by repetition only the positive signs of the presence. Now he perfected this observation by noting discontinuity in repetition, the separating link between left/right, in/out, and the binary systole and diastole, the ultimate yes/no of counting by discrete units: the yesses one after the other —*les numéros les uns après les autres,* as Benji had once described the fundamental arithmetic mystery—and the noes in between, to keep the positive integers apart, letting them be.

In his mind's eye, duality within unity arose in negative creation as he experienced that minimal contraction of infinity, the infinitesimal shift that makes the finite, a saying of *no* to nothingness. He *knew* that a moment before he conceived this, all he saw, heard, and felt had not been *there* as such; or rather had not been there as forms, but was infinitely open and free. To that shift, that marginal contraction, he had contributed a name. In a wordly universe, everything speaks its name. He was newly aware of his capacity to vocalize this sound, and of its potential. Was this a power? Did it have a purpose? The answer came to him from all sides, from above and from below, from wherever he turned head and eyes. The purpose could only be a knowing, a knowing of a special kind, never construable as particular privilege. Inhabiting a wordly world, *everyone* knew, and no move could be made without such knowing. It was given in front. A search is intrusive, for it changes what it searches. Its outcome in language is little more than a description of the search itself and thus a most limited insight into the object of cognition.

It was the nature of Tallini's travail—a struggle for transcendence within an ingrained immanence—to be a blinding ray for all but its own unfolding, for which it shone as a beacon of truth. Accompanied by moments of such acute intuitive perception in visual and aural intending, long patient labors seemed like mere ballast on soaring inspiration. His theme was Promethean: the conquering hero, having much to be forgiven, carries a proud guilt.

As if transfigured, Tallini stood amid the rocks. Had time elapsed? Could the same spring be twice heard? Or was its sound sempiternal, and what he heard was heard forever? Taunted by thoughts, he spurned them, but also watched them forming and unforming. He distinguished random associations from all that was so graciously coming down. Both modes of thinking were effortless on his part. The former consisted of arbitrary formations whose usefulness in a variety of disciplines and arts he did not contest but whose potentially distracting interference with the new—the independent, autonomous, and nonassociative—could not be denied. The state of active receptivity that responds to the always surprising new descent is delicate in its inner contradictions. He sensed it as an emptiness that yet is not *nothing*, as an absence presumably indwelling whatever receives. Pure noncontradictory receptivity would produce a psychic void conducive to nothing so much as the dreams of both sleep and wakefulness, and in that cessation of attention, the exercise fails.

With his new sense of open receptivity, Tallini's awareness—located in his inner ear—intuited a presence in the spiral of sound, a presence more intimate than the light of objectivity that shines from the eye, from a self. He knew that when the fact comes down as sound, it bypasses a processing by the unified self through the cerebral cortex. Once received by the nervous system, sound does not lend itself to objective analysis as does the image made by light. Tallini did not learn this through a knowledge of anatomy but from an ancient mind as yet unfamiliar with conscious senses, a mind still sorting out the effects of seeing, hearing, and a tentative thinking, and one that was still close enough to its origin to remember perfect silence as pure obscurity. This mind experienced the first intimations of light as a break in the silence. It was the silence in the ear that had been the unknowing. And there could have been an early, practical discernment between a sound that is seen and a sound that is heard, that is *only* heard. The sound that is *known* can always be seen; it is the sound that can be thought. Only the sound that is *not* known, *not* thought, expands in perfect obscurity.

◐ ◑ ○ ○ ◑ ◐

He heard a sort of twittering and warbling behind him, although he had never seen birds in these hills. The sound came from the spring, but by a peculiar echo, it reverberated from the rocks and made itself audible behind and above him, persisting in the silence of his contemplation as it developed a full array of sounds. Again he was made aware of his body's rhythms, now keeping time with the sounding spring in its infinitely variegated tones: silvery bells and distant gongs, sighs and whispers ludic or lewd, joyous or weeping. His attention suddenly musicalized, he heard the flowing water's endless melody, sung by all that vocalizes and played by entire orchestras, even by vinas, okarinas, bagpipes, cymbals, marimbas, cembalos, and by instruments unnamed because not as yet invented to produce the sound now assuming volume within reach of Tallini's hearing. No words, but all these sounds were rising to his ear from the patter of a spring within the silence of its site. It was as if the sound had appointed *him* as its center by the fact of his rhythmic receptivity, his own heartbeat pounding a bass line not only to his own immediate corpo-reality but as a rhythm of authority to the limits of his sway, whose sphere extended as far as his sensorium reached. Thus his dominion assumed a pervasive presence in every signification, hypothesis, and calculation. Such cognitive immanence may contravene scientific tradition, in which the observer is independent of the object of investigation, yet it offers inscriptive, evolutionary experience to less acquisitive, less aggressive approaches, such as the termless thinking of true contemplation, a feeling of abstracted touch, which was at the moment Tallini's sole sentient presence.

But now he no longer felt the touch coming from above. Before, he had thought of it as a lifeline or as an index finger that extends the reaching arm, in turn compelling his mind to reach toward the image of his own finger's opposing touch.

212

This linear approach and Tallini's response never favored a more diffuse contact, but the mere fact of connecting was the first step. Only now, when the feeling did not manifest as a concentrated flow but rather was felt spreading and enveloping, did he see into its very depth: oneness out of duality, and dualization in oneness. Number was his paradigm of becoming: the first step of contact determines the second by division, demonstrating a tertium quid in this coupled unification. Henceforth, there is constant alternation between this complementary duality, the sameness of both that makes for the one. After the ternary there is multitude, each individual with its unique characteristics, its number. He had heard Benji extoll the merits of the dual as portrayed in ancient grammars. Perhaps this linguistic expression of twin action harked back to an initial cognizance achievable neither within unity nor in multiplicity but solely by such double action as manifests an initiation.

Now the feeling was surrounding him, and it came from the hills. Oblivious of the extreme heat of the day, Tallini stood there for some time, in full sun, exhausted and dehydrated, light-headed and empty-minded, listening to the source. When he finally looked around to find some shade, a remarkable sight arrested his move. In the distant semicircle of hills, he apprehended unfamiliar forms, and the phenomenon fixed him to the spot. Calmly, without surprise or alarm, he discerned looming entities gradually approaching to encircle him. Some seemed to emerge from the rock formations, others from open space, out of an atmosphere he sensed as contact with the cave people. These beings were without physical bodies, but manifested very approximate human form of wavering contours. At first he saw them as fluid silhouettes, almost entirely diaphanous, with a gradual translucency toward the outline and an opaqueness at the boundary.

He did not, at first glance, search for detail. However, when he looked at one of them more closely, its transparency was replaced by layers and layers of the sheerest sky-dyed fabric lightly swathing a vaguely human shape. But as he shifted his gaze to another, the first figure became transparent again, whereas the object of his attention, transparent a moment earlier, took on layered substance. Apparently they were inherently transparent, becoming available to the eye in direct proportion to the waxing and waning degree of attention they received. Thus, when Tallini's unthinking, unfocused sight was sweeping over the assembly that formed about him, he could distinctly see the rising ground behind them and the hills in the distance, albeit through a filter that diminished light and eliminated color. But as soon as his look came to rest on a particular entity, a translucency intercepted his view and stopped it at a certain depth, as if a thick fog had absorbed the visual impulse. And the moment he joined mindfulness to observation, layers of sheerness whipped up a surface that arrested his eye, so the moving and weaving integument seemed a living being, possibly a hominid.

To be seen, they were dependent on another's glance, gaze, observation, attention, and eventually mindfulness— each stage escalating their progressive visibility. Under persistent attention, these apparitions had a trick of occupying the entire visual field, obliterating peripheral vision, so that a background had to be *recalled* by the observer for him to see it again. This essentially linguistic action could replace them, however briefly, as focus of attention. The effect of the distraction was instantaneous. They would fade back to their outline, minimal sign of a volume to which they pretended, to which, for reasons unknown and mysterious to him, they had a right, though they lacked the power to actively occupy their volume, a power possessed by even the lowliest material object. He noted with interest the profound influence they exerted on the phenomena around them, whose laws of visibility they modified to their own requirements, extending their own inconstancy to the rest of the visible world by forcing it out of the picture. The disadvantage of this power was that they grew fainter in the absence of another's attentive consciousness. By themselves they were nothing, invisible. Having never before encountered so aberrant a vision, Tallini left himself out of the equation altogether. The error of this disjunction dawned on him only in later reflection.

He knew that if he was to communicate with these entities, he had first to understand the principle, if not the mechanism, of their being, the laws of their existence. Every passing second held a clue and revealed further facets. Thus he realized that his attention, which filled them with visual substance and color, also kept them too distant for dialogue. But in the circumstance to which he was adjusting, question and problem coincided with answer and solution. This allowed him to eliminate from his attentiveness a bias that had relegated the forms to that distance. By burdening a purely perceptive function with a frame of expectations these entities refused to recognize, he precluded closer contact with them. The impetus behind such intrusive probing ranges from banal curiosity to a morbid fear of experiencing the unknown. To thrive, the entities needed Tallini's total openness and the attention of a mind devoid of all constraints. A reflexive action of negation, therefore, had to precede the effective creation of these forms. Acquisitiveness and inquisitiveness, each one breeding the other, are both rooted in the same ground of seeking, of wanting. This intrusion in one's daily contacts, the mental acquisition of the other that comes with knowing him, is hardly noticed any longer in everyday life. Corresponding to the mind's outward inquisitive bent, there is the return of information, which is identified, classified, and then assimilated. That is an acquisition.

Tallini's insight—a new depth of understanding of the event—and the subsequent reflective moment that neutralized his own participation were rewarded by dramatic changes in that strange assembly. The apparitions were amazingly responsive. Tallini, having fixed on an entity and offering it the elixir of form until it displayed substance and color, had deepened his self-conscious attention to intense contemplation when he became aware of the figures' displacement toward him. Meditation apparently brought them closer. And this happened not by their moving from one location to another and by logic and language covering the distance between the one and the other. No, while he was absorbed in watching them, they simply disappeared from his field of focus while simultaneously reappearing at a point closer to him.

He noted their independence from the laws of perspective. As they advanced in his direction, neither their size, their girth, nor their aspect changed with proximity; nor did they offer greater detail than they previously had. Perception evidently caused them to appear and could bring them closer, but it could determine nothing further about them. To his surprise, his vision quickly adjusted to this anomaly, so that he no longer imagined them shrinking in size with every forward bound. He was amazed, in the bewilderment of this visual irrationality, at the logical persistence of his own mind, still compelled to question how, in a group of indistinguishably fluttering entities, he could assume that there was not a multiplication of them but a repetition, a reappearance of the same ones, those already seen, only transmuted in time and space. Clearly the gaze was the motor for the change, being as it was the only outside factor acting on the scene.

Tallini never doubted he was in the presence of a mind, unanimous despite its multiple appearances. Why presume that if there be no body—and how could fluttering color be interpreted as "body"?—there can be no presence of a mind? In his experience, bodily presence could actually hinder the presence of mind, a fact his Rajasthani guru's discipline aimed to demonstrate. Guruji maintained the body's automatisms are so hugely valorized today that the mind's function turns into a mere accompaniment, at best a sort of counterpoint to the body's action. "Life for most people is mainly a matter of the mind following the body around," Tallini remembered him saying. "What they are doing is expressed by their bodies rather than by their minds, and their minds are rarely in their actions." He had gone on to criticize the Western scientific ideal of objectivity, seeing that the undisciplined body, be it a layman's or a scientist's, is rarely *out* of the action. "Under those conditions," he had concluded, "the aim of barring the body from the cognitive act in order to comprehend the object by the mind only is naïve wishful thinking. Such a bodiless mind is an amusing conceit: an illusion, and absolutely counterfactual!"

With his own mind neutralized and entertaining the forms around him with open and empty attention, Tallini allowed such bits and pieces of information on the mind/body theme to rise to the surface of his consciousness. The problem of scientific objectivity was one of Benji's recurrent topics, and Tallini remembered putting forward guruji's opinions for him. Now Benji's discourse came back with stunning accuracy.

"The predominant importance of the body in the average human life can easily be judged by its incessant displacement to achieve its aims. Nowhere is this more in evidence than in the scientist's mind. It shows every morning when he has to pick himself up and move to a laboratory full of machines in order to obtain cognition, as if one couldn't know all one had to know right at home. So in the scientific case the mind, whose professional existence pretends to be unmoved by the body, must be moved to a special place for the work of cognition even to begin. This circularity is a limitation those scientists should examine, the limits of the scientific mind, and this they can do at home. This is essentially what fascinates you about your friends in India, those living saints you filmed, isn't it so? Not only have they grasped this, intuitively or intellectually, as I believe many people have, but they *live* that cognition, live it out, which is a rare accomplishment. What is the action that corresponds to this particular realization? I mean, what does the body do that corresponds to it? The answer is that it must remain unmoved, immobile, certainly a first principle of meditation. Surely we agree on this point, don't we? Then the question is: What action?"

The fluttering colors of the forms Tallini was observing and thus nourishing seemed to be a clear expression of a mind's mobility. Better, he considered that the fluttering color *was* mind, that it was mind just *because* it had no body and yet could be perceived. For a moment, his attention flagged as he tried to relate these forms to the Moors he had glimpsed earlier in the plain. But there could not have been any relation between the two. Those Moors were there by themselves, they didn't need *his* attention, they had been there centuries before, even before he had ever seen Spain. And they would be there after he left, because they are, through their history, part of the landscape as much as those Spaniards now living there. No one would dream of speaking to them or imagine them speaking, at least no one in his senses. No, the Moors belonged to another, much more common realm, the realm of ever-repeated generations of physical existence. Whereas the entities that had appeared by the source, those that were encircling both him and the source whose trickling sounds never left his hearing, these presences were of a special moment, a moment without return: the moment of beginning.

It was clear to him that they pertained to his own realm. In a very fundamental way, they were human, as human as he himself. What was surrounding him so assertively was an anonymous gathering of a basic, inchoate humanity, before experience, virginal. Or rather, these beings were experiencing incipient experience, elaborating a consciousness of experience in the initial experience. No doubt they had appeared because he had summoned them all along, conjured them by his preoccupation with them, ever since the first days in Paris —in the library, at Ladsnik's reception, on his walks and travels. They alone would have the answer, he thought, but instead, the nearest form seemed to be questioning him. Not the kind of interrogation that could be heard, at least not in the way one thinks of the ear's hearing audible waves to which meaning can be attached. No, that was not it at all. Only the sense was there, not the sound, not even the word, and yet a general setting, an atmosphere.

The term *wordliness* came to him. Yes, something like that was certainly prevailing, pertaining to a human experience. Without it, how could he have understood? He did understand that the state these beings were manifesting had existed, forever, and it was evident that they had been together in it and not apart, already knowing one another in a close way in the silence. They were clinging to a same staff— first two or three, then all—all clinging to the same staff.

218

Tallini understood a common attention was meant. But then had come the sound, the call, everyone with a different call. The few who spurned the call banded together and fell behind. This sound was distinct from all the sounds of nature, it was the sound of sense. And the sense was ineffable. Not the sound. Everyone had the sound and everyone had a call—they were common. But sense was unique, and it was the same for all. This is how Tallini read them.

● ◐ ○ ◯ ◑ ◕

One of them had now come quite close. Its presence was greatly empowered, so that Tallini discerned a radiance of sorts, feeble but qualitatively like the touch of the ancient ones. This he perceived as an embassy, and it was radiating communication. They were emissaries, they were representatives. Representation to the devil? The moment this occurred to him his attention ebbed again, and the form grew pale and receded. Catching himself and reversing its decline, he decided to sit, a better position for this activity.

In a single fluid gesture, he sank cross-legged onto the ground right where he had been standing. Sitting, lotus-locked, he no longer felt the heat of the sun, engaged as he was in converting and processing that sunlight into an existence for this creature, which along with its companions changed its appearance in conformance with the vantage point of his seat. By losing half their height, they approximated roundness. These beings were present; they were there in a special way. Yes, it was like the feeling of the cave people when they were in touch. It was a being/nonbeing quality, hitherto abstracted and therefore defying description or else conceptualized into a spurious logic.

This development opened a floodgate of remembered discourse, sending the forms of attention into retreat. "The logic of creation is without negation," Tallini heard, "because creation itself is negativity denied. Negation is reductive in all other situations but not when it negates itself, not when it eliminates itself for the furtherance of positivity. Creation is a second power of negation. After that initial creative gesture, which absorbs all possible negativeness, it unfolds without negation, its arithmetic without zero, no nothing, no naught, its logic a thoroughgoing positivity, but only thanks to the original conduct of the second power negative.

"Does it sound plausible for a creator to produce the inexistent? No, he does *not* produce the inexistent. If negation is not of itself, it is reflection, and therefore has already abandoned the creative path for the joys of representation. This is the entry into a counterfeit creation where entities are no longer themselves, or in themselves, but are *like* themselves, deceptively similar to themselves. Abstraction becomes relativized, equations become differential, creative logic becomes methodology. If creative positivity retains even a trace of the negative, it's no more than a faint shadow in the essential openness it posits.

"The Eastern mind very easily effectuates this replacement of emptiness by openness. Perhaps it intended openness to begin with, and it came out as empty negativity, maybe through errors of transcriptions or translations. For the Western mind, nothingness is a problem, and thus easily takes on shades of nihilism. It's important therefore that the formalization of logic itself be without negation. And the second power negation in the creative beginning does not negate some positivity or other, invented for the purpose, but negativity itself, in the only realistic position."

But Tallini knew that what *he* was experiencing now—what he was seeing with his own eyes—was nonbeing that did not negate the being, a positivity of a special kind, a positivity that could encompass its negation without opposition. It acted through the affinity between yes and no, and struck him as a more evolved, a dimensionalized version of the boulder system. At the same time, his experience of these faceless forms was casting a new light on experience itself, illuminating the deeper questions about the sense and nature of experience as such. These he had taken for granted, and thus they had remained invisible, transparent. Was it because the entities were featureless that they allowed this experience of experience? What was the *sense* of it, and did it have *direction?* And what determined the sense of it, and its direction, presuming it had such qualities? Or did one just let experience occur, vaguely reacting to "what's happening"?

"Experience is how you know," Tallini heard a voice declare. Then another, "What you know." Yet another, "Who knows whom?" "Who knows who?" boomed one more. Many voices speaking all around him, all different, yet all one. Asserting, questioning, answering, affirming, denying. And somewhere— perhaps not even inside his body, in a place not himself and yet connected, wired for the senses to the center of his brain, to the pit of his stomach, to the beat of his heart— colors flashed propositions in those hollow entities. But Tallini no longer bothered with this code. He had grasped the teaching so vividly transmitted and felt no further need for its representations. The embassy was accepted and would be honored, but the messenger was to be dismissed. Who cared about him, the courier, a mere means to an end? Who cared what he might opine, he

They are still close to the mastery of the hand, and the hand raises questions. Things are less like other things now. The hand has made the difference. The fire has grown from it, domesticated along with the gentle beasts. But when the hand kills the fierce beast, the killer is still in-dwelling the beast, suffers with the beast. With fire, the beast has become more other. Hand and fire practice separation from the beast, from the other. The hand that is biggest with the flow teaches separation, out of the beast, out of the fire, out of the other. It teaches signs that look like the other, like the fire, the Big Fire, round like the eye. The hand, the fire, the eye, the sign. The hand has signs for the other and for the hand: pressed in the wet mud, it stays. It is he. Every hand now is he, by the stones it carries, by the stick it holds, by the mud it fashions, by the flaked edge of its stone, by the herb it finds, by the signs it marks. With the fire everything grows. The hand, with four against one, has brought numbers and questions and the signs show difference and separation. Now they are less the same, some are more hand, some less. All now know the difference, the others left, they went away. They couldn't question, the hand was dumb.

who has not read the acts, although throughout the long journey they never left his side? The messenger is the body of the deed, the bearer of the action. What could be his office once the message was delivered, once the deed was done?

But before he had time to dismiss the company by turning away, the closest one, on whom Tallini had been fixing his attention, took yet another leap still closer to him, occupying his entire field of vision. Whereupon all propositions coiled into one single question: What is experience? This question was the one that exposed his entire life to doubt. Had he lived it in an illusion concocted by his brain, in a construct of his own fabrication? Was this merely an unfinished structure assembled with materials left behind by previous builders and now his to complete? Only within the bounds of evidence could he answer, only within the ends of probability and possibility—that is, with the ready-made imagination and calculation that formerly had triggered his understanding. And this was no longer valid in a moment that was radically improbable, impossible, unimaginable, and yet full of reality.

There had been hitherto little doubt in his mind that experience, if it was to be more than a passing parade, had to accommodate him at its center in the special manner unique to his species. Wherever both mind and body were involved, there would be experience at whose center *he* experienced and interpreted this experiencing as the means of knowing *himself*. This wisdom is hardly ever called into question. It has come down the ages and was honored by the West long before the cardinal points were named.

Tallini had accepted this tradition. When its insight was new to him it was creative for a time. Benji held that the most creative phase of an insight *precedes* its formulation. Then as it imperceptibly becomes obvious, it loses all efficacy until—Tallini realized this with a start—it becomes visible again, reaffirming itself, this time by its own negation. Experience has become inexperienced in knowing itself. Yet a certain activity of an assumed self continues, willy-nilly, "to happen." The experiencing observer, the one who manifests at its center, is therefore suspect of being superfluous to the experience. The principle of "know thyself" stands falsified by an absence of subject.

● ◐ ○ ○ ◑ ◕

If Tallini later refused himself the pleasure of communicating this exciting realization to Benji, it was because he wished to spare both his friend and their friendship. And himself as well, by avoiding one more lecture on nihilism versus *syntactique*. Also, he recognized, by then, a necessary distance between this doubly reflexive adventure and the theoretical expertise to be expected from Benji. In Paris, contemplating Arvan's collection from the outside and through a plate-glass window, Tallini had felt a similar distancing from the views of the specialist, notwithstanding his valuable assistance in other ways.

Now it seemed as if an understanding in such elusive matters was too subtle for pundits who could never admit ignorance and are always constrained to take a stand. It might be that in certain matters no stand is to be taken; perhaps there is no place to stand, no ground. Such a postulate, arising from the mystery of his adventure, would be unacceptable to Benji. His refusal of it would be all but occulted by commentary that would be bound—and perhaps was intended—to cloud the pure simplicity of the realization. For the first time in his thinking life, an idea, the idea about his experience, struck Tallini as too precious to be marred by discourse. What he would choose to share with Benji was a set of terms abstracted to the point of harmlessness, which could in no way reduce or dilute the experience that was more than concrete. It was, indeed, *creative* of concreteness: the landscape encompassing and producing the entities—soil, rock, vegetation, life, air, sky, the universe that stretches far beyond—a space in which he was in no way central yet which needed him for its experience as surely as did the apparitions who languished without his attention. What he kept to himself was the reality of this bond and the unreality of its split into an unexperienced world opposing an autonomous observer.

Rising to his feet, Tallini slowly pivoted away from the forms. All at once, the one that for an instant had monopolized his entire vision disappeared from sight, leaving behind a voice in Tallini's ear, a familiar voice, but one he could not locate in space. As he moved, Tallini passed in review the remaining forms and realized that they had been striving for their turn in his full attention, that they had requested a life through his consciousness. The voice in his ear was speaking while his gazing attention trailed off, allowing them to disappear. Facing the murmuring spring, he became aware of its patter, which had certainly been there all along, although he had stopped hearing it.

Because the ear, unlike the eye, cannot shelter itself from its medium, and because its contact is "in the round," inattention, not lack of audition, must have caused the lapse. This realization induced in Tallini the *experience* of the volume of sound, complementing the flatness of sight. Had Benji not spoken of something like this, at the café, in a world remote in time and place? The café! Were they still sitting at those tables, while *this* was happening? Was it possible for something else to happen while this was happening? Or when this was *not* happening!

Tallini was *listening* to the source as if to a voice. Was it a reason to assume, because he didn't know its language, that it was ignorant of his own? Certainly the cave people who lived in the hills had *heard* this source—and if not this one, then another—long before their language was implanted in their pharynx and established their tongue. The speech in his ear could come only from the closest entity, he thought, from the form that had jumped into an instant of full vision, suddenly sharply delineated, a concept, the grasp of a whole. But no, the voice he was hearing was his own, and it came from the source. The patter that had been hiding the message now fell away, and a rhythm organized the flow, establishing order in time and thus, inevitably, a theme. He learned that only the concept came from the entity, from the form, whereas the endless language of its definition came from the source, constantly adjusting the form.

It was his own voice, directed into his ear by the conceptual entity under his attention, his own voice, revealed from underneath the patter constantly passing through his brain. This was not the particular voice he could make to sound if he could bring himself to speak. With his parched throat and under this hot sun, his voice would be but a hoarse croaking. The voice in his ear was in no way affected, however. It was his voice as it always was, the voice he alone could hear. But now he discovered it anew, sensed it under the indifferent flow. Heard what it could tell him, if he would let it speak. What it said belonged to him alone: the secret of his life, as only he could tell it to himself.

He felt a lightness in his head, and a vague motion of the ground under his feet, as if he were drawn toward this flow and swept by a current. For the trickling source was turning into a stream, but no longer of water, no longer a flowing *over* or *through* something. It was like a warm ocean current not of liquid but of fire, by nature inimical to water. In this conflict, form is given by negation without opposition. A differentiation coupled its two differentials, one colder, the other warmer. The result could be a Gulf Stream of the mind, real enough, specific enough to bear a name. He felt the flow of this current, felt that the one who observes and experiences is designated within a universal medium of language, and that only a reconciled differentiation holds him together and keeps him formed and informed. It might take no more than an act of the mind to leave the current and disperse back into the medium.

This intuition raised an apprehension in Tallini—as might a hazardous temptation—and brought him back to the voice in his ear. This time, however, he clearly understood that it was *not* his own voice modulating and articulating in the flow of the linguistic medium. It was his *tone* that emerged from the patter in an aura of familiarity, the purl of language being merely its support. The tone was his, and the language of intonation was perfectly transparent to him. He followed every inflection to its ultimate meaning, took the jab of each accent, suffered every stress. The understanding of this language was to hear the tone, to recognize it. Whatever else might be said didn't matter to Tallini; nor did it matter that the language was unknown to him. It didn't matter as long as it allowed the tone to stream in the medium audible to his ear.

But now the rhythms and cadences of this free flow fell into patterns through repetition. The message suffused his entire body: "Dance, dance with the flow to know the source, dance, dance. . . ." For the source had now amplified its stream and was no longer murmuring but commanding him to dance with the flow. The current moved his feet, and now he was stepping about swaying and waving his arms in time, as if directing what had become an immense orchestra. As he danced to the rhythm in the flow, great melodies wove through the musical medium.

It never entered Tallini's mind that he was here performing an ancient ritual. He was in a state of bliss, floating through the current, having received as inevitable the source's invitation—a natural idea, the essence of evidential conduct. This was not a sound to *listen* to, not yet—or no longer. These complex rhythms couldn't be grasped by the act of comprehension that differentiates listening. Once heard, they had to be danced to be experienced. No listening could comprehend the thousands of sounds, no tympanists could conceive the instruments, the sound makers, that constituted this sound, thus proving its comprehension. He was at the edge of music here, but it was too early. He also knew that it was not the first time this source had been danced to in the manner it wanted to be danced to now.

The heat was forgotten, and he suddenly craved more contact with the elemental medium in which he now found himself flowing. Without interrupting his dance, he stripped his clothes off piece by piece, slipped out of his shirt without

226

losing a beat, kept the rhythm going with his body while he untied his shoes, kicking them off as hard as he could. Then he tripped and hopped out of his pants and ripped off his shorts. Stark naked in the sun, he jumped and turned and scooped and looped, twisted and bounced and danced, danced until he collapsed in a heap and from there slowly slumped face down, and with a last reach and kick, ended up spread-eagled in a murderous sunbath.

TWELVE

ASSOCIATIONS

On one of the last warm days of autumn, late in the afternoon, Benji was crossing the Luxembourg Gardens, where any number of indolent drifters and aging *parisiennes* passed their time on the park benches, many feeding pigeons. Scattering the birds here and there with his purposive gait, Benji sifted some idle thoughts about the satisfactions to be reaped from this time-honored charity: a sense of doing modest good, companionship in a lonely life that lacked even a pet of one's own, or perhaps a modicum of affection from these fowl far more at ease with city life than their marginal benefactors. Shaking his head at his own speculations, he continued the brisk pace toward St.-Germain-des-Prés, where von Ostheim would be just about to close his shop. No need to worry about missing him, though, as he would, as always, be preparing to spend a good while in his office after hours, looking at prints, making order in a perpetual confusion of papers, files, and portfolios of all kinds, or simply reading a brochure or an article.

By the time Benji reached it, the gallery was indeed already closed, but von Ostheim could be seen through the display window hanging some pictures. He seemed at the moment to be deep in contemplation of what he had just hung. He was at the far end of the gallery, and Benji was unable, from where he stood, to see the subject of the work. Von Ostheim had stepped two or three paces back from the wall and was pursuing his observation in a rather strange posture, his left hand tucked in his right armpit, his open right hand raised to his face, covering part of his chin and cheek, with long fingers stretched out halfway over his ear.

As von Ostheim seemed extremely absorbed in his contemplation, Benji was unwilling to disturb him and, although a bit uncomfortable with his indiscretion, he attempted to read what his friend might be expressing in this stance of his. He was surprised at his incapacity to deduce anything whatsoever from the posture. It vaguely resembled a gesture of Benji's own, performed when faced with something disagreeable and usually accompanied with an *"Ach, du Lieber!"* But now von Ostheim tilted his head slightly, without moving his hands, perhaps attempting to judge whether the picture was hanging straight. This was a virtual obsession with him, and he was constantly nudging a corner of a frame somewhere or other in his gallery. But that couldn't be it, as he didn't approach the painting, and now it seemed to Benji he looked vaguely as if he might be suffering some pain in his jaw. Whatever it was, Benji marveled at how one and the same gesture could express so many feelings, fit into so many contexts. This, he mused, was of course the case with words as well, and even entire sentences could fit a variety of situations. And he remembered the beginning of Tallini's boulder letter, the enigmatic, epigrammatic "everything speaks." If every gesture spoke, then certainly so did every animal attitude and every plant growth.

Benji tapped at the glass of the window. Von Ostheim turned with a start, and seeing the other wave at him, raised his hand in a vague greeting and came to let him in.

"What on earth were you looking at there, Ostheim? You seemed a million miles away. Perhaps you have some problem with your jaw, or was it perplexity? I tried to read your attitude there, but couldn't without knowing what you were looking at."

"Yes, yes, I was absorbed. Such an interesting thing. I've had it only a few days. Take a look."

He led Benji to the back of the gallery and pointed at the wall. Hanging there was a lead pencil drawing, manifestly from a past century. Between a foreground of rocks and shrubbery and a distant background of hills nestled a spacious house in rustic style with outbuildings, surrounded by an open field and trees. These were located close enough to a town, only faintly adumbrated, to warrant an imposing bell tower, portrayed in detail and very dominant in the arrangement. At first glance, Benji found the composition most engaging in its un-self-conscious manner, quite striking indeed in its subtle amateurish quality. It made him take a closer look. Why would Ostheim, who knew the business better than anyone, have a *croûte* on his wall, a mediocre piece of work?

"Well, what do you make of it?" By the trace of glee in the dealer's voice, Benji knew the old fox had something up his sleeve. It was von Ostheim's game with him. He would submit an odd and obscure item and impassively expect Benji to give an opinion. This presupposed a recognition of sorts, if not a direct identification, a judgment as to century, at least, and a good approximation of the decade, as well as some ideas concerning school, style, and so forth. It was a procedure not unlike the analytical tasting of wine.

Benji usually acquitted himself rather honorably, keeping the game interesting. He had his bag of tricks, a manner of hinting and talking about and around, all the while getting his clues from von Ostheim's almost imperceptible reactions. Moreover, Benji was steeped in history, had a classical background, and was multiculturally versed. He possessed, as well, a central European appreciation of intellectual and artistic value and an uncanny feeling for style. There were times he had been fooled, of course, as when he took for Peruvian a statuette that turned out to have come from a Tibetan peasant hut. But he had rarely been found utterly defenseless, or even totally stumped. Even when proved in error, he could weave the most persuasive discourse on the similarities of the two styles, convincing von Ostheim that it *could* have been Incan. And although for the moment he would have been unable to utter a syllable pro or con, he had been given clues that were begging for interpretation.

Had he seen this piece from the corner of his eye while strolling by any second-rate art dealer on the boulevard or along the quays, he could have judged it with dispatch and absolute certainty. It was a production that had undoubtedly at one time fulfilled some individual—artist was here *not* the word—and it was not like Benji to disparage an amateur who sketches the phenomenon. Quite to the contrary, he frequently encouraged his interlocutors to attempt a sketch of what they were describing. When shown landscape photographs, he often lamented that Monet or Fragonard had not been at the scene, or even just the photographer, sans camera, but with pencil and paper.

It was a topic he had exercised with much wit on Tallini, who at first refused to take him seriously. But soon enough Tallini took his advice, since it seemed to help his eye, as he said. Benji pointed out the creative opportunities offered to one and all by the aesthetics of modern times, when fortunes are regularly made in persuading the public that *anyone* can draw, which is both true and false. In this way, Benji showed the depth of his regard for the status of art in his day. The eighteenth and nineteenth centuries, when *not* everyone could draw, were crammed with anonymous sheets somewhat like this acquisition of Ostheim's—a glut on the market. In those enlightened days—in England, France, Germany —everyone was drawing almost everything, everybody was studying art, playing a keyboard, clavichord, harpsichord, piano. Or fortepiano, rather. Yes, that was where this drawing belonged, to the time of fortepianos. Say 1800. And that bell tower, of course, could only be German. From the south, toward the Czech border. That region was associated with rather unhappy memories, and Benji let out a groan.

"*Ja!* Any ideas?" Von Ostheim was prodding, confident. He could hardly wait to drop his bombshell.

Benji remained silent. Although he knew perfectly well no answers were to be found in the drawing itself, he gained time by appearing to have launched into a minute examination of the piece. From the point of view of workmanship, any dilettante could have been the author. But not just any dilettante could have his work hung by von Ostheim. If not the quality of the work, what then determined its presence within these reputable walls? Was it the scene depicted—was the house in this setting perhaps Ostheim's ancestral home? Nonsense, that would be quite out of character for a man who shunned nostalgia and cultivated no sentiment for his past, at least none that Benji had ever observed. Anecdotal significance in the absence of artistic value, furthermore, could never sway Ostheim to exhibit a work.

Ostheim, if Benji remembered correctly, was a native of Danzig, and the landscape was definitely southern Germany. Hadn't he seen this kind of tower in villages around Weimar? Carried away by an evident interest in the bell tower's architecture, the draftsman had robbed it of all atmospheric perspective by representing its minute particularities, details he couldn't possibly have *seen* from where he stood. But it was this same knowledgeable treatment applied to a rock formation in the distance that put Benji on the right track. Here was a man who tempered, to an extraordinary degree, what he saw with what he knew. Even the clouds didn't originate in a pure sensorial realism but rather seemed to indicate a general type of formation, a cirrostratus complete with a refractory phenomenon haloing the sun. That observation was decisive.

"I believe, dear Ostheim," he declared calmly, "that what we're facing is an effort of our own Johann Wolfgang von Goethe." He continued his sham examination of the picture, thereby affording his friend the leisure to compose himself.

"Excellent, truly excellent," said von Ostheim, who was inured to life's small disappointments, and gracious in defeat. "A Goethe drawing, indeed." Benji couldn't tell whether his guesswork had been received as expertise or had in itself been deemed worthy of compliment. Not that it would have made any difference. The fact of the matter was that he had identified Goethe's hand. Could anyone contest it? He had been correct, and there was no one to question the legitimacy of his method, if method there had been. He heard von Ostheim say, "The source is reliable and it comes with good papers. And reasonable."

A Goethe drawing! Benji couldn't help observing how the work had suddenly changed in his eyes. Before his attention had been diverted, in the search for clues, from the object proper to its circumstantial context and new owner, the amateurish quality had been the dominant impression, even more so than the steeple, the only particular he fixed in his first glance, and then with far less interest than disdain for its contravention of the perspective illusion. Now this amateur quality had entirely disappeared. Every pencil stroke took on interest.

"Wait a minute," said Benji. "I believe I've seen something like this somewhere, in reproduction. Isn't this . . . let me see, is it . . ."

"It's a view of Schiller's garden in Jena," von Ostheim blurted out, to ward off a possible double whammy.

"Of course it is." This was not quite what Benji was going to say, but it was his ultimate parry. As the drawing's graphic aspect captured his attention, the game with von Ostheim vanished. Following Goethe's many competences through the picture—from regional architecture to geology to meteorology—had certainly been rewarding. But this latest information, or confirmation, was intriguing in that it brought into play one of the great man's favorite investigations: botany, and more precisely, the plant world in its most personal and original setting—the garden. In Weimar, his patron, the grand duke of Weimar, had given Goethe a park for use and planting to his purposes. Now he, Goethe, stood on a knoll above Jena, looking down on Schiller's garden. And here, in contemplation of what Goethe saw, were Benji and von Ostheim. Benji knew how to appreciate such a conjuncture, and once again, the drawing changed. Through the power of what it assembled, it acquired a magnetic component. And through what it enabled, became a "work of art," as von Ostheim called it over Benji's shoulder, "a jewel of feeling and thinking."

"Which it certainly was *not* in the days when Privy Councilor Goethe was sketching landscapes. Time will make art out of most anything that endures, don't you think? And make caricatures out of the rest. Yesterday's *croûte* is tomorrow's avant-garde. And yesterday's avant-garde becomes tomorrow's *croûte*. But seriously, Ostheim, in his time was Goethe's graphic production ever looked at as art? No more so than his physical experiments, his work on color, or his morphology were thought of as science, I'd bet. Or, for that matter, his epistemological considerations on fact and theory as philosophy. How different it all seems today, this picture here, and all the rest. Is there any artistic merit in this work we're looking at? Or is it meant only as a sketch of a friend's house, the sort of thing a photograph does today? And speaking of photographers, I have two letters from that Tallini fellow, rather interesting. We'll get to that later. It astounds me how this drawing has changed in the short time since I first saw it! Changed for the better, I must say. One thing, though: whatever it represents, it doesn't look like much of a garden."

Benji had straightened up from his inspection, and they stood for a while side by side, in silent contemplation. "Doesn't look like much of a garden, " Benji repeated.

Von Osthein, redundantly: "Schiller's garden."

"Seen by Goethe," Benji completed the thought. They looked at one another in amusement. They shared a mother tongue that had known unprecedented degradation in their own time. Having ceased to be a fit medium of truth, it had driven poets to suicide. That it recovered can be attributed not only to the courageous writings of a few individuals of their generation, but as well to the foundation laid by an equally restricted number of outstanding artists, from Heinrich Schütz to Goethe.

"A garden cultivated by Schiller might indeed seem a bit rigid and dogmatic to Goethe, don't you think? Come, Ostheim, play the game! What would you have thought Schiller's garden to look like? And there isn't much nature left in this garden, just what looks like a field with rows of cabbages, these little curlicues, separated by straight pathways. The whole thing is laid out with great care; one can almost feel a rule behind it. I'm certain that in Goethe's garden there was no preconceived idea of what a garden was supposed to be like. There were only individual plants, and growing wherever Goethe either found them, or where he felt the plant would like it. No other rule. Neither aesthetic nor utilitarian, but an occasion for those insights that Goethe treasured beyond all else."

"What fanciful ideas," said von Ostheim. "What have you been reading?"

"Not so fanciful, Ostheim. Goethe has a lot to say, and he's doing so in this picture. Surely that must be why you're putting money into it."

"I'm buying it for its signature, because I don't deal in autographs. That's how I make my best deals. No doubt you noticed that Goethe's autograph is missing from this sheet, and with that absence I'll make my profit. If it was present, I wouldn't touch the work—it'd be too expensive for me. The absence cuts the price in half, but not the value, as Goethe's signature is all over the drawing, in one way or another. That's how you recognized it, how else? So for the one who knows enough about the subject—and the subject includes the artist—the value is there, and it's an excellent deal for me. All I have to wait for is the fellow who doesn't need the autograph to know the author and enjoy the work. And the fools who pay double for a bit of dried ink or a few penciled letters are not my clientele. For anyone who knows his business, my price is excellent, irresistible. If you weren't the miser you are, you'd buy it for yourself and make an investment. Things like this are getting rare, and you're obviously fascinated by it. Take it today and you get another five percent off."

Benji admitted to temptation. It would look great in the space between his desk and the bookcase. It would just fit, and he could mount a little light above it and look at it from his chair. But he knew he would waste hours fantasizing. Besides, whatever Ostheim thought, he could no longer afford such caprices.

"Not this time, Ostheim! Find yourself another victim, I don't need the thing. I've already taken the best from it.

What's left is just nostalgia, reminiscence, dreams of excellence in a world long gone. But the best of it has now become idea with me, I've made it independent of the thing. With me, it can come alive in a way the drawing can't, by itself, because Goethe didn't really have a great graphic artist's line and expressive power. So for all the rest, for all that's *not* idea in this object, for all that is perception and contemplation—for all *that* I'll go elsewhere. If I'm to spend my time contemplating man-made things, then let it be for the sake of the object itself and not for its subject. A man-made object reflects the *hand* of an artist, even if the subject be a bloody side of beef or an old worn peasant boot. The subject is entirely idea, and it's the object that has a chance of being artistic, esthetic.

"And you see, we are now wondering about the role of subject and object in the creating of our perceived world, so we're quite close to Goethe and Schiller in one of their chief preoccupations. And being that close, why not look at a *real* production of theirs that is not primarily idea, but not primarily art either: their gardens. Neither one of those two poets was creator of objects, in a painterly or sculpturesque manner. What you're selling is not a work of art. You're selling its *subject*, the idea, not the art. And the subject is delicious, this reflection of Goethe's on the garden of his friend, in the light of what we know of their relationship. Enough to occupy you for an afternoon, and then some. But for this, we no longer need the picture. So I'll save my money and still be fully satisfied. For when I've taken all that it has in idea, what remains becomes a curio, and a fairly mediocre one at that. But not to worry, Ostheim, you'll find your man for this. You always do."

"Authenticated by Schnitzlach," von Ostheim retorted, "don't forget. He personally knows the family who's selling. Seems that some female ancestor had received it from Goethe, under what circumstances they didn't know or choose to tell. With Goethe it doesn't take much imagination, of course. A point that might interest you: we have a date for when he was in Jena to visit Schiller, 1795, April to May, but we get this in letters, not on the drawing. That's how Goethe met the young woman, through Schiller. In his garden, perhaps. Seems she was of the local literati, if I may, the crowd around the university. I was offered the letters too, but again, I don't deal in autographs, so I declined to see them, which is polite in a case such as this, when you know you're not buying. They were being very guarded, anyway, very secretive."

"*Quel dommage!*" Benji's tone was a judicious mixture of irony and regret. Von Ostheim was a shrewd salesman, under his genteel manner. But Benji wanted his garden game. "Come now, Ostheim, a little flight into the might-have-been, please. How did they differ, those two gardens?"

"What is it you want from me, *Mensch?*" Von Ostheim had stepped away and was going through the motions of straightening a sketch that was perfectly level, a representation of some musicians in a landscape, with ladies in broad-brimmed and beribboned hats. "Now if it was a Fragonard whose garden you wanted me to describe, I could oblige in detail at this very moment, and it would be signed and certified. I have that garden under my eyes. But for the Goethe, although it is 'Schiller's Garden in Jena,' looking at that drawing tells me nothing about the title. Where is it, that garden? Is it hidden behind those tufts of trees in the median plane of the picture, already quite distant from the observer? Or is that field part of it? And if not, why does it take up half of the picture? What happens in that huge foreground? Is this really what you want me to do to this poor drawing, I'm asking you?"

"All right, Ostheim, you win, I'll leave you alone. I never meant our knowledge of the gardens to come from representations. You know that as well as I do."

"What else do I know about their gardens, if it's not pictures of them? I'm surprised that Schiller could afford to keep one, and anyhow, he's much too delicate for manual labor. As for Goethe, I happen to know he spent clement afternoons with shears and trowel pruning and digging here and there, and I know about his work in botany. But I'd wager that he was in that garden mainly for the blue eyes of a gardener's daughter, beautiful and under age."

But Benji, not to be put off, persisted. "You said 1795? Isn't that the year of Schiller's essay on poetry? In his later years, Goethe called it the seed of the classic/romantic distinction. An engaging juncture, don't you think? And not unrelated to my drift. In fact, it takes me back to the correspondence I mentioned to you when I arrived—Tallini's letters. It sounds more and more as if the fellow was undertaking a sort of rapprochement with a world he has so far neglected: the world of nature. And it seems to me that he was motivated by a formative drive not at all unlike what energized these men of a century and a half ago: Schiller into poetry, Goethe into science—where, in his own opinion, he did his best work. The only difference is between then and now, purely temporal, but the spirit behind all this activity leads to the same interest, a common inquisitiveness, with different ways of understanding the task and going about it. Art, philosophy, science, logic—the instruments of knowledge of our civilization, the Greek. My friend Tallini is brushing them aside because they have lapsed. He is living in a different age, and so he must use different means. These have to do with a certain presence and the consciousness thereof, an awareness of experience.

"Consider what we so candidly call 'the outside world,' and you might eventually find that it's in large part contingent on a contact we establish. This banal fact is more difficult to comprehend than it seems at first blush. What will be the quality of the contact? Will it be categorical like Schiller's, empathetic like Goethe's? In other words, will it depend on—or at least be thoroughly influenced by—the intellectual persona who happens to be present and experiencing? Tallini is beyond all this, his *time* is beyond it, and he is dedicated to experiencing *in his time.* That's the basic premise, life in the moment, a postulate that implies the simultaneity of inside/ outside, as a conceptual necessity."

They had been strolling through the gallery, and now von Ostheim stopped and said with brow wrinkled in mock indignation, "Hold on, aren't you reading too much into that Tallini fellow? I mean, alongside Goethe and Schiller, really!"

"Same energy, Ostheim, believe me. Same pursuit. Closer to Goethe, and yet with more than just a touch of Schiller's idealism hidden behind the pragmatic. But what different gardens they all do cultivate! Take for example Goethe and Schiller in their first meeting, with Goethe trying to explain how his botanical investigations managed to isolate an essential plant form, the primitive plant for his metamorphosis theory. Goethe was quite certain he was spending his time—or better, his life—with nature, with the *outside*. But Schiller declared this was not an experience of some kind of vegetation, not at all. He thought it was an *idea* Goethe was contributing to the general greenery. An idea! Can you imagine the blow? Poor Johann! A wonder he didn't turn on his heels and slam the door behind him. He later admitted— to Eckermann, I think—that it took a bit of self-control. As you probably know, he welcomed this notion of ideas he never knew he had, signaling that he saw them under his eyes, which must have sounded like gibberish to Schiller. He didn't let on, we must surmise, because he was a kind and civilized poet and certainly also because he badly wanted contributions from Goethe for his magazine.

"What happened in that meeting was typically a disagreement on the nature of the outside/inside contact. They become friends because they are both so intent on the question —and not because they liked each other. Once they knew each other, they both profited, and profit is the ultimate cement in such affairs. I'm speaking of intellectual, spiritual, artistic, creative profit, of course. They were both smart enough to realize it. There probably weren't so many people around, even in those days, who could discuss the matter creatively."

"And I gather you believe Tallini could have entertained those two?"

"No, not discursively, but he could have shown them a thing or two on proper action. Schiller was totally blocked, experientially speaking, with ideas to which no experience can possibly be fitted, by definition. Goethe had no use for such structures. He was much closer to us today than Schiller was; his interest was in the *quality* of thinking. In his approach, Goethe didn't want a sharply defined concept separate from the senses. He wanted an approach to the world by a contemplative thinking, which in my mind is a step toward a nonspatial inside/outside, joining a contemplation of the outside to a function that to all appearances exists—or at least is anchored—only inside the human being. And again, this relates to Tallini, who goes this one better by experiencing that this human being and his inside is itself part of the outside. He places himself in the world, and in this truly engaged posture, he lets it think. And acts and feels according to that thinking. Now you tell me those three wouldn't get along?"

Von Ostheim permitted himself a guffaw, but reminded Benji of Schiller's frequent indispositions that must have made his work even more difficult. "And before calling him 'totally blocked'. . . ."

"Ex-pe-ri-*en*-tially speaking," Benji intoned with a slight edge. "That's what I said and it's not anything he would deny, if he were here. In fact, I now recall that he did admit something to that effect—in a letter, I believe . . . now where was that? Let me think . . . ah! yes, Restif de la Bretonne, that's it! Are you familiar with Schiller's letter to Goethe concerning Restif? Schiller is hugely entertained by the writings of this heroic womanizer, and at the same time repulsed by the licentious aspects of this catalog of conquests. And he wouldn't be Schiller if he hadn't neatly formulated and packaged these countercurrents. He found the descriptions invaluable, as he had never come across a nature sensuous to that degree, and to be thus introduced to a multitude of entities—and if I recall correctly, he brought out that they were mainly female—this is of interest to him, because as he says—and here is the point I'm making—he himself had had little opportunity to observe the human condition in vivo, to draw on the outer world for his experience. I can't recall the precise terminology, of course, but the text gave me the impression of a Schiller who made too much of the inside and not enough of the inside/ outside contact we were speaking about. So he must find his experience in a book. It may be unfortunate, and perhaps not coincidental, that this confession should arise through the agency of such an exhaustive individualization of erotic behavior, but it's fair nevertheless to extend it to the rest of his objectivity. Neither he nor Kant are as yet overly concerned with the disembodied mind."

"And I'd be willing to wager that it'll be extended to Schiller's *garden* before you're through."

"Very kind of you to remind me, Ostheim. There is no doubt in my mind that Schiller's garden would be one he'd have read about rather than visited. But to get back to what I said about Tallini, it's not that he thinks it all through. To the contrary, you can bet he doesn't. He's *living* it through—and not living through it! The concept of the inside/outside structure is a minefield of logical conundrums. So there is little gain in *thinking* such a concept, unless the thinking becomes the experience. And that is what I don't know, what I can't tell: will he break into that wordless cogitation? That's where it lies, the experience he's after. And to my mind, he has the qualifications for that adventure.

"For those who think in words, like you and I, there's nourishment in the inside/outside dualization, or better, there always has been, up to now. And it's only now—I mean in our time—that there has been dissatisfaction with the concept—real logical qualms, not just emotional rapture. It's a change in evidential definition, the old saw of what goes without saying. Actually, *nothing* does. Before it gets a chance at being known, *everything* has to be said. And something, if only its name, must be said of everything before it stands a chance of being known.

"You know what special kinds of nouns names are. At universities, they're throwing books at one another to discuss what names can do and what they can't. And all words are names, aren't they, for anything that has appeared to us and been heard and felt and smelled and tasted—in brief, experienced. That realm of words, Ostheim—it's getting a bad name. Some thinkers want out, into a postwordly world, but out with the benefit of cognition. To put it clearly, they want pure experience. And they don't confine themselves to physical existence any more than they do to logical brainwork.

"Behind it all is the breakdown of the dual inside/outside and the attempt is toward a unification. That this be a *reunification* is a contested point, as is every stepping-stone on this loaded terrain. The predominance of the temporal in this unifying effort grows from necessity. Spatial coordinates and the geometry of the solid are the very best proof of the existence of an inside/outside structure, and therefore antithetic to unification. You could say that spatiality is incurably afflicted with the condition of inside/outside. A spatial attempt at unification invariably disappears into identity, often in a cross-legged oblivion of the structure altogether, and therefore of the philosophic problem. Experience on that path is usually curtailed to a minimum, to the narrowest expression of an outside world. It's a trade-off between intensity and breadth, and that's why it couldn't capture Tallini. He needs a broad experience of the world, but I believe that at one time he was sorely tempted by the intensity of a mystic solution. There remains a touch of it, from that contact during the living saints film. I saw the change when he got back. Not to be discounted. Came back a different man, a better one. And as he's not the type to sit, he sets out to do the work where he finds it, in the daily experience. I'm telling you, Ostheim, the man is doing his job. It's a big story, Ostheim, and we're right at its source."

"Well, well, how involved we've become in these events!" Von Ostheim had been leading Benji slowly through the gallery, hoping for a comment on his exhibit, which he thought especially successful. "Have you turned into this man's biographer, perhaps? You're giving this affair a lot of thought, maybe a little too much, no?"

"Sorry, Ostheim, I'm all wound up. And of course I haven't discussed any of this with Tallini at all, not in these terms. To be sure, it's my construction of what's really happening. Tallini was here in Paris for a day. We talked, and I'm all the more persuaded that he's taking charge of himself. He wants to shoot some footage, with the idea of a new documentary. He's even working out a script, I think."

"Well, that's fine," von Ostheim said, while Benji fell silent and stood staring into space. "I just think you're taking all this a bit too seriously. Let's go to the office. I've got to get off my feet."

"How seriously *should* I take it? How seriously would be serious enough?"

They moved toward the office. Benji was eager to get out of the gallery, where he never could fully convince himself that Ostheim was actually listening. He was at every moment distracted by his own exhibition—each piece a friend, a story, a hope, a gamble. But to Benji it was a distraction with which he couldn't compete. In the office, his audience of one could not escape. They would be sitting across from each other at von Ostheim's desk, an arrangement to which Benji was partial, habituated as he was to meeting in cafés. He liked to sit in von Ostheim's office, but he wasn't always invited. It was an elegant little inner sanctum, crammed with overflowing portfolios, and there was only one painting on the wall, hanging right behind the dealer's desk chair: a Manet, *Bull in a Meadow*, 1861, from the dealer's private collection and not for sale. The bull's head was lowered as if readying to charge the viewer, or in this case, into von Ostheim's back.

After they settled on their respective sides of the desk—actually a venerable kitchen table from a Burgundy farmhouse—there was a lengthy silence while von Ostheim aimlessly shuffled some papers. Benji observed him without expectations, observed him simply because they were sitting so close to one another, Ostheim's thin and frail body obscuring but a minimal slice of Manet's charging bull. What did Ostheim see in this painting? Although a fairly early Manet, it had grace and solidity. Perhaps these were the qualities that appealed to Ostheim. Or perhaps he envied the aggressive stance, the hard neck and strong shoulders of the beast. Perhaps. . . .

"Seriously enough to consider that all this busy effort of Tallini's might be just another try at the Delphic *gnôthi seauton* Socrates pushed way back when? Antique and antiquated, if you ask me. What else will he get to know in those hills, if not himself? I thought by now everyone had noticed the redundance that has crept into this precept over the years."

"More than that, Ostheim, much more, one can be far more adventurous than that today. And so Tallini is, bless his soul, adventurous, just like a true fool."

"Ha! A true fool, that's good. Not redundant, at least, but self-contradictory!"

"Hardly, my friend, although a true fool is not so easily identified, and yet kings in their time wouldn't have dreamt of reigning without one at their side. But for a good text on the true fool, you have to turn to the Tarot cards. The joker of the modern playing deck is a fake of a fool, an extra card, situated *outside* the deck, with domination its only characteristic, coupled with universal fit. It's become a wild card, uncivilized, untamed, and by that fact, extraneous, a deus ex machina. In contrast, the true fool of the Tarot *belongs* to its deck. It's a card like all the others, none worth more than another, none in competition with another, but all in the relative harmony or disharmony that characterizes any situation. Each card is unique and indispensable to the deck in its entirety, the sum total of all possibilities. Now with the modern deck, where the fool has degenerated into a mere joker, any decent card game can be played in the absence of that joker, and more smoothly at that, without its irrational interjection of absolute power, and its chameleonic adaptability to any suit, any sequence, any grouping—an equally irrational universality that demolishes all proper character. So you see, Ostheim, there are two kinds of fools, and there exists a place to study them."

"You gamble?" Von Ostheim was suddenly interested.

"Haven't touched a card since I was sixteen. But before that, I put in a few intense years playing with my grandmother, who was shrewd and dedicated to *bésigue*, a fairly old game that valorizes the marriage of the queen of spades to the jack of diamonds. I gave some thought to card games and the Tarot in later years, and it looks to me as if Tallini is playing

244

his game in the age-old deck, and not in the modern. The modern is based entirely on the relative strength of the cards, which is constant. Besides that relative strength, each card has the faculty to *fit*, which is circumstantial. Except for its suit, the modern playing card provides no message save for its power and the power of configurations when related to others. This is no longer a game for our man Tallini, who had abandoned the power game even before I met him, if ever he took part in it. And he certainly refused to adapt to the modern deck from which he was dealt. Tallini won't fake. He's taking his place in the deck of the true fool, a wanderer with a bundle on a stick upon his shoulder; one step over the abyss, yet never falling. According to the adepts, the Tarot tells us who that might well be."

Von Ostheim was still shifting papers about, apparently without purpose, on the timeworn surface of the massive kitchen table. Its top had so charmed him that he had traded a Kokoschka charcoal for it—a minor sketch, but one close to his heart. The tabletop was scored by the preparation of centuries of meals and exuded a sense of reality and purpose, satisfying a criterion for basic living. Such gauges were wanting in his profession, a domain of illusionary values where fashions and psychology established prices rather than creative worth. This had always bothered von Ostheim, as if something had got lost in his life. The patina of the surface assuaged this sorrow, and when he first acquired it, the desk had been a daily solace, until the papers got the upper hand. Having accumulated relentlessly, they encroached upon ever larger territories until the tabletop came to be covered in its entirety with letters, bills, catalogs, newspapers, articles clipped from magazines, photographs, prints, ledgers, and notebooks. For some time, he had done periodic cleanups, thus obtaining, every once in a while, a view of the treasured surface. But his housekeeping slackened, and then it stopped altogether, and all that persisted was the gesture, an automatic moving of papers from one pile to another. Benji knew nothing of the table's history. He often wondered about its massiveness, but assumed it was part of von Ostheim's scheme for a subtle intimidation of buyers and sellers. He considered that Manet's charging bull might fit in the same class.

"As to a Delphic Tallini on a quest for self," Benji resumed, "it's simply not in the cards. It's not in character, take my word. And your objections to such a pursuit are well taken. From the point of view of vocabulary alone, the Pythia's syntax is disastrous in our day, seeing that we have come to know less and less not only about ourselves, and the self, but about the very notion of knowing. Consider the nineteenth century, how secure we were not only with our process of cognition but also with our being in earthly experience. Now everything is once again up in the air. The possibility of knowing is put in question, and so is the very existence of a self. The best thinking, in my opinion, finds cognized experience a worthy object, and that's where it endeavors to keep the mind. But the mind likes to wander when imposed upon, so it's no easy task.

"I think Tallini is experimenting with an alternative. If the mind has trouble adapting to the experience, then we should adapt the experience to the mind. He chooses and determines an experience that captures his mind entirely. You might say he's obsessed. But obsession often breeds imaginative inventiveness, and I'm convinced there are moments when he *is* the very caveman he is after."

"And I suppose you claim that such behavior characterizes an approach to the inside/outside simultaneity you mentioned earlier?"

"It does indeed, and I appreciate your attentiveness, my friend. I'll also beg you to keep in mind that spatiality was eliminated from our construction and that we are therefore left with a *temporal* simultaneity, which in fact reflects the current everyday experience taking place in our reality—that is, within the limits of the speed of light. This condition obliges us to disregard the time it takes from brain to eye and back to the other who's outside, to disregard that time in our experiences, and therefore to assume a simultaneity whenever we're in contact and communicate, specifically in a visual context. Whatever happens as we sit here in each other's presence, we assume it happens to us simultaneously. It's a practical assumption, and it seems to work. Perhaps we're just unaware of how badly it really works!

"In any case, it no longer satisfies the more astute demands placed upon such notions as knowing or self or the combination of the two. It's the margin of error of the temporal, and it doesn't please the purist. So this persona, who lives in the very same world he wants to know, who *is*, at least in part, the same world he wants to know, this "individual"—misnamed to begin with—invokes a present moment in order to neutralize the temporal: the present moment of experience, unlivable in space but experiential in time, as a live point of contact between past and future. That's the crosshairs of Tallini's sighting, that's where his aim is taking him. We rarely get to speak about such ideas in very precise terms. He used to have trouble coming up with the correct term, although that's changing now. He's a man who has trouble expressing what he doesn't *really* know. But on his path, he'll first have to know *less* before he'll know more.

"No doubt you've heard of beginner's mind. It's an Oriental conceit, and most provocative, borne out in many inventions. The fresh, the pristine gaze can beat volumes of theories. The new, that's what he's after. And how can he see the new if he's not himself new? You'll have to grant him that logic for the sake of his enterprise, Ostheim, even while you scorn my philosophizing.

"You'll also have to grant that whatever we come to know is new, for if it weren't, it would be remembered and not really cognized. A lot of mankind's efforts go into memory, remembering—or better, into not forgetting. That makes for culture, but perhaps it doesn't do all that much for cognition, when you consider that human error is the norm, not the exception. That kind of knowing is a constant correcting and shifting of the old, the learned, the received, with no truly fresh beginning ever. Some say there's a better way. I guess Tallini doesn't want to spend his life learning by heart and then repeating the tune—he wants to improvise. Now there's something I have from the horse's mouth; it's the sort of thing he'll talk about without any problem. He feels he knows all about it, from the music he used to play. With him the contact of inside/outside undergoes a qualitative change.

"Both Goethe and Schiller still occupy themselves with a world, with an environment and nature that exist and are perceived as existing in Newtonian terms. Goethe is already in revolt in his own specialty, the nature of color and light, but he certainly doesn't extend this critique to the substantial and the material. Their physics is still atomized, their matter an indefinite supply of basic building blocks, with a given world that is what it is as perceived by an evident *individual*, a unified self, a concept that has been propped up by equally flawed evidence of an ultimate *atomic* entity, a smallest solid, a point of matter. Once all this is exploded, as it evidently has been for Tallini, what he contacts exists in a different reality, a different outside, and with this ultimate materiality breached, evidences mutate.

"That's essential to Tallini; it's like the air he breathes. No need to be an expert to draw one's own conclusion as to appropriate conduct in the act of knowing. His experience is different because he no longer attempts to contact a materiality, a generality of order, of species, of genre. So if it's not material form we contact out there, not something that already exists as such, then it is wise to examine the senses and what they contribute by their nature, beyond what they all have in common, which is the faculty to contact. They differ elementally in *what* they contact, so that what you see is no longer light but fire, and what you hear no longer noise or sound, or even words, but tone, and therefore overtones and harmony. And so on, to trace all the senses back to the elemental and project a transcendence. Don't you think the earliest people, Tallini's people, are closer to *that* kind of vision than to our conceptualizations? Of course they are! And it's by such originative perception and imaginative mimicry that Tallini intends to join them."

There was a silence during which von Ostheim, armed with a magnifying glass, examined an area of his desk fortuitously uncovered by his shuffling. Benji was accustomed to such activity, and he knew it to detract in no way from his friend's attention to the subject at hand. In fact, he idly fancied that a word, too weighty to complete the flight to Ostheim's ear, might have fallen to the desktop where it was now being minutely inspected.

Von Ostheim took his time to answer. "I wonder," he said at last, "whether your friend Tallini would recognize the image of him that I now have in my mind, based on all you have told me. If not, what good, then, all this information? I don't even know what he *looks* like, except for his hands. Stonemason's hands you called them, as I recall. Hard to know a man when you don't know what he looks like. And I'm curious to what extent this man actually enacts the ideas you are elaborating. In other words, how much is Tallini, and how much is you?"

This concern seemed reasonable to Benji. "There's always an interpretation, I don't deny that. To the contrary, I maintain it's a necessity, and doubly so with Tallini. His letters are cryptic, they're coded, and he has difficulty speaking about what he's after. But I know what he's expecting, and you can wager that when it comes true, it will happen in a cave. A great eolithic renaissance, hitherto overlooked! I don't know what form it will assume, and I don't think he himself has any idea about that—he keeps an open mind, an empty mind—but whatever it is, it'll bring him evidence of a great tradition spurred by the domestication of fire.

"Here's where organized language takes over from the uproar of animal sounds, the barks, grunts, and shouts that must have exercised the larynx into this moment. Before fire, there was no drive toward organization, no possibility of retaining notions, no order, no sequence, no model for it, no history. Now they have light and heat at their command, a giant step. What did they do with this new light? Once in possession of the fire, they recognized it in themselves. Or perhaps it was because they recognized it in themselves that they came into possession of it. Achieving the mastery of it must have made them discover it everywhere.

"It must have been their first generalization, Ostheim. This is all of a sudden very clear to me. Nothing like a bit of dialogue to bring clarity. Of course, they would have recognized the fire that sleeps in things unburned, they would have seen it in everything, notwithstanding the differentiations expressed in the forms. They had discovered a constant. They had discovered. . . ."

By the time Benji left the gallery, dusk had fallen on the city. As always with von Ostheim, he felt it had been a stimulating conversation.

THIRTEEN

COMING TO

When Tallini came to, he was no longer alone. His eyes opened, but save for that flicker of attention, no fiber of his body stirred. His breath was less than faint. Was his heart beating? His consciousness was a flowing liquid. Before, there had been nothing, but "nothing" is already something, though lacking all qualities. The liquidity challenged nothingness to reveal a solid mode of being. He felt himself streaming out of a heavy hardness; he was liquid, just as the rock had liquefied into the spring now trickling out of it. Water and rock are both mineral, one liquid, one solid; these two states join in the mineral so one may issue out of the other. The origin of the liquidity he felt could only be the immobile heaviness of his arms and legs.

The minimal motion of raising his eyelids enabled him to register another liquidity beyond, past the single blade of grass next to his cheek and toward a patch of grass nurtured by the nearby source. In its eager affinity for water, grass was literally growing out of the puddle, which mirrored a liquefied heart in him where nary a breath hovered over the waters. The miniature pool seemed an infinite ocean. His liquid body emerged from the petrified darkness now being vanquished.

At the circus, where the promise of the final attraction had drawn a big crowd, young Piero had told Marpa, already while the lions were jumping through the burning hoops, that he had to pee, but she had never been to a circus before, and in her excitement became totally distracted. Failing him in this dire moment, she told him—barely looking at him, so entranced was she by the Trio Fontanelli on the grand trapeze —she couldn't miss the finale. He kept waiting while more clowns came into the arena, their antics striking him as silly now that he had to go so badly. Then everybody stood up, and he could no longer see anything at all. Just as he went in his pants, there was a big boom, and a great shout of admiring amazement filled the tent. Beyond the human wall that separated him from the arena, a man in red tights, the human cannonball, sailed through the air across the big tent and into a net. While his body dissolved with intense relief, Piero followed in his mind's eye the flight he couldn't see but could imagine, just as the master of ceremonies in black tails and top hat had announced it from the ring.

Seemingly forgotten soon after it happened, that circus incident now relayed the same melting feeling to his receding swoon, easing the burden of solidity. That there should suddenly be this lightness flowing through his mind was in itself a relief, because in that first second of coming to, he had had nothing in mind. He woke up with his head completely empty and his eyes staring at the ground, at the little green pool produced by the trickling source.

But his eyes moved, and their movement enlarged the scene. It now included the tip of a boot, just behind the wet spot, a discovery that should have galvanized him, were it not beyond his present assimilative powers. He focused lazily on the puddle that had become a huge watery eye staring back at him. At times, while photographing, one eye peering through the viewer, he may have experienced similar intimations of this sort of reciprocity with his subject. The current was circulating in the object through him, and it moved again in him from the object, creating the commonality that ensured a visual exchange, and therefore an existence hitherto obtained only by postulation, like a discipline guaranteed. Such postulations—and perhaps such disciplines—seem irrelevant, obsolete to the experience of the visioned and visioning fluidity of the mineral. The certitude of a common existence in a shared volume could be transmitted through the eye's vision, the most exposed, most forward nervous emissary (state-of-the-art "speed of light") and returned, reciprocity hinging on the seeing eye's receptiveness open to temporal flux and reflux, the function of impulse and reaction. The receiver reads the cipher returned by the other, and the circulation back and forth weaves a net of mirrored circuitry.

For Tallini in his coming to, the ultimate reality of this experience lay simply in the certitude of being looked at by an object he held in his attention—the little pool of water. His head was empty, and its very emptiness made it a privileged site where natural affinities could reign without fear of a self-conscious mental activity pregnant with presuppositions, received ideas, hypotheses, and the like. His mind was open, furthermore, to an array of opportunistic thought-forms that might find in his diminished state their chance for expression. He discovered an intrinsic naturalness in this reciprocity of vision with what he perceived. On its end, what the puddle-eye was seeing was this fluidity through him. As concept, it was available solely to a mind, but could in turn be structurally ciphered only by the self-same mindless mineral that constituted the puddle-eye itself.

When the mineral moment is totally dominated by its fluid quality in contradistinction to the solid, there—in that extremity—water flows. Which does not mean to imply that mineral in such a case loses all solid qualities. To the contrary, it retains them more securely, by a transcendental overview, on a more general level. Liquid does not dissolve the solid, it springs from it as the source from the rock, to provide it with superior generality, so that liquidity can come about through a wet participation in the world of the solid. Only then does the latter become the cipher of reality. Liquidity, in constant motion, is a fact of life in the world of time and is therefore essential to the solid cipher. A world of the purely solid, where chronology is lost in duration, is unknowing of this motion. By the emergence of motion through fluidity, the solid turns to its opposite, a cipher of change and thus of time. In this duality within oneness lives the elemental world. This universe, whose etiology resides in a duality contravened, en-globes all elements, allowing sound to be carried in air or supporting the light of fire, which is its visibility, and, in fine, permitting all forms.

All this had lain open in Tallini's empty-minded perception, and he had simply let it be perceived. No rationalizations were elaborated, no conclusions to the effect that if there be earth in all the other elements, then the other elements must all occur in the element earth. Apparent to his present state was such a vision of fire in earth, where the white germ appeared—became visible—like a spark of solar life, after moisture had cracked the seed to tap the liquefied blackness of the putrefying grain. Whiteness was brought forth, the negative side of being without color. The black of putrefaction is the colorless chaos of all colors. While whiteness is extreme color dryness, a breakthrough point by excess on the side of nothingness, blackness is the breakthrough by the fluid motion of all. As the white, out of black, pushes toward its genitor, the golden sun, *all* the colors appear out of the juncture of these extremes, out of unification of all and nothing, of black and white, of dark and light. Carried by air in the space between white light and black earth, the vegetating germ turns green. Before it has lived fully, it will have produced all the colors, aging toward the reddish browns in a return to blackness, toward the next cycle. Its agent is a fluid fire, a mode the dry/hot element discovers during its journey in earth. The fluidity of humid fire circulates between air and earth as sap in water and as respiration in air.

To his vacant mind, it had seemed perfectly natural that the puddle should stare back as he observed it. The more he looked, the more it stared. Given that his vacuity, like all emptiness by nature, was open and susceptible to fulfillment, he was seeing much more than he would have were his head already charged with ideas.

What brought a sudden end to his viewing was something that as such was not visible at all: the fact that he was not alone. What he did make out, the tip of a boot, once seen, had to be deciphered, and this set his mind to work. The tip of a boot, and not just any boot. Cogitation now processed the rough leather, clumsily but intricately tooled and tinted: a homemade boot tramped through Tallini's head. A second look of confirmation followed, and then deductions, conclusions, and eventually actions. Yes, he was no longer alone here; there was another, a booted other. Confining his reaction to the slightest movement of the head, his field of vision now encompassed a very tanned individual in black pants of cheap worn velvet and a fresh white shirt with frayed collar and cuffs. He was sitting immobile on a rock, no more than four or five paces away, a broad-brimmed black hat shading his angular features.

Tallini's convalescent vision, still somewhat blurred, ascertained that this man had never been seen before. The generality of the vision indicated an unwillingness, an incapacity perhaps, to assign its observation to a particular self, a rightful subject, were the proposition enunciated in an active voice: he himself had never seen the man before. Instead, although he had seen and registered the vision, it was easier at this time for him to think that *it had been* seen, and *it had been* registered. This passivity hindered a "responsible response" that would allow identification. Wasn't it the case that he had failed, moments earlier, in just such a challenge from the puddle-eye, when, distracted, he had abandoned a longer, deeper look, giving in to the perennial temptation of seeing more instead of looking better? In his weakened state, and assailed by indecision, he availed himself of the passive voice, adept at accommodating the noncommittal.

In the absence of a visionary self, the activity of seeing was lexically and grammatically impersonalized, with no one asking, Who sees? and with no one held responsible for the vision—the other, in this case the man on the rock, who played the role of objectivity by being seen—and nobody asking, Seen by whom? On whose authority? Although a logical *object* of attention, the stranger, the other, was promoted to syntactical subject of a passive grammatical voice. The epistemological subject, the seeing self, abdicating its visionary primacy, dilutes the act of vision. It need not be specified who does the seeing; anyone could have done it. Another, earlier Tallini might have defended the right to one's selfsame observer, whatever the nature of the object/one's subject under attention. Now, experiencing the absence of a ready-made self, he came to appreciate the impersonal, disinterested view to be obtained through an eye other than the selfsame.

The essence of his present experience—his slowly coming to—lay precisely in nothing being the same, where the accompanying semantic evidence of "nothing," in that case, had to be taken as the only sameness. Nothing being the same, furthermore, by no means implies that everything is different. As with the old/new, so for the same/other. Nothing is all new, nor can it be all other. There is a remainder, unchanged, that measures the new or the other, proportioning it for a fit. This process is a drafting of distinctions. The distinctions of the new and the other depend on the remainder prior to the fact of difference: fully the same, old through and through. This conservative residue can stretch from the narrowly specific to a quasi-universal generality. Clearly, if the "same/old" is of long standing, strongly rooted and in command, the new, the other, will have problems of access. On the other hand, and ideally, the restrictions on newness might be minimal, as when oldness and sameness are restricted to mere three-dimensional appearance or bodily existence in time. With such an unspecified remainder, every event is new, except for the basic commonality of flesh and bones. Within this experiential context, spontaneity in the present moment is the proper gesture.

Tallini had never seen the man before. His empty mind received him impersonally, as it did all else. Since the emptiness had opened to thinking—a thinking that had surprised him—Tallini was following a strong bent for generalizing, for seeing things impersonally. Because he had never seen this man before, it was plausible no one else had either. This was certainly true of this particular soggy spot in the dry and rocky wilderness, where he could safely have wagered that this stranger had encountered no third party. But the generalizing trend held here also, for he felt it to be true in the world, in the cosmos—the man had been seen only by himself. He had, after all, not been there before. Or should he perhaps think that the man *had* been there before? Before what? The man was sitting on a rock, near the wet place created by the source, with the wooded rise in the terrain behind casting a thin and spotty shadow over him.

Tallini didn't even have time to wonder who he was, for the man, who had been watching him, spoke. *"Soy Angelo,"* he said, *"para servirle a usted, señor.* I work at the smithy in town, sometimes. Perhaps you never noticed me, but I know who you are and I know why you wander around in these hills. It is not safe. You are foreign here, *señor,* you don't see the dangers."

Tallini tried to fathom the implications of what he was hearing, but he sank back into an indifference close to the unconsciousness so recently overcome. He had two distinct sensations, however: the vibrancy of the man's voice and the dull throbbing headache that was sending platoons of boots thumping through his skull. Yet the headache was not responsible for his mind's uncharacteristic slovenliness. A conceit —more sense than idea—that filled his empty opening mind had been evolving while he was regaining consciousness. The visual feeling of a blade of grass was at once nothing yet space enough to accommodate the entire physical world. Tallini felt an animal urge to settle back, with a sigh of relief, into the comfort of well worn fits and patterns, sensorial, cerebral, and emotional, which were crystallizing around a familiar entity remembered in detail from beyond the blackness. He had always known this entity, and although it evolved in time, in step with the world's universal genesis, it has remained the *same,* a continuity that has an ontogenic beginning and a phylogenic past. As such, it has been recognized by the *self.* Recognition presumes a symbolization, a language, a logic; and it is linguistically that a first-person singular is awarded her "I" as if a diploma. Now she's on her own. With the gift of the mind's "I," she will have to make up her own.

On the impersonal agenda of coming to, of coming back to himself as a *former* self, the vision of the puddle-eye was a first hitch, and a decisive one. Eccentricities of this nature are unacceptable to a process whose exclusive drive is the desire to revisit well-worn and rigorous automatisms. The puddle event had no standing in the bureaucracy of circuits processing his recovery. Could Tallini's indifference to recuperation have signaled his guarded reaction to that particular "old" point of view but not to a more general vista that might include the "new"? What conjured the naysayer at this juncture, when all systems were primed for coming to within a familiar consciousness, back to everyday life? Was it resistance to the yoke of automatisms and a break with the unexamined hand-me-downs of habit, so that the spirit's agent might have its day? Or was it simply a failure of the will in the face of the difficulties of the everyday, a dread of strife and competition? Tallini was in no condition either to pose or to answer such questions, but the stranger, who had sat there unmoving during Tallini's long silence, might well have wondered what was detaining the manifestly conscious patient in a mute reticence. He offered his diagnosis. "Too much sun, *señor*, that was the problem. Too much heat in the head. *Insolación*, a sunstroke. It is a good thing you were not alone."

Tallini was only vaguely startled to hear he had not been alone. He had assumed that at the moment of blackout, during that inspired dance of his, he *was* alone. In the past, he would certainly have been disturbed by such a contradiction and would have tried to resolve it by proving one side wrong and the other one right. Now, however, he did no more than silently note it as an event in itself. The situation was manifestly out of the ordinary, without an etiquette to dictate a procedure. In such an extraordinary ambiance, contradiction might well be a norm. For each other, the participants in the event would have the opportunity to be themselves as well as the other. Whom to observe, to assimilate, if not the other? But the other is also a self, so it too is both self and other. Such are the conditions on this isolated stage, with the authors/actors their own sole spectators. No motivation entered here for playing anything but oneself; yet conversely, the other is unavoidable. Was this why the critical appraisal of self and other became so urgent?

Beyond that, there was nothing special about the encounter with this very civil fellow, distinctly Gypsy, who evidently knew a thing or two not only about Tallini's recent past but also about life in the sun, life among rocks. Here was someone who was infinitely closer to this terrain to which Tallini—as he suddenly realized with a pang—felt he had staked a claim, and to which, through its earliest inhabitants, he felt he had a commitment. The other, this Angelo, was certainly not someone to dance naked in the subtropical midday sun, even at this late season. Though rough-looking, he was polite, reserved, and soft-spoken. There was no reason he could not just have passed by at the moment of Tallini's dance. What was remarkable about the situation was not *what* had happened—common enough, to all appearances— but its happening *at all*, happening here, at these obscure coordinates. Somehow, this conundrum was not eased by the apprehension that if the man was *there* at a specific moment, it was because he had been *around* all along.

Tallini was surprised by his lack of reaction to the thought that the fellow was following him, observing him. Under any other circumstance, Tallini would certainly not have hesitated to vent furious displeasure at having been tailed. Without his having been aware of it, an eye had been fixed upon him, an eye he had never seen, never felt. Even now, the man's eyes were invisible in the shade of his wide-brimmed black hat. Tallini was entitled to expect a healthy pair of eyes in that tenebrous brow, but that discovery would hardly be comparable to the revelation of a vision through the puddle-eye. If he was able to see a puddle-eye seeing him, what, then, would be the status of this eye behind the brim, an eye he *couldn't* see? There was no doubt in his mind that the look of the puddle depended on his seeing it. Was this Angelo fellow's look from behind the brim equally empowered by Tallini's sight of him?

Then Tallini noticed he lay in the shade, under some cover, under an improvised structure of bamboo covered with

259

cloth. Where had it come from? He lay there, waiting for the throbbing in his head to subside. He wondered what Benji would think about what was happening. To think anything about it at all, Benji would have to have been lying here where Tallini was lying, with a perfect stranger a few paces away observing him with unseen eyes. That would never happen, of course. What was happening, however, was that Tallini was experiencing an unusually vague grasp of his own person, and this insecurity somehow translated into an equally unusual level of empathy with his absent friend.

Then Tallini suddenly sniffed a vivid odor he could not identify until he moved his head once again, ever so carefully, and found not only that the headache was subsiding but that his head was resting on a thick and well-worn pigskin jacket, which could only belong to the stranger. The old leather and the sweaty wear and tear of it was giving off olfactory signals. At metabolic and instinctive levels, they were hugely stimulating, offering him an animal energy he lacked. It was an odor of primary-primitive activity, the smell of the human animal. Close to the natural fact, the odor seemed to fuel in him metamorphic capacities of which he had been unaware, and which perhaps had never even existed before his dance in the sunlight. It seemed like another extension of the dimension that gave him the puddle-eye, the visual exchange of form and liquidity, a partnership of solid matter and fluid time, and the flow that chronicles the self through the "I" of the observer.

This lively circularity was new to him and brought to mind the lessons of the old, the now, and the new. But his woozy mind still refused rational action. His entire body, coming to, reborn in a sense, assembled as one in his mind, revealing a range of faculties akin to what futurists dream about when they write of telepresence. Not that Benji would have "appeared" to him, both of them having "materialized" at a table at *Chez l'Alsacien*. No, Tallini's experience was not fantastic, and it was at once simpler than a mechanical feat of remote control and infinitely more complex. Telepresence is but the next logical step in a technology that has already produced the sequence: telegraph, telephone, television. It would be, perhaps, a crowning testimony to a particular interpretation of such concepts as space, time, world, life, and meaning. Tallini had experienced nothing of the dizzying electronic networks that would produce this technological wonder. Its simplicity lay not only in interpretation, not only in language—*"it is the tool par excellence of multiplicity. In any case, the idea of telepresence is as old as the act of creation, and you can follow its success in myth and in folklore. Certainly if a deity created the cosmos, it did so as a telepresence of itself, for itself, as it itself continues to exist, according to theologians, and despite Nietzsche's talented exploitation of the proposition that 'God is dead.' I presume one never hears, in reputable theological quarters, that God became the world, does one? I don't really know, but it seems unlikely. As you are aware, I'm not very versed in this domain. But Zeus certainly was a great abuser of telepresence, producing himself at considerable distance from Olympus, halfway to Hades in fact, in places such as the pond at the bottom of Leda's garden or in Danae's boudoir, where all that gold could be readily caught in the bedsheets. Not to speak of the bull and Europa, a terrifying aggression that was bound to leave grave geographical traumas. The bull's reward for the prestation of his form is a cool celestial abode, while the wronged Phoenician princess for all indemnity receives an earthly continent where her particular violation becomes endemic in generalized violence. So much for divine justice in the eyes of some ancestors. But let's take a second look at these metamorphoses, into Zeus's zoo and his treasury of precious metals. Are these not his emissaries, just as his light and lightning are? Mind you, when it suited his purposes, Zeus was not adverse to traveling. We know of a sojourn in Ethiopia, for instance, where he was especially pleased with the local sacrificial offerings. But when it comes to projecting his powers, to dubious effect, among unsuspecting mortals on earth, he often chooses not to leave his habitat. By mimicry and metamorphosis, he makes his appearance without leaving Olympus, as bull, as swan, as*

261

golden shower. In this telepresence of Zeus, the quick changes are no more symbols than is the robot on the other end of our line, the dummy that will lead our life for us, act for us, and some say, think for us. I will not bother to comment any further—you know how I feel about such developments—from a point of view of syntactique . . ."—but in an experience that possessed a *corpo-reality.*

It was Benji speaking, and Tallini hearing and understanding. His responsive reception completed the other's statement, made it whole by a final overview the creative speaker could not make. Improvising, never quoting without referring, never reciting by heart unless performing, nor repeating by ear the oft said and heard, the creative speaker at no single moment holds the idea-as-a-whole, not even in a sentence. Understood as a whole, the enunciation belongs to the receiver who can keep an open, empty mind during the flow of language, applying himself solely to the quantitative relations that persist in that open emptiness, through interior and exterior auditory functions. This allows mind to apply itself uniquely and exclusively to a syntactical relating of subordinate components—discursive and contextual—as foundation for the emerging idea, the qualitative elemental relation.

● ● ○ ○ ● ●

Tallini was torn away from this unusual tête-à-tête by a presence very close to him. There was no doubt Benji had been speaking; the sound of his voice was still in Tallini's ear. It was Benji in Paris, the context they had in common. But now, the presence he was feeling was not Benji but Angelo. He saw the stranger, but as yet his most sensitive attention was occupied by the pigskin jacket, the odor of which was for certain not entirely attributable to Angelo. Nevertheless, he did relate it to him and not to the pig, true creator of the garment.

Angelo now moved one or two paces toward him, indicating his intention to come closer, and a more obscure desire as well—unconcealed, but coded—to keep a certain distance.

Tallini had known Andalusians, *gitanos* in particular; the gesture was not lost on him. There remained a political distance that would have to be reduced by paraphrastic dialogue and further gestures, advances, retreats verbal and physical, until the distance became personal and therefore adjustable in time and by actions. After the two paces, Tallini knew he wouldn't have time for these conventions. Reading the signs of this particular mind-set in—if not *into*—the man's comportment helped to put Tallini at ease, boosting his confidence in the self that had turned so volatile since it became subject to the "I" of the observer. What was it the man had said?

Tallini's earlier indifference seemed already to belong to a different time, when the black and blank heaviness still weighed down his physical body. During this moment of lesser consciousness, increased gravity must have affected this indifference. There had been only an absolute blackness, one remove from deep sleep, into which everything had disappeared. This emptiness persisted in the recovering consciousness as an inner silence he had not yet managed to break. Perhaps this indifference, so unusual for him, had simply been his physical debility in the absence of an intellectual or even moral grasp of the situation at hand. Perhaps it was an instinctive, proprietary reaction of having been there first, for instance, and perceiving the other as intruder, whatever his actual intentions. He never considered that the other, fully and uninterruptedly conscious, could very well assume the role of host, to greet him heartily as he came to—metaphorically, to welcome him home. It was, however, much more the Gypsy's home than Tallini's. The Gypsy could claim primacy on chthonic grounds, on counts of both fact and consciousness. Perhaps a measure of embarrassment hid behind Tallini's naïve and misplaced territoriality. There could be no doubt that the stranger had observed him for some time before he fainted. Perhaps he had been the secret companion of *all* his expeditions. What could this man have made of what he saw? A nap in the shifting shade of a boulder? A wild nude dance around some vegetation to the tune of a gurgling spring?

Just before the turn of his head allowed a full face view of the stranger, Tallini, at last, *heard* what the latter was *saying.* He not only comprehended what was articulated, but marveled at the unique ways the lexical sounds were falling together meaningfully. Uncertain of sense though they were in places, meaning yet was conveyed by them as it is by a signing gesture for the deaf. And there was meaning in the man's paces as he moved toward Tallini. Moments of meaning appear, then disappear, and yet they remain active, with the one meaning transcending the many instantaneities. So in language: at the end of the phrase, the one meaning transcends the many sounds. There is a pattern in both cases, and Tallini followed its temporalities. The miracle was that he *understood.* What he had always taken for granted—light, sound, sense, language, the fact as such—now demanded his overt participation. He had to voice and act meanings.

A hierarchy of evidence, determining the horizon within which the play is sustained, also contributes to the complex environmental network upon which the action builds, providing the background that sets it in relief, or the circuitry from which it emerges. Therefore the play is deeply affected by changes in the nature and thresholds of the evidential, and such changes demand corresponding inscriptions and alterations in the script. The evidence of sunset and sunrise long sustained a coherent cosmology that only very slowly surrendered to heliocentricity, considered a higher level in the evidential hierarchy. Much of the same can be shown for the evidence of matter in physics.

Once doubt corrodes it, evidence becomes topical. The imposture is doomed and will be revealed; it loses its invisibility. The now visibly falsified "evidence" is captured in a syntax or a computation to join the fate of other hypotheses. It will be subjected to a multitude of possible propositions and calculations, free, like any other conceptual entity in the general linguistic ensemble, to influence the scene by its opinion, to vie for themes that might promote it, perhaps to change existing themes and propose new variations—in a word, to assay various visions. On this level, the determinations of yet another, a new invisible evidence, remain unnoticed. The history of science represents such a chain of successive evidence—in modern times principally attained through developments in instrumentation. Benji sometimes referred to Plato's cave, where evidential reality could dissolve into shadow when the true light-source is faced.

Tallini's case was somewhat different. His turn was out of darkness toward light, whereas the Hellenic descent goes from light to light—as Tallini had gone, before he had known the empty darkness now turning to clarity. Going from light to light implies an actor, an acting self that is pure evidence, invisibility at a hierarchical acme. But there can never be a self emerging from dark emptiness. There can only be an opening to the new, to the never-before. That nothing comes from nothing is yet another evidence firmly entrenched on the path from light to light, but everything that now came to Tallini came out of nothing. Not that it did not contain karmic elements, but they fell together in a new way, illuminated by a different light—not a light of brighter *reality*, as in the move from light to light, but a light of *being*, creating a *mise en scène* that included *his own body*.

Certainly this was not of his own doing. It couldn't be, as the evidence of "his own" was in the process of being corroded. An openness had been produced by the blackout, through the disjunction with a past. He was in a turn, like the one required of Plato's deluded shadow-watchers if they are to gain fuller understanding. They turn from a light taken for granted, however, one that fits shadows into evidence. For the invisibility of the light, shadows come to express reality. That light of invisibility in itself, as such, was what Tallini pursued, Benji thought; it was the ultimate aim of his endeavor. First focused by photography into a rhetoric on qualitative facts, his striving was approaching a privately experienced ontology. The last push would require a cave that could become his athanor to fire up a personal vision the likes of which had never before been seen.

As the Gypsy tilted his hat back and Tallini turned toward his gaze, Benji's voice in his ear proffered analytical considerations: *"The idea of 'the seeing eye' is a metonymic substitution of tool for opus, you will admit. The opus is the vision accomplished, the tool is the means."*

But now, the impending eye contact added yet another sensory region to Tallini's synesthetic crossroads: a feel of cloth against his skin, registering his being fully dressed, when it was stark-naked that he went into the dark! Of this circumstance he was fairly certain, though consciousness *had* been interrupted in this peculiar manner he was only now getting to know—to wit, that the one who passed out was no longer the one who came to. All he could conjure up was a lame "last thing I remember." The other matter, by contrast, had at this instant become undeniable fact—he woke up fully clothed. It was easy to conclude that the stranger had helped him into his clothes, although not a shred of this remained in his memory.

Once he might have minded being thus manipulated by a stranger, but not this time. Indifference had turned to trust. With Angelo, he had been in good hands from the beginning, even if there remained no consciousness to confirm the fact. As far as the words were concerned, he had caught the name and registered the proposed explanation of his physical condition. Everything else had been lost, for his attention was totally absorbed by the Gypsy's extraordinary first-person singular assertions: "I know who . . .", "I know why . . .", which were more than Tallini could have said for himself at that moment. What, in fact, *was* he doing here? And why? Had he ever confronted the questions to which this stranger claimed answers?

Their eyes met in a powerful visual lock, revealing the full force of the query, a near-mystical "who" and "why" more searching than any technical "how" or pragmatic "what-for" could ever have been.

"After all, the eye is a controlled transparency to light, a translucency, and literally, it is not the eye that sees. And that unseeing membrane beween the two polar sources of

light, inside and out, is put under great stress and assumes tremendous stature when eye contact is maintained, which is a unique moment of vision."

Angelo's eyes were sad and patient, demonstrating what Benji's voice was saying. They were expressing the importance of the event as eyes best can, and only can when gazing into another's.

"Now the eye no longer filters another's reflection, but clarifies its own vision in a direct return of the other's light. Beyond the sustaining of the gaze, there is no representation in this case, though the effect of symmetry peculiar to the horizontal mirror image is obeyed: in sustained eye contact, a right eye gazes into a left, and vice versa. This is no trivial occurrence, not with what is known about left and right and their difference. What can be said for certain is that when the other looks back, there is a complementation."

Angelo's eyes were saying that this entity they belonged to, which the other didn't know, this Angelo, if it was to be here at all, was here in order to look into your eyes. "For I know who you are and I know why you wander around in these hills."

◗ ◖ ○ ○ ◐ ◑

By the time Tallini was on his feet, he was certain this ocular exchange had marked a serious commitment to something other than himself. It had betokened a decisive step toward his goal in these hills. The newness of this silent gesture, its otherness, displaced all prior associations into different terms: contract, trust, pledge, friendship, love, and so forth, some of which might contribute to, but none embrace the totality implied in the wordless barter. No doubt this feeling of wholeness was furthered because of the impersonality of the engagement, clearly not a compact between him and the carrier of the link, the Gypsy. Nor was there any hesitation or calculation, as had mostly marked earlier commitments, in terms of affection, responsibility, sacrifice, compromise, or even profit.

This openness between them was in no way disquieting. It removed the limitations that had so frequently proved fatal in other relationships. His intention, he was slowly realizing, was not toward his human peers or anything concrete, not toward an abstraction or an idea, but toward an activity— rather, toward acts. This *commitment* fully expressed a sense of bringing together, without specifying the participants. Until recently, the concept of work—in contrast to making a living—had been the impetus of his enterprises. But contact with the cave people, from the beginning, had little by little displaced "work" with a notion of "mission," which now found its proper context in terms of this new and profound engagement. This entire complex was epitomized for him in the evidence that he was no longer alone.

Standing up had been somewhat arduous. When Angelo interrupted their shared gaze, breaking the circuit, fatigue once more settled upon Tallini, his heavy eyelids closing on a lingering still of Angelo shifting his hat, so that the broad brim shaded his eyes again in a harlequin mask. It was Tallini's first exposure to the quick and precise maneuver he would come to know as part of the man's presentation of himself. He had an uncanny ingenuity for finding even the least bit of shade where cover was scarce, at the same time ensuring that he saw more of others than they saw of him.

"It would be good to get on your feet, *señor*, it is bad to go to sleep now," he urged. The admonition spurred Tallini to make another effort to stay upright. The Gypsy kept his distance, making no move to help. Tallini's head was still throbbing and every fiber of his body resisted, but he managed. From this physical effort came a deeper understanding of his *no longer* being alone, an awareness of companionship. Finding himself in the Gypsy's company conveyed a broader application of fellowship than what might be implied by his actual physical presence. Tallini had never thought of himself as being solitary, but this encounter so amplified his sense of communion that it seemed to dwarf previous relationships. Even loves, perhaps. He had never closely scrutinized such associations, as he considered them a by-product of living. He didn't miss them at times when they were rare, nor did he refuse them when they offered themselves. In neither case did he ever desire them or seek them out.

But this encounter would make him realize his past loneliness within professional circles, in the Paris rhetoric, and—notwithstanding Benji's friendship, where an abstractive distance remained—even in his ideas. Intense relationships were not unknown to Tallini. He had lived them in the field as a young man, under fire in Zaragoza and along the Ebro. At that time, the depth of life claimed by such profound bonds was manifested through the abysmal, unfathomable proximity of death, an ever-present third at the killing game. Similarly, every serious twosome eventually produces its third entity, a mutually conjured witness belonging to neither one nor the other but subsuming both. Engendered as it is by both parties to the association, it is thus fashioned by their every thought, word, and gesture. Without it, the relationship drifts into banality. Only rarely is this third created along with the incipient partnership, as it may be when life itself is at stake and death is hovering. But in this encounter it was given, and Tallini recognized its arcane value.

When he finally stood facing the Gypsy, he could think of nothing to say but *"Gracias, Angelo."*

"Por nada, señor," the other replied. "Why don't you take my place in the shade—your legs are shaking." And he pointed to the spot where he had been sitting, the only shade in sight except for the bamboo structure Tallini had just left. "I'm being paid to watch you, and I believe that includes watching over you, when necessary. Do not be upset, I am not one of them. It is an easy way to make some money, to work for them. I will tell them whatever you like."

As Tallini recovered, he said he preferred to move around. His headache had abated, and he was glad to be where he was, and to be alive. The man's connection with the *Guardia Civil* didn't disturb him in the least. There was something so marvelously real about him that Tallini trusted him without hesitation. As things stood in this country, anyone who worked, worked for the *Guardia,* in some way or other.

"*Con permiso, señor,* I'm not paid to tell you what to do, but if you want to risk your life in places where no one dares to walk, I shall try to stop you. The last time I was too far away and you were already on that dangerous slope. It was better to let you proceed and not to startle you. But now that we have met, I will stay closer. There was a perfectly good path a little higher up to get where you were going."

Tallini did not feel he had to explain he was going nowhere. He didn't quite know how much the Gypsy would understand, although he had an inkling it might indeed be a lot. Would he understand that another voice besides his own had been and was addressing him? Tallini knew full well, of course, that only the Gypsy's voice was modulating sound waves, but nothing could dissuade him he was also hearing Benji just as clearly. His doubts about his identity applied to his location as well, and he finally asked the question de rigueur: "Where am I?"

There could be no question that the loquacious Benji was speaking at *Chez l'Alsacien,* the only place shared by Tallini and Benji. The Gypsy's few words, although they didn't *say* much, seemed to *mean* a great deal, more perhaps than Benji's, which were by far more plentiful. Both strongly vied for his attention. He was torn between the two sites, in a manner that took no account of the actual setting of his physical body. It suddenly seemed natural to him that his body should provide the means for a dialogue with Benji in Paris while standing here on a Spanish rock. This had to exist, just as the inner volume of the boulder existed, after the passage through the plane. Back then, his mind had fitted his three-dimensional sensorium, as consciousness, into that plane like a drop of ink fits its spot on a blotter. And now as he evoked it, it demonstrated to him the mind's bidimensionality. A similar perfection of fit is not to be achieved in three dimensions, where the fit is always imperfect.

"*In the plane the mind is master. Look at geometry, the perfection of the theorem on the paper! A universe perfectly defined. This is where the mind has certainty, in a written language, in number, in a syntactique. For the volume, no definition has yet been found, at least none that isn't imme-diately tied down and reduced by a writing, by a calculation, to an inscription onto the plane. No, the volume has to be experienced in the round, and that can be done only by the body.''*

Tallini was unsure whether he was hearing or sensing, so much did these words complement his experience. Revisiting the boulder had been a desire, but he knew there was no way back. Now a new understanding seemed to crown the experience and send him onward. The plane surface had even-tually impelled him into a puncticular dimensional unity, but his need now was for polydimensionality, the opposite direction. But where was the tridimensional surface that could act as skin of that higher dimension, an agent of contact that would be the gateway to the ultimate other, who would have to be comprehended without even a trace of commonal-ity? He knew in advance there was no finding, yet the search remained. He had been through it with himself a thousand times, in another life, before the blackness. If it counted *there*, how much more here! Was he wrong to shed the indifference? Was this not a transition from dark to light?

He walked and stretched and felt his body come back to normal. He saw his musette bag and suddenly felt hungry. Angelo approached and offered him his *bota*. "I usually keep wine in it, but for up here, I fill it with water." Tallini drank some water from the wineskin, then he drank some more. He sat down under his shelter and took out one of Giorgio's sandwiches. The Gypsy returned to his shady spot and, rolling a cigarette, began to talk.

"I come from a family of dancers, but I myself was not allowed to dance. This was because of Tio Ortiz. I called him *tio*, but he was no relative. He took care of me when my parents were killed; he was my *compadre*. He used to spend a lot of time with me and talked about our people. He was the wisest man in the family, and I was closest to him. He pre-pared me for my life. I became his disciple, and he didn't want me to dance. He said I would either be very good, or no good. If I was no good, I'd be like all the others, so what for? But if I

271

was very good, I would soon be dancing in nightclubs and be seduced by the stupid life of the *señoritos*. If I *had* to work, he said, it was better to work hard with my hands instead of trading burros and cheating people. Work with metal and fire, he said, and so he made me an apprentice at the smithy. There one learns something, he said, and now I think so too. But I don't work regularly. And I have a business of my own, jewelry. We used to go to the fairs; the others danced and sang, and I sold gold work and stones. Opals and amethysts, and sometimes an emerald, no questions asked.

"Then there are other duties, and they have to do with being in these hills. The *Guardia*, they sent me up here to spy on you, and they don't even know I live here! They are afraid of these hills, the Spanish. They tell stories about the hills, about people disappearing, about ghosts—none of it true. Our people once knew these hills, but only I alone am left, and now nobody knows I live here. Oh, not that I have my wife and children up here. No, I rent a little house in town, of course, next to the last house on Calle Caraveo. But my life is up here, and I spend as much time here as I can. Now all my people have gone off in all directions, and I have stayed alone. *Señor*, I ask you, is that a life? My wife, Faraona, especially is lonely for her people. They went north because they have a boy, very smart. They say he will go to a big school. Tell me, *señor*, what would life be without such dreams?

"But about Tio Ortiz—they called him '*Brujo*,' a sorcerer, which is not a bad thing to be called, with us. *Brujos* have a very quiet power, something the Spanish do not understand. He had knowledge of medicine. Everyone knew he had a secret in these hills, a secret that had been passed on from generation to generation. Yes, I'm a fortunate man, *señor*, and not only because of my wife and two little boys. I also have these hills and their secret, told to me by Tio Ortiz. Now I will tell you all he told me. You see, *señor*, my family is dispersed because they came to feel that the old traditions and the old ways are no longer called for. With so many people everywhere, there is no longer room to be apart and free. It becomes too difficult, my family thinks, it becomes impossible to be a *gitano*, and they end up in cities, working as waiters or maids.

"But now it is my turn to break the old rules and traditions. Until now what I will tell you could only be told inside the family. You see, *señor*, at one time the family was very large, and one could always find someone to carry the secret, and so the secret remained among the people. There is a rule, a law you might say, but not like *your* laws. Only two people at the same time know the secret, the one who has been given the secret and the one who gave it. The rule is that you have to give the secret to someone who will understand its value. You can see that it is difficult to find such a man—to make sure he understands, one has to tell him what it is, and once he's been told the secret, it's done, he carries it. And if it turns out he doesn't understand, such unfortunate errors of judgment have brought the people close to ruin. And you might ask, *señor*, and wonder if perhaps Tio Ortiz and I have not understood the secret, because the family has gone so bad during our service as *brujos*. You can see that I bear a great responsibility. Not that anyone reproaches me. Those who don't know have very little concern about things like this.

"Of course such dispersions have happened before in our history, and then in better times we come together, finding each other again. Always we come back here. The way things were going once Tio Ortiz left us, it was important that I should give the secret, but there was nobody in the small group, nobody, and finally they all moved away. It was a constant worry for me. Some may even have thought that I kept the secret for myself, a sure sign of not understanding, wanting to keep the *brujería* for oneself. But I found no one left to carry the secret, no one who could understand. I would have recognized him. Tio Ortiz taught me to distinguish people, and when you have learned that, then you can be chosen and become *brujo* yourself. But the only way to know that one is a true *brujo* is to choose correctly the next carrier of the secret. You see that it is complicated, and questions about how a secret can be kept and how people can be distinguished were the principal teachings with Tio Ortiz. It is important to our life, we Zincali, such questions.

"I pondered many years, without solution, and then you arrived. At first I paid not much attention, but everybody in the village was talking about your trips in the hills. And when I looked at you one day in the street, I was sure there was more. Perhaps I recognized you already the first time, but of course I thought it was impossible, you were not family. And then I understood who you were. I recognized you, and realized that a great change had to come, for a new time. The secret is no longer needed by the family; now it is needed by *you*. That is why I told you I know who you are. Although you were a foreigner, I knew I could make you part of the family. I would adopt you. Well, it is done, and very easy to achieve as I am the only law left in these hills.

"When I heard you were looking for a cave, I knew I was correct. The secret *is* a cave, *señor*, and you don't need to find it. We have already found it. It was found by the first *brujo*, and finding it was what made him a *brujo*. You must understand that this is not a cave like the others that were found in the hills. Of course we knew those other caves too, but they had nothing special. They were used much later, when a lot had already been forgotten. So we allowed them to be discovered. Do the authorities really think they could find something in these hills we have not already found? What they find is what we want them to find, so perhaps they stop looking. But the secret cave they will not find, as long as there is a *brujo* to protect it.

"But now times are different, and my people know none of this. They do not know why they move away. They find reasons, they make up reasons. But I know why. The hills don't need them anymore; the secret cave needs a different kind of guardian. I hope you see what I mean, *señor*. Perhaps my words are not well chosen, but I know them in our language, and there are special words. So for the first time, this is all being said in another language, in Spanish, not even Andaluz, but in a *payo* language. I know my people would think I have gone *loco* to do this, but they do not understand.

I now know why Tio Ortiz chose me to carry the secret, what it was he saw in me. It was the ability to do this which is against the law, but do it to show that the law has become too weak, too limited. And with this I have confirmed to myself that I am a *brujo*, for I have done the impossible—to make the law stronger by breaking it."

The Gypsy stopped, much to Tallini's regret. He could have sat there for the rest of the day, listening to this remarkable tale. That he was a major part of this story, that in fact the entire story was but the historical background to his entry into action, was very clear to him, and it felt perfectly natural it should be so. It was a changed world he was living in now, and it suited him. Another part of the riddle had unwound with every twist of the Gypsy's discourse, at the end of which, full stop, here he was, Piero Tallini himself. For the first time in his life, he felt he was the right man at the right place and time. But of all the words the Gypsy spoke, only one stood out: the *cave*, and with it the absolute conviction that this was "his" cave. It was the cave he had been looking for.

'What is different about *this* cave?" he wanted to know.

"That is what you must find out, what you will find out, because I have distinguished you as the man in the legend, the last, *el último brujo*. The *brujos* know this cave is different, and whenever there were two, they have sat in it together to recognize this difference. And they have talked to each other about the difference, making up words to talk about it. You must know, *señor*, I am the first *brujo* who can write a little, although I am very slow. But it is difficult to write when it is not clear what is to be written. Until now it was enough just to distinguish the difference, what makes the cave different.

"Oh, there have been some who wanted to do more, like Paco, *Él del Tambor*, a famous *brujo* many years ago, but still remembered in the words, because he was *loco*, like a saint. Paco started to say that if it was different, then it was no longer a cave, and it would have to be called something else before they could say anything about it. That was the way it was different, he told his partner, who told the next one and

275

so on, down to me telling you. No one ever paid much attention to Paco's talk, but what he said about that was one of the things Tio Ortiz told me, things that had come down to him. Another said it was the chapel of a black virgin who had given birth to Balthazar, *el niño más negro,* the first king of the Gypsies. But these are stories from another time, they are not for our time—that was the conclusion of Tio Ortiz and his companion. They concluded that the secret is contained in the cave.

"There is nothing in the cave, you understand, *señor,* only stones, and nothing has ever been touched. That is the order that has come down, nothing must be touched. But it is there, you cannot miss it if you sit down on the stone and listen. Yes, all the *brujos* hear it and know it is there. But none has been able to say what it is, *señor,* and I am no exception. *You, señor,* I'm convinced, you will hear and you will also be able to say—though not to me, who knows but need not say. All the *brujos* have just been the keepers of this, until the moment comes when the *último brujo* is discovered. And I have discovered you, *señor,* and as you are the last, you will need no companion. I shall be leaving for the North, after I have instructed you here."

"And the cave, where. . . ."

"Not today," said Angelo. "I can see you are again strong on your legs. The sun is already low, and the nights are cold up here. You must return to the village. You must not stay up here until I have shown you the cave."

And without another word, he picked up his pigskin jacket and started downward, leaving Tallini no choice but to grab his musette bag and follow.

FOURTEEN

ACQUAINTANCES

The Gypsy knew his way around those hills, and his path down was much more direct than Tallini's usual route. There was no visible trail, and no one but Angelo had gone this way in recent years. The highway was entirely eliminated from this itinerary, which ended in the backyard of a small property. Some sheep were penned next to a modest stone structure, neither house nor barn and probably both in one. Someone was sitting on a stool next to the house, picking a guitar. When he saw the two men approaching, he stood up, still holding the instrument. Angelo made a vague gesture of greeting, but didn't say a word. The other just stood there. Neither man spoke.

When Tallini joined them, he was introduced as *Pedro el Italiano*. The man's name was Pepe, and he was the brother of Antonio, the town's taxi driver. The brothers owned the property and raised those sheep. They also sold goat's milk, Angelo explained. Pepe said nothing at all, but grinned in agreement with everything he heard. Then Angelo explained to him that *Pedro el Italiano* would be using the path. The man nodded. He barely looked at the stranger, but with a glance that would never forget. Angelo turned toward Tallini: "Take only this path. We don't like to make new trails. There is nothing up there for *payos;* why make another trail? Pepe doesn't mind anyone crossing his property to use this one, as long as I've introduced him." He gave a dry laugh. The guitar player nodded, waving them on when they left.

Tallini and Angelo soon arrived at the edge of the cobble-stoned village, with its whitewashed façades and red geraniums spilling from black-grilled windows. They walked toward Angelo's house on the Calle Caraveo, and just before reaching the doorway, Angelo said, "I will not be in the hills tomorrow, for sure. And I don't know about the day after. But on the third day from today, it will be new moon, so we can see the stars. Go up the way we just came down. I will definitely be there, and I will find you if you don't find me. *Y que vaya con Dios.*" With that he turned away, took a few long paces, opened his door, and was gone. "He had to stoop to enter," Tallini noted to himself as he continued on toward Giorgio's *posada.*

A sudden confusion overtook him, his head empty again for a moment, as it had been when he first recovered consciousness. He wondered, "Is that what happened, I lost consciousness and then regained it? Who lost what, and what was regained by whom?" He certainly did not regain what he had lost, not he who was now walking toward his hotel along the Calle Caraveo. Hadn't Angelo just told him who he was? And was he really the one Angelo had described, the one who came at the end of a line of vagabonds, street peddlers of mythopoietic bent, into whose ceremonial grounds he had stumbled? But in the one Angelo had addressed, something was saying "I am Piero. If anyone, it's I, Piero." And suddenly the "I" to which he was subjecting himself lost meaning. He had been totally absent from it in his swoon, and as he reentered consciousness, the witness to his dancing never gave him time to recover it. His body recovered—the nerves, muscles, blood, and bones. But the Gypsy had given him no opportunity to reintegrate all he was to himself: "I." His senses awoke to the puddle-eye, and exercised themselves on the tip of an ornate boot, allowing its occupant to take command, but they gave *him* no chance to settle back into his self. He had to concede his return to that former self was being foiled by whatever had slipped in at the juncture of his absence/

presence, between old and new, and had driven a wedge at a vulnerable point of rational contiguity, akin to the scission between wakefulness and sleep.

Now the old, the returning self, seemed an unknown masquerading. True, there had been a reanimation, a reestablishment of something interrupted. That much was familiar and essentially unchanged, the hiatus counting for very little, if not for nothing—a mere blip in a continuity. All else, however, was new, and here the breach was immense. The new was interruption itself, it arrested the old and rent the continuity. Who had reasoned that the new had to retain a part of the old, if only for purposes of recognition? Evidence or *petitio principii*? Everything was new, save what could be reanimated. What was reanimated *remained* old; the new was animation itself. Interruption can never be excised from a chronology, which is the logic of the old. The new *exists* by interruption, the event of the new when the old is left behind, abstracted. It is a moment of great import in states of ecstasy, in epileptic fits, in mantic intoxications. How long had he been out? "Not very long" was the best he could get from Angelo. Anyhow, the question had been irrelevant, he now knew. It was a last measure of the old, coming on the heels of "Where am I?" The old changes, and the changes continue the old. Matter is old: "Nothing new under the sun." *Le plus ça change. . . .* The new is not a change, it is creation. Contemplating this notion, he reached the *posada*.

● ◐ ○ ◑ ◐ ●

He entered the lobby. Giorgio was performing in the kitchen, and the first dinner guests had arrived. Tallini took the stairs to his room and bedded down for twelve hours of dreamless sleep. The next morning, he was unable to ascertain the slightest ill effect from his adventure, but he felt fresher and more alert than he had in a long while. This, as well as his rapid recovery, made him doubt Angelo's diagnosis of sunstroke. Rather, he surmised that his course of action had called for a break, an interruption that would permit the entry of a new element, and this was made possible by his temporary incapacitation. As the striking new element was the appearance of Angelo, whom he was beginning to esteem as a kindred soul, the Gypsy was foremost on his mind as Tallini descended for a tardy breakfast.

Giorgio volunteered some news that shifted his train of thought: "Mademoiselle hasn't yet returned, but she called. She won't be back for another few days. It seems she was invited down to Torón by a friend of hers, an aficionado—flamenco, you know." Giorgio snapped into a castanets pose, but Tallini was not amused. The world Giorgio's words conjured up was infinitely far removed from his state of mind, although he himself was a longtime enthusiast of that Andalusian specialty. He suddenly realized that with all his preoccupations he had not yet given a thought to tracking down this secretive music, which had been a distinct passion in his life when he was here in Spain years ago. It seemed like a perfect occasion to make up for this neglect.

Giorgio was fully informed, familiar with all the *cantaores*. "Yes, in Torón de la Frontera, they're famous for it. Not yet commercialized, and very few foreigners know about the place. For the music, go to *El Gallito*, best flamenco south of Granada. No way of knowing when anything will happen, of course. How far? An hour down the coast, no more!"

Before long, Tallini was requesting Giorgio to arrange an excursion to Torón, to rent a car and a driver—no one who worked for the *Guardia*, of course. Wasn't there a local fellow who drove a taxi, Antonio by name? Perhaps he would be free. No, not today, tomorrow would be better. He would have an early breakfast, spend some time on the beach, work in the afternoon, and then an early supper—*lasagne* in his room. He knew enough to leave the Ferrari in the garage, so as not to draw undue attention. True flamenco is elusive, spontaneous, rarely obtained for the price of a ticket to a concert hall. It requires a certain uninterrupted ambiance to make it happen, a vital bonding of performer and spectator. It needs, if not an intimate locale, then at least an exclusive one, definitely not a nightclub.

280

Tallini had been lucky to happen upon flamenco during that most uncivil war, when it was drenched in blood, yet indomitable. Years later, again quite fortuitously, he found himself driving through Provence one August, just at the time when Gypsies were converging on the Camargue to bathe an ancient icon of a black Virgin in the sea. All day and night, next to trailers, carriages, wagons, and Cadillacs that had pilgrimaged from all over Europe, there had been flamenco. And most hauntingly, a young girl who danced to her grandfather's guitar and her brother's singing. A circle of Zincali had formed around the trio, and Tallini found himself in a crowd of *jaleos*, their syncopated hand-clapping, stamping, and encouraging shouts of *olé* meant to spur on or to challenge the performers. He had always been struck by the pure energy generated in this exchange, the clear give-and-take between performers and audience. On such an occasion, he became truly cognizant of *duende*, not in its debased sense of a performer's charm but as the singer's electrifying gift of inspired improvisation, of activated daemon, capable of magnetizing the spectator's inner spirit into the drama of the song. Because he had witnessed such impromptu creations, there was a certain depth to Tallini's understanding of the art.

After breakfast, with arrangements for the next day's excursion confirmed by Giorgio, Tallini walked out to a solitary spot of coast where the beach disappeared under a rubble of giant rock masses. It was an inhospitable site for bathers, where he was not likely to be disturbed. Sitting cross-legged on a high promontory whipped by the tide, he could view the horizon as from the bow of a ship at sea. Indeed, he felt at sea as he thought about Angelo's story. To begin with, he was not at all certain of exactly what had been said. How strange that the fellow had made such demands on his attention, just when he was coming to! Or had it all been timed to take advantage of his vulnerable condition? But then Angelo had done nothing of the kind, as far as Tallini could tell. The Gypsy had begun his tale so abruptly that it had taken Tallini some minutes to realize what was happening.

In order to remember all he had been told, Tallini tried to

recreate the scene. He didn't recall whether the monologue was spontaneous or provoked by something he himself might have said. But if the beginning remained obscure, the end stood out clear and complete in his mind: the "different cave." He had been chosen for that special cave, yet this election was terribly vague in his mind. Was this part of *his* life, or was he living someone else's? All he knew for certain was that he assumed himself to be the subject of both these lives, before the blackout and after. As for the latter, he felt he had spent his entire life in preparation for this unique distinction: Custodian of a Different Cave, a summons for which he was without doubt superbly prepared, suited, and *available.*

This last condition was no mean qualification under the circumstances, the Gypsy having indeed been severely restricted in his search. Remembering Angelo's speech of recognition, Tallini wondered how much his own trips to the hills and his interest in caves—well-known in the village—had drawn the Gypsy's attention. Instead of having been chosen, he would have preferred to earn the merit by his honest involvement. Although Angelo was unaware of Tallini's mission to contact "the early ones," this, along with his serious approach, might have established an aura capable of attracting him. Then again, the Gypsy certainly played no role in the final act that precipitated their meeting, Tallini's wild dance and collapse. In this manner Tallini tried to persuade himself that he was, with this new adventure, still in command of the conduct of his life.

At first, Tallini's eyes had been excited by the endless variety of detail within his horizon—the seascape proper, with its hills and dales and snow-capped mountains. Then he wondered about the invisible components commanding the spectacle, hidden agents of this marine *perpetuum mobile*, forces enthralled by the moon, at work in the heavy depths of brine. Inducing huge streams and currents, they heave the surface of their element and give the winds a hold. It was a game of barter between water and air, the silvery haze of which, carried by the breeze, settled on Tallini's face like a cool pellucid veil. The colors in all these changes flowed from swirling murky greens to flashes of lapis lazuli flirting with the mirrored sky. And in the white foam of transformation, millions of diamonds exploded light into the full glittering of its spectrum.

Perched on its heights, Tallini, watching his promontory's prow cleave the incoming waves, listened to the swishing and thundering of their flux and reflux. The production was doubly impressive, first, as a colossal clockwork measuring its own perpetuity, then as an animated being surrounding him, twice daily embracing this rock—his solid world—to seduce it, grain by grain, into sand. As he shifted back and forth from one impression to the other, the first, with its eternity of repetitions, filled him with the anxieties of cosmic boredom. Here the only rational activity, the only human control, is the count: one wave, another wave, a third, a fourth, *les numéros les uns après les autres.* There will never be more waves than numbers, and thus each and every one could be named in a delusional thesaurus of the main.

In his second impression, no trace of such a rigid order is to be found. Here fluidity is construed into the internal rhythms composing the basic regularity. For unless it be mechanical, even the most relentlessly repetitive movement— repetitive in what it *is* and in what it is *not*, in short, a *regular* repetition—contains inevitable variations. Thus, for Tallini, the sound of every wave was different, and yet there were categories of waves by sound—hissing waves, howling waves, and the whiz-bang of artillery when a breaker slapped the rock side's smooth flatness with a pane of water. And then there were the ever-different melodies inspired by the size of the wave, the height of its crest, the magnitude of its movement. Tallini had long memorized these shapes that curl the sea into liquid organ pipes through which he could hear the winds whistle, hum, and wail.

He had closed his eyes the better to hear the waves. Now they made music, keeping time measure by measure, and no longer in an arithmetic progression. Yet there was a counting, and he marveled at the difference in the count, in this instance a melodic conduct full of life and variety, filling time with its beat. This was the *life* of the sea, a fluid mass so huge as to achieve its own movement in harmony with other worlds yet subject to measure wherever it touches a shore. Opening his eyes, Tallini gazed in wonder at the show, until its infinite variety diminished to hypnotic sameness. Then he slowly raised his eyes to the horizon, vision's ultimate conceit to hold infinity within its bounds.

Suddenly Tallini was certain that *they*, the early people, had also seen this, that they had sat here on the rocks of this coast to contemplate the fluid continent. The hills and their caves were formed in the same turmoil that carved the coast with its bluffs and giant promontories. Both coast and hills must have existed in their present general aspect at the time early humankind awoke in Adam's Fall, with humans feeling their way toward accommodations suitable to their mission. And wouldn't the slope of the terrain have favored a downward course for their wandering, an inertia bringing them to rest at zero elevation? Faced with the enormity of this watery expanse, could they—at first sight and without entering the waves—have sensed the crucial difference between this elemental reservoir and the water they had encountered on terra firma, in pools of rainfall, for instance, or in trickling springs, or in lakes and rivers, if they had wandered from afar toward these hills whose caves would shelter the first clues to their destiny?

As Tallini contemplated such questions, his certitude grew. The manifest autonomy of this boundless sea and its incessant activity would surely have been perceived by the early ones as the majestic power of a living entity. There was no need for Tallini to emulate this perception; it came to him naturally. He felt it was close to a quality he had already once encountered and described as "everything speaks." He saw them approach to test the liquid land; he imagined their eventual, inevitable immersion in it.

Then suddenly it struck him with the force of revelation that it hadn't been like that at all. Their discovery was but a reunion, for they had once been united in a symbiosis lost and forgotten in the depths of time and sea. In truth, they had *come* from the sea in the first place! Not as maritime conquerors in vessels, needless to say, but in some fashion that they would recognize when they arrived again at the shore. It would *have* to have been a recognition and not a memory. For had they fallen into water, their initial survival—necessarily as aquatic organisms—as well as their long and slow recovery to a form allowing exit from the deep would require transformations that would have precluded all memory.

And with the provocative jolt of such revelations—because the insight is so inexplicable as the product of thought —the agent of their identification came to Tallini as his tongue touched his lips: *taste,* the sense of taste, and *salt* its vehicle. They had tasted salt before, in the sweat of their brows, in the blood of their wounds, in the tears of their pain. It accompanied all the great events of their lives, and now they knew the mother of this taste, as well as their relation to this expansive body of water.

◗ ◐ ○ ◑ ◑ ◖

Tallini spent the next day writing in his room. In a letter to Benji he wrote that the quality of his experience turned the discovery into evidence of a better kind, independent of faith, knowledge, or intent—a quality "inherent to this occurrence." He would be shown what had to be, regardless of his striving. It might not be the cave he imagined nor even what he had been looking for. In fact, he expected the unexpected. This common parlance was quite fitting because his losing consciousness, the puddle-eye, Angelo, his story—none of it fitted into the world of his imagination. It was simply of another domain, or better perhaps, of the domain of an other.

Yet this alterity brought him no closer to the cave people. Since the fainting and the Gypsy's subsequent appearance, the former tactile sensation had been replaced by the calm certitude that whatever was absent from the moment was bound to be unnecessary to it. This was the obverse of the certitude he had brought from the hills after the boulder experience—that the man one meets on the street is *there* by the irrevocable necessity of all the steps that brought him there, and if he appears in that moment, be it ever so marginally, he is necessary to the moment, which could not have come to pass without him. There was a corollary realization. The absence existed in the moment *because* of its nonappearance, and this existence as absence had to be taken into account. Without it, there would be no constant other, there would only be another of constant change. And could there possibly be a self when every other is change?

Tallini stopped writing. He rose from his chair, stretched, yawned, and approached the window. What did he think he was doing? Recounting the experience of a living moment? Giving it form, building it into a word-organism, subjecting it to a logic of cause and effect? Laughable! A living moment shared by all and everything that appears to the senses, that forms the perception, informs the mind? Insane! "Everything speaks," he had written in an earlier letter. Now he was becoming aware that *everything sees.*

He could hear Benji: "When everything speaks, it speaks because I hear. But when it sees, it sees because I *see.* Weigh the difference, it's considerable." Two different levels of energy indeed, Tallini acknowledged, two modes of appearance, one based on reception, the other on origination, action, creation. But what would Benji make of the *absence* of the other? "An ultimate other," he could hear him, "after we've worked our way through the endless repetition of the 'changing other,' which is no other at all but an extension of ourselves, always different, always the same." Yes, always the same: always different. At the boulder, absence had come into play in a dilemma, a perfect neutrality confronting two possible trips, with no inclination one way or the other. No antecedents, no preferences, no will. Absent was what was not chosen, the trip on the path not taken, the other. Once more he heard Benji: "This ultimate other is different. Unlike the changing others you encounter on the path you take, this absent ultimate other is self-contained, self-sufficient, autonomous. There is poiesis in the path *not* chosen."

● ◐ ○ ◑ ◑ ●

A knock at the door. *"Le lasagne, Piero."* Giorgio himself had come with it. He found his guest in a rare mood, quite talkative. *"Siediti un attimo,* Giorgio, while I eat, if you have time. I see you brought some Rioja. Splendid. And *two* glasses, so I needn't bother to invite you. Help yourself. Forgive me, I haven't spoken to anyone for a long time. That isn't exactly so, it just feels that way. I mean *really* spoken. . . . Never mind, Giorgio, it's only that with a *paesano* like you, it's easier. I simply feel a different man when I speak Italian. You too? Fine, then let's be different together, if that's possible. It doesn't seem possible, though, when you look at it more closely. Because being together must mean being the same in some way or other, don't you think? If only being in the same place, at the same time, like you and me here, together. Because if we were totally different, we would also be at a different time and in a different place.

"You must forgive my exuberance; it's the air in those hills. And I slept remarkably well last night. I got a bit fatigued the day before yesterday, and it was very hot for this season, a terrible sun. I wasn't exactly feeling well, and then this local fellow came around, this Angelo. You don't know him? Possible, he may not be someone you would necessarily meet—a blacksmith, lives on the Calle Caraveo. Rings no bell? There's no smithy in town? You don't say! Perhaps he made it all up! Ah, in the next *poblado* there's a smithy? Well, perhaps that's where he works. No matter, a nice guy, he helped me out, he really did!

"Yes, thank you, my project is doing quite well. I just heard from an associate in Paris—no, not telephone, you know how I avoid it—I mean mentally, I heard with some kind of inner hearing. I seem to get in touch. I tell you this *in completa confidenza* and only because I know you'll understand, as we are both Italian and we have a more vital enthusiasm than do Frenchmen and Spaniards.

"The French are snobs and they have, *dans l'ensemble,* already a northern chill, and the Spanish are still under a Caudillo's heel, so it's up to us to perpetuate Europe's Mediterranean sparkle. Neither one has our imagination. Look at our opera! Majestic! The others push philosophy and myth or else do minuets on *pointes,* but for Italians, it's the spectacle that counts, Italian opera, *grandiosa*—the exaltation in our souls we try not to show too much when among French or Spaniards.

"That exaltation makes me say I *hear* my friend. I'm not crazy. But I say 'I hear,' and I say that this should not be surprising. I even believe that perhaps at one time it was normal, yes, Giorgio, normal to communicate with someone at a distance. You'll ask me to what avail, when we have the telephone, but you forget that not everything that is to be communicated can be communicated by telephone. Not everything will be able to be squeezed through those wires and come out on the other end the same as it went in. Not interference, noise, and static, my friend. I'm talking about the substance of what is said and what is meant. There are things that cannot possibly be communicated by telephone, and they are precisely the things that can be communicated at any distance, but not in language such as we use it in daily life. Will you believe me that I had to go into those hills to find out what this means? But I had some experiences that have helped me to understand better.

"In a way, it is quite simple, a logical endeavor, in two steps or in three, we'll see how it goes. We start with language, the very same we are using at the moment. And straight off there is the matter of being *in* language in a certain way, instead of just *using* it. You and I here, in our common language, we are using it. What else are we to do? Perhaps we are in it, but we are unaware of that. All our attention is on what is said. Rightly so, you say, but there is more to it! There is the language itself, which is bigger than what is said with it. Language has to be turned around to have it be much more than what has now been achieved, the kind of understanding people have with each other when they speak.

288

"Turn the language around. It has happened before, goes back to Adam, the first to hear a voice not his own, and it is happening in our time, right now. I believe that this is what my friend in Paris means. He has a name for that kind of language. He calls it *'syntactique.'* Not that I have ever found the name very helpful, nor will you, I'm sure, and you mustn't feel that you don't know what I am talking about, just because you don't know the word. You'll tell me you know it *now*, that word, and that's an error, I'll permit myself to point out to you, being your *paesano*. The word you think you know, that 'word' is a misnomer. It's not a word at all; it's a *term*. This difference is something I've heard much talk about from my Paris friend, and it's written about in books, although in different terminologies. I may even be contributing to this talk at times, because by now I have some experience in it and some ideas about it. Now I confide to you, my friend, as I could to no one else, and I tell you because I know you will not laugh at me, *caro*, because we are Italians, and although I prefer to live in France and you in Spain, still, it is not Italy, *non è vero?*

"Speaking about books, philosophy—you may have wondered as I did when I was younger, what it was all about. I went and looked, not formally, of course, just by myself and for my own pleasure, and I can assure you—*detto fra di noi*—most of what is in them concerns what everyone knows before he even starts. Most of it is what I call 'given in front.' *Time* is an important topic—it occupies many shelves in most libraries—as is *space* and how they fit together and *life* and *death* and *love* and *hope* and *hate*—and how the world is made up and how it turns, or if it turns at all. We know about all those things, don't we? And it is evident enough, if you will just look around you. Trouble is, some things seem evident one day, but no longer the next. And once you start *thinking* about it, *attento!*—you'll never get to the end of it.

"Look at the things that once were evident and today are a big mystery. Think of a flat, immobile earth, or of matter as a solid hunk of something, and you don't have to go very far back to have it hailed as evidence. *Dunque*, how good, how helpful is all that thinking, anyway, under these conditions. Of course it's not a question of just getting rid of the thinking, although more and more people seem to go that way, whether they know it or not. They have no idea what causes the sickness of the language. They have never heard of such a thing, but they are playing out the effects well enough.

"From what I understand, there has been an accomplishment in the language, a completion, and there have been others before, mythic, mythological, logical. And now there is an overflow of language, a flood of it, all of it *using* the language but unaware that there is nothing in it. One has to experience that, as I have, in my business—and in yours as well, I bet— with the kind of people to whom one has to talk. They believe they're thinking! And that's what it has become, believing. If only they could think their thinking, but it pours forth unthought and means less than a spring I heard bubbling in the hills, much less. Here is where the turn must come this time, yet another turn of language, and it's got to do with *thinking* that language, not just using it, not just thinking *with* it and by means of it and as a means to something else —not just thinking *about*. I'm sure you can appreciate the difference, my friend, between thinking in itself and thinking *about*. Intransitive/transitive, according to grammarians. Just some way language works. But the fact that it 'works' a certain way can be a problem when you try to think in it. It might turn out that *it* thinks *you*.

"Anyway, some people believe you should be able to think without language and get away from everything that exists ready-made in language, as a way to clean up the language or to clean up their minds, which is somewhat the same. It's such a cleansing that prepares language for its turn. There is only one problem with that cure—it's being administered to the wrong patient! They have forgotten, or they probably never knew, that inside the unity of language there's a distinction between words and terms. Once the distinction is made, they will see it's not a *word*less language they need but a language freed from *terms*.

"It's a condition of meditation, as I found out in India. Of course I didn't find it out in words but in experience. Only after I had understood did it become clear that it might be possible to think in words totally devoid of terminology. Well, perhaps not totally, that may be impossible. A trace will remain, perhaps, not even a silhouette, just a fingerprint, almost nothing. But whatever remains is unique to that particular term. Enough to identify the absence of the term but not to establish a meaningful image. That's how the word remains free yet available. It is quite an uphill struggle because in everyday language the use of terms for human transactions is practically all there is, with very little wordliness left. Thinking in termless words has in our time become the luxury of the few who are able to limit their contact with the ever-present terminology.

"I have myself experimented with such a discipline, and I can tell you, *caro*, it's best to stay in your room or to sit in a forest or on a desert island if you want to deal in free words. Thinking in termless words—it's the *'in'* that's important! You want to know what will be eliminated with the term? In the beginning, practically everything: the grammar, the syntax, the evidence on paper or in sound, the form, and most important, the image. But once one is well established—and it is a practice—one can slowly and carefully reintroduce terminological elements. Because the term has its place, its importance. In language, after all, it's the substance of the written word, and the evidence of a language lies in its terminology. Humankind can exist purely terminologically, at least for a while, and in our technological age, it does so, for all practical purposes. But if ever humans will set to *thinking* intransitively in a language, they'll want a wordly body to express the language, and eventually *all* languages, instead of bits and pieces thrown around to communicate, like a ball game. A game with a special twist, perhaps, but nevertheless just the same fragmentary waifs passed around in the service of everyone's personality and interests. But in termless thinking, the language as a whole exists as medium for the thinker, like the air he breathes as he speaks. That's how I understand it, as a substance that nourishes him."

Here Tallini remembered his *lasagne,* which he had hardly touched, although the bottle of Rioja was well on its way. He couldn't recall when he had spoken so freely, with so little difficulty. Giorgio was stunned: *"Che bello, Piero, bellissimo . . . sei un poeta, caro."* While Tallini ate, the innkeeper seized the opportunity to say how it was for him to hear all this, although he didn't know whether he really understood, since it was much too much for him all at one time. But he also was often sick and tired of the conversation he had to engage in with his guests, always the same things, mainly about the weather and the state of the sea, and at the bar in the evening always the same jokes and nonsense. And what a pleasure it was to hear his native tongue spoken and to hear such interesting things. Of course. . . .

There was a knock at the door. *"Ya está el coche, señor."*
"Already? Tell the driver to wait for me in the cantina."

    ◑ ◐ ○ ○ ◐ ◑

Tallini opened the door on a remarkable scene. Amidst half a dozen tables of late diners, a bearded man of dark complexion was standing, speaking. His dress was simple but elegant, his beard neatly trimmed. That is what Tallini took in at first glance, and it would hardly have been remarkable had it not been for the fact that the man was speaking in heavily accented French and apparently addressing the Andalusian clientele. A foreign tongue is still seldom heard in small out-of-the-way villages such as Torón. Among the fishermen, bull breeders, small merchants, *Guardia Civil,* farmers, carpenters, stonemasons, housewives, and children gathered here, it was certain that no more than one in ten understood any French at all, and certainly not one in a hundred could grasp the man's syntax.

French was a language Tallini knew well enough, but the sounds he heard upon entering the hall did not readily translate into meanings. From the entryway to this glorified fisherman's hut, he could see the open kitchen in the back and long tables crowded with people supping on gazpacho or paella and drinking Jerez, a classically Andaluz scene. The voice was euphonious and expressive, but Tallini's attention was drawn to the three other people seated at the table where the speaker was standing—two men, clearly Spaniards, and a woman, Hephysta. He assumed she was unaware of his entrance, so intensely was she gazing up at the bearded fellow. This man was speaking a sort of hybrid French—not speaking, Tallini now noticed, but reciting. He had a sheaf of papers in his hand and glanced at them from time to time. Black, but not swarthy like a Gypsy might be, he was African, and seemed to be giving a poetry reading.

Sidonie did in fact notice Tallini enter, but in a reflex movement of avoidance, she had turned toward the speaker. As Tallini was orienting himself in the noisy, smoky room, she debated with herself whether he had come in pursuit of her or had been led here by chance. Undecided, she turned back toward him as if accidentally, with an expression of surprise on her face and the faintest of smiles. He interpreted this synchrony of reciprocal discovery, not *altogether* engineered, to be fair, as her having sensed his presence, and he felt in his gaze a way of bringing her alive—to him—quite in the manner by which the puddle-eye had come into existence under his regard. He looked back at her, and as their eyes met, she brought her right index finger to her lips in a little girl's gesture of silencing, as if all disturbance issued through the mouth.

The gesture had arisen almost despite herself and was anything but premeditated. No doubt it sprang from a protective feeling toward the speaker's performance. Whatever else might have provoked this signal, the intent was solely a reflex of the moment. Had Tallini been aware of this, he could have saved himself a wayward interpretation. As it was, the gesture struck him as incredibly patronizing, almost demeaning, as if he lacked all manners and had not the slightest idea how to behave. The unlikeliness of the signal's provincialism elicited a different interpretation from Tallini, more literally in keeping with the action where index in fact seals lips by crossing them. The silence she demanded couldn't be an absence of

293

noise, as the place was not exactly a mausoleum. Although the late diners might have been keeping their voices down a bit in deference to the foreign orator, their conversations continued unabated, pots and pans clattered in the kitchen, orders were shouted, all at a fairly high decibel level.

The silence she indicated was vocal; she didn't want him to speak. Implausible in this absolute negativity, the clause, when correctly complemented, expressed a distinct possibility. To speak about what? The only thing they had to converse about would be a slight past in common and a rendezvous he hadn't kept. Now they were about to meet again and she didn't want to talk about any of it, most likely because of that Francophone chap holding forth at her table. Tallini's interpretation may very well have been correct, but he would have erred had he thought her aware that her gesture was expressing her will. The interdicted lips had come about through a mechanism all its own of which she knew nothing. She did realize that her gesture assigned the moment to quiet, secrecy, and prudence. It risked a conspiratorial link, a bond he might relish, although it embarrassed her. She also sensed he read too much into it, as indeed he had.

Like a few others that evening at *El Gallito*, Tallini's ear was attracted to the sounds uttered by the speaker, even before having fathomed the language, its meaning. Entirely different from the flamenco usually heard on the premises, there were nevertheless rhythms and modulations that had an appreciable quality not unrelated to *el Cante*. The delivery, though not sung, yet generated an unmistakable surge, the message conveyed through the sound. Despite the undertone of conversation, an ebb and flow that gauged a performer's relative dominance, no performance here of any kind went entirely unnoticed. But usually the bid for attention had to compete with business deals, family reunions, or the dialectics of past bullfights. The saving grace was that the patrons were usually locals, knew their *canto*, and therefore had a fair judgment of the good and a gut feeling for the bad. Perhaps it was because of all this that the best singers came from *El Gallito* in Torón.

On the occasion of Tallini's visit, the lively spirit of Torón's public ear was challenged by the sounds of an exotic poet. Later on, the locals, though hardly mentioning the linguistic aspect of that evening's fare, often recalled the striking sounds with which the foreigner had come forth. They discussed the nature of the difference in the sounds, how they evoked not guitars but woodwinds, even horns. Minimizing the language difficulty, they had given the performance a chance, as they did for any newcomer willing to try his soul at *El Gallito*. Everyone was in agreement that by local standards, the offering had been minimal; four or five short-lined stanzas followed by a kind of refrain that included a word everyone understood, notwithstanding the skewed accent that missed the nasal in its tonic rise on the final vowel: flamenco. The word is fully part of the general lexicon, and its appearance in the common tongue is no longer specially noted. The Spanish ear, however, picked out the periodic emergence of the known from a sea of incomprehension at its very first repetition. If one was uncertain, at first, of having heard correctly, the first repetition not only confirmed the word, evoking the noble art to which, as aficionados, they were dedicated. It also gave away the formal game, the rhythms of stanza and verse. This furnished a badly needed lead to listeners bred in the specialized monolingualism of remote provinces, where a regional pride restricts the linguistic horizon yet further, to a dialect, to a local patois. For such an ear, trained by repetition not only linguistically, but in seasons and plantings, by winds and seas, this rhythmic device is appealing and universally understandable. For polyglots like Tallini and Sidonie, the challenge was far more intriguing. Ostensibly, the poem was a eulogy in praise of flamenco.

Suis que je suis l'esprit d'ici, duende bien chaud dans ma peau

A ten- to fifteen-minute piece, all told, including a low-voiced prelude introducing himself as Mantikos, and a few charming remarks directed to the lady at the speaker's table. Tallini missed this part, as he had entered during the second stanza.

But he understood perfectly the sotto voce coda, although the voice barely carried above the din. A tentative *olé* at the third refrain was insufficient to sway any mood, and then the performance was over. Some patrons, less alert, perhaps engaged in animated conversation, might have actually missed it altogether. But for Tallini, it was the center of the tableau into which he had stepped.

The visual/gestural exchange with Hephysta had halted his advance into the room, and he recalled what had happened up in the hills in a space similarly polarized, where a proper gesture was to determine a political distance—as *this* one undoubtedly was as well. He had spun Hephysta's reflex gesture into a filigree of feelings quite transparent to her. Not that she saw through them, but rather she failed to see them at all. And yet there had been, if not an élan by any means, at least an acceleration on his part toward her, brusquely braked by her indexed lips. The censure in the gesture was what made him sit down at the table nearest the entrance. He looked away from her during his move, and when he gazed in her direction once again, she had turned her head and was looking at the speaker, so that Tallini was seeing her in profile. Strange, he hardly recognized her. He had known that it was she, known it intuitively as he entered. In their sweep his eyes had brushed the pale blue of faded jeans under the table, and the only female silhouette not overtly Andalusian. But his gaze was arrested by her sudden turning toward him.

Once again their four eyes met head-on. Such eyelock, Tallini realized, cannot accurately be described as a seeing of something, unless likened to the fixation of a point on the horizon, a "seeing" to infinity. The true lock is defined by the fading of all background, for however short a moment, so that only *this* remains. It is a vision very different from an observer's recognition of colored surface and formed volume within a vista that opens perspectively. The locked gaze, in contrast, is a translucent contact point with an energy of sight. In a flash, left eye looks into right, a twin polarization by opposition. What could be more opposite than left and right in both the mirror image and in the living other, vis-à-vis?

Leaning forward, elbows on the table, he clasped his left hand with his right while meeting Hephysta's eyes, left to right, right to left. But he overlooked the complementation of visual touch in his own clasped hands. They did not fit as does a handshake, which is the grip he was seeking, the fit realized in a traditional tactile greeting, with a harmonizing complementation like the meeting of eyes, an intimate touch at a distance.

Hélas, je demeure dans un temps qui meurt, futur kif-kif bourricot

Again she turned away, and as Tallini looked closer, he recognized her less and less. There had been a change, but a change more likely to have occurred in his own pliable psyche—the inner vision remote yet within his ken—than in her physical features. It struck him that the very distance, the space between them, underscored this mode of cognition. With binocular vision no longer deluded by a remote object's reduced size, the laws of perspective and scale remain a *reductio ad absurdum* of the ways in which distance affects a phenomenon.

He recalled his encounter with a stranger, back in the village after his boulder experience, and his speculations about their sharing of time and place—an infinity of past directed toward the event, never repeated, of crossing paths on a sidewalk. This seemed to him relevant to the drive—or perhaps the natural predilection—for closeness in cognition. The hand's first grasp is appropriation rather than approach. The handshake, the disarming clasp of mutual touch, invites the other within a personal range. One turns from an image ever so slightly reduced by distance to touching the entity itself. Within this domain of tactile proximity, where no reductive image ascertains perceptible distance, there is evidently a spectrum of contacts, as when they are generalized in the lover and her embrace.

He mused how closeness is prized as the only counterforce to distance. For cognitive pursuit, the closer the better, as the human constitution seems to indicate. There exists an ideal of identification that provokes images of melting and blending, of fusion and confusion, of divine chaos whenever its predominantly Oriental experience succumbs to Occidental descriptions. East and West, however, both hold distance as essentially negative, to be overcome, to be reduced. While the East brings eternity to this innermost task, the West works on speed of displacement. In the end, both positions indeed *cover* their distances, the Eastern tenet of identity best fitting its ideal by a unification *in the mass*. The other, a world removed from such unifying absorption, invests in mathematical precision to reap extensive practical results. Here a specific well-defined distance from the objective is valorized and maintained for optimum cognition. Tallini had encountered both these extremes, the first in his meetings with the living saints of India, the other in his readings and in Benji's various epistemological moods.

At this moment Tallini recognized the folly of impatience in the face of distance, the inanity of sorrow, resentment, rage, or despair at the imposed distance that knows but one scale: human distance. A distance *from*, from what one wants to know, from what one desires. Evident distance, path of separation, true measure of what is apart and must be trod every step of the way as the very experience of separation. The insight was elusive; he could not quite fathom its effect on his inborn faith in the visual perspective, its implications for a signification of space. But he received it with the emotional twinge that marks an inscription, and he simultaneously realized his energetic intent was no longer directed horizontally toward Hephysta, in the frozen gaze. The action was elsewhere and the distance not horizontal, as he had assumed, but vertical. He realized he was in contact again. Feeling and words were coming down, in the midst of his surprise at the fragility of evidence in human cognition, of the way evidence eroded with every conscious step.

Qui habite la caverne de mon coeur? Flamboyante Madame Tarot

When Sidonie turned back toward Tallini, a smile had reappeared behind her eyes. It was meant to reassure him, as she couldn't be entirely certain his presence was not accidental, that he had sought her out. She couldn't be sure, but she thought it was likely. The smile was meant to hedge her bet, although the odds were in her favor. By all rights she could have afforded a temporary coolness, a slight reticence. If there were a purpose in his coming this far, then there would be persistence, perhaps even challenge, and he would certainly not be offended by a diplomatic pout. Were his appearance fortuitous, however, he might feel embarrassment at the coincidence and be discouraged by the thankless job of making himself believed, by the sheer impossibility of it. He might choose to flee rather than put up with the situation. Or he might think he was intruding, and although he now sat down, the door was still very much within reach. At least he hadn't bolted on reflex, as she might well have done had she been close to an exit. Who knows? She might have disappeared, if only temporarily. All of it felt excitingly literary to her, if this, then that, if . . . how everything can be achieved with two small letters! The world always took on a literary cast for her when events moved out of the ordinary, as they were doing that evening at *El Gallito.* With Mantikos, things often were indeed out of the ordinary. Endowed as he was with a feverish imagination, he required them to be so and would treat them as such, whether they were or not. He went to great lengths to transcend the ordinary, possessing ample mental and physical predispositions for the task.

As she looked from one to the other, the two men seemed very different one from the other, more so than they had seemed before their different worlds had intersected by her agency. Perhaps this feeling was heightened because of the difference in her reception of them, the fact that they came to her by way of such distinct means—the one a sensorial contact through the eye, the other through wavy fluctuations in the ear, where a hidden process impresses upon the tympanic membrane a range of vibrational frequencies serving to situate sound for the auditive mind, logically in words, musically in song. The thought of this sensory distinction, measurable in wavelengths, held for her a unique plenitude yielding to a dimensionality beyond volume, as distinct from volume as the latter is from plane and once again removed from line and yet again from the puncticular. Surely every conscious being is in some way aware of the ladder of dimensions on whose rungs it climbs from undefinable point to the tridimensional experience sufficient unto itself. And so it was for her. Through her education, moreover, she became aware of a scientific multidimensionality that transcends the trinitary. She had studied the subject in philosophy and even in physics, and absorbed, whole and unquestioned, an academic version of the day's erudite cosmologies.

As the moment of eye contact blotted out everything but itself, she had no idea what might have reached her through his eyes when he first saw her from the door. But in an inner site vacant of all visual concerns, the ray of light that bound them for that instant flashed a vivid thought-experience: a field of empirical components—not terminologies or symbols, which were her usual fare, but the essential content of the experience as such. She came to the realization that at one time all these components were formed by words, but that the locked gaze does not have ears. Without sounds, terms are jettisoned, terminology is an empty shell. The field is a galaxy of essential experiences, each relating in innumerable ways to countless others, clusters of experience that move in changing relations. Neither promoted nor restrained by outside forces, wide open yet self-contained, local foci of adequacy and fitness occur, gather, and assemble through flexible reciprocities. An infinitely connected alliance works itself together in pursuit of common experience. Within the changing equilibrium of global self-adjustments emerges a world of momentary mutual satisfaction.

Ailes éternelles! Je te rappelle: nous étions jadis tous oiseaux

Sidonie/Hephysta got the distinct impression that this image was somehow coming in part from Tallini's stare, and she discovered in a flash the ancient power of eye to eye. Even at a distance, this contact was capable of launching and sustaining an energetic circuit of sight. In any other regard, this energy explodes into color when intersecting form, be it at the surface skin of an object or a living being or the blueness of the sky. When eyes gaze into eyes, however, the look encounters no obstacles, no limits, no demands of chromatico-formal creativity, only the total surrender to the directedness of this mutual gaze. For its comprehension, pure unconditional direction invites a principle of circularity, the serpent biting its tail—two facing pairs of eyes occupying the diametral poles of head and tail on an energized circumference. One energy, two poles, four elements to create this phenomenon. Again, this vision did not flow from her as though her own; rather, it was constrained by the visual stream they shared and that was passing through both. In her, it was filtered through innumerable fragments of academic experience and books, but rarely in actions. Here, now, in their mutual scrutiny, the vision was not exclusively, solipsistically, her own. This particular visual gesture reached her from the other in the only way both pairs of eyes could simultaneously behold one and the same sight from one and the same perspective.

The ordinary look that scans at random knows no facsimile; it has no equal. It cannot be duplicated or emulated. It is fleeting and on its own. From that point of view, as many worlds of visual certitude exist as there are observers. Yet it is no less true—infinite points of view notwithstanding—that the world, allowing for every gamut of regional styles and idiosyncrasies, *appears* much the same to all. Disagreements exist, of course, as proved by multiple witnesses to a single event, particularly when sudden change is involved. Yet among those who observed an event with their own eyes, agreement is rarely wanting on fundamental grounds—the fact that something occurred, took place, existed at all. Were this ascertainment within the ken of language, it would employ a present tense. But there is no tracking the present with language. This ground, this taking place, is where distinction ceases between the worlds of the sad and the glad and all the others. It is one world for the being.

As Hephysta entered this floating sourceless thinking, years of unconvincing and often tedious philosophical soundings now tumbled into place, into a point of view so distinct from her intellectual routine that it hesitated before imposing itself as her own just at the moment its light was shared not in a construct, but in transparency. She resisted accepting this insight. It meant losing control, and she was beset by a flurry of doubts and hesitations, the obstacles and dangers in what she suddenly perceived was a process of conversion. Incomprehensible to her until now was Pascal's mysterious submission, after a revelatory November night, to an elitist sect of predestination, and his arrival at Port-Royal armed with Epictetus, Montaigne, and a style all his own. His toys were left behind: the plane geometry reinvented in childhood, the conic sections invented at sixteen, a calculating machine two years later. It was the middle of the seventeenth century, and he found himself in the right place and time with a sensitivity for natural law, atmospheric pressure, the stability of liquids. The fount of his creativity was eclectic: calculus of probabilities, the hydraulic press, a theory of roulette. Then, a night of sudden grace, a privilege, divine design. Result? He packed it all away. Self-conversion. Self-transcendence. Henceforth he devoted his style to a transfigured Christianity. Surely a change of vision accompanied such an experiential shift.

Though at a far remove from Monsieur de Saci's conceptions, the change in her was nevertheless in some measure related to Pascal's night. Not as if lightning had struck, neither for the one nor the other. Pascal had been frequenting Jansenist meetings for years. Yet, as is its hallmark, the conversion was sudden; she knew now that it hadn't taken any time at all. The vision was changed, as was her own. Better, she felt that for the first time, there *was* vision where a sort of blindness had been, and she felt certain Pascal would understand. She was amazed, as she had been informed she would be, informed by the same classic sources that speak of lack of insight and then describe how "the light on goes." Most of these sources—at least one of which surely graced Pascal's reading table—she had long despised as irrational poisons. But the contact with Mantikos had gradually become an antidote of sorts, introducing the possibility of a life beyond reason and yet penetrated by thinking. Not that they had ever talked of such a thing. She had gathered it from his actions, from his gestures, and put it into these words. What philosophy Mantikos had mastered, he had done so in his actions. He meant to define poetic life for his time by living example, by staying, consistently, "drunk on poetry." All else was subordinate to that plan. He called it "surconscious" and "the seat of poetry," involving as it did a certain time-tested "systematic derangement of the senses."

Mon seul désir pour pur plaisir: aimant-noyau du flamenco

It was the end of the African's address. The two musicians at Hephysta's table jumped to their feet. One of them already had a guitar in his hands. A few chords sounded, and there were shouts of olé Manolo, olé Pichuco. Without a thought, Tallini made his move to the door. To Hephysta/Sidonie, it was as if he had vanished into thin air. One moment of inattention on her part, and he was gone. Outside, Tallini stood and listened to the preluding guitar proposing cadences to the singer who cut in, tentatively at first, then breaking into a Cante:

> Aquel pajarito, madre
> que canta en la verde oliva

But it was not an evening for Tallini to listen to this music, which demanded concentration and attention, an unencumbered mind and a free soul. At the moment, he could have mustered none of these, hence his reflex of flight. But he also felt he had accomplished what he had come for, yet without a clear sense of what that might have been. He had made out to meet Antonio, the driver, in a nearby café. They had hardly spoken a word to each other on the drive down the coast. Tallini had been distant in his brooding preoccupation, and his chauffeur knew when a customer wanted to be left alone. Now Antonio was sitting at a table with two other men in rumpled suits, tieless in white, buttoned-up shirts, stained fedoras on their heads. Tallini approached, and Antonio invited him to join them, introducing him, to his surprise, as Pedro el Italiano. Tallini sat down and the three men continued their conversation in a language Tallini didn't understand. After a few minutes, the other two got up, waved a vague gesture of farewell, and left.

"Family," said Antonio after he had ordered some Montillo. "They trade horses, travel all around the country. You didn't stay very long at *El Gallito*. You didn't like the music?"

Tallini said he had just gone to leave a message for someone, and the music hadn't yet started. He would come back some other evening when he had more time.

It turned out that Antonio knew everything about everybody in the region. He had dozens of funny anecdotes and turned out to be very pleasant company. He called himself a compadre and associate of Angelo; they had plans for the future, big plans, abroad. For the moment, they both worked for the *Guardia*, like everybody else who didn't want to starve to death. It would also be handy, when the time came, in getting papers to cross the border.

"But don't worry," he assured Tallini, whose features were showing some signs of dismay, "we tell the *Guardia* nothing, at least nothing that is true. Angelo was ordered by the station in the town where he works to follow you and find out what you are doing in the hills. And I was ordered by another station to follow Angelo, because they don't trust him and want to know what *he* is doing in the hills. *Son tontos*, they are fools, one and all."

So Tallini had an enjoyable ride home, and was in an excellent mood by the time they arrived back at the hotel. There was a warm handshake in parting and some mutual taps on the shoulder. But as Tallini opened the door to Giorgio's *posada*, he had an idea, and he turned and called after Antonio to come back for a moment. Then, when they were facing each other again, he stuck out his right hand: "Shake my hand again, Antonio, but do it with your *left* hand." And the taxi driver, somewhat surprised, kept trying to fit his hand into the other's for a good grip: "*No cae muy bien, señor. ¡Es que no encaja!*"—"*Verdad que no, Antonio*," Tallini replied, absolutely delighted. And with a few more taps on Antonio's back, he turned away and entered the hotel.

FIFTEEN

THE PATIO

On the day of new moon, Tallini was a man of cautious expectations as he set out toward the path starting from Pepe's sheep corral. He climbed steadily and energetically, and when he paused to rest and look around, he was already deep into the hills. Once he had caught his breath, he became aware of a great silence, and in that silence, everything reminded him of Angelo. Not that he detected any perceptible sign of the Gypsy, but he felt a distinct sense of his presence. He thought back over his recent experience with the forms in the landscape—forms of attention, as they now seemed—not very far from where he stood, but at a lower elevation. The forms then had seemed to be drawn *out* of a background landscape, almost pushing it from the field of vision altogether. Focused attention had been of the essence in defining these forms.

Now, to the contrary, the forms of nature were more impressive than he had ever perceived them to be. The empathy they invited brought him an acute awareness of the vegetative organs he shared with them: the roots of digestion, the breathing leaves and blades of the respiratory function, the circulating sap as both chyle and blood. Their difference was a pumping heart in the one, a drawing of the sun in the other, yet both served an identical function. It struck him that understanding the refinement from sap to blood was bound to be instructive, and there was no doubt in his mind about what came next. Thinking was the ultimate refinement of the flow, and this last step seemed to him of giant proportions and special difficulty, because it was the thinking itself that revealed the thought system. This idea caused him to lose his perception of the landscape for an instant, and then Benji's voice was in his ear: "Same function, different form. That's certainly one way of getting to know something. But don't you have to know the function before you can detect it in two different forms? Or else. . . ." But Tallini didn't want Benji's arguments to confuse his vision, and he refused to listen to his voice, whereupon Benji faded.

Again he felt Angelo's presence in the landscape as he drew closer to the low patch of vegetation he had observed earlier. As his approach had been against the light, with the sun in his eyes, it was hard for him to distinguish it clearly. From a distance it looked like a single shrub with gnarled branches. But now he distinctly saw a row of vines sprawling on the ground, a few still clinging to poles tied with esparto hemp. Some rusted wires on the ground showed abandoned attempts at training. These grapevines, once cultivated, were now surviving in defiance, almost out of spite. Although they looked dead, their trunks as dry as twisted ropes, he felt the humidity of sap at their core, detected it as surely as he knew the blood in his own veins. At some incredible depth, rootlets were still gathering water and minerals in sufficient quantity to have produced, after the rainy season, green leaves long since turned brown.

As he touched one of them, it glided into his hand, and he absent-mindedly crumbled it between thumb and fingers. Was it a reflex action that made his tongue mimic this gesture against his palate? Suddenly the sharpness of young Montilla livened his tastebuds, but without the usual bite of a first sip of this highly alcoholic sherry. Omnipresent aperitif in these parts, he knew it well and recognized the heady power endowed by the sweetness of its sap. Nor was this phantom taste altered in the least by the residue of bitterness sometimes left in the wine from the open earthenware jars in which fermentation runs its course. It was the wine *before* this process he was tasting, the ghostly sweetness before the souring, the sap's potential before countless cellulose vessels refined it to liquid fruit. In fact, he was tasting the vine, not its fruit, and the vine was not only the vessel but its circulating content as well.

As he looked at the vine, he had no trouble situating that taste, the powerful elixir of the fermented fluid, which had metamorphosed from water to sap to fruit, a process of creative spoilage that gathered fire and water into wine. He was tasting this particular vine the way oenologists taste vineyard and vintage. And then the flavor that was forming between tongue and palate rose to his nose and the liquid taste turned to aerial scent. He was no longer tasting the vine, he was smelling it. The core of water in these woody tunnels and hollows sent its most ethereal message to his nose: the nose of Montilla.

Wasn't this what was meant by "knowing the vine"? For a split second Tallini had lived a vegetative destiny in that familiar bouquet, and the fleetingness of the event only intensified his impression. It took its place with the other unusual experiences of the past days and weeks that had left him cogitating their overtones of eternity and infinity. The difference was the extraordinary buoyancy that tinged this latest experience. Truly contained in the moment, its immediacy carried no reflective or speculative sequels. This was a knowing without thinking, and it seemed ever so much more profound. But though he was convinced this instant exploration had let him know the plant as surely as one knows a familiar face, he also was aware that such knowledge was absolutely private and uncommunicable. And it struck him that life in a world made up of such knowledge would be a lonely journey indeed.

It came to Tallini that what he had tasted—in this realm that certainly belonged to taste rather than to vision or audition—was the vine's *thinking:* it had communicated an idea precisely. Not only the town that had given the taste its name but the people within its whitewashed walls, the vineyards and hills surrounding it, and the chalky soil—all thinking "Montilla" for those who could taste not the substance of the wine but its scent bearing the very idea. While he deciphered the vine's thinking communication—the sweet by the tip of the tongue, the sour at the sides of his mouth—noble esters rose in vapor through his nostrils and were trapped in the nasal cavity. There, in this *bain-marie*, this water-bath of scents, they once more condensed to liquid. Now moisture performed a dissolution transmitted through nerves centered in the olfactory bulb. Tallini did not *think* the circuit; his whole being was in this bouquet, and the bouquet was in his nose. He was conscious then that an aroma would have to produce its own terminology, as he couldn't *think* while determining a nose! But once the nervous system is engaged nothing can restrain the flash into memory. This ultimate transmutation occurs in the temporal lobe and the line to the cortex is therewith clear.

"*Buenos dias, señor.*" Suddenly Angelo was standing in front of him. "Welcome to my country home. You are looking at my old friends, yes? They have been good *compañeros*, they have, these vines, for as long as I can remember. But I have known for years that I would eventually have to abandon them. I had spoiled them with an easy life, so I have trained them to survive on their own. You see, *señor*, the spring where I found you the other day, it is behind that knoll in the distance. It is quite a way to carry water, but it is the closest to the cave, which is in there." And he pointed to a nearby rock formation of considerable height. Tallini now noted that between the vines and rocks, the terrain was unusually even and devoid of debris, almost as if it had been cleared and leveled by hand.

"Yes, there is water there on the surface," Angelo continued, "but here it is deep under the ground. I know where it is, and so do these vines, one can feel it, *señor*, but . . . not with those!" And he pointed at Tallini's feet, which in turn made Tallini aware that on this occasion the Gypsy was barefoot.

"My shoes?" Tallini couldn't believe anyone would elect to go without shoes in this terrain of rocks, cactus, snakes, and scorpions. Then he recalled his naked dance at the source, which Angelo had very likely witnessed.

"Yes, *señor*. These hills are special for us Gypsies; we all know this ground very well. But this particular *sitio* here," and he indicated the seemingly domesticated plane Tallini had just noticed, "this is something more for me. It has been my home for a long time, and I have received much strength from the earth. It will be difficult to leave it, I shall never find a home like this again. So here I don't need shoes, nothing will harm me here, no snake and no cactus and no stone. And here I can feel what is below the ground, I can feel the water, and so do these vines. For the last five years, I have given them no care, and only during the drought we had two years ago, with almost no rainy season, did I supply them with a little water. This year they will reach the water underground, I can tell. But they will bear no fruit. Perhaps you will care for them, so they will give you fruit, *señor*. You will not regret it. These grapes are unlike any others you have ever tasted."

Tallini was hardly listening. It occurred to him that he had known the vine just now much as he had known the boulder, with an unconventional use of his senses and his body, outside of language and mind, and in a kind of sharing and exchanging that surmounted a barrier of his own making. The plant had been there all along, open and giving. Now his ignorance of a world in the midst of which—and through which—he lived was a frightening realization. Had he been spending his time in a waking dream and allowing reality to pass him by? The dread of this possibility was assuaged by his recovered access to this neglected relationship, which filled him with joy. He rejoiced in the functions he shared with the vine. All living things could be known in this fashion, and only when thus known do they live. And if the boulder lived, as it had shown him clearly enough, then what did *not*? He was reminded that everything speaks, and he understood all living presences can be known by the echo they project.

"Soon the mountains will be covering the sun," Angelo was saying. "We can sit over here and watch." He led Tallini a little way farther, where a flat slab of rock made an excellent westward-facing seat. They sat in silence and contemplated the sawtoothed Sierra. There were no clouds, and the sun vanished without show. "It takes a dirty sky to give good colors," Angelo said afterward, and then suggested they eat. He reached into his sack and brought out a jar of bright orange paella and a sausage gnarled like the vines. Tallini took two sandwiches out of his musette bag and gave one to the Gypsy. He hadn't said a word since remarking his shoes. He hadn't liked the sound of his own voice. It didn't ring true. It wasn't he. The new Tallini didn't have to speak, and he simply nodded in affirmation of what the other said. Angelo ate slowly, talking between bites.

"It will be dark soon, and you will go into the cave. I have spoken much about myself and my people. But I must now tell you all I know about the cave. Some of it I couldn't have said last time because I myself didn't know then. I told you I wouldn't be in the hills these two days, but I spent them in the cave because I felt I would understand something better. And I did. It is what our *brujos* do when there are great decisions. And if the *brujo* stays long enough in the cave, sometimes the cave gives answers.

"The very first night I found out what I had to know: the cave must be closed. There had always been talk among our *brujos* that the cave would some day have to be closed, but not by anyone of the family. You see how it all fits together, *señor,* and how it was meant for me to spot you as the one to take over our secret. Now I must turn the cave over to you and instruct you to close it.

"But the one who closes the cave must first understand its secret. And then it has to be preserved—that is the important part. Perhaps the secret of the cave has to do with where we come from, we Gypsies. I hope it does. We were always told we came from Egypt; even our name seems to say so. And we worked our way through Africa and up to Spain, some as horse traders, some as thieves, but many as blacksmiths for honest wages. Always outcasts, though, because people were suspicious of the power of the forge, our handling of the fire, and the sparks and flashes that surround us when we work. But if you will discover the story of my people back to the first one, then it will prove I was right in recognizing you. And then we are truly brothers, are we not? You are not a Gypsy, *hermano*, but you are restless and dissatisfied just as we are. I will show you the cave and you will understand.

"One strict order has come down—from the first *brujo*, so I was told—and I am telling you now: *nothing* in the cave is to be moved. There are only rocks in there, of course, of all sizes, and they must not be moved. You ask why this is so important? Tio Ortiz didn't know for certain, but he thought the secret might be disturbed if anything were changed in the cave. I don't know if this is true. You must yourself *feel* the secret of the cave, like *we* feel it. When I recognized you, I knew you could do that. That is the end of my instructions. Now do you have any questions to ask me, *señor?*"

Tallini didn't have any questions, but hesitated to say so. For a while he said nothing. Overwhelmed by the prospect of being shown a special cave where he was going to spend the night, perhaps even several nights, he could not imagine what else there was to know. It didn't occur to him to wonder how long it might take to find whatever the Gypsy had instructed him to find, or if he ever would find it at all.

Angelo seemed to understand his silence, and went on: "You will go into the cave when it is dark. I have made torches from some resinous wood that grows on the other side of the mountain. I will lead you in and then I will leave. Tomorrow at the first light, I will come up from the village and put a jar of paella in front of the cave. At night, you will leave the empty jar for me. I will come up every day, until the day I don't find an empty jar. Then I will know that you have done your work and you are closing the cave.

"We shall not be together again, although it would be a great pleasure for me, of course, *señor*. But these things are not decided by me or by you, and perhaps you will see it is wiser this way. We *gitanos*, especially those of us who work in the forge, we know much about secrets, and if the secret of the cave was something you could come out and tell me, then it wouldn't have been much of a secret at all. Anything that can be told will never be a secret!

"But whatever it is the cave has to tell, somehow it must be preserved. You will find a way to do this. What you will discover is for *your* people now, no longer for us, and in some ways, we are glad. In these times we live alone, or if together, then we live together by choice and not as a family that none of us has chosen. It is very difficult, *señor*, and even being together by choice shouldn't really mean it is *our* choice, yours and mine, because we don't even know what we are, so how can we choose? Who is choosing, *señor*? I ask you.

"Gypsies don't like to choose. They let it happen, they let things choose themselves. They know *they* can't do it— they would choose wrong much of the time. So they don't do it and therefore have no expectations. Or if they *have* to choose, they choose knowing there is no choice. It was our way to live, *señor*, but now everybody wants to go the easier way and do like the *payos*. Forgive me, *señor*, but I myself am content with leaving because it is not my choice. And I did not choose you. I *recognized* you; it was fated. How could we choose the inevitable? Because one thing that made us Gypsies is now disappearing, and that is our freedom. We've sacrificed many things for it—a real house, country, security, position—many things for that freedom. But now we're going the other way. As for me, I will also be leaving—as soon as I see there is no empty jar. Antonio has gotten papers for us to cross the border."

Then Tallini at last had a question. "Tell me, Angelo, do you know what is meant by 'closing the cave'?"

The Gypsy was rolling a cigarette, looking straight ahead. He took a while to answer, and he did so in a low voice and without shifting his gaze: "I know nothing about it, only that I will not visit the cave ever again."

Somehow that simple statement went straight to Tallini's heart and kindled there a sense of responsibility neglected in his excitement. It occurred to him now that closing the cave for the Gypsy might well be the price for opening it to himself, and his responsibility might well consist in judging the extent of this opening. But these considerations would have to wait, as Angelo was already on his feet. "It is time," he said, and the two men made their way toward the rock formation the Gypsy had pointed out earlier.

A dozen paces from the looming outcrop, Angelo told Tallini to stay put while he went ahead. In the gathering darkness of the moonless night, Angelo was close to invisible. Against the shadowy rock, only his white shirt could be seen clearly. Tallini strained his eyes and observed the Gypsy run a searching hand over the stone surface, then crouch down ever so slightly and lean against the wall. Tallini saw him wriggle a bit, and then disappear. He thought his eyes were playing tricks on him. He had to restrain an impulse to step forward—he had good reason to take the Gypsy seriously on matters of protocol. Just then he saw the man, crouched as he was when he went in, wriggle out of the wall again, straighten up, and wave for him to approach. Not until Tallini was at arm's length from the wall did he notice that at the place where Angelo had performed his sleight of body, what looked like a recess in the stone was actually a crack, an irregular opening, in places barely broader than a hand.

"What happened?" Tallini asked, as if he didn't know.

"Perhaps you want to know how I do it." The Gypsy sounded amused. "I will show you, *hermano.* You see, the opening only *looks* small. It's an illusion, and it protects the cave. It is like those animals that can look like a rock or a branch, and nobody pays attention to them. This looks like just a little crack in the rock, like a thousand others. Even when you stand right in front of it in full daylight, there's no light coming through from the other side. Only our *brujos* know about this. Come, I will show you now how it is done." Arching his back in a peculiar catlike manner, working his shoulders up and down as he moved his feet, Angelo seemed actually to slip right into the very wall. Tallini stood amazed, peering into the dark crevice. He heard Angelo's voice on the other side: "I'm coming back, stand away." And already there appeared his shoulder and the white shirt that seemed to attract the day's remaining light. "Now you try it," said the Gypsy, dusting off his pants.

Tallini approached the wall for closer scrutiny. Indeed, the crack turned out to be much wider than it looked. The narrow opening reached about shoulder high. He felt the smoothness of the stone on the inside surface of the rock, polished, he assumed, by many hands. Then he turned sideways crouched, and fitted his head and shoulder between the two sides of the break, in what seemed to him the only possible way. He wiggled a little and wedged himself between the walls. Pushing forward, he might have gained an inch or two, but then got quite stuck. He felt Angelo taking hold of his free hand. *"Cuidado,"* he heard, *"Asi no,'mano!* That's not the way to do it! I thought you were watching me!"

Tallini pulled himself out and felt foolish. Of course he couldn't get in there—he was much taller and heavier than the Gypsy. "Oh no," Angelo replied, shaking his head, "Tio Ortiz was at least as big as you are. It's just that you didn't go about it right. Now watch me well." He stepped close to the wall, crouched, set his shoulder to it, moved his head back and forth a few times, shook his upper body with an almost rotary motion Tallini hadn't noticed the first time, and with three tiptoed steps and a twist of the hip, he slid right between the rock walls and disappeared into the fissure. Tallini looked in and saw nothing. *"Ya vuelvo,"* he heard the Gypsy's voice as if behind a curtain, barely muffled. And then he saw an arm, a shoulder, and with the same movement the man reappeared once more.

"But it's a dance!" Tallini exclaimed, amazed at his own discovery. Angelo looked at him with equal surprise as Tallini repeated, "You're *dancing* in and out!"

"A dance?" Angelo was baffled. "I'm doing a dance, you say?" He stood immobile, thinking about it. "You may be right, but nobody ever called it that. But now you say so, yes, it is a little like . . . like *bulerías, por Dios!"* And he took a stance and clapped his hands in a rhythm, and his body started to move, the shoulders, the hips, and then came the three tiptoed steps. *"Si, si,"* he chanted. *"Olé, se-ñor ami-go y her-ma-no, si, si!* It *is* a dance. *Olé!"* The rhythm and the mood were infectious. Tallini was thankful for the exhilaration, for he was passing through a nasty moment of doubt, feeling he was in over his head. The importance this affair was assuming had wholly dawned upon him. A failure now would be disastrous. It would certainly be the end of his life, of his new life, barely started, that had already effaced the old. All this occurred in a fleeting moment, the time it took the Gypsy to get into and out of the wall.

"Dance!" Tallini heard, and the voice turned into a murmur in his brain. "Dance with the flow. . . ." Already in his ear, the hand-clapping came to him easily, and he moved his shoulders and hips and tried the three little tiptoes. Then to Tallini's astonishment, his guide suddenly broke into a way of moving that was still the same dance, but with an awkward stiffness—heavens, the man was imitating *him!* And he was doing it so successfully that Tallini felt himself dancing over there, in the Gypsy's motions rather than in his own. This brought immediate results. He perceived the Gypsy's movements all stemmed from one single region, an unmoving center within him. They flowed from that source. And as he knew it in the Gypsy, he felt it in himself. His body relaxed, and he felt everything that moved connected to everything else and flowing from his center, and he himself was not involved in any of it.

"We will try again." Angelo stepped up to the wall and motioned Tallini toward the breach. "Here, don't forget your musette bag." Tallini grabbed it and fell into a feathery gait, leaning into the darkness. This brought him into a space entirely surrounded by rock, but before he could look around, he heard Angelo: "Now come back, *hermano,* to make sure you can get out. Exactly the same way, but in reverse." Tallini's mindless body obliged as Angelo gave him a tap on the arm. "Get back in there, I'm right behind you."

● ◐ ◖ ◗ ◑ ●

"We call it 'el patio.' " They stood side by side in an arena whose amphitheater seemed entirely cored out of the rock. Tallini, looking about, felt his hand touch the wall behind him, and once again he sensed its unexpected smoothness. Perhaps his hypothesis of many hands was wrong.

"And the cave is over there," Angelo pointed diametrically ahead. But Tallini was preoccupied with quite a different phenomenon. His eyes were adapted to the starlight, but as he danced in and out of the crevice, he got the distinct impression it was *lighter* inside the rampart than out. By all rights it should have been just the contrary because the high walls were bound to restrict the light's access. It was almost by second nature that he perceived this, by the habit of the camera, which had sensitized his eye to available light. After each crossing he had felt in his hand the narrowing and widening of the aperture, a gesture that never lies. He briefly thought this light differential might be an effect of adaptation, but that didn't make much sense, when it looked to him as if it were getting even lighter.

"The light, Angelo," was all he said, but it drew an unexpectedly strong reaction from the Gypsy, who suddenly pulled up straight, opened his eyes wide, his nose tilted in the air as if to sniff the word he had just heard. He turned his head from side to side slowly in concentration until his face broadened into a grin. "You are right, *hermano*. This light, it is something that happens sometimes, we don't know why. It is a tradition not to tell the new *brujo* about it. Let him find out by himself, if it happens for him. Knowing about it before it has happened is dangerous, because wanting it to happen, you will imagine it, and you will become dishonest. Now we will sit while the light is with us, and think about the ancestors who lived in the cave."

He led Tallini to the center of the "patio" where there were two facing rocks roughly shaped for seating. Angelo took his place on one of them, but Tallini settled cross-legged on the ground as he had been instructed by the yogis in India. "This light," Angelo explained once he was seated, "it often came for me when I stayed here for a long while, when the vines were still bearing fruit. Then it started to happen less, and lately, I no longer distinguish any difference between in here and out there. Until just now. I saw it as soon as you said it.

"For Tio Ortiz, the light appeared also more often when he was younger. He thought it has to do with the stars that shine into the opening. If it is the right combination, it happens. But then why would it become weaker? The stars come back always the same, do they not, *amigo?* No, it must be that we see the difference less and less. It is a change in us, not in the stars.

"You know the stars are very important for us, as some of us read the future. So we look much at the stars, and we are certain our ancestors looked at them also. And it is clear that if two people look at the same thing, they have something in common, they are a little bit the same. And so we can be in touch with them, and make conversation." And he leaned back in his stone throne, silent in the contemplation of the many suns and ancestors.

Tallini watched him in this unusual luminosity, which was, if anything, on the increase. Had a moon risen somewhere out there, it would certainly augment this cylinder's available light. But wasn't this night specially picked by Angelo because of the new moon? Hadn't he said so when he made the arrangements? Tallini wasn't certain. So many remarkable things had happened, but he simply ascertained the sense of a new moon night. Furthermore, the luminosity surrounding the two men was clearly not the silvery sparkle of lunar reflection observed in the absence of its ultimate source. Turning away from the Gypsy, Tallini lifted his head and saw the stars as if through a huge telescope, with himself at the center of a giant's eye to observe what Angelo was observing, thus to enter into a dialogue on this slow beam of a very distant flame.

It came over Tallini how it was that in its proximity a direct solar flash blinds. He marveled that the evidence of the sun is always reflected before it strikes the eye, and the moon is but another means of this phenomenon, albeit a special one. So one can look at the moon, but what one *sees* is the fire of the sun, as we see sun everywhere around us erupting into all its lively colors. It is yet another aspect of fire, as is also the sap in the tree. But whereas the latter is part of the vivifying flow, and available to experiential examination, the former is a leap into the unknown. The eye cannot see the sun, yet the sun is everywhere the eye sees. Never comprehensible as such, a fire beyond all fires, it is taken for granted in its parts as a first nature. The grantor, however, is a *second* nature, one of habit. But is the first not necessarily part—and a significant part—of that second, which flowers from it and is entirely human?

Language, in fact, is the salient difference between first nature and second, between One and Two. What is seen is explosively creative, an autopoietic fireworks we can tolerate by sight only in a reflected form. Why had this never become livably meaningful to him before now? For what reason was he only *now* able to live it in his thinking? This is the eternal question behind evidential amazement, and he knew its answer was deeply buried in the past. It did, however, make him aware of the possibility of *forgetting* he had fallen into a swoon and came to be changed, to be other, and to be in the presence of Angelo. Beyond that, such questions matter no more than whether it be Tallini or Benji who answers them— as long as it is not *he, Pedro el Italiano!*

Dizzied by the vastness opening in these starlit instructions, Tallini lowered his eyes and caught the beam as it struck the rock wall and flashed to life, bouncing off at a crazy angle onto another section of wall, gaining speed and luminosity while Tallini sat in the middle—*"Un osservatore, per avventura!"* He perceived this moment dovetailing with that time at the table *Chez l'Alsacien.* Both moments were qualitatively identical, so why shouldn't he experience them as one qualitative fact? Both are approaches to an amplification by means of an acceleration.

318

Benji had called the question of the speed of light and its limit "a matter of perspective. And," he continued, "there are two master perspectives according to which all derives: the *addition* of One and One to make Two, or the *division* of One into Two. The former is a direct affirmation of positivity and a practical constructive use of One and its infinite linear successions. The other is a conscious negation of an ineffable One and its unfolding into dimensions. Each gives us its kind of duality, and everything else that comes with it." The speed of light and its limit could be found in the first perspective of the cumulative building blocks. The second needs no absolute speed and in no way limits light, thus fitting the qualitative fact of his experience. Tallini understood the limited speed of light as a figment of a materialistic physics, useless in the interpretation of this event. Not that there wasn't a speed to that ray of starlight, slowed as it was by the distant stillness of its source and so arriving softly, almost lazily, in the amphitheater. There the touch of the stone wall sparked the beam's energy, speeding its reflection to a further site, hence repeating the process as the beam went racing round and round the circle, suddenly cut off from its near-infinite past. Caught in a limited gyration feeding on itself, it kept accelerating, its luminosity increasing.

Now Tallini remembered the smoothness of the rock he had felt both at the entrance and inside the arena, and he realized that for this light amplification the reflecting surfaces had to be as smooth as he had felt them to be. Rock cleavage was not rare in these granite formations that had thrust themselves up into chalky coast, some rich in mica that could easily yield the desired surface. But how could such breaks have occurred so as to arrange the smooth planes in this enclosure? Considering the matter, he became aware of the earthshaking convulsions that must have torn the crust asunder to achieve this feat. Extremely vivid were these cataclysmic images evoking the mountain building and volcanic eruptions of a world in the making. When the raging calmed, his fearless sight rode the starlight's soft speed through rock, crust, and mantles, straight into the heart of the core's colorless fire, to reunite the two radiances. There could be no doubt as to the continuity of the *outer* fire *in* the rock—as well as in every living thing and being. In fact, he sensed the inner fire of the earth pushing its way out, pushing against the soles of his shoes.

Astounded by the ease of his gestures, he observed his own fluid motions as his hands untied the laces and he slipped out of his shoes and pulled off his socks, his feet now contacting the ground. All the while his thoughts harked back to that divesting at the spring when he was seized with a wild, undisciplined frenzy for maximum merging and moving in the ambient air. Then he had kicked off his shoes, sending them flying through space. Had he had wings, he would have taken flight himself! Instead—and unlike the airborne Daedalus—he crashed *before* takeoff, but emerged from a sea of blackness as *other*, another whose otherness he now experienced. Asked later about this otherness, he would say no more than it was new, and that the oldness whose comprehension made it new was the world *as is*, namely, Tallini's universe. But Tallini had no doubt he inhabited the same world as the other. And yet there was another, and wouldn't the other demand another world?

As his feet touched the ground, the push of the inner fire—hitherto a faint but steady pressure from below—shot through him like a weak electrical current instantly communicated to every cell of his body. Each and every cell was alive in him—it always had been, although never consciously lived as such. The excess of consciousness—new and other—now investing this enormous aggregate of cells, destabilized an existent state. Such disruptions are always energizing, in contrast to the reign of the old, a debilitating stability. This excess energy leaves its signature, branding flesh and cauterizing bone. He was aware it marked him, confirming the new and other he was, or was becoming. He would have felt himself in the throes of a Tallinic initiation of sorts, were it not for a voice, clear and articulate—and female: Hephysta!

"Ah *bon*, Monsieur Pierrot is no longer satisfied with geometry, he needs stronger medicine. At least it will keep him busy enough not to spy on young ladies when they go to listen to music with friends, nothing more! But what is it you are doing here barefoot in the night with this delusive *romanichel?* I am unable to compete, I'll admit, with such thrills.

"To tell the truth, I don't have a competitive nature. But you challenged me, Monsieur Pierrot, perhaps because you saw I am a simple provincial schoolteacher, on an extended paid vacation, the last for some time, and we live only once, *n'est-ce pas?* You see I am tied to my world, and I will never pursue you in those hills of yours, so you feel free to ask me for my definition of the point because misled by a gust of wind, no more, you think I am reading geometry. And you forgot our rendezvous. But there is no sense recapitulating these events that have sufficiently preoccupied me. As to your definition of the point, I believe you would have had a question like that for any other thing I might have been reading, from the Bible to the Marquis de Sade, and they all would have said the same thing. But I gave you a few answers, did I not? I was responsive to you, no? We are not savages, after all. But it is *your* responsibility, not mine, and that is what I came to tell you. And also to give you the true answer to your question, because perhaps you may be able to use it now.

"The only serious answer for this frivolous world of ours is that there *is* no definition of the point; there is only discourse about it. It doesn't exist because the point does not exist, and you know it as well as I do. You were teasing, monsieur, you were toying, and you never bothered about your responsibility. You were too busy asking other questions elsewhere, no doubt. And what is the question you are asking here this evening, Pierrot? What definition are you asking for tonight?" The sound of the voice stopped abruptly, leaving Tallini with an aftertaste of artifice.

Suddenly Angelo was standing next to him. Tallini had not noticed him moving. And it had turned dark, the only light from a few flickering stars that could be seen in the aperture. "I will make a fire there, where those ashes are. You sit down." He pointed to the ground ahead, but in the dark, Tallini had to crouch and probe the ground until he encountered a few charred pieces of wood and the silky feel of ashes. Angelo disappeared briefly into the cave to fetch some wood shavings, dried leaves, and straw. On the bed of ashes, he arranged the heap through which the flame was to draw its first breath. "We never use paper," he explained, "and we always draw the flame from stone. Those are the two rules for making fire, and I understand the first one very well. Paper leaves a mess behind, like a black crust through which nothing can breathe. And it has no endurance after sudden heat, and unless some wood takes over, it's gone or else clogs itself in its own *mierda*. And makes too much smoke and useless light, which only gives it away."

After another foray into the cave, Angelo returned with kindling, which he leaned delicately, stick by stick, around the flue. "I have always obeyed the second rule also, because it is the rule. But now I think it is different. I can no longer find the reasons for it, as I can for the paper. I know the teaching about fire says the flame must come only from heaven or from earth, either from lightning or from fire stones, and it is a different fire if it comes from one or the other. This I once believed also, because it was told me by Tio Ortiz. But for some time already, I can believe it no longer. He said the fire must never come from phosphorus and sulphur or other chemicals. I have obeyed the rule, but in my heart, I have come to believe that it can't make any difference where the fire comes from, that once it is fire, it is all the same. I have come to believe it is a superstition from the old *brujos*. Some of them were blacksmiths like me, and people I meet working in the forges still believe it. I tell you this because for today we are going to use friction matches. But first I'll bring more wood."

This time he stayed away a little longer, offering Tallini the leisure to contemplate a somewhat ironic situation. The

Gypsy's declaration of disbelief acquainted Tallini with a hitherto unknown consideration he nevertheless recognized as qualitative fact. A vision that was seemingly forsaken by Angelo was replaced by the evidence of an everyday event. Whether heavenly or earthly, this flame was immediately meaningful to Tallini as a qualitative aspect of the fire fact. Fallen to earth, fire is a celestial gift bestowed by an act of natural power, whereas the stone's spark depends for its striking on no other power but the human hand. This is a fire humankind has always possessed, a fire no divinity can withhold. The quest of Prometheus is therefore not the flame of a candle or of a phosphorus stick, nor the million flames of a forest blaze—it is the *seed* of fire he purloins from the hub of the sun wheel. The flame from above wastes its awesome power on a ground, at best leaving only fiery footprints. He wants this fire *before* it strikes earth, before it is trapped in it and constrained to burning itself out laboriously. But between heaven and earth, this power is apprehensible for humans exclusively as *light*. And so the sharp-eyed volatile is chosen as agent of punishment—or is it a teaching?—after Prometheus' stealthy theft of the fire's dormant seed. What the eagle destroys is traditionally designated as the ever-recrescent seat of *personality*.

Angelo returned with some twisted pieces of wood that looked like dried-out roots. He rattled a box of matches. "It's the first time I use these up here, but you are not a Gypsy, you are here only for closing the cave, so I know I will be forgiven. There are fire stones in the cave, but they take practice, and I don't make a fire very often, only on special occasions. The fire could be noticed, so we make small fires, and with this very dry wood that is stored in the cave, there is little smoke, so nothing can be seen from outside."

Soon Angelo was fanning a little flame. It seemed quaint to Tallini, reminding him of the campfires of his youth. "For the torches we need the fire," Angelo explained. "They don't light very easily." Tallini felt a tide of impatience welling up in him. Angelo brought the wooden sticks. Then he fanned the blaze, built it up a bit more, and when he was satisfied it had taken, stood up and told Tallini he was leaving, and no, he shouldn't move, he would rather remember him thus, by the fire. And he said there was a large plastic jug of water inside the cave, fresh from the source; he had filled it yesterday. And because it would be better if he had water with him all the time, he gave him his own *bota*. Then, certain he had taken care of everything, Angelo turned and went his way.

● ◑ ○ ◔ ◑ ●

Tallini sat for a moment, his mind a weave of confusion and clarity. Now that it was all there for him, now that it was all "his," he felt a sudden letdown, which he attributed to a release of tensions, or perhaps he was feeling the chill of the stars. Then came the discovery that the other, the one he had become, didn't really *have* much "his"! Had it not been for the elation that accompanied this new state, he might have slipped back into the old, which was full of things "his": the old Tallini was an Italian, he was a photographer as well as a friend of Benji, an acquaintance of a Sidonie he had named Hephysta. Each one of these relations defined him, formed his attitudes, fashioned his life. At the bottom of all these *his's*— his mother tongue, his country, his flag, his profession, his friends, his acquaintances—was the one who had blacked out and had never come to. That is how it must have happened, although the switch was not immediately detected. Only by becoming a *brujo* had he taken the giant step.

But now, while he sat there, this *brujería*, this witchery itself lost its uniqueness, for he realized he had been a *brujo* before, and not only just once. Several occasions now stirred in his memory when he had felt a similar elation and had been equally changed, renewed. Had he not become a *brujo* when he was very small and saw himself for the first time in a mirror? And on the ledge of the quarry, when he thought he would die, but disappeared in a sound with that same elation? And later, every time he fell profoundly in love? What was different now was that Angelo had actually *named* this state,

324

this elation of renewal through the other, be it one's fellow man or one's mirror image, be it even but a perception, a sound, in his particular case. The nomination lent it a quasi-official status—*el brujo*—at least in Angelo's clan.

This multiplication of the oracular moment was a second giant step. In a quick review of those earlier instances, Tallini ascertained that in each, the *other* existed in a special manner in which he, Tallini, had been invited to participate. Perhaps such moments could be multiplied through some activity of his own, a will, or perhaps, quite to the contrary, a yielding. And yet despite these revelatory insights into repetition and alterity, or perhaps because of them, Tallini felt the need for something more. Called for here was a participation he was not only willing but anxious to offer. It was up to him, and he was ready. He was elated at having succeeded, at having achieved the aim, yet even to himself he couldn't define that success and achievement. Crowning it all was a marveling incomprehension of the way everything could have happened so simply and naturally.

Nevertheless he experienced a touch of apprehension at how quickly and how far he had gotten involved in this—whatever it was that had started out as a search for ... he knew not what, but it had evolved into this *brujería*. Only now did it occur to him that, once again, he hadn't even brought a camera along, he had never even thought of bringing the Leica he always used for unobtrusive reporting. Remembering he hadn't put it in his musette bag reminded him of what else was always in it: a small flashlight with reserve batteries. The bag had remained at the center of the patio where he had watched the starlight. He got to his feet, intending to fetch it. But when he stood up, he went over to the hearth, picked up one of the torches, lit it in the fire, and waited until it was burning brightly. Then he took the few paces toward the mouth of the cave and crossed its threshold.

SIXTEEN

CAVE DWELLING

Tallini took a few careful paces forward. The corridor he had entered almost immediately turned to the left, past a curve lined with kindling and small logs, and then it narrowed, the walls at one point touching his shoulders. With the next sharp turn, the passageway widened again, and the walls stopped twinkling in concert with his torch. It seemed he had stepped into a spacious hall whose obscurity at once enfolded him. Holding the torch high overhead, he continued on with confidence into its shallow glow. When he stopped, it was as if his body sensed that many others had stopped here before.

He looked up beyond the flame, trying to make out a ceiling, but could see nothing at all. A draft appeared to be flickering his torch. There was ample space all around him now, and that waft of strangely chilly air. Peering about, he realized he could easily become disoriented, and decided to move closer to a wall that would lead him back to the entrance. Because of the configuration of the entrance corridor, he assumed that even in the daytime no outside light could reach this hall. And if the cave turned out to be empty, then the only objects of investigation would be the very walls.

Turning to the right, he almost stumbled over a small heap of stones. His reflex was to push them aside with his foot, but he caught himself in time. In this enterprise, Tallini intended to live by the rules, and Angelo was insistent that nothing be moved. By leaving the flashlight in his musette bag, he had already begun to prove his commitment to proto-col. But did the prohibition refer to the rubble one would, after all, expect to find in a cave? He hadn't yet encountered anything that *could* be moved, and these particular stones, probably fallen from the ceiling, were the first objects that might qualify under the hands-off rule, so he let them be.

Lowering the torch for a better look, he saw this was not rubble at all, that it was a heap of small stones, none bigger than a fist, and most much smaller. They appeared to have been not simply gathered in a pile but stacked up with care. Perhaps they were some sort of votive offering. Parts of the heap still showed deliberate arrangement, but some stones seemed to have been displaced, perhaps by animals or by a past *brujo* who had stumbled into it as he had, with an inad-vertent foot. But were Tallini to break the rule, he could not have blamed his feet, which would have continued straight ahead had *he* not decided to stop. He remembered having so decided, and then turning to walk toward a wall. Or perhaps this heap was a marker, a sign, a boundary post, a *term* before its time, and powerful enough to stop him short—for what reason, he couldn't imagine. In any case, the pile of stones had arrested him, and he was grateful. He memorized its as-pect from where he stood, then walked all around it one time, assessing it as a possible compass. This closer inspection con-vinced him these were the remnants of a purposeful arrange-ment that betrayed a *hand*. The smaller stones scattered at the side of the heap led him to envision higher layers of the structure, layers that had collapsed.

He thought of sitting down in front of the stone heap. By revealing a work of the hand to him, the pile of stones had turned itself into structure in his mind. Had it been a con-scious effort? By whom and to what purpose? Angelo might have furnished some clues, but in his absence, all Tallini had to go by was here in front of him. Yet he hesitated—the torch was burning low, and it had been a long day. But mainly, his own reaction baffled him. The tortuous entry had been a surprise, and by the time he had reached this chamber what-ever lofty expectations he may have entertained were fading.

These stones reminded him there was more, that there were rules of engagement and, therefore, responsibility. Did his behavior correspond to what was expected of someone on a mission to close a cave? Angelo had said nothing about exploration nor had he described the cave, except for the comfortable stone slabs near the entrance, wherefore Tallini had envisaged that area as still accessible to daylight, or even moonlight. Now he bit his lip in chagrin. What was he doing here, anyway? Was this murky tunnel really the cave of his quest? The letdown mood that had set in with Angelo's departure deepened with every step. Instead of exploring, shouldn't he go back and sit on those slabs near the entrance as Angelo had done, sit and await instructions? Hadn't Angelo said he would find out how to proceed once he was in the cave? In spite of his powerful attraction to the heap of stones before him, he felt it was time to regain the entrance, so he turned back.

Tallini had to walk on much further than he anticipated, and after coming to what he thought would be the wall, he found it to be but a fairly narrow panel of stone, beyond which was absolute darkness again. Yet he persisted in this direction, only to encounter another panel, this one larger than the first, but it too stopped abruptly after a while, leaving him once more in black emptiness. Drawn by the unknown, he progressed gropingly, almost automatically, to several other panels. Then the torch burned his thumb, reminding him it would soon be spent. The burn pulled him away from the magnet drawing him on, only to lead him into a maze of stone galleries as he attempted to retrace his steps. A touch of fear caught his breath and sped his heartbeat, the fear of the quarry and the crag, the dread of their stony indifference in the moment's need. And indeed, as he attempted to retrace his steps, the rock offered no assistance. Everything looked different. Soon it seemed to him he had walked much farther back than he had come, and still he was surrounded by these vertical partitions, which seemed to be ever more densely set. Without knowing why, he turned again. He no longer heard the hollow echo of his footsteps. As he raised the torch, it hit the ceiling and collapsed into sparks, falling to the floor, smoking and glowing faintly. Save for that glow—which lasted no more than a minute—it was as if he had been blindfolded. His first thought was of the matches Angelo had left with the kindling at the entrance. Confused and panicking, Tallini felt hopelessly lost.

Once his breath and heartbeat had settled back to normal, he inhaled and exhaled deeply several times. His body wanted to move, but an intuition kept him from leaving that spot. Not through reason would he work his way out of *this* predicament. Centering in his mind the configuration of the corridor and entrance into the hall, he planted one heel on the rock floor and started pivoting round and round. This circular movement seemed to satisfy his conflicting requirements for bodily movement and psychic immobility. Like a clockwork mechanism slowly uncoiling, and in total and exclusive mindfulness of the corridor, he turned on his body's axis until he regained his bearings. Moving ahead again slowly, he came to a familiar partition and then, recognizing the hollow echo of the hall, he knew he was out of the stone woods. Following a wall and certain the entrance was near, he was advancing decisively when he hit his shin and lurched forward with a curse of pain.

Tallini sat rubbing his leg until the pain subsided. He closed his eyes and tried to think of nothing. Not only did he immediately succeed, but it became unusually easy for him to maintain this imageless state. The cave seemed to be absolutely dark; it appeared the same whether his eyes were closed or open. What was this, then, he perceived looming before him? It was the surface of darkness. The *volume* of that darkness remained unavailable, although he *knew* he participated in it. Strange this should impress him now, when he couldn't see any part of it. All he could discern was its black surface, which couldn't be part of the volume, only its limit—a volume is volume in its entirety. Black? Not the absence of colors, but their chaos, spectrum in all its shaded detail, but devoid—as yet?—of prismatic order. Had it been truly a perfect *black* he was seeing, black would have been alone among all colors to achieve its own ultimate unshaded and undifferentiated whole. But it didn't, for in this perfect darkness, vision was busily dappled with light, fast moving designs shooting through the dark: light seen in total darkness, a chaos of orderless night light.

He remembered what this surface was called by the yogi who had instructed him to close his eyes in meditation and to let them rest without effort. "Rest on the frontal plane," he had said. But with the sound of that voice the frontal plane had ceased to be a surface of nothingness. No longer black, it was filled with colors and forms in the sun of that Jaipur afternoon. Taught to make the image disappear, he contemplated it with indifference, out of boredom, until it faded. Yet the frontal plane remained, it needed no input beyond a perceptive consciousness. Of itself it formed designs and images, and wasn't that—he asked himself—but a small step away from everyday daylight vision? And was that distance not a *quality* of light? It wouldn't have been the first time he experienced vision in darkness by the light of meditation, but now he understood its logic. The light of day is wed to volume, whereas the light of darkness is inscribed in volumeless space. That space he had felt inside him, obscurely. Here light was shed on this obscurity. As the volume is inside out, so space is outside in. He knew that such complex relations could be subjected to a geometry of forms and formulas, and yet, in a very different manner, he also knew that on the page they could never capture his experience of their realization— not a simple understanding but a making real by a bringing-into-being.

Then a silvery dawn arose inside him, the rigor of the frontal plane weakening as a motion rippled through and turned it into a veil that fluttered as if in a breeze and then was gone. All his feeling functions rushed into the unknown prospect of sensation and perception that had opened, poised to vibrate and to act in this new capacity. Without sense objects, however, and in the absence of a frontal plane, the turbulences of the mind no longer found a screen on which to

330

project their fake light play. A word came: *chaos.* It lasted but a moment, yet Tallini sensed a total reshuffle of components. A metallic illumination rose within him, surrounding him with a precious mineral aura. Guruji's voice arose in his heart: "The messengers of action return, not as source of information but as powers of cognition." Why had they been searching for stimulation in this field of pure disorder, those messengers of his? But already they had adjusted and found their mark, which could be nothing but stone. Not the action at the surface—best left to the sense of touch—but cognition in depth of stone where primordial qualities are housed. Could the network, which Tallini had experienced by *mineral* components inside the boulder, now be known by *tissue* from without? The messengers located a central fire and returned bearing strands of light, the same silvery light surrounding him. The center of the stone glowed with the light of day, illuminated by sunlight, just as fiber, processed by time, releases captured sunlight when it burns. Light in stone is like the fire of the eye.

As every volume has its tone, this universal sound component of all physical things and beings joins the fiery light at the center of stone. Because sound itself is volume, it permits audition in the round of any volume, a service light vision is unable to provide for the eye. In Tallini's dark and silent circumstances, the two prime senses of sight and hearing no longer served the sensorium's need for stimulation. This made it possible to explore a deeper sense of sight and hearing, which escapes thermal and tactile sensing: a fire that does not burn the hand and a volume the hand cannot touch. Here, light and sound pertain to eye and ear, but do not yield dimensional perspectives. Under these conditions, the messengers —Guruji called this sensory function *"indriya"*—no longer report to a static reception that interprets and forwards them for representation. Tallini's entire being was immersed in the light of fire and in the volume of sound surging from stone. And then this plenitude spread to all senses; volume was odoriferous and light left a taste of flint in his body cells.

He felt disoriented, but as his body sought stability in the support of the stone floor and the slab on which he sat, all differentiation between stone and body vanished. The sense of touch, no longer confined to the skin, was activated throughout his body. Thermal and tactile sensations, pain and pleasure acknowledged life activity at every single point of his body, and at every point he felt suspended in and sustained by a pervasive substance exempt from gravity. And then he realized this substance was a weave of strands carried by the messengers from an infinity of stone centers, filaments of light that had filled the volume of sound with a mesh woven through the tissues of his own body. He was suspended in this spatial illumination, and a great number of connective patterns were evoked between him and the stone origin.

Then, to the perceptive integrity of a body that had attained the primitive wholeness of a single sense organ, a presence made itself felt, a presence he vaguely remembered as from a distant past. He neither heard nor saw nor felt it, though if it were to speak, he was quite sure he would recognize it. Neither by sound nor by form did he perceive it, nor by any other quality, but as an undivided whole commensurate with his own totalized perceptivity. And thus in his own silent inner voice he interpreted to himself the sense of its communication.

First you will learn the seat of all clarity is stone, and you will remember that ultimately nothing survives which is not set in the mineral. Stone is first and last, and all you desire from stone you can find here in this enclosure. This was something proved, coaxed out of the rock by those on the threshold of time. They are the beings you are searching for, they are the ones who came to me once the rock was cool and solid, once the air had become light and the water thick, and their own bodies had settled into the form that is also yours. Their ancestors still had lived entirely in partnership with plant-nature, learning from vegetation and using the fire power of its seed. Then came great changes in all forms, their own and the elements'. They had to leave their vegetative life and felt exposed and vulnerable. With the thickening of the water, they lost the benign fire power of the seed and turned to the fire that now could burn in the thinning air, a fire that gave them protection. With that they were ready to enter the earth.

I am the indestructible spirit of the mineral, and I exist even in the smallest grain of sand. I am most powerful where the earth is hollow, and they were driven to the hollows of the earth. They did not yet think or reason, but they possessed the capacity of imaging, and their lives were lived in those few images gathered from their limited and repetitive lives. So close were these images to their lives that they were as yet unable to separate themselves from them. And while they had not yet a language of thought and reason, they had a small number of powerful sounds that gave them dominion over those images by a force unknown to your thinking tongue. And it forged for them a new link with nature to replace the lost partnership with the plant world.

After a long time in this state, they came to me to find what they required and desired, and were given the eyes to see the stone so they would be able to do their work. This is the work you have come to find, and I will give you the eyes to see it. When they left, they abandoned the stone and in time forgot the images, having started to speak. But during their stay in the cave their eyes were clear, and once they had mastered words, they walked like gods. They accumulated a treasure of feeling and of being together with their own kind, and with the animals and the plants. What they found in the hollows—consciousness of self and language—would cover the earth, although the sovereignty of stone was to be diminished with the advent of bronze and then iron. Yet these are also in stone, all the times of the future are in stone, for those who can read them. But when they began to inscribe the stone with their chronologies and their impressions and beliefs, they neglected the practice of their remembered images. It enfeebled their penetrating vision because they began remembering in words; this practice caused their eyes to be covered by a translucent shield. The sickness of your life is this shield that defends you from what you perceive. Now *you are as blind as were they who had never seen. They came for assistance and found it in my realm, the mineral, where it is always alive. It was they who lived in this cave, who worked on the stones until they brought forth this clarity. I will lend you their eyes.*

◗ ◖ ◯ ◯ ◑ ◕

Tallini lay on the stone slab. Had this been a dream? He didn't feel as if he had slept, but he was pervaded by boundless lassitude. He couldn't move as much as a finger. No thought came to his mind, no sight to his eyes, no sound to his ears. His awareness was dimmed to the soul's night light that guards the breath in conscious sleep. A massive heaviness pulled him downward, down through the rock, down toward an unknown center. A dull pressure against his shoulders at times penetrated this twilight, as if soft amorphous shapes were gently nudging. This was accompanied by eerie sounds and noises, moans, growls, and whistling. All sense of time or space had vanished. The descent could have lasted an eternity or taken but a moment, and soon it was as if he had found a new equilibrium at zero gravity. Infinities of time passed in an instant as consciousness abandoned him completely.

A female vocalise of breathtaking beauty lingered in mezzo range, as if to gather strength to open immense expanses stretching back to archaic times. Then it took a brief flight, fell back, and after a few long plaintive vowels, soared again until it reached the full soprano of its upper range, where it hovered and floated in a delicate melisma. It sank in decrescendo and broke the spell with crystalline laughter.

All around now were female voices in peals of laughter and excited chatter, soft shouts and mellifluous exchanges, the patter of bare feet and the rustle of flowing robes. Again, in the distance, a few voices were testing a close harmony. Then suddenly a hush as a dark contralto commanded the domain, forceful, severe, and tender all at once.

"Enough—enough of play! Can ye not hear the soil above

that clamors to be nurtured, she who lies barren while ye sing and jest! Not for dalliance were ye chosen and recalled to these depths of Origin, but to practice poise and revitalize thy fertile essence. Off then, ye Nymphs, to quarry Our veins of generative power, to garner fertile essence from that mother lode, and then, duly charged, be sent aloft to spread Our tidings teemingly. And when above, remember these majestic halls for yet another cargo, and do not fall to loitering in shallow grottoes and pleasing some frivolous lover with lascivious dance. And ye, quarrelsome Meliades, already charged with fruitful burden, get ye above and to an ash, ye daughters of Uranos. And all the other Hamadryads, why do ye tarry! Seek out the arborescences whose destiny ye will share and with the dowry We bestow, inhabit them and cajole them into mighty trees, and waste not further time in gossip here below. And now be gone, I have a visitor!"

Turning to a recumbent Tallini:

"Welcome to these archaic vaults, intrepid mortal. Do We detect Our distant cousin's greeting, that blameless soul, dweller of the superficies and trafficker in crystals, long known for his assistance to your kind! Be advised those eyes he lent you for exploring his realm are useless in Ours, which tolerates neither distance nor perspective. But you have the ear to hear Us, and We shall tell you everything necessary to know of Our domain, which now seems but darkness. We have not seen the likes of you since the Rhenish Doctor, philosophus philosophorum, and note with pleasure that the stench of singe, so dominant on him, plays no part in your appearance. The other came with dubious references and on a selfish quest. He purloined our incense brazier, a precious heirloom. We suspect the complicity of one of Our brothers, fearfully called 'the Rich,' merciless master of the lower depths who lets no one return unfettered to the living once they taste his sojourn's bitter grain. His own niece even. . . .

"Ah, but We have mourned sufficiently and need no longer dwell on wretched family feuds. Suffice it to assure you that your fall was not toward his shadowy reign. It was *a fall but for your senses' heaviness, and not in truth. 'Tis not Our brother's nether realm you've reached, but the work-place of the goddesses. Not death reigns here, but deft left hands weaving the fabric of life. It is the Magic even before magic, the fount of everything that lives above, of Mater and Matter, Might and Making, the root of all roots, the cosmic taproot of all earthly life. Benighted only can you touch this midnight mystery, as no expanse as yet accommodates the light of eye. Direct it inward, then, where eye and world are one, and put your soul to sleep, so that it leave you free of image. Here time is without motion and space without dimension, existence beyond measure and before even One-ness. And yet the Nature of Our domain is of time and space and measure, but dormant yet. Not for your understanding, but for discovery within yourself, as you yourself contain this pristine stage of being. Here you may live life's birth and thus unravel the mystery of your own. For the origin is always present, of cosmos and of heaven and earth, as well as of whatever you call yourself, so that you may truly know who you might be. Achieve this state and live in Paradise. We leave you there."*

● ◖ ○ ◗ ◑ ◐

Had aeons passed, or had there been a lightless flash, a second that contained a million years? Or had Tallini had a dream? No, this was not a "having," but a "being." Then had he *been* a dream? That more correctly fit his feeling. A dream in the Mind that had addressed him, the dark contralto in his ear. He recalled nothing about it he could put into words, but he felt a state of reverence pervading his being. As this was all he retained, he fastened on to it in a calm and effortless concentration. And opened his eyes.

He was no longer in the pitch-black cave he had entered by torchlight, but surrounded by a faint yet steady luminosity like a long-forgotten landscape revealed in the sudden turn of a road. There was no doubt as to the nature of such clarity, and Tallini greeted this indirect trace of sunlight like a long-lost friend. Perhaps these others—the torchlight, the metamorphic light of the frontal plane, the silvery mineral light, the no-light of the depths that had no space to spread, a light no eye could see—perhaps they had been no less natural than this faint glow of daylight, and they almost certainly all had one and the same absolute source. But only this one could warm him, body, heart, and soul. However dim, this was the reassuring gleam of daylight, and it made him sit up with a start. The stone slab on which he had been lying was next to the cave wall; on his right was a large hall in which five shafts of diffused light broke through the roof. As he followed the shimmering rays from ceiling to ground, he noticed each illuminated an irregularity on the floor, and he scrambled to his feet when he realized it must have been one of these heaps of stones he had inspected by torchlight! When had this been? Certainly not just the night before! It was as if an eternity had played out during that short night, as if he had lived innumerable lives. But he couldn't dwell on the past, for as he drew near the stones under that natural spotlight, he felt they contained a future.

He noticed how the light beams assumed specific shapes when they struck the cave floor, a fissure in the rock ceiling permitting the light to penetrate only in spots. There was no way of telling whether these were natural apertures or deliberate cuts into the rock. He spent a little time at each heap, going from one to the other, rigorously obeying the taboo against moving any stone, although he could not resist touching several of them. As he ran his fingers over them lightly, he noted some had rough surfaces.

A gnawing sensation was drawing attention to his hunger, and this brought to mind the paella jar at the entrance. Angelo must certainly have come and gone by now. No matter; Tallini decided to replace breakfast by a brief meditation on the stones before him. But no sooner had he enthroned his subject in the frontal plane than a distinct want made itself felt in the palm of his hand. What was it, after all, that was preventing him from picking them up? A prohibition that had come down through generations without plausible reason for its observance. Confronted with the unknown, past *brujos* had preferred to follow tradition. But he had witnessed Angelo's own disregard of another such rule, the use of flint to light the fire. An examination of the stones seemed essential now. Perhaps breaking through this particular received tradition was the first rule of closing the cave. Thus his meditation ended before it had begun, as he reached over and picked up the stone closest to his hand.

◗ ◖ ○ ○ ◐ ◑

Unlike Arvan's Paleolithic tools, this stone didn't readily conform to his grip, nor did it have a sharp edge bespeaking its function of cutting and scraping. Tallini carefully laid it down next to him and tried another and then another, each time with much the same result. Most were far too small to be used as utensils; what they all had in common, however, was one more or less flat side that had been invariably placed facing upward in the stack. Holding a stone with the tips of his fingers around its flat face, Tallini's grip seemed to correspond to some willingness of the stone to be thus held. Did he imagine it, or was this edge indeed more polished than the rest of the stone? As he moved it back and forth in the beamed light, the irregularities of the surface threw tiny shadows that lent it depth. Suddenly a face appeared in the stone: turbaned head, bearded countenance, deep-set eyes—a stunningly realistic image. As he moved the stone ever so slightly, the image disappeared, and he had some trouble finding it again. Instead, partial representations appeared, a profile here, a landscape there, or some architectural motif.

Tallini set the stone down and picked up another. It was marked by fracture lines forming various shapes, geometric surfaces, mainly parallelograms. He turned it in every possible way, but it yielded only these abstract shapes. He tried a third stone, and turning it round and round, he produced a variety of images, some representative, some abstract, as well as some possible faces, more or less distorted, and in a few cases, landscapes with structures that reminded him of sanctuaries he had visited. He examined several more stones, until one fact seemed absolutely clear. Each had a relatively flat side, which in this particular light yielded a variety of shapes and images. Could this be the reason for these collections? But although the stones, sheltered here, might have remained unchanged for thousands of years, certainly the human eye and brain had not, and what he, with his sophisticated vision, was detecting was certainly not what the ancient ones had seen in their time.

Then Tallini remembered the voice that had promised him eyes, *their* eyes, and this now became clear to him. He was being given eyes to see what he needed to see in the cave. Yet here he was, stupidly regarding the stones with his *own* eyes, which had seen all he had seen and were controlled by a brain that had thought a lifetime of thoughts, and knew what it thought it knew! Those eyes were patently useless here. Could the ancient cave people conceive a turbaned head, for instance, when they had never seen a piece of woven cloth? No, he needed new eyes, he must forget all he had ever seen and all he knew. He had to regain the eyes of a child at the onset of the human species' many tens of thousands of years of conscious and self-conscious seeing and thinking. The eyes of that child must still be within his, as the voice had assured him. In Jaipur, he had learned to locate interior states of utter simplicity, and he now proceeded through the steps of this discipline, whose daily practice he had continued. Never before had he been able so directly to attain the denudation of all artifice of thought and feeling. This inner austerity evoked a sense of truth. A purity of purpose evolved until there emanated the reverential state that is the aim. The pupil was now ready for his meditational work.

Thus by the time Tallini opened a pair of eyes both newest and oldest, the cave had come alive inside him. Maintaining his contemplative state, he kept his regard from roaming, from attempting to ascertain the nature of the change. He was looking straight ahead through a cornucopia

Someone has come to lead, no one knows from where. He is called the Wizard. He speaks of waking up, says their doing is sleep, and their sleep, death. He wants their sleep full of dreams, and a waking that is known. He speaks of waking the soul *in dreams and the* thinking *in waking. Only few follow him, the others stand aside and make the sounds of danger. Their bodies remember what is seen and done, and can repeat it; that is all they want. The Wizard shows the hand stretched outside; now the thinking must be stretched inside. He says those with fear are still in the whole, in the egg, where there are no questions. They remain the same and see no difference between in and out, between each one of them and the other, the world outside. The Wizard teaches the other. He leads some of them inside, into the cave, to find what they have not yet seen and done, and to teach what cannot be seen. He brings them stones to practice. The seed of all is in the stones. Some understand, others only follow. Before the Wizard, sky and earth were only one sound, the same. Now they are different, blue and green. And always looking into the stones for the other, all the difference that is to come.*

of light that shone down on the stones in front of him, after which his gaze, seeing now with no more than a haze of peripheral vision, plunged blindly into the dusky cavern as if into an abyss. Yet now he seemed to be detecting what he ordinarily would have thought was going on around him by a kind of sensory palpation. Perception of the ambient cave merged with his own interiority. Along with this realization came a desire to exteriorize these beings who were part of him, yet who were also sitting as he was before piles of stones. He wanted to establish a distance between them and him, to make them into something he was not. But they seemed not truly to exist separately in the volume outside of himself, although he knew them well in the cave of his inner space. They were participating in his state of reverence, infusing it with a nuance of awed amazement that strengthened his own resolve. And as he reached forward to pick up a stone, in a slow, measured movement so as not to disturb this state, he was aware his gesture was being mimicked all through the cave inside him. More than imitated. *Their* gestures and his were simultaneous; they were moved by his movements, multiplying them as if linked by an invisible bond. As he lowered his eyes toward his hand, they didn't adjust to the change in distance, and his vision was blurred. He could barely make out the rock in his hand. He looked at its fuzzy contour, but he had forgotten why.

How long until the eyes would learn to focus on the nearby object? Weeks, months, years, a generation? There is no duration in this work, not yet. Sitting cross-legged, absorbed in what he had not yet seen clearly, the others with him in his interior cave, Tallini felt as one with his ancestors. And slowly his vision sharpened, the stone surface was clear to his eye. Now he saw the stone. Before, he had only held it and heard it. The holding came first, in the fist, for throwing, for hitting, for scraping. Then the teaching that from hitting stones together came the hearing of rhythm, and the rhythm accentuated the feeling of flow. Many tried practicing the rhythm of the flow, and some persisted and learned stones were all different because they had a different hitting sound, thereby giving a different feeling to the flow. Gathering good-sounding stones, they invented lithophones and in groups practiced making the stones sound together. It was a time of liberation for them because there was movement now where there had been confinement and immobility.

Later there came the seeing and the teaching of the seeing. With the use of stones to create sounds and rhythms, but especially with stone-gazing, great changes came to the cave people. Before that, each one was alone, each one a world without extension or alterity, a unison precluding harmony, identity concealing consciousness, and an incommensurable sameness. No time present, past, or future, only isolated moments of happening, and few needs, always the same, demanding fulfillment. No questions, no decisions, no striving, but also no felt soul and no contemplated sky. Yet there was an aura of origin, half paradise, half purgatory.

Such was the state of sameness that would be weakened by rhythm-making and broken entirely by stone-gazing. As time passed, difference was slowly drawn from the stones by those who practiced their contemplation in the interior cavern. But not all could follow the way of entering into the cave, and some were unwilling. For yet others, the focusing skill was difficult to acquire; it came only to very few. These few used the diffused light that broke through the ceiling, letting it play on the stone so something was revealed, and they learned to see that something and name it, with a breath-sound. They in turn taught others, who put order in the stones, classifying them.

In the sounds transmitted to him, words like *library of stones* came to Tallini, and with those words came the realization he was once again seeing through his own eyes. With *their* eyes he may well have viewed what happened and how, but he would have to inscribe the experience through *his own*, and this was now possible. However, until he did that, what he had seen with the eyes lent to him would not be accessible as memory.

Tallini sensed the presence of other stone-gazers, yet he kept his eyes on the rocks, neither looking up nor turning around for fear of chasing them away. Evidently they were the same entities whose fragmentary messages had been coming down for some time, but now he found himself *surrounded* by them, which meant he was present on their level—or they on his. Unlike the entities that had appeared out of the landscape at the source, these didn't require his attention for their existence. In fact, he was certain they would shy away from any notice he might take of them, that they would scatter and disappear. Deciding they had been attracted by this activity they shared with him, he redoubled his concentration on the stone he held, a particularly cryptic specimen covered with linear markings that might well have portrayed a script. He tried to grasp the significance this particular design might command for humans who, even if they had achieved expression by sounds, certainly had no conventional writing.

So as not to distract them in any way, he tried to make himself as unobtrusive as possible, to remain in a meditative mode, focused entirely on the stones. He tried to limit the thoughts going through his mind, fearing they could disturb the cave people around him. Being new to thought, these humans were still very sensitive to it, he felt, and more readily able to detect a thinking process in another. His thoughts all at once seemed to be reverberating through the huge cavern in a most disturbing manner. Their thinking—if that was the word for what reached him—was not directed toward any aim. It was not used for knowing or comprehending, but was at most a silent sound of their perception. This inarticulated sound was the only sign of their ambient presence. It registered in his inner ear, but never entered the auditory canal, nor did it vibrate the tympanic membrane. It was an internal sound, speaking from soul to soul. And slowly it infused him with the spirit of their time, a time of transition.

His presence in their gazing chamber, his interest in the stones, his ease of concentration seemed to have raised expectations among his unseen hosts. Were they waiting for his interpretation of these rocks? How could they fathom that these pebbles, whatever they might do for *them*, would not be the same for *him*? Tallini, gazing into stone, did no more than *recognize*, without attaining even the basic inspiration illuminating the discovery by these early ones who were in the throes of original cognition.

What was the flaw in his approach? Tallini became certain that his error was in looking backward, trying to contact the cave mind in a past, a retrospection entirely foreign to those he was attempting to emulate. Not only was his conduct contrary to their travail, but it implied they were aspiring to his own present state. And as he deepened his introspection to correct this egocentricity, it came to him with utter clarity that his error lay deeper yet, that the very underpinnings of his intuitions had to be revised. He was making *temporal* presumptions. In fact, the construction of past/present/future was *his* problem, not theirs. Origin without past is an insight of pure logic. But its being futureless, and its distinction, thus, from a mere beginning—an ever-present origin—such a realization belonged to an ontological domain. He had projected a future onto the archaic mind where it simply couldn't be absorbed. Time, Tallini now realized, was not the early ones' concern at all; he had been projecting it onto them. Neither retrospection nor prospection could reach them, engaged as they were in the most elemental conquest of space, the struggle for a basic perspective, for a dimension that would break through the identity enclosing them in a cosmic egg of sameness.

◑ ◑ ○ ○ ◐ ◐

Tallini's gaze turned into a stare, the stare dissolving into a blur as the stone he had been regarding lost all objective characteristics. It had become part of the hand that held it, part of the arm that grew out of the body that was part of the cave that was the world he was, and there was nothing outside of him. "Before thought, before mind," those were the last sounds to reach him as oblivion beckoned with an infinite naught. In terror of this nothingness, the hair rose on the nape of his neck, yet the world's fear, pain, and misery begged for its blessed annihilating power. On this balance, what was it that averted the fatal tilt to madness, and lifted him up in the face of a new dawn? He was to think it was a will, not his, but a will alive in the cave. The will of those who lived in that preternatural darkness and had never yet faced a world not themselves, who lived without dimension, without perspective—and craved release. To that avail, something had to form outside of them, something somehow separate from them. That feat could be achieved only through the Herculean task of breaking an unconscious oneness, splitting the one that has no parts, the one that swallows up everything including itself, an identity identical to nothing but itself and thus unknown even to itself, ever unchanged and unchanging, an indistinguishable sameness of singularity absolute. How could this state even suspect there might be another but the same, and how had a least heterogeneity initially made a minimal distinction?

For the first time, a focus of two beacons, the eyes, errant and diffused until then, were reined in to meet at a precise distance, not on an object as yet, but in a singular perspective: on a point. Two beams trained on a new oneness, the unity of dimension needed for that focus. However, through the fractured identity that allowed an outside point to be located, light was let *in* as well, filtered by the soul's lens barely wiped clean of its primordial sleep. Mirroring the outside focus, there was a convergence of energies on the inside as well, a coordination of faculties, a clustering of hitherto scattered elements toward a center—in fine, the kernel of an inner self to which the outer point referred, and which related to it. A differentiation had been achieved, in the world as well as in the human being who broke through to a miraculous creative state. And a relation was established in the sense not only of a point perceived by a specific being, but also of the latter's *possession* of this point. It was not acquired as a point in the world, but as the world in its entirety, and this point-world represented the entire content of the incipient consciousness. Here began a process of repeating and relating. Once a point was secured, others could be acquired and related to the first. Soon the effort of focusing became automatized, and an image formed. Such was the training of the stones received by Tallini from his invisible cohorts.

He soon felt confident enough to raise his eyes and look around. Here, he would be surrounded by his ancestors in their work of world creation. The cave might remain empty to his sight, but it was forever alive in his intuition of these archaic presences. Every stone of the great library was occupied by gazes at various stages of awareness, all gathering points of focus to nourish the quickening soul, weaving these events into experiences to awaken emotions long immobilized in the soul's big sleep. He picked up each stone again, forcing himself to disregard the first image that corresponded to his own mind replete with ready-made images. He constrained his imagination until his sight relented, so that complex scenes yielded to simpler objects, sometimes even to the primitive sighting of puncticular focus. Appraising the inexhaustible wealth of the collection, he moved from one heap to another, until he had visited all five.

He was about to return to the entrance for a little rest on his stone bedstead when he noticed a glimmer of light coming from the depth of the cave. Could this be another ray of light on yet more stones? He hesitated, judging the afternoon had to be well advanced, with the available light diminishing. Between him and the glimmer was a pitch-black stretch, but he carefully started to make his way, eyes fixed on the faint light ahead.

An atmospheric change accompanied his progress, hindering his movement. An oppressive languor, as if laden with a heavy perfume whose scent had long faded but whose essence remained suspended in the air, penetrated both mind and body. Again he heard the inner sounds, now distinctly like voices, a rising and falling in tone, a back and forth as in an argument. The sounds and scents had a narcotic effect upon him: his legs felt leaden, and the faint light he was ostensibly approaching now seemed a mocking phantom that receded with each step. As he struggled onward, a distant voice could be distinguished, a forceful voice he had heard before, long ago it seemed, though he couldn't remember where. It was a low and majestic female voice that soared over the confusion of the crowd, and although he distinguished no words, he caught the warning in the tone, imploring him to turn back. But an immense desire drove him on, and no danger in the world could now have made him desist. As he summoned all his energy to overcome the invisible resistance facing him, it seemed he was no longer advancing through space but regressing through a backward chasm of time. Leaning hard as if into a storm, he drove forward for what seemed like hours of slogging through wet sand—and suddenly he stood in front of another small heap of stones illuminated from the ceiling.

The relative intensity of the light showed that only a brief interval could have passed during his approach, yet his effort must have been real, for it had exhausted him. He stretched out flat on his back, his eyes level with the stones whose reddish hue soon excited his attention. He sat up and took one stone from the pile for closer inspection. It was unlike any mineral he had yet seen in the cave or, for that matter, in the region. It looked rather like a pink Italian marble with brown and white splotches and veins. As he presented it to the light, moving it back and forth, the pink areas took on the substance of human flesh, and vaguely ithyphallic forms appeared to be actively engaging a distinctly female figure. Tallini whistled through his teeth. "Why, the scoundrels!" he muttered to himself with a chuckle. Where did they get this? Was that the reason for the color? Could these stones all be. . . .

At that moment, somewhere above him, he heard an ominous rumble rapidly drawing closer and growing until it thundered and roared and pounded right over his head. Amplified by the cavernous sound chamber, the noise was even more terrifying due to the uncertainty of its cause. Hunkered down on the shaking ground, Tallini had a vision of the cave's collapse and of himself crushed by the mountain. But for all its fury, the commotion was brief and was followed by the same total silence that had reigned here before. As he carefully raised his head, he saw the dying evening light, enlivened by a cloud of dust, streaming down from the ceiling and the manifold reflections of turbulent particles. After regaining his composure, he was astounded by the thought that in this noise were the first sound vibrations to reach his ears since he had entered the cave. And yet *that* sound had an air of unreality about it, whereas the others—the speaking and singing voices he had heard, or the eerie sounds that accompanied his drop through the rock—all purely internal phenomena, had yet kept their guise of special authenticity. The cave had turned reality inside out.

Then, into the dusty silence, the rich contralto with a shattering accusation:

"The scoundrel is *you!*"

Tallini crouched even lower under this blow. Although not fully grasping the deeper significance of the epithet's ominous damning, he wondered if his eyes had betrayed him, if what had been gained with the first stones might have been wrecked on the fleshy rocks of this second find. And yet, beyond his vision's indiscretion, he had to wonder what common theme might well have motivated the sequestration of these colored stones in a corner of such laborious access. Granted he had seen only a single one of them before darkness engulfed the cavern. Not that he likely would have looked at any other had there been sufficient light! For his last glance at the heap had left him with an ambivalent vision of entwined human sinuosity, and never had stones seemed so alive. He envisioned the enigma of discovering a secret inexistent before his scrutiny. And if his eyes had betrayed him with this unveiling, he in turn, as their master, had betrayed whatever entities reigned over the site.

Having failed in his mission, he wanted out, seeing flight as the only solution. Though by now the cave was utterly dark, he started threading his sightless way through the stone streets of this subterranean city. Difficult as the passage had been on coming in, he felt literally ejected as he was seized by an intense impatience to get into the open. He fancied a new life awaiting him out there, a life that had never heard of caves or rocks to read or ancient voices and all the rubbish that had recently filled his life. He longed for a clean slate. He would go to America.

Stumbling into a pile of stones, he sent them flying. When he reached the wall, he followed it carefully, one hand stretched out low until he located the slabs. He found the corridor without trouble but encountered swirling dust that made him cough. As he took a few more steps in pitch darkness, he ran into rock. With a sinking heart, he judged it to be a boulder that reached up to his chest. Evidently there had been a collapse of the roof somewhere. His heart stood still as he gave in to the realization that the exit was blocked and he was entombed, locked into this sunless dungeon of a cave for good. Remembering what Angelo had said about the isolation of this place, Tallini let his shaking body slide to the ground, then dragged himself toward the slabs and stretched out. Hunger pangs now reminded him of the paella, and of the jar he had never gone to get. The only person in the world who knew his whereabouts was a secretive Gypsy, long gone.

He lay there, exhausted, trying not to think, dozing fitfully. Not to give up, that was most important. He would look around when the light returned. Now he had to rest, to save his strength. The hunger pangs would subside. He knew he could easily go two or three days without food, and luckily he had the *bota* of water with him. He dozed off again, and awakening with a start, he found the cavern was no longer dark. To his surprise, he saw a circle of luminosity, well defined, in which there seemed to be some movement. Tallini thought he heard voices, but before his eyes had adjusted to the sudden light, he noticed the approaching figure of a man. Not until they were face to face did Tallini recognize him.

"Ladsnik? Is that you? What the devil? . . ."

SEVENTEEN

EARTHPLAY

"Of course it's me. What did you expect? One minute to curtain! Remember, you come join me on stage when you feel the moment's right. Spontaneity is everything here. But don't wait too long." He turned away and took a few steps toward the circle of light. Before Tallini could wonder about the producer's newfound style, he heard the first of three measured knocks on wood—incongruous in this mineral environment—announcing the beginning of a theatrical performance. Ladsnik had just enough time to turn around and give him a sarcastic look. "I like your costume. Break a leg!"

LADSNIK *(advancing to center stage, which is bare except for several stone slabs disposed for seating):* Distinguished audience and friends, I speak to you as a producer who this evening has the good and rare fortune to bring you a true work of art, and this, I gratefully report, without having been put through the exhausting labor that is the usual burden of any production. Tonight in this great hall, I bring you a masterpiece that will compose itself by itself, using all means at hand, including your own presence. Rarely has the public been offered such a unique occasion to participate in the creation of a work. I say "unique" advisedly, for this play, whose script is never to be written, will be performed tonight, and then live on only in our memories, and, if I may be so bold to presume, in yours. This play is meant to bridge the entire history of theatrics, from its earliest beginnings—authentically represented among our esteemed audience, I believe—to its very latest, its most contemporary style of acting, demonstrated by our own thespians, professional troupers all. As close to the beginning as possible, and as close to the end as we've come—those two poles and various stations in between will be given a chance to face each other and to interact. And we welcome a free exchange between the two, which I am certain you also desire, and this because everything must have a start, and nothing goes on forever, and . . . ah, but here is our friend Pierrot, certainly no stranger to you, come to rescue you from my philosophical musings. For with him our show opens, and with him it must close. That is the only certainty we have about this performance. So I wish you a fruitful evening in this play of life, and ask you please to welcome the intrepid, the inimitable *Petrus Lunaris! (points to the approaching Tallini and steps back into the shadow)*

TALLINI *(dressed in a white silk tunic with a deeply pleated ruff and big black buttons reflecting the stage lights; the fullness of the sleeves echoes the fullness of the white silk trousers, ending, like the sleeves, tightly cuffed, and revealing patent-leather slippers whose black shine, emphasized by white silk stockings, accentuates the black satin skullcap completely encasing his head. His face is caked with flour and he carries a mandolin-like monochord. Some scattered applause is heard. This costume is stitched so it can be easily shed as the action progresses.):* I sing a fearful plaint on this one string. A kingdom once gained, lost for a single word, left me with longings and desires. Confined forever to the bowels of the earth, the moon my sole companion, the wine of moonlight a sweet tasting for my eyes, thrilling intoxication to my senses. *(He sits down on a slab, plucks the string of the monochord and fingers a few notes. Meanwhile, a second figure is coming on stage from the opposite side. It is Benji. Tallini stops playing and looks up.)*

BENJI *(wearing an old overcoat with manuscripts sticking out of its pockets. He is pushing a cart piled with books and paper bags.*

He looks like a homeless person.): This seems like a fine place to finish my article. Already looks like the world of my predictions. *(notices Tallini staring at him)* Piero!

TALLINI: Benji!

BENJI *(in total disregard of his friend's costume):* Thought I might run across you here. Hadn't heard from you for some days. *(looks around)* Seems like a propitious place for anthropological pursuits. Have you made any interesting contacts? I myself happen at the moment to be looking for something along your line, although in the opposite direction.

TALLINI *(gets to his feet, sets the instrument down on the slab, and walks toward Benji):* I'm waiting for something or someone and don't know for what or for whom. But now in this moonlight I breathe again the sweet scent of fairy-tale time. And so you appear and together we'll ride the pale floods of my longing upward and far from here, back to the foothills of Bergamo.

BENJI: Travel? Now? But I just arrived! Brought enough food for a few days. And a couple of bottles of wine. So let's celebrate our reunion. *(Pushes his cart toward one of the slabs, unpacks a roast chicken, a ham, cheese, bread, a bottle of wine and two glasses from his paper bags. Tallini begins eating greedily. Benji pours himself a glass of wine and walks around, monologuing.)* I took to the road because I got stuck on my technology article. It looked like I had done all I possibly could at my desk. Just had to get away, do some field work, so to speak. Like you, I'm after a certain aspect of humankind, but mine is future, not past. Some questions I need answered from the future. You see, everybody who has any brains left knows we can't continue the way we're going, with our outdated idea of technological progress. Mind you, not that there is anything wrong with technology in principle. There seems to be a technical bent in the human being, which manifests itself in the fashioning of tools. *Homo faber*, after all. The problem is the sort of technological arrogance that overcomes people when they see what they can do with their minds. But time's running out, the thing's got a will of its own by now. In any case, it's here, and it's not going away. So we must . . . *(he is inter-rupted by a voice from the audience)*

FIRST VOICE FROM AUDIENCE *(coming from the north side of the circular stage):* I am a voice from long ago, when elders still talked about those blessed early days when all was alive in every way. They spoke of the first ones who lived in the land of the living, when earth and sky were the body of the Great Being through whom everything lived, the sun its living right eye, the moon its left, the stars countless souls and spirits sustaining their lives. Their power still resided within them through the entirety of the Great Being, and they raised stones to the glory of its power, living monu-ments of live stone. Nothing was needed yet beyond their bodies, the power inside sufficed for their works, all of which were great and none of them frivolous. This was called the time of the living, the time that knew no dead.

In our day, there was already need, and some power from inside was going out into wood and stone, to meet the need, to ease the work. We knew the dead and were taught the sounds and gestures to return them to the earth, so they may rejoin life after their voyage over the Sea of the Dead. Those are the sounds that conquer death. That is how it was with the early ones. There is now too much need in you, and little power left inside, all of your life given into your machines. Much and many are dead, and the dead are dead forever.

TALLINI *(who has slowly approached Benji during this speech and is standing beside him, listening intently, for a moment showing some animation):* That voice, I know that voice. Although I have never heard it thus, it has spoken to me silently, in my heart. *(takes two steps toward the audience, in the direction of the voice)* Speak to me, my friend, we must . . .

BENJI *(grabbing his arm to hold him back):* Hey there! Hold it, man! You're on stage, remember? It's just a voice. But the ideas have merit, I must say. Exteriorization is what it talked about. About a beginning time, a principial time, I should say, of total interiority, and therefore without action to affect the world and without language to express it. A state of perfection, without necessity, without desire. Like Paradise, it couldn't last. The voice talked of need and death, and I believe they are one, it's only that they take different responses, the one by action, the other by words. The words seeded a first narrative, a justification for the shocking fact of death and the voyage toward another life. Where there was only life, there was no need for language. But the narrative of death couldn't be divorced from action, and so we have the first burial rites—the dead brought into contact with the earth and thus rehabilitated, so to speak, from their scandalous betrayal of ubiquitous life. However that may be, one thing is certain: we've just heard from a historian who's given us ground for an investigation into technology—language and action. Two aspects of exteriorization, the first of mind, the second of body, the practice of tools. We'll see them come together, much later, in a crisis of ethics.

TALLINI (dreamily): He's talking about building a world. It brings back a distant force once known, creative, solar. Ah, but it is a hard world of striving he would build. Better to stay where the only pain is a crystalline sigh and the pale moon's blooms can be plucked in consolation. Too high a price to pay for that new world. What was so intimately lived inside is now laid out there, appraised, measured, and numbered. The power that goes outward is lost to insight, and soon there will be two powers, and no way to bring them together. What strife in the mind and the soul!

SECOND VOICE FROM AUDIENCE (coming from the east side of the circular stage): What has possessed him, the harlequin? I recognize him through his disguise because I knew him, next to me, around the consecrated stones of learning, come from afar to be with us and understand. He watched us struggle with our vision, laboring to see all we had been hearing inside now extended in front of us. He heard us struggle with the sounds, he helped us make them into words. Does he no longer remember? He was an inspiration to us, as we watched him reach with sureness for the stones, grasping them firmly at the first try, as if that vague and unfamiliar prospect belonged to him, as if he were a part of it, and it of him. Why is he now without will, and forlorn?

BENJI *(to Tallini, who has slinked back to his slab and fingers the monochord, but without producing any sound):* What have we here? An acquaintance, perchance? Seems you made a good impression in these parts, offering lessons in objectification. This was bound to stimulate their potential for action, or hadn't you counted on that? And you must tell me about those learning stones around which you and these chaps got together.

TALLINI: Ah, the stones. . . .

FIRST VOICE FROM AUDIENCE *(his delivery more hesitant, with intervals that allow for Benji's interjections):* The stones, little by little, gave us everything . . . after he left. Before that there was only this . . . form, which had not been there, nor did it come from outside, it came . . . from above, above the head . . .

BENJI: Intuition . . . wordless insight . . .

FIRST VOICE: There were forms of sound, hearing forms . . . They had been coming in, just floating, inconsistent, ungraspable . . . until the practice of the stones. But first the great confusion about the new outside . . . the bodies of things, were they still alive out there? How to fit them with the old living inside that used to be everything.

BENJI: Grasping the psychophysical whole . . .

SECOND VOICE: The practice of the stones brought power over the outside, knowing the distance outside and understanding the form of it inside. For the early ones there was only the enduring, the continuing being, now with the stones at a distance showing the forms, and the images of the world at a distance, this enduring knew a here now, and a coming and a gone . . .

BENJI: Psycholiths! Opening a perspective.

SECOND VOICE: Inside form and outside bodies were joined in the work of the hand. The stones made clear the forms from above and they became words. The images in the stone were also in the world, and the world of images could be reached by the eye and the hand. And the form that could be touched contained the possibility of change. Some began breaking stones and using parts for cutting and scraping, and they changed good branches into spears. And later some brought out of the stone the bodies inside it, each one a sacrosanct figure to be venerated . . .

BENJI: The Venus of Stone.

FIRST VOICE: But before that . . . the language was not yet complete. . . . It was each one alone with the words, and the single words alone and not joined to others . . .

BENJI: Language as such, noncommunicative . . .

SECOND VOICE: Everyone was together with the body, but not yet with the words. The females brought the change. They brought their own stones to the males on a night of great moonlight. *(Here Tallini, who had continued the silent fingering of his monochord, looks up, becomes increasingly interested, stands, and approaches center stage again.)* Because the stones do not give images in full sunlight, the males only looked at their stones in the cave, when the thin light came from the top. But the females' stones were different, they were the color of skin and showed forms of males and females, apart and together. While the males were looking in the stones and moving them so these images moved together and apart, the women hit stones together for sounds, struck the lithophones and stamped the ground to show their compact with the living earth. As the males looked at the moving forms, a new feeling arose inside them, as if they were moved as they moved the stones. But the females did not allow the males to approach, so the males were away from them, just as they were away from the image in the stone.

BENJI *(with newfound gravity):* Those were the erostones! The stones the women brought were erostones! And their new feelings, that inner motion, those were emotions.

TALLINI *(to himself, while taking off his skullcap and tossing it on his stone slab):* I think I've done more than hear about those stones!

BENJI: Practice of the psycholiths gave a perception of distance. It's clear the women were acting out a cosmological ritual. By the distancing effect, could they have interpreted the contemplated erostones in terms of their quasi-erotic ritual movements?

TALLINI *(ripping off his ruffed tunic under which he wears a T-shirt):* I can conceal it no longer. When I ran across those stones, a thought came to my mind, and a word escaped me . . .

BENJI *(disregarding Tallini's pronouncement):* Once distance is created, there is space for an erotic tension introduced by the feminine element, in a desire to suspend immediate contiguity. In a complementary and contrary motion, the erotic becomes a vehicle for language, a means of overcoming distance through communication.

TALLINI: I understood it too late, the cosmological context.

SECOND VOICE: After the night of great moonlight, the females entered the cave and took for themselves and their wizardry a space deep in the back of the cave, and their arts became powerful. Then according to the new rules they established, each one could be distinguished by a sound and was receptive to one male only.

BENJI: Is he speaking of a transition to matriarchy? *(addressing Tallini)* This whole discussion, however fascinating, seems somewhat removed from my original concerns. But I have a feeling it relates more closely to yours. Am I right?

TALLINI *(shedding the rest of his costume by slipping out of the white silk pants under which he is wearing jeans, and wiping the flour off his face):* I didn't understand it until now, and it remains fraught with mystery and emotion. I stepped into a sacred circle unprepared, took a profane stance while on hallowed ground, thought a word in the mind instead of gathering it in the heart, and unwittingly broke a circuit of which I had become a part.

BENJI: Pathologies of exteriorization! Language to begin with, the inner wisdom of the word, is free in its own improvised reality. And then by necessity it's exteriorized in a terminology to enable communication. Living subjectivity is exteriorized at the cost of suffering, dead matter, and irreconcilable duality. Pornography, for instance, isn't it a pathological result of erotic exteriorization? Now I understand what I didn't fathom even a moment ago, that the problematic aspect of technology is also a case of pathological exteriorization. Let the presences from ancient times bear witness and help us to further understandings!

FIRST VOICE: At first it was necessity that drove us outward.

SECOND VOICE: But it soon was understood that what the need had created, this outside helper, was the only thing that was dead without ever having been alive. Only through contact with the hand that had made it and that controlled its purpose could it participate in life.

THIRD VOICE (*coming from the south side of the circular stage*): For the sake of better understanding between my venerable companions and this excellent troupe of entertainers, I feel that certain circumstances need elucidation. Thus it must be made clear to these performers that it is a grave misnomer to speak of us as *presences*, when we are but effects of the salt of our bones.

TALLINI: What do I hear? Are these more mineral voices?

THIRD VOICE: We are indeed, but mineral that broke away from rock and was slowly worn down to minute particles, and thus captured by higher organisms at every level of the chain through which it circulates. In this way mineral life participates in the experience of higher realms, becoming their memory inscribed in permanence.

BENJI: I never thought I'd hear this narrative from the very substance itself!

THIRD VOICE: And let it be further understood that my honorable companion who spoke first may well have witnessed the earliest human inventions, and his testimony is most welcome. But he cannot furnish inscribed memories beyond the last great ice cover. It is not known what happened to his bones. Perhaps they were encased in a frozen mass that holds them to this day on some remote northern glacier. Or, transported by rocks and pebbles, they came to rest in a barren moraine, their vital minerals useless amid infertile rubble. Until the salt is leached and washed away and a further caprice of nature brings it into contact with a generative loam where vegetative roots can reach it, there is no opportunity for it once again to become magnetic nucleus to incarnation.

The same holds true for my other esteemed friend who came later, as he mentioned, and who spoke second. His memory reaches somewhat further, but still not quite to our time, as his ashes were collected by a doting wife after his fatal disagreement with authorities on a matter of doctrine. Gathered in a thick glass vessel specially commissioned for the purpose, the salt of his bones, to my knowledge, remains deeply buried in some mountain wilds. Thus both my honored friends have stepped aside in their time, while the great and unrelenting game of life passed them by, for better or for worse. For better, if it spared them an era degrading to their permanent essence. For the same capricious fate that held them back will likely someday throw them in again to rejoin the play pristine, and thus present a fresh and unconditioned outlook as they once more incarnate to the specifications of their salt. Such special points of view can lead to inventive contributions.

BENJI: The strategy of Pharaohs, their salt presumably forever set apart through mummification and protected by a mountain of stone!

THIRD VOICE: Or perhaps for worse, because discontinuity, excessively prolonged, may rob them of a wealth of experience, so their reappearance, inscribed with insufficient context, might find itself disoriented and alienated. But enough of all this. My two good friends have furnished us valuable intimations of existences not yet encompassing the dimensions of modern times, and I am here to take over where their competence ends.

BENJI: A fascinating account, to be sure. And may I inquire where you last have left your own mineral remains, and are they freely circulating and exercising their powers of attraction?

THIRD VOICE: Kind of you to ask, dear sir. I come indeed from a very uncommon place, and as an emissary. A special site because of the extraordinary accumulation to be found there of this living salt to which we all are eventually and periodically reduced, and to which all the living owe their form and continuity.

TALLINI: An apprehension grips me. He speaks too glibly of this unnatural condition.

BENJI: It's true, I feel the same. Speak up, tell us who entrusted you with this embassy?

THIRD VOICE: Those like myself, of course, who provided the substance for this vast mine of experience. A very stable mineral, I might add. A fixed salt, it has been called. When residing in bone, it becomes sensitized to emotional experience, which it registers in what we call, somewhat metaphorically perhaps, an inscription. For the vegetal, we know something of the effects of an accumulation of this salt. There have been experiments . . .

BENJI *(interrupting):* I've heard of this. Raise a plant and grow it to seed. Burn it, add the ashes to the ground and use the seed to grow another plant in the same earth. Repeat the process a number of times, and mutations occur, isn't it so?

THIRD VOICE: Couldn't have said it better myself. But of course we must be aware that a plant has no bones to store its minerals and the notion of inscription is impermissible on a prelinguistic level. Whether the chlorophyl experience is emotional for the plant must be left to speculation. But it certainly is the predominant—if not the sole—experience of the vegetable kingdom.

BENJI *(impatiently):* A course in philosophical botany perhaps? Now to the point!

THIRD VOICE: I'm only showing difference, sir, the better to appreciate similarity. For while human experience is diverse in general, we have a special situation in the case here represented, where the bones comprising this vast ash deposit had all inscribed the selfsame experience, specific to our age and impossible before, because dependent for its mass exploitation on present-day techniques. Inscribed it, furthermore, as ultimate experience, not merely the seconds, minutes, or hours preceding their destruction. No, this shared temporalization was calculated to drive their carriers to a state where human emotional inscription into salt had become impossible; in other words, they were systematically dehumanized. The means to that effect may have varied, but the common pain and degradation thus translated into a single inscriptive style. The tortured registry of these terminal inscriptions on the delicate saline palimpsest obliterated all previous experience and etched this last indelible record in heavy strokes. And left a characterization so narrow and in such massive repetition that it became epitomized in one single signature standing for all.

And now, sir, in the name of this signatory, I ask you and your fellow entertainers the question I am charged to represent. If the function of this permanent salt is to invoke a suitable form for fulfilling its potential, what subject would take upon itself a destiny so exclusively characterized by suffering, and how would it fulfill this necessity?

BENJI (*after a long pause, with absolute silence in the hall*): A devastating indictment!

TALLINI: I know whereof he speaks. But these consequences are. . . .

FOURTH VOICE (*interrupting, coming from the west side of the circular stage*): Wait, a few more words to be added here to complete the picture. What we have heard is indeed dreadful enough, but there is more to report. To reduce a permanent salt to a condition no longer apt to attract human form is a criminal assault not only on its particular carrier but on the entire species sustained by the mineral. Yet despite its degradation, this salt stays in existence. It endures and it will circulate, so the possibility remains of eventual redemption through the presentation of an adequate form. There remains hope of a recovery in such a case, a prospect of survival.

But what of the frenzied technological inventiveness that devised a means of fissioning the hitherto fixed nucleus for the sake of its terrible power, and then loosened this power in an unstable chain reaction that destroys all mineral salt within its range? No survival here, no possible recovery. In this case, death has been doubly final, both for the individual and for an accumulated experience forever lost to a future humanity. This second death, even when understood, and although disastrous for the individual, might in the immediate present appear—quite mistakenly —as a sustainable loss to humanity. A second death, hitherto only a metaphysical speculation, is in its actuality too recent a phenomenon for its long-term effects on the species to be ascertained, let alone evaluated. It is, however, certain that such nullification will leave a void, a negativity bound to spread in its ramifications, as if a ghost. Nor is the damage of unstable chain reactions limited to the salt of living individuals. Any handful of soil anywhere on earth maintains fixed salt in progress. The destruction of the storehouse of inscribed experience poses a threat to the *humanity* of a future humankind.

BENJI *(stands center stage, facing west as he begins to speak. Tallini has moved to the north of the stage while the Fourth Voice was speaking. As Benji begins his speech, Hephysta appears at the south side of the stage and haltingly starts moving very slowly north across the stage toward Tallini, who equally slowly starts moving south, toward Hephysta):* So at last the future human being is considered! Does anyone give him a thought? Does anyone care about his life in the world he will inherit? I would like to hear from him, and perhaps these salt effects that are manifesting here can put me in touch. Having inscribed the past, perhaps they can decipher the future.

My research led me to realize that the globe's spoliation by unbridled so-called progress in technology might degrade conditions of existence to a point—reached long before the planet has been made totally uninhabitable— where life becomes undesirable by our notions of human dignity, of man's function on earth.

It is true that in our day the mass of the globe's inhabitants live in conditions disgraceful enough to belie humankind's status at the pinnacle of consciousness. As to the human purpose in nature, which might be intuitively assumed to bear a relation to that status, it has until recently remained a topic of endless philosophical speculation, but seems to have found, almost by default, a conclusion in modern times. *Technology* is humanity's calling, we are told, and indeed humanity falls in step and in tacit acceptance acts out this destiny. Meanwhile, industry and marketplace are flooded with inventions whose future effects are unknown or ignored, and for which no one in particular can be held responsible yet the species as a whole must be called to account.

How will future humans cope with these enormous problems? Perhaps the future will have to lower its standards and still find life worthwhile. People might be forced to abandon any calling and be satisfied with a brief moment of self-contained existence.

SECOND VOICE: Did I hear correctly? Our efforts to gain an outside helper for our hand, that stillborn thing of our making, at our beck and call—it has been lent an artifice of life, been allowed to build itself into a monster now out of control! Is that what we are to learn from this entertainer?

BENJI: An unavoidable progression, once it's launched. You did it yourself when you took up that stone, which was nothing but a stone, yet it was *all* stone with *all* its qualities, its potentialities. And then you noticed it was hard and could pound on other things, drive a stake into the ground, for instance, and you thought of it as *hammer*. That instilled it with usefulness. But with its new name, it lost its qualities of *stone*. Its usefulness is the artifice of life of which you're speaking. And so began a long chain of events of ever greater usefulness and dependence, which grew into the complex instrumentation now indispensable to our way of life. So do not blame us entirely, for it was you who set the monster into action.

TALLINI *(Hephysta and Tallini have been approaching each other in slow motion during this exchange, taking small steps, dreamlike and somewhat like automatons. At a certain point, they raise their arms as if preparing to embrace one another. Hephysta wears white elbow-length gloves, very visible on her deeply tanned bare arms. As they come within a few paces of each other, Hephysta, in continued slow motion, her arms held shoulder high, now removes the glove from her left hand with her right. In so doing, she turns it inside out. Tallini stops and observes the procedure. Once the glove is off her hand, Hephysta throws it to the ground at Tallini's feet, limps past him at a normal pace, and exits north. Tallini, also moving naturally now, picks up the glove, examines it until Benji has stopped speaking, and then declares, his eyes still on the glove):* Inside out, left becomes right. But the white glove remains.

THIRD VOICE: If the stone rolled, it never rolled far from the hand. The only power ever given to our tools was the power of our hand. And now and in the future, we know what our tools can do: they have no power of their own.

TALLINI *(his normal self again, stuffing the glove into his pocket):* He's right, whoever he is. The responsibility lies in keeping things in hand.

BENJI: A very limited horizon for human action, if taken narrowly. But if the hand is an extension of the mind into space, so can the mind become an extension of the hand into time. For what we must have well in hand is the effect of our instrumentation in the future, even a distant future. The mind can evolve a cognitive equivalent to the hand. For such a foreseeing mentality, things would never leave their inventors and creators. And as the hand gives life in the immediate, so the mind as the extension of the hand will give life into the future. It would bring the universe alive once more.

TALLINI: What you are thinking and saying I am feeling in my bones.

◐ ◑ ◯ ◯ ◑ ◐

With this, Tallini opened his eyes. A haze of daylight streamed from the ceiling apertures. It was as if his brain now housed this extraordinarily vivid dream in all its details, fixed in a tableau of perfect simultaneity. His body calm, infused with energy and very much alive, he stood up and concentrated on locating another exit from the cave. Soon he found himself outside the zone of ceiling light and in complete darkness. Arms stretched out in front of him, he advanced step by step, checking the space over his head periodically, until to his great relief, he touched a wall. Instinctively, he followed it until he saw a dim glow in the distance, which, after all this blackness, struck him like the entire universe of light.

Having recently seen all that can be seen in absolute darkness, he blinked a few times to make sure of what he saw —but the light remained. In his excitement, he took a few rapid steps forward and hit his head on the ceiling, which was suddenly lower, so he had to proceed on all fours, hampered by his sore leg. Soon the passageway narrowed, giving him the impression of entering the neck of a stone funnel. At the same time he realized the opening was quite close, as a faint waft of fresh air reached his nostrils. By now he was flat on his belly and could see a space filled with air and light. He wriggled forward, and placed his hand on a ledge just beneath the opening, whose oval aperture he judged to be about fifteen inches wide. He might be able to stick his head out, but not his body. Panting and sweating, he lay there, unable to advance, unwilling to retreat, looking at the light outside, thinking of a means to overcome this impossible situation, thinking, thinking—until something snapped in him, and he let go, encased in rock, all thinking stymied.

He remained for a long time with his mind devoid of thought, his body relaxed to the point of feeling almost comfortable in its stone enclosure. Having abandoned the striving toward the haven of light, air, and freedom so close and yet manifestly out of reach, he floated in the vast serenity of his acceptance. Equanimity reigned in his being, spiked here and there by a bittersweet image of a lived incident incongruously flashing through his mind.

No longer came the slightest thought of backing out of this funnel; there was no thinking whatsoever. He had come straight to this exit, had been guided here as surely as if he had *known* it existed, and if it were not intended for him, looking elsewhere would be useless; it would in fact be counterproductive. His absolute surrender to the situation was the pure expression of the conviction that as things now stood, so they were meant to be, having been brought about by the sum total of his actions. He had carried out his assignment, and if a tinge of regret remained that he would not walk into the light again, an equally strong sense existed that everything was perfect as it was. None of this was really thought—it went through him as no more than the vaguest of sentience. In fact, he was so totally relaxed that he was on the verge of falling asleep, perhaps never again to wake.

Then this sense of well-being no longer conducted an autonomous state inside him, but made itself felt as a subtle energetic current from outside, traveling through him as if he were part of the rock that was hugging him so closely. It left behind impressions that spoke to him as they had once before, in his own silent voice. And it seemed to him he heard a mocking laugh.

"We meet again," and Tallini recognized the spirit of the mineral, "but this time with a little daylight, enough for you to see my face. You will remember that my power is greatest where the earth is hollow, but reduced in large spaces where it is much diluted by air. But now you have come to visit in a hollow just large enough to fit you, a space made just for you. That is why you now feel my power going through you, for we are made of the same substance, as you know. When last we met I lent you a special pair of eyes. They were of use only in the cave, which you have already left, one way or another. You can now apply to your human eyes all you have learned."

Tallini was staring at the small surface of rock illuminated by the light from the opening. The voice inside him, his own silent voice, was connected to that rock face as surely as the speech sound in the ear would be linked to the countenance of an interlocutor.

"Still thinking *about* me," said the spirit. "But to reach me, you will have to *think* me. Thinking *about* will yield only aspects, and will remain on the periphery. To get to the living essence of me, you will have to *think me*. And your thinking will have to stay with me, not oscillate between us in order to measure and compare and relate. While thinking about me can be conducted without sense perception—in which case it will yield more information about yourself than about me—thinking me can be initiated by a seeing and a hearing, sometimes also by a touching, as is happening now. The fiery element alone is contacted by seeing as the light of the eye penetrates the fire of the object, the quality that makes for visibility. Touching penetrates the object's earthy qualities and furthers intuition. The ear captures its harmony, and in the name it hears, grasps the harmonized unity."

Although this thinking was, strictly speaking, not his own, it contained components and overtones of ideas Tallini had at times entertained, which seemed here to receive an impersonal confirmation. This was complemented by the three sense perceptions that had been evoked: his hands pressed against the rock, his eyes fixed on the rock wall's spot of light, and his inner ear interpreting the mineral discourse.

"These sensory intuitions must penetrate the thinking, which in turn lends them configuration. But the unity that was heard in the word is yet to be *experienced* whole. Therefore, with ample meditation on the object, a sense must form within you especially for this apprehension. Only then can you say, 'This entity is known to me.' "

Tallini shifted his body just enough to allow his hands some freedom of movement as his fingertips grazed the rock's grainy surface, a texture invisible at this distance from his eyes. But the blind digits gave him a clue that the sharpest view could not have furnished. This was sedimentary rock, and he remembered having read at the Paris bibliothèque that these coastal hills were composed of marine limestone, with igneous intrusions of granitic mica.

All at once he felt strangely troubled by his abysmal ignorance of the limestone world encasing him, this soil he trod so thoughtlessly, despite the relationship—a family bond, almost—that tied his bones to skeletons of silica and calcite shells. He was acutely conscious, suddenly, that his experience of this rock was limited to a mere snapshot; yet the reality of the event had been thousands of millions of years in the making, and this becoming could not be left out of a true participation in the present fact.

Trapped as he was in this mineral embrace, it seemed as if the stone were now allowing him to penetrate its timeless genesis through the endless downward float of the sea of plankton, suspending him amid myriad radiolaria and foraminifera caught in their biostratigraphical enterprise. Drifting leisurely in the pelagic blue, he contemplated the extraordinary productivity of these protistan migrants. Biologically situated, this planktonic congregation formed the lowest level of a food chain that stretched from their microscopic cells to the huge mammals that shared the oceanic realms. Without the modest and prolific plankton, this magisterial domain of animation would be a lifeless giant uselessly sloshing about at the bidding of the moon.

Tallini was traveling in a haze of protoplasmic filaments, pseudopodia projected by the individuals of this radiolarian cloud whose host he had become. In his excitement at this adventure, he barely noticed that his vision now transcended the limitations of scale, and he could appreciate these marvels of natural workmanship and the extraordinary formal inventiveness expressed in both their macro- and microscopic sizes. The siliceous shells of these single-celled animals took on the most admirable and unexpected forms. Infinitely varied as their structures were, the shells were all pierced with holes of various sizes, at times assuming the aspect of delicate lace, at others a fisherman's netting. Their fundamental motif appeared to be spherical, but, with a fantasy that knew no bounds, the animals devised endless improvisations on this basic theme. The sphere was wont to adopt direction, develop polarities, or be influenced by gravity. It could elongate to express the existence of poles, or grow large protuberances to mark their sites.

Defensive adaptations added another theme to the improvisation. The shell could retain its roundness and cover itself with thorny spikes, like a sea urchin's. A remarkable feat of engineering (a more sophisticated expression of defense, or perhaps merely of privacy) was revealed through the relatively large apertures of a fully spiked outer shell—a second and sometimes a third and fourth concentric sphere, inner sanctums held in place by a system of posts, like Chinese ivory balls carved one inside another. Then again, as if in anticipation of reaching solid ground, the sphere might metamorphose segments into three projections of equal length, equally spaced around its girth, so the result resembled a tripod supporting a dome. Or it might sprout a cylinder from which the dome balloons like a perfect soufflé. An anthropocentric vision with a utilitarian bent could conjure helmets, hand bells, pitchers, vases, even a military drum—a world of objects—from such formal reminiscences.

Drifting lower into colder zones, Tallini noticed how his subaqueous companions were turning more robust, with thicker shells. Daintier and more fragile entities, caught in a sudden eddy, were hurled from the ocean's surface down beyond their depth to a frigid death, their frail bodices torn to pieces in the swirl. At times a chilling current from the deep swooped up into the warmer regions, producing a planktonic hecatomb. All this detritus floated downward again, and when Tallini reached the ocean's lower depths at last, he found countless skeletal remains suspended in the thickening ooze, calcareous first, and finally, in the abyssal zone, siliceous from the debris of radiolarian hulls. As he felt the solidifying texture of the sedimentary environment, his powers extended: he not only observed the microscopic life, but experienced its destiny in time. Likewise, he witnessed the process of multimillenary compaction reduced to a fraction of a second, so that before his eyes, an island grew, a continent perhaps, built with the primal life of a faraway aeon.

He was able to observe the energetic chemistry transacted in the briny milieu, where acids and metallic radicals romped, precipitating their salts into a clay reddened by iron. Being assembled here was a receptor of physical memory, virgin mineral salts bound to rock, from which in time they would leach into open nature and circulate as the individual grounds and full potential of inscribed human experience. It seemed as if the gigantic enterprise of continent building found its ultimate meaning in that eventuality. To fulfill this destiny, the submerged continent had to become terra firma, and yet by the very logic of this becoming, it would never on its own be able to break through the water's surface, because its growth depended on marine creatures that would rarefy as the construction approached sea level. Furthermore, the surface waves would sweep clean any loose sediment that might settle. Although the process was still far from this limit, Tallini could already notice a distinct slowing of growth. Somehow he intuited that this land could not be stopped, that nature would eventually force it to the light of day and have it play its role.

An untenable equilibrium was reached when this underwater land could no longer feed on marine beings, when it was ready, ripe, but still sea and not yet earth. Bathed in the same amniotic fluid that had been nurturing a continent on life, building it up with life and therefore meaning it for life, he sensed a moment of great stillness and knew the time had come. Beneath the sea, the earth split open, and from its secret center a mountain of pure heat and pressure pushed through, to be quenched in an ocean of vapor as the new continent, broken in half, reared into a bloodied sky, and crumbled into a few huge fragments that settled back into the white hot matter, already beginning to consolidate.

Where was Tallini? This metamorphosis staggered his senses, and he heard nothing, saw nothing, felt nothing, and yet experienced it all. The world revolution of billions of years ago had come upon him, overwhelmed his being and englobed the total experience of his quest. In this transformation, the quest itself was metamorphosed and no longer confined to this cave. Nor was it in any way related to his earlier life and enterprises: the light-machine and camera, the laws of harmony, and his experiments in difference—no, not even to the first glimmer of consciousness of self, that self he no longer could acknowledge, that illusionary self suddenly standing unveiled as imposture, not even there. It belonged to the Earth itself, with this continent that was born and that was *all* continents.

This was Terra Firma, the world that had become inside him and on which he stood and moved and acted. The Earth that was born was himself. He was terrestrial being: Earth-Man. Yet even that horizon could not hold him. Beyond it was another, *the* other for an Earth-Human, the cosmic object to be embraced in his Being. For the calculating mind of the individual person, itself a minuscule part of Earth, that universe of stars and nebulae would remain an awesome and unlimited immensity, utterly irrational by any measure, as millions of light-years is no measurement at all, but a notion, a conceit, a fancy. Only embraced by an Earth-Human could this universe become Cosmos, encompassed by the Being of Earth, the living, thinking Earth, the conscious Earth, the Earth of consciousness. As Earth-consciousness expands, so does Cosmos. The furthest limit of this Cosmos is the limit of Earth's consciousness. Alone the consciousness of the Earth-Human limits the Cosmos, and is able thereby to know it to its limit.

EIGHTEEN

RELEASE

Where was Tallini? He had seen a light too brilliant for sight, a sound too loud for hearing, an event too gigantic to be conceived. But now all was becalmed. A soft curtain of light lay on his lids, and he was bathed in a tranquil, steady sound. He recognized the sound of life and opened his eyes.

He was lying sideways on a slope, looking at a brilliant Andalusian sky. Behind him was the mountain, in front of him a pane of rock. Most important of all, he was out in the open air. He slowly sat up, facing the mountain. Close to his feet was the opening in the rock wall. He didn't understand, but he could not think about it, not now, perhaps never. He knew now that certain experiences might not be furthered by thinking. He stood up. Beyond the pane of rock, the sea stretched out to the horizon. A voracious appetite for life and light had entered his soul, pervading his entire being.

Behind him the mountains were just covering the sun. As he looked straight out over the water, his heart, guided by the changing light, escorted the great Fire into the hushed coolness that followed its interring. His body's heart was like an inner eye for which the Fire did not die or vanish. He continued to follow its path by the warmth that would remain even after nightfall precluded visibility, the warmth stored not only in his heart and in all hearts, but in every body and object on the globe as well. Aware of the Fire in back of him, behind the mountains, he imagined it changing, traveling in its trajectory, now feeling it underneath him, while he remained immobile, centered, certain of a survival that was tied to the great star tracing the limit of his world.

The night he entered the cave, a bundle of countless nocturnal suns, stars beyond the solar limit, had touched his heart, only to chill it with icy rays. This alienating greeting in fact offered the sole experience of outer space to be gathered by a natural constitution; all the rest was calculation and instrumentation, and, as far as perception was concerned, only a step removed from fantasy. How different the situation within the sublunar earthly realm! Here all senses and faculties were trained to specific tasks of recognizing and identifying a totality in which they took part. And yet great nations were squandering energy and treasure on the conquest of desolate sidereal realms, where, encapsuled in an artificial environment, humans would be incapable of experiencing their hollow triumph.

The sea shimmered like a velvet carpet in the dwindling day, conveying a sense of surface never obtained by a landscape of geological accidents. With dusk obscuring the horizon, not a hint of the earth's sphericity remained. Tallini was breathing easier now, more deeply, the weight of volume fading from his perception. All that was left had been transformed into transparencies he was incorporating in his progression. As volume dissolved, time integrated into pure present. Inside/outside, past/future—these oppositions vanished, their tensions polarized within oneness. The realm of quantity that he had always interpreted as "facts" unraveled to reveal its underlying qualitative functions.

As the reality he had known melted away, he understood this was a death—not directly his own, but of a world that had been part of him and in which he took part. The recapitulation of life that is said to occur in the instant of death now presented him with such a momentary revelation—not of his own life, but of the life of his world. With this tableau of mineral, vegetable, animal, and human becoming and being, his own odyssey stood revealed. It filled him with an intense love and longing for the miracle of life, a loving longing filling every cell of his body and transforming it into a new Earth that took shape around him and of which he was the center. But not he alone. Every other human consciousness would thus find its center from which to recreate a body of Earth. This commonwealth of consciousness was no longer a planet whirling around a sun—itself a vassal of Sirius and the extra-galactic sidereal cosmos—but a conscious and autonomous Earth come of age, free and responsible for itself, a spiritual-ized Earth whose sun merely lent it a physical visibility.

Was that all? No, for this total recall included an origin, indistinguishable from the present moment. And with the setting sun, an invisible light rose in his heart. It was a feeling of joy, and Tallini smiled.

ACKNOWLEDGMENTS

To my *querida editora* Nancy Peters for a patient early reading and continued support, and to Will Marsh for his incisive edit, as well as to Philip Lamantia, Marcelly and René Zahles-Gruber, and Rosette Letellier, for assistance at various times and in various, sometimes subtle, ways.

Special gratitude to Christopher Bamford, for the many helpful conversations, with admiration for selflessly shepherding this flock of words to a safe corral not even his own.